Sea Panther

A Crimson Storm Novel
Book 1

Dawn Marie Hamilton

Sea Panther ~ 2013 Golden Heart® Paranormal Finalist

ISBN: 978-0-9899642-3-4

This novel is dedicated to Frank.

May the wind fill your sails.

ACKNOWLEDGMENTS

So many individuals helped bring this book to fruition, and I thank you.

Thank you to Cindy Davis for editorial guidance. To the Celtic Critters, past and present, for critiques and vital encouragement. To Nancy Lee Badger, Sarah Hoss, and Melissa Stark for unending support. And a special thank you to Derek Dodson. Words cannot convey how important you are to me.

Thank you to the members of Celtic Hearts, From the Heart, and FF&P Romance Writers for keeping me sane. To all the judges who've judged the manuscript for *Sea Panther* in RWA® chapter contests and the Golden Heart®, a heartfelt thank you.

Most importantly, I thank Frank, my husband, best friend, and personal hero.

CHAPTER ONE

December 6, Current Year
Moored at Sandy Hook Bay in New Jersey

Robert MacLachlan licked the corner of his mouth where a droplet of blood lingered. A precious taste. Rich on the tongue yet bitter to swallow.

He paced the deck of *Sea Panther*, his ninety-foot, black-hulled sloop, allowing self-loathing to course through his veins along with the woman's blood.

"Cursed fool." He smacked a palm against the cabin top. Coming on deck hadn't eased his torment. Not even the briny tang of the sea breeze soothed him.

Dawn neared. He retreated below to the sanctuary of his cabin. Only on this sunrise a lass remained sprawled across the bed. His stomach clenched when he slid his gaze over the naked woman lying so still on the bunk. He curled his hands into fists, disgusted by his gluttony. Having gone too long without feeding, he'd taken too much blood. Her ashen skin, a stark contrast against the deep green velvet coverlet, provided a painful reminder of the monster he'd become.

Bloody hell. Why hadn't Colin removed the wench?

Though his hunger was fully sated, the faint pulse at the woman's neck beckoned Robert forward. He gritted his teeth against a wave of bloodlust. A compulsion to finish, drink the last drops of her essence, drove his fist into the wood above her head.

"Satan, take me." The fervent plea burst unwelcome from the depths of his anguish.

He winced and shook out his throbbing knuckles. The pain would be fleeting. Damage to the fine teak bulkhead, as with the scar across his cheek, would be a lasting symbol of his lack of restraint.

Sea Panther's first mate slipped into the cabin, a syringe in hand.

"Shall I return the lass to shore?" Colin's gaze flicked to the shattered wood before focusing on Robert.

"Aye, that you would," Robert answered his keeper's question. Barely did he recognize the raspy hiss of his own voice.

He need not worry. The redheaded Colin MacEwen knew him well. Tonight his faithful servant and friend of over twenty years would clean up the mess. Though appreciated, the necessity was damn galling, enough to make a man want to slam his skull into something hard.

Colin was a burly man yet he handled the woman gently. Robert flinched when his friend inserted the needle into her vein. Her eyelashes fluttered for a moment before she lost consciousness again. The drug cocktail would ensure deep sleep and quicken blood cell production. God, he hoped she survived.

"Don't be too hard on yourself. She came to you willingly," Colin said, always one to sense Robert's dark moods.

"That makes it worse. I should have protected her from..." He let the words trail off. They both knew he should have kept away from the lass.

Colin wrapped her in a blanket then twisted around to face him. "You can't help being what you are."

There was no sign of condemnation within the depth of his friend's eyes yet Robert was condemned. The injustice of his life burned like acid in his chest. The need to growl, the need to pound fists, the need to beat something into submission threatened tenuous control.

"This time I went too far." He reached deep within and clamped down on the aggressive desires. He'd been a bloody fool to allow the young woman with the purple-tinted hair to pick him up at a bayside bar. Dressed in black lace, leather and chains, she'd told him she wanted to hook-up with a vampire. He should have been wary.

"How she learned what I am is a mystery. I ought to have stopped when the warning alarm sounded in my head. Walked away." He swallowed, and guilt settled in his gut. "Instead, I gave her what she wanted and almost took her life. I have little compassion left. Time is running out. I must unearth a cure."

"You will, my friend. Have faith."

"Soon it will be three hundred years."

Too long to be cursed. Too long to live as an animal. Too long to live as a vampire.

Robert rubbed the ache building at the back of his neck. "I am tired."

"Has Dr. Knight made any progress?"

Hope beat in rhythm with Robert's blackened heart. The much-acclaimed ethnologist, who specialized in Caribbean Voodoo, was the most recent addition to the staff at the scientific foundation he funded in the Florida Everglades. The world believed the assorted experts in his employ researched the endangered Florida panther.

He choked on a dry chuckle. Their true objective was to find a cure for his malady. Dammit, they had better discover a solution soon, or darkness would claim what little remained of his humanity.

Colin watched him expectantly.

"The good doctor is diligent, searching through piles of dusty historical texts. There are a few theories. Nothing concrete." Robert released a frustrated breath. "I realize after tonight how desperate my need has become. I must return to Florida and undergo more tests. One of those expensive scientists on my payroll better find a cure before I destroy another human life."

His friend clasped his upper arm. "I'll see to the lass."

"Aye, and arrange to have blood delivered at each port of call. I will not risk any more innocents."

With a grunt, Colin hefted the bundled woman over a shoulder.

"I'll hand her off to Jagger. He'll take her to a safe house. She'll be well cared for until she recovers." He adjusted the weight of his burden. "When do we leave?"

"Tell the crew we sail on the tide."

* * *

December 9
Cape May, New Jersey

Cheerful carolers serenaded from hidden speakers. The way-too-joyous music taunted Kimberly as she wandered along the Cape May avenue, peering into storefronts glittered with holiday decorations. She crossed empty arms and hugged herself. She hadn't purchased anything. What little cash remained in her stash would be needed when the week's reprieve ended.

The chill of the evening wasn't a bother. There was no need to hurry. Besides, she had nowhere to go. She halted in front of a display of sinful pastries. Along with the tantalizing scents of nutmeg and cinnamon wafting from the bakery, an overload of better-time memories swept over her. She blinked several times, refusing to get weepy.

After spending a better part of the day trying to rise above the malaise, she still felt like crap. Neither the seasonal splendor nor the afternoon of window-shopping had done much to dispel the remnants of the nightmares.

The memory of the dreams and the related sensation of being chased made her shudder. And if that wasn't enough to frighten, the thought of a hit man—

Enough of that. Kimberly stiffened her spine and turned away from the images in her mind. A prickle teased the base of her neck, and she increased the pace. Could the rumor be true? Was someone following her?

The anxiety stealing her breath was probably ridiculous.

After all, she strolled with well-dressed couples along a very public main street on a Friday night.

She bit her lip, feeling the deep pinch. The reflection in the plate glass window of a gift shop showed only normal activity: shoppers, traffic, candy wrappers blowing past. No skulkers. No dangerous-looking men. Come on, get a grip.

The December wind whipped up, and she shoved cold hands deep into the pockets of her overcoat. She crossed the street and stepped onto the snow-dusted sidewalk in front of the corner diner. Stopping under a streetlight, she nonchalantly turned around.

Her breath left her lungs in a whoosh.

The *drop dead* gorgeous man who stood before her oozed sensual heat from every pore of his over six feet of muscle clothed in black jeans, form-fitting leather jacket, and biker boots.

The gaze she ran over the length of him was probably too obvious. Irrepressible though. The man's short, tawny-brown hair with a slight reddish tinge was styled to spiky perfection. A firm square jaw filled out a rugged face. And his eyes...

Humor flashed in the expressive cinnamon-brown gaze and his sexy full lips parted into a slash of a grin, displaying perfect white teeth. She couldn't refrain from gasping.

A Bad Boy. Her spine tingled with—could it be attraction?

Without a sound, he moved closer.

Her stare froze on a scar. The thin line marred the side of his handsome face from the corner of the right eye, across the cheek to his chin, making him appear... *dangerous.*

Muscles in her chest constricted. Adrenaline pumped through her veins. She took a step backward, ready to run. How could she have let her reaction to his good looks lower her guard?

"You dropped this a way back." The man held out her scarf.

A yummy Scottish burr stroked her like a physical

caress, and a delicious shiver slid over her shoulder blades. What an idiot to think he meant harm. He only intended to return the scarf. He wasn't a hit man sent by a powerful ex-client.

"Thank you." She slipped a hand from a pocket and reached for the woolen tartan. The brief touch of their fingers sent electric tingles dancing across her skin. Previously cold cheeks burned with unexpected heat.

Laugh lines crinkled at the edges of the man's eyes as his smile widened. "Good eve'n to you."

With a respectful nod, he whirled and strode down the street. Kimberly stared after him as if she'd never seen a man before. Gathering scattered wits, she entered the brightly lit diner.

While waiting for the hostess, she perused the want ads pinned to a bulletin board next to the counter. One in particular drew her attention and she read the notice a second time...

> *90-ft. sloop SEA PANTHER seeking fifth crewmember for coastal cruise, leaving Cape May on 11 Dec., docking Charleston, SC for refit, continuing on to Florida and the Caribbean. Experience required. Fair wages. Inquire at Rusty Scupper.*

If only she'd the nerve to reply to the ad, she could sail away from all her problems. Taking off would be a major cop-out, but the fantasy of escaping from a messed up life offered a certain appeal. And she did need a job.

"Would you prefer to sit at a booth or the counter?" A college-aged girl with a blond ponytail interrupted Kimberly's thoughts.

"A booth, please." Kimberley's stomach gave off a soft gurgle as she slid into the offered seat. Hoping no one heard, she pressed a hand to her belly and concentrated on the menu.

Nothing appealed. She hadn't had an appetite in weeks. Not since learning the offshore deal she invested her savings in, along with the money of a few clients, failed.

God, her life was such a mess.

After taking her order, the server returned with a sad-looking wilted salad. Kimberly pushed the limp lettuce around in the bowl with a fork and imagined having the courage to apply for the crew position on the ninety-foot yacht. Jumping at the job would be a short-term answer to the situation. If only she could...

Nah, she couldn't do it.

During her teenage years, she had loved to sail with her father. That was until disaster fell and he died on night watch while the rest of the crew slept.

A tear escaped and slid along her cheek. She'd refused her father's request to go along on that ill-fated cruise and went on a stupid date instead. If she hadn't, maybe the accident would never have happened. Whenever they sailed together, she stayed up and shared the night watch. Had she been there, the sailboat wouldn't have been on autopilot, and he wouldn't have been swept overboard by the boom during an unexpected jibe.

Kimberly couldn't take the job. She brushed away the moisture. She hadn't sailed since that night, and vowed never to sail again.

On the way to the door, she glanced at the ad. Maybe it was time to jack up her big girl pants. She grabbed the index card from the bulletin board and stuck it into a pocket.

* * *

The simple act of returning the woman's scarf had taken a dangerous turn when their fingers touched. Robert managed to control the vampire by sheer will alone. Nonetheless, the power surge coursing through his veins from the brief contact with the lass awakened the panther. He barely made it to the tall grass on the outskirts of town before being claimed by the transformation.

He chose not to fight the change. He welcomed it with every fiber of his being.

Heart raced. Blood throbbed at his temples and a tortured curse escaped his lips. He discarded his garments and clenched his teeth. Muscles ripped and tendons snapped and bones distorted to conform to the panther's shape. Coarse golden fur tipped with a reddish tinge rippled over bare skin, making him quiver with urgency.

Nostrils flared, he sniffed the salty breeze. There would be precious few moments for his pleasure before the beast seized complete control.

He darted through the salt marsh, paws sinking into moist earth. His growl sounded out a soul-wrenching lament on the injustice of his life. Robert couldn't shake the feminine image of the tall graceful woman with brown curls and haunted chocolate eyes. The desire to mate shook him to the core.

Far from the trappings of civilization, he slowed to a rhythmic lope. He hoped no one found the tracks. The headlines would be sensational.

Big Cats Return to South Jersey

Cougar Tracks Sighted in Cape May County

On closer inspection, a zoologist would recognize the smaller pawprints and attribute them to the Florida panther, Puma *concolor coryi*. Researchers would bombard the foundation with inquiries. His secret would be in jeopardy.

The panther reared its full power and forced away Robert's human thoughts.

A raccoon moving through the reeds caught his keen gaze. He pounced on the prey. Yet on the fringes of consciousness remained the unquenched desire for his mate.

* * *

Sofa to sliders, a glance through the glass at the lit balcony, and back, Kimberly paced the sitting area of the upscale B&B room. Thoughts bombarded each other in her brain. How to make things right? Being homeless was a frightening future. A future that could only be delayed a few more days—until the prepaid week ended. Good thing her fiancé—ex-fiancé—hadn't a chance to cancel before taking off to the Cayman Islands with his administrative assistant.

Jason? How could he have dumped her right before Christmas? And just when she really needed him?

Kimberly rubbed a stiff neck and forced the overwhelming thoughts about the catastrophe that ruined her life to the back of her mind. She promised herself she'd enjoy the mini vacation without dwelling on the carnage. When the week ended, she'd worry about how to move forward.

The incessant ringing of her cell phone coiled her nerves tighter. An unfamiliar number showed on the display. She chewed on the edge of her lower lip. Should she answer?

Curiosity won the mental debate. She grabbed the purple cell phone from the coffee table and plopped onto the comfy sofa. "Hello?"

"Hey, I'm on break. Had to borrow a phone. Battery died in mine. Had this feeling. You know, felt like I needed to hear your voice. You okay?" The familiar tone and clipped words spoken by her sister Sarah allowed Kimberly to relax.

"Fine." She hesitated, suppressing a twinge of guilt for lying. "I met a gorgeous guy tonight with a sexy Scottish burr."

Crap. Where did that come from? Kimberly hung her head and silently groaned.

"Thought you swore off men."

"I did. I'm not planning to date the guy or anything. Dropped my scarf, and he returned it, is all." Oh yeah, and the exciting sensual spark she experienced when their fingers touched. She didn't dare mention *that* fascinating tidbit to her sister.

"You don't think he's the hit man your ex-client hired? Do—"

Static blared from the speaker. "Can't hear you. You're breaking up."

"Can you hear me now?" Sarah popped her gum.

Kimberly laughed. "Yeah. Loud and clear. You sound like the guy from that annoying old phone company commercial."

"Forget that. Could he be the hit man Mr. Romano hired? Were you followed to Cape May? Jerky Jason might have told them where to find you. I've felt negative energy for days."

Unease bubbled in Kimberly's stomach. Her sister sometimes had a sixth sense. "Don't be overdramatic. There isn't a hit man. Jason hoped to scare me with the warning. He didn't want me to enjoy my stay in Cape May." Kimberly brushed an unsteady finger over the smooth fabric of the floral sofa. "Besides, Mr. Romano is a respected businessman. Even though I lost a lot of his money, he wouldn't hire a hit man to kill me."

"Yeah? Well, he might belong to the mob. Please, be careful. You've already lost too much." Sarah paused. "As for Jason, I'm glad he won't be my brother-in-law."

The last thing Kimberly wanted to do was think about Jason Reedman, or any of the disaster that had become her life. Couldn't her sister understand that?

"Let's drop it."

"But I feel so bad. I'm really sorry you had to sell the condo to pay off debts."

Kimberly held back tears threatening to leak. She had lost everything. "Thanks for the support, sis. Things will work out." *I hope.*

"I have a couple thousand saved."

"I don't want your money." Kimberly twirled strands of hair around a finger appalled by the idea she might be desperate enough to borrow money from her younger sister.

"What will you do when the week in Cape May is over?"

"Crash on your sofa, search for a job, celebrate Christmas." She wished Sarah goodnight and ended the call. She needed to think.

Who would hire her after what happened? Who would trust her?

* * *

Neptune was throwing a temper tantrum, and the early

morning light enhanced the display from where she sat on a blanket in the sand. The sea had always drawn Kimberly, especially when at its fiercest. Her father used to joke that she'd been washed up on shore—the long-lost daughter of the sea god.

She tried to ignore the familiar tug in her chest.

Another white-capped wave crashed on the beach, thundering in her ears. She covered them with the tartan scarf to muffle the sound. The wool smelled of male musk, coffee, and cinnamon.

The scent of the man who'd returned the scarf.

A thrill caught her unaware. Something about him had connected with her on a unique level. Silly, really, she'd never see the man again. Shrugging off the tingling chills, she snuggled deeper into the warmth of her coat and returned the wave of a wetsuit-clad surfer.

He grabbed his board and plunged into the churning sea. The guy must be crazy to brave the water on such a cold morning. Moments later, he became a silhouette against the pink and gold colors of the sunrise as he rode a curl to shore.

Shaking her head over the lunacy of thrill seekers, she gave up the perch in the dunes where she'd fled after waking from another disturbing nightmare.

Watching the sunrise had been a soothing distraction, but it was time to head back. She strolled across the street to the Victorian B&B and the hot breakfast hopefully waiting. After slipping into the foyer, she hurried past the noisy dining room and ran up the stairs to drop off the blanket and coat. With most of the guests already downstairs, the empty hall seemed too quiet.

Kimberly slid the card key into the slot, opened the door and—froze.

The curtains performed a macabre dance, billowing in the breeze from the open sliding glass door.

No! God, no.

Denial screamed in her mind, turning to fear as her gaze frantically darted around the room. Closet doors hung ajar. Drawers from the dresser sat on the floor in disarray.

Clothing lay scattered on every surface.

She stumbled back and ran along the hall and down the stairs. The rapid pounding of her heart made her stomach churn. Panting, she rushed through the parlor to the office.

* * *

After spending most of the morning making a report with the local police, Kimberly leaned against the hood of her car in front of a grungy-looking bar and grill. She stole some warmth from the noon sun while debating whether to walk in. The ad in her pocket had sent her driving to the outskirts of town to a place called Paradise Point. After getting lost a few times, she finally found the tavern. The dilapidated bar didn't look like it belonged in paradise.

The sign over the door hung from one hook. There were two, fifty-dollar pickups parked in the gravel lot. Not exactly encouraging.

A chill breeze tickled her cheeks, and she shoved her hands into deep coat pockets. The sun sat high in the cloudless sky. If there was a better time to get this over with, she didn't know it. The last thing she wanted was to be here after dark.

Kimberly stiffened her spine and marched to the door, the crunch of frozen gravel overloud, then pulled the index card out of the pocket and stared at the masculine penned block letters. *Rusty Scupper.*

This is the place.

Layers of chipped black paint and battered hinges. Looked as if the door had been kicked in dozens of times. The owner of the B&B had hinted this section of town had a seedy reputation. Guess he got that right.

Maybe it would be better not—

Get a grip, Kimberly. You can do this.

She grabbed the grimy knob and twisted.

CHAPTER TWO

The dank smells of stale beer and perspiration and moldy wood, mixed with a hint of urine, assaulted Kimberly as she entered the decrepit bar. Her eyes required a few seconds to adjust to the dimness.

Three salty old men stared at her from bar stools twisted in her direction. The other stood behind the bar, drying a streaked glass with a stained linen towel.

She swallowed, suppressing an urge to run out the door. Lead took up residence in her legs as she walked across the sticky plank floor to the bar. The bartender smiled, showing tobacco-stained teeth. Kimberly fiddled with the tattered index card in her hand.

"Can I help you, miss?" The bartender dropped a cardboard coaster in front of her.

"I'm interested in the crew position on *Sea Panther*."

Three sets of eyes widened. Not a good sign.

The scruffy guy seated on the closest stool rubbed his gray beard. "You want to crew for the Panther? You're a brave girl."

"Isn't that wise?"

The bartender shot the patron a scathing glare, and the man stared down into his beer mug. The door creaked open with a burst of cold air; everyone glanced in that direction. A tall, brawny man with red hair and ruddy complexion sauntered in and approached the bar. The bartender handed him a foamy mug, which he downed in two gulps. Then he sat on a stool at the end of the bar and pushed the empty mug toward the bartender. "Another, Mackey."

Mackey laughed. "Have a bad day, Colin?"

"Aye, you might say that. Worked up a heavy thirst."

"Well, your day is about to improve."

"How so?"

Mackey tilted his head toward Kimberly. "This lady here is interested in crewing for the Panther."

The redheaded man glanced at her. One side of his mouth quirked up, and he shook his head a couple of times. Then he measured her with a stare and gestured to the barstool next to him. "Join me, lass."

Another man with a Scottish burr. Were Scotsmen taking over South Jersey? Kimberly hid nervous amusement behind a cough then shored up her courage and slid onto the stool next to the big man. Either she had impeccable timing or fate had taken an interest.

"Care for a drink?" he asked.

"No thanks, too early for me."

"Suit yourself, though I'm sure it's happy hour somewhere." He grabbed the refilled beer mug from Mackey and took a long swallow. Setting the mug on the bar, he spun on the stool to face her. "Colin MacEwen."

She laid the index card on the bar and shook the outstretched hand. "Kimberly Scot."

Colin's gaze shifted to the card, and he smiled. "I see you found one of my wee advertisements."

"Are you the captain?"

"First mate. My distant cousin is the captain." Keen hazel eyes once again roamed over her.

She fought not to squirm under the earnest inspection.

"Why do you want to crew on *Sea Panther?*"

"I need a job."

He grunted. "Do you have experience?"

"Yes." Kimberly held his gaze. "You may have heard of my father. Jimmy Scot?"

Would he recognize Dad's name? Colin remained

inscrutable. Alrighty, then...

"He was an international racer. I sometimes crewed for him when he wasn't racing. He died several years ago."

"I've heard of Fast Jimmy." Colin's face softened, and he took a swig of beer. "*Sea Panther* sails at a leisurely pace, making frequent stops along the way. Would that bore you?"

"No." Kimberly stilled, holding in the relief. He was considering hiring her. She didn't want to blow it now.

The man frowned. Hesitated. Then seemed to come to a decision. "You'll need to meet with the captain. He'll have more questions."

"Sure."

"Meet him here at eleven tonight. And don't let him intimidate you."

"Here?" Kimberly squeaked.

"Problem?"

She glanced around the barroom, trying not to show distaste.

Colin chuckled. "Where do you live?"

"I was staying at a B&B in Cape May."

"And now?"

Kimberly lowered her gaze to the well-worn surface of the mahogany bar. "Nowhere. That's why I need a job."

Colin reached for the index card on the bar and flipped it over. He pulled a pen from a breast pocket and jotted an address on the tattered sheet. "Here." He handed it over. "Be there at ten o'clock tonight. I'll make sure the captain is at the club, and I'll tell the lads you'll be coming."

He chugged the remainder of his beer and tossed a ten-dollar bill on the bar. "Take care, Mackey." He inclined his head to her. "Good day, Miss Scot." Before walking out the door, he called back, "Be there at ten. Don't be late, the captain hates tardiness."

He chuckled and pushed out the door.

Kimberly exhaled sharply and glanced at the bartender. He stared as if mesmerized by a favorite reality show on TV. She smiled. Now that the course was set, she wanted a drink. Needed one, actually. As the mate said, it must be after five somewhere in the world.

"A glass of red wine, please." She swiveled from side to side on the barstool.

"Right away, miss, but you should have let Colin buy the drink. His captain is swimming in money."

She leaned forward. Now she'd get the real poop.

"Colin is okay, but the captain is strange," the patron who'd started to speak earlier said.

An uneasy sensation settled in her chest. "What do you mean?"

"He's never seen other than at night...and there are rumors."

"What kind of rumors?"

"Dark tales."

Kimberly bit her bottom lip.

Mackey scowled at the man. "Do shush, Tinker. Don't be scaring the lady."

"Aren't you afraid to crew for the Panther? He's a hard man." The other bar patron dressed in a black wool fisherman sweater finally spoke.

Kimberly didn't understand the urge to jump to the captain's defense. She'd never met the man. Didn't know his name. "If you know a reason I shouldn't crew on *Sea Panther*, I wish you would tell me what it is."

"Well, there's rumors is all," Tinker said.

These men thought she should be afraid. Why? "Please, tell me more."

"Captain MacLachlan's a reclusive billionaire," Mackey said.

"Some say he's," the man in the sweater looked around the barroom wide-eyed as if fearing the walls hid listening ears, "a pirate."

* * *

At nine-thirty in the evening, Kimberly stood on the sidewalk across the street from the address Colin provided. Hip club-goers entered through a pair of lacquered black doors.

She took out her cell phone and entered a speed-dial sequence. *Come on, answer.* Sarah better have recharged her phone's battery.

After two rings, her sister offered a cheery, "Hey."

"Hi." Kimberly's chest tightened but she plowed on. "I might not make it for Christmas."

"Why not?"

"Ran into a bit of a difficulty. I need to lay low for a while."

"What happened? Are you okay?"

"Someone ransacked my room at the B&B this morning." If it wasn't bad enough knowing someone broke into the room, that they touched her personal stuff made her cringe.

"Did they steal anything?"

"I no longer have anything of value worth stealing. I pawned my electronics and most of my jewelry. The police said maybe one of the other guests disturbed a robber and they ran off. Though, I don't think the cops believe that any more than I do."

"Do you think it was the hit man?"

"Don't know. I'm scared." The ache in Kimberly's belly burned. The rumors about a hit man must be true. But why would he go through her stuff? She'd been an easy target while sitting on the beach. A perfect kill.

"Then you should come here. I'll get one of my big guy friends to protect you."

"I'm not putting you or your friends at risk. I found a crew ad for a ninety-foot yacht sailing to Florida and the Caribbean. I plan to be on that boat when it departs." *And if there is a hit man, he won't be able to find me.*

A long shrill whistle sounded from the phone speaker. "Are you losing it? You swore never to sail again."

"I know, but desperation changes things."

"You don't have to leave. I can lend you some money and—"

"I don't want you mixed up in this mess."

"But—"

"Let it go. Please."

"You're too impulsive. You can't take off with strangers on a mega-yacht."

Kimberly winced. It wasn't as if she hadn't considered the risks. "I did an internet search on the yacht. The owner is a wealthy philanthropist who operates a panther research facility in South Florida. Above board. I'll be safe."

"Oh, Kim, how do you know for sure?"

"Don't worry. I'll be fine." Kimberly refused to allow her sister's grave sigh to sway her.

"I can't talk you out of this, can I?"

"No." There was no way Sarah was changing Kimberly's mind. She was determined to be on *Sea Panther* when the yacht set sail, even if it meant stowing away.

"Be careful and call me often. I need to know you're okay."

"I will." Kimberly disconnected the call and shoved the phone back in her purse. She waited for a black sedan with tinted windows to pass before striding across the street. She'd do whatever it took to get on that damn boat.

* * *

Colin sent a woman for Robert to interview. Why? The man knew better.

Before he could wrap his mind around the why of his first mate's actions, a knock sounded at the door. "Enter," he yelled and continued to stare at the garden through the private dining room's paned windows. He was acting rude, but he wanted to assert control over the battling beasts before facing the woman who managed to wheedle Colin into giving a recommendation.

The sound of a feminine throat clearing stiffened his spine, and he whirled around to face the woman. Oxygen left him in a rush. There stood the lass who haunted his dreams for the past night and day—since he saw her on the street and returned the damn scarf. The simple touch of their fingers had produced sparks. Remnants of the intense jolt of power that released the panther from tight restraints continued to surge through his blood.

He needed to be wary of this dangerous woman. He couldn't hire her—have her near him, night after night, for the entire duration of a cruise. Too great would be temptation.

Robert studied her tall, slim form. She appeared elegant

even though casually dressed. Soft chocolate eyes peered from a sculpted ivory face framed by shoulder-length curly brown hair. His gaze fed on lush lips that begged for passionate kisses.

When a pink tongue darted out and moistened those lips, every muscle in his body clenched. Fire raced through his veins. He was lost.

He couldn't allow it. He strengthened his resolve. "Please, have a seat," he reluctantly offered.

Her eyes glimmered with recognition, and she smiled. "Captain MacLachlan?"

"Aye." Robert waved toward a chair. "Sit."

He clenched his jaw. Was it his voice that sounded so gruff? Just as well, he didn't want to give encouragement.

She dropped into the chair. A perplexed expression played on perfect features.

"What is your name?" he asked.

"I...I'm sorry." She jumped up and reached out a hand. "Kimberly Scot."

"Robert MacLachlan, Captain of *Sea Panther*."

He hesitated before shaking her hand. Would her touch produce the same effect as on their last meeting? He tightened control on the vampire and the panther, and grasped the slender hand.

Zap.

Her eyes widened.

He yanked his arm away and extinguished the unwanted flame of lust hardening his loins. This woman meant trouble.

"Sit," he barked.

Though her hands trembled, she did as directed.

He trembled too. Needing time to rein in the chaotic emotions, he poured wine into two goblets from the bottle on the wet bar. He handed her one, careful not to make physical contact again. "I own this establishment. The wine is excellent."

"Thank you," she said and accepted the glass.

He grunted. God, he was being rude.

He paced a few feet away. Far enough not to reach for her. The lingering sensation from their brief handshake made him edgy. The pulse at her neck called to the vampire. The panther, demanding his mate, fought against bonds to which Robert tethered the animal. Robert forced control. "You want to crew on *Sea Panther?*"

Uncertainty flickered in her eyes. Was she afraid?

Aye. He smelled trepidation. Although it was best she fear him, the thought didn't sit well. A strong need to protect his mate blasted his frontal lobe. Damn panther.

She held his stare. Finally, she answered, "Yes."

"Why do you want to crew for me?"

"I need a job."

"I see."

Dark brows rose in a graceful arch. "Do you?"

"What experience do you have?"

"I sailed with my father when I was a teenager."

Robert ignored the pinch in his chest and slid his gaze over her too-slim form. He lingered on the curve of her breasts before gradually directing his gaze higher, satisfied when she blushed. "Not to be insulting, but you haven't been a teenager for a long time."

The angry tilt of her chin exposed the sweet, soft, tempting length of her throat. His fangs punched through his gums, and he labored to concentrate.

"My father was Jimmy Scot. I'm sure you've heard of him."

Indeed. Fast Jimmy had won more international yacht races than any of his contemporaries. Why did his daughter seek a job on *Sea Panther?* Although the lass wore quality garments, Colin believed she struggled without resources.

"When was the last time you sailed?"

"Before my father died." She pinned him with an irritated look. "Listen, I need a job, and I'm a good sailor."

Sea Panther needed another hand. No one else had applied. Robert sighed, feeling cornered. Hadn't she heard the rumors about him? Didn't she believe the stories as all the others did? The lass must be in a dire situation if there was no one to turn to other than him.

She held his gaze and waited for a response. Her imploring brown eyes slashed his defenses. Robert didn't want to give in. He should send her away.

He retreated to the other side of the room and sat on the red leather sofa. With one leg crossed over the other knee, he tried to appear unaffected by her presence. He observed her while morosely pretending to sip from the goblet of wine, wishing the crystal glass contained her blood.

CHAPTER THREE

Kimberly struggled not to fidget under the scrutiny of her host.

Dressed in form-hugging black pants, a starched white tuxedo shirt open at the throat and stretched across a broad chest, and with the scar on a dangerously handsome face, Captain MacLachlan did look like a pirate. An eye-patch and sword, and a kerchief over his short spiked hair would complete the swashbuckler effect. Kimberly tried not to sigh at the image. She had to stop watching those classic old movies.

From his charming smile on their first meeting, she wouldn't have expected him to be such an ill-tempered man. Tonight, however, his dark expression unnerved her. As did the odd sensation when they touched.

She rubbed her palm on her thigh—the palm still tingling from their handshake.

From the way the captain snatched his hand away, she would have thought him stung.

Silence stretched. Kimberly couldn't stand the suspense. "Will there be other women onboard?" She burst out with the question that worried her most.

Captain MacLachlan arched an eyebrow. "Do you have a problem working with men?"

"Of course not." She wouldn't allow him to think her a

sexist. "But I do wonder if they'll have a problem working with me."

"My crew will do as I order."

"That doesn't mean they'll want to work with me." Kimberly rose from the chair, unable to sit any longer. She'd been shocked at the pub to learn Sea Panther's mysterious captain was the same man who owned the yacht. What a coincidence she'd met him on the street the other night. She flicked glances in his direction while she paced.

His penetrating stare tracked her every move. "It might ease your mind to know my sister will meet us in Annapolis and will sail with us until we reach Florida."

A surprise and a relief. "Does that mean I have the job?"

Kimberly held her breath. He had to hire her. He just had to. It would be the perfect opportunity to slip away. No one would think to look for her on a yacht sailing south this late in the season.

The captain sprang from his seat. With graceful catlike movements, he crossed the room to tower over her. She refused to be intimidated, and held her ground, allowing him to crowd her.

"Why do you want to crew for me?" he demanded with a sneer.

His rude manner got under her skin. Air left her lungs with a soft hiss. One. Two. She silently counted to ten and swallowed her pride.

"I'm homeless. Crewing for you will give me a place to live." She gazed into the most alluring eyes. Her stomach did a somersault. *Idiot.* She couldn't believe she was attracted to the infuriating man.

He remained quiet. Time ticked by.

He sipped the wine and pursed his lips as if it tasted sour. "All right. You're hired. The salary is $750 per week. Does that meet with your approval?"

"Yes." She took a step back. "Thank you."

"Be at the boat before first light. My first mate, Colin, will explain your duties. We set sail early. I wish to sup in Chesapeake City." He set the wineglass down and strode to the door. "Be prepared to work hard," he said over his shoulder.

He left. The door closed with a thud.

Kimberly breathed a sigh of relief. The room seemed less stifling without the captain's overwhelming presence. She strolled to the window and peered out at the spotlighted winter garden. Cottony snow capped a collection of sculpted evergreens.

The old men at the *Rusty Scupper* had it right. The captain was a strange man. Like the actors in her favorite old movies, his speech and mannerisms imitated a bygone era. Was it an affectation or did it come naturally to him?

She savored the last taste of the cabernet. Raspberry and plum aromas with a hint of cassis flavor. In truth, the wine was excellent. As she placed the empty glass on a table, the door opened again. She tensed and swung around.

Colin stood in the doorway, a grin on his face. "So you've ensnared the captain."

"He hired me if that's what you mean." She couldn't help returning the Scotsman's smile.

"It is. Do you have a place to stay tonight?"

"My car."

"That doesn't sound comfortable. Meet me at *Paradise Point Marina* at midnight. We'll stow your gear, and you can stay aboard."

Colin ushered her to the club's entrance. As she got into her car, the creepy feeling someone watched caused the fine hairs on the back of her neck to bristle.

* * *

At midnight, Kimberly drove across the frost-hardened gravel and frowned. Finding a parking space would be difficult. Boats that had been pulled onto the hard for the winter occupied most of the marina lot. She drove around until she found a spot close to the floating docks in one of the few spaces available under a lamppost and parked.

She speed dialed her sister. The phone rang several times until the annoying voice on the other end said to leave a message at the beep.

"Hey, Sarah. I'm leaving tomorrow on *Sea Panther*. I

need you to retrieve my car from *Paradise Point Marina*. I'll call when I can. Have a wonderful Christmas. Love you."

Kimberly pressed the End button and slipped the phone into her purse. She'd miss spending the holiday with Sarah, but had little choice other than to disappear for a while.

She reached across to the passenger side and shoved the leather valise containing personal papers and a thumb drive into her duffle bag. Leaving the thin briefcase in the locked car proved a good call. Otherwise, the intruder might have stolen it during the break-in at the B&B.

Taking careful note of the surroundings, she slid out of the car and shivered. The uneasy sensation someone watched still bothered her. Forcing the anxiety aside, she shouldered the large duffle bag and carried the tote along with her purse in the other hand. The stench of fish guts had her wrinkling her nose as she passed a few fishing boats tied to the dock and made her way to the launch waiting at the end.

Colin waved. "You didn't change your mind?"

"No. I need this job."

"You're sure?" His brow furrowed. "There's no need to be embarrassed if you changed your mind. If you're uncomfortable—"

"I'm sure." Kimberly managed a strained smile.

He nodded and loaded the bags. She liked the man. He reminded her of a big redheaded teddy bear. She helped cast off lines then sat on the cold bench. "I didn't have an opportunity to ask the captain about the rest of the crew. Who will be sailing with us?"

"A motley crew." Colin's loud voice boomed over the hum of the motor. "Timothy Eagan is our navigator. Good man. Then we have John and Davey Walsh. Twins from Boston. Won't find a better group of lads. They won't give you any trouble if that has you worried."

One of many worries, but why admit it?

"Including me and you, that makes five crewmembers. You hired me as the fifth. Don't you count the captain?"

"We need to be able to sail without him."

"Oh?"

"We must always be prepared to set sail whether he is aboard or not. Robert is the head of *Panther Enterprises*, a large conglomerate with offices all over the world, which necessitates a considerable amount of travel on his part."

"He lives in Florida, right?"

"You've done your homework."

"I wanted to know what I was getting into."

"Good girl." Colin chuckled. "Robert has a compound in South Florida with a fine house though he considers *Sea Panther* home. We'll visit the compound before sailing on to the Caribbean."

She didn't care where they sailed to as long as it was away from here. Away from rumored hit men and break-ins and unemployment.

Moonlight exposed a silhouette of the yacht. When the moon slipped behind a cloud, the mast light became a beacon in the dark. As they motored in close, an eerie chill raced over her skin. Fear? Partly. But more...something akin to *fate*.

Colin pulled alongside the yacht, and a yellow-slicker covered crewmember assisted her aboard. She waited while the two men secured the launch.

"Davey, this is Kimberly. She'll be replacing Willy." Colin inclined his head to her. "Our lad here has night watch."

They exchanged hellos, and Colin directed her to the companionway. She stepped down into a luxuriously fitted salon with red leather settees and teak tables. The light-colored wood also covered the bulkheads and cabinetry. The European décor felt masculine. Similar to the yachts she sailed on with her father. Her chest tightened as her heart twisted with a twinge of sadness.

Colin joined her a moment later, and she forced a smile. "Is someone always on night watch? Even when in port?"

"Aye. We take security seriously." He took several steps. "This way to your cabin. Stow your gear then we can go on the grand tour."

Relieved by the apparent security measures, she trailed behind, through the large salon, past the navigation desk, and into the well-appointed galley, where a loud kaplunk made her jump. "What's that?"

"Ice."

"Wow. An ice machine?"

"Convenient when you want to make a frozen cocktail." Laugh lines appeared at the edges of his eyes when he smiled.

"I'm impressed."

"Don't be. No washer or dryer."

No disappointment there. She hadn't expected laundry facilities onboard.

He headed aft, and she followed. Inside a small passageway, he stopped in front of the first of three teak doors. "The captain's sister uses this cabin when she's aboard." He pointed to the two other doors. "The one on the right is yours. The other is a head."

Kimberly opened the door to the assigned cabin and smiled, surprised to find a double bunk and a small hanging closet. She laid the bags on the mattress then checked out the head. Toilet and sink with a handheld shower. Not bad for low person on the totem pole.

Or sailboat mast, as it were.

She followed Colin back into the galley where he showed her the adjoining engine room behind a reinforced metal door. Exiting through the salon, they entered another passageway, and he pointed to the closest door. "Timothy's." After a few more steps, he said, "The twins share this cabin and mine is the single across the way."

When she walked on, Colin stopped her with light pressure on her arm. "The captain's cabin is forward, off limits to crew."

"I'll keep that in mind." She preceded Colin into the salon then turned to face him. "There's something I neglected to mention."

His eyes narrowed. "What would that be?"

"I have a fear of heights." Kimberly bit the corner of her lower lip. She should have owned up to it sooner. No way could she ever climb the mast.

"I'll pass the information on to the captain, but I don't see that it'll be a problem."

"Good." One less thing to worry about.

"We rise at 0600. After breakfast, I'll acquaint you with the upper deck and explain what the captain will expect. Have a good rest."

"I will." She started to walk aft, but glanced back at Colin. "Thank you."

The man's face reddened. "Just do a good job."

Kimberly nodded and went to her cabin, but found it difficult to sleep. She tossed and turned. The sheets twisted around her limbs. The nightmare began like always. Somehow, in her subconscious mind, she knew she dreamed, as if she watched a movie where she was one of the actors.

He followed her. She ran and ran as fast as she could.

Branches tore at her clothing, scratched her bare arms, slapped her face.

The man was gaining on her.

She ran until she came to the edge of the cliff. Hands on knees, she panted, trying to catch her breath. Her pursuer was too close. She veered away, dashed along the cliff, the stranger right behind. She sprinted along the edge, praying she wouldn't trip and slide over the rim. That she'd find a way across the jungle-like ravine.

She didn't look down, couldn't look down. Fear threatened to strangle her.

Out of breath, she stopped and glanced back. The man still followed. He moved closer, his face hidden in shadow.

He moved as if in slow motion, as if the projectionist ran the film frame by frame.

The man reached to push her over the edge.

This night the dream took on a bizarre twist.

The man shuddered and morphed into a big cat. A mountain lion or cougar.

She froze.

The scene sped up.

The animal growled. A blood curdling sound that raised the hairs on her arms. Canines bared, he leapt toward her. Lunged for her throat. She toppled backward; fell over the edge, screamed.

She woke with her body covered in sweat.

Another growl echoed in the night. This one sounded like a tomcat yowling, though louder. More frightening.

Kimberly bolted up in the bed. With a shaky hand, she reached for the switch and turned on the reading light over the bunk.

The cabin door swung open.

The captain stood in the doorway. Gorgeous cinnamon eyes bore into her. His intimidating breadth and height pressed against the edges of the small portal made him appear larger. Dangerous.

She moistened dry lips. "I...I'm sorry. Did I scream aloud?"

An abrupt nod was his response.

"Had a bad dream." Could she feel more embarrassed? Surely, her face must be flaming.

"I had not realized you were aboard until I heard you cry out."

"Sorry," she said, wishing he'd hurry and leave.

"Nae worries." To her relief, he backed toward the doorway. Then his gaze locked on her breasts.

Kimberly glanced down. Her at-attention nipples pressed against the thin fabric of her sheer cotton undershirt, emphasizing the dark aureoles. She pulled the sheet up to her neck and glared at the smug jerk. The least he could do is look away.

His gaze rose to her neck, and she saw his struggle to swallow. The unmasked expression of blatant desire within his eyes chased away her annoyance. He stared at her as a starving man might view a well-stocked buffet table. Consumed her with his gaze. Her insides melted.

He cleared his throat, but his steady regard remained intense.

"Captain? I..."

His gaze jerked to her face. "Excuse me," he mumbled as he eased out into the passageway and shut the door.

Great way to start out, Kimberly.

Her watch displayed four o'clock. Another two hours before she needed to start the day. She flicked the light off and squeezed her eyes tight.

God. How awkward. She flipped over and slammed a

fist into the pillow.

She'd never fall back to sleep. Not after glimpsing the captain's expression of hunger.

What would it be like to make love to such a virile man?

CHAPTER FOUR

Not in three hundred years had Robert been this turned on by the sight of a pair of budded nipples. He almost imagined the feel of those perky breasts whilst his teeth grazed over the thin fabric covering them—imagined moans escaping her lips. *Kimberly*. His blood blazed with unquenched desire.

Violent need throbbed with each beat of his heart. His aching erection strained against the fabric of his trousers. He undid the zipper in a hurry.

Damn. He'd reacted like a green lad who'd never bedded a lass before.

Robert clenched his jaw as the beasts attempted to rise. They fought for supremacy. He refused to allow it. Not on this sunrise. He dropped his pants and freed himself. With a deep breath, he wrapped a trembling hand around his cock and rubbed the thumb over the head, massaging the moist tip. He fantasized Kimberly was stroking him. Breath caught in his lungs as the fire in his groin intensified. He leaned his ass against the bunk with both feet firmly planted on the floor, and pumped until sterile seed exploded from his body with a fierce shudder.

Despite the ferocity, the orgasm felt hollow. Nothing like the heights he believed Kimberly could bring. He dare not think on that. Dared not allow her close. The two beasts living within were too dangerous.

Damn Colin. What had the man been thinking to suggest—no, insist—he hire a female for crew? And not just any lass.

"Kimberly." The name whispered on a breath. Something about her quickened his pulse as no other woman ever had. A growl threatened to escape his throat. He choked it back. What emotion remained within him was too raw...too wild.

Of any time in his eternal existence, he needed to be careful. Vigilant. Hold a tight rein on the monsters lurking within. He dared not contemplate what would happen to Kimberly if the beasts seized control.

* * *

Early in the morning, loud voices and the aroma of frying bacon wafted from the galley. The time had come to make an appearance in the salon, but Kimberly's pulse raced with dread...with excitement...at the thought of seeing the captain. She couldn't get the ravenous yearning that had burned in his eyes out of her mind. Though uncomfortable to admit, deep within her blazed the same fire.

Great. Just great. She couldn't afford to lust after her employer.

Forcing aside the image of Robert's hungry gaze, she inhaled a deep breath and headed for the galley. Colin stood at the three-burner stove, whipping up what smelled to be a yummy breakfast. No doubt, she'd gain ten pounds crewing with big guys with hearty appetites.

"Ah, Kimberly. Good morn to you, lass. Go on into the salon and get acquainted with the lads."

She hesitated for a moment, waiting for the nervous churning in her belly to ease, before joining the rest of the crew. Three sets of eyes checked her out with curiosity. She'd met Davey the previous evening, but had no idea which of the two identical, blue-eyed blonds he was.

The third young man, a tall lanky fellow with a shaved head spoke first. "I'm Timothy and these two nut cases are Davey and John. Will take you weeks before you can tell them apart."

The twins gave game smiles. She relaxed a bit and responded with a finger wave. "Hi. I'm Kimberly."

The greeting, "Welcome aboard," repeated three times.

One of the twins leaned forward. "Davey." He pushed up the left sleeve of a navy turtleneck shirt. "The one with the awesome sea maiden tattoo."

Sure enough, the multicolored image of a mermaid swam on his arm.

"John," his twin said. "I saw you on the beach the other morning while surfing."

"You waved to me."

"Yeah. You looked sad."

Thankfully, Colin carried in a tray laden with five plates, and the guys grabbed for the food, saving Kimberly from having to respond to John's comment. She didn't want to explain her depression.

"Hope you lads are being nice to Fast Jimmy Scot's daughter," Colin said.

"You didn't tell us your father was Fast Jimmy." John stared with renewed interest.

Kimberly shrugged. She'd rather Colin hadn't mentioned her father. Guilt mixed with the other anxieties swamping her. She hated having resorted to using his name to get the job.

Quiet ruled while the group chowed down, the only sound the scrape of forks across plastic dishes. When the men finished, she still had half a plate of food.

"You didn't like my cooking," Colin accused.

"It was great, but I'm afraid my appetite isn't as big as the rest of yours." Kimberly swept her gaze over the group of muscular men at the table.

Colin chuckled. "Will be after you've sailed with us for a time."

"Doesn't the captain dine with the crew?" she asked, relieved he hadn't joined them yet curious about his absence.

Timothy and Davey exchanged glances.

"Sometimes for the evening meal," Colin said easily enough.

Still, an uncomfortable tension filled the air. What had she said to put the men on guard?

Colin rose and gathered up the plates. She reached for an emptied coffee mug, but he waved her off. "Spend the next hour getting acquainted with the lads and learning about *Sea Panther*. When we set sail will be soon enough to lend a hand."

John laughed. "Timothy will introduce you to *Robert's lady*."

"Lady?" So much for inappropriate interest in the captain. The man had either a wife or a girlfriend.

"*Sea Panther*," John said with a wink.

"Oh." Heat burned Kimberly's cheeks. She hoped the boys didn't notice, but Davey's shrewd smile proved he caught her heightened color.

"*Sea Panther* is a fast, hi-tech, Italian racing sloop," Timothy said. "The captain had her custom built in 2001. Her hull is carbon fiber. She has a seventeen-foot draft. We need to be extra careful to stay away from the shoals along the coast."

Kimberly panicked, doubting her rusty skills. "Colin didn't tell me we'd be racing."

After all, it had been a long time since she last sailed.

"We won't be," Timothy said. "The captain doesn't enter *Sea Panther* into races."

This time John and Davey exchanged glances.

What did all the sideways looks mean? She shrugged off the question. Might be a guy thing. Until she proved herself, they wouldn't give their trust.

"Her length overall is ninety feet, with a beam of twenty-one feet." Timothy continued with the lecture, and she listened attentively.

"You're wrong, Tim." Davey smiled devilishly. "*Sea Panther's* beam is only twenty feet, six inches."

"They're major geeks," John chimed in.

"Let me finish." Timothy leaned forward over the table, getting into the topic. "We run a single diesel, 325 horsepower engine. The boat carries 434 gallons fuel and 647 gallons water. Her cruising speed is ten knots, but we've gotten her to twelve knots with favorable winds."

"Nerds!" John said.

"Tell Kimberly about the electronics," Davey said, voice rising with excitement.

She laughed at the interplay. "What else do I need to know?"

* * *

Kimberly assisted with the sails when Colin set the yacht on a southerly course a couple of hours later. While they cruised, she hung in the cockpit and listened to the boys trade friendly insults. Captain MacLachlan didn't appear on deck until dusk.

The arrogant man swaggered to the wheel and claimed control of the helm. Unusual for a sailor, he dressed in black jeans and shirt. If his stature and clothing didn't set him apart from the rest of the crew, the heavy biker boots he wore certainly did.

He looked damn sexy though, with the top three buttons of his black silk shirt open at the throat. Kimberly would have to be dead not to notice. She couldn't stop staring at the man. Whereas, he didn't so much as acknowledge her existence.

Maybe she misjudged his interest when he came to her room.

When he ordered everyone below except Colin, she made a point of stopping in front of him. He ignored her and spoke quietly to his first mate. She gritted her teeth ready to interrupt, but thought better of it and stepped through the companionway into the salon.

It wasn't a surprise that as soon as they secured the anchor in the small harbor near Chesapeake City, Colin and the captain left in the inflatable dinghy. She had a hunch the captain avoided her. He hadn't said anything since their nocturnal encounter after the nightmare. Could he be embarrassed too?

"Come on. John drew the short straw and has watch. Me and Davey are taking you to the best place in the world for garlic crabs." Timothy extended a hand and helped her into the hard-sided launch.

"Absolute best." Davey pulled the cord to start the

motor.

"Sounds great," she yelled over the engine buzz. She watched the inflatable heading for shore in front of them until a large motor yacht crossed their path and blocked the view. By the time the boat got out of the way, Colin and the captain had disappeared into the shadows.

Chesapeake City turned out to be a cutesy tourist town on the Chesapeake Canal with small, multi-colored Victorian buildings. At this time of year, the place seemed empty.

The bar restaurant they went to smelled of Old Bay seasoning. Brown paper covered the table and a roll of cheap paper towels sat on top. They ordered pitchers of beer, which they drank from clear plastic tumblers. To her amazement, she got into the spirit and shared in the consumption of three dozen large crabs. As Timothy predicted, the blue-claws tasted excellent.

Two hours later, the three of them swayed, arm in arm, strolling through the dimly lit streets toward the dock. As they passed a dark alley between two shops, the crash of a garbage can banging the ground stopped them. A shadow moved away from the light, and fear raced across Kimberly's nerves.

"I think someone is there." She made a move to run, but Timothy tugged on their linked arms and stopped her.

"Probably a raccoon picking through the trash. No harm will come to you, darlin', while you're with us." He gave a cocky grin.

She rolled her eyes, and he chuckled.

Suddenly, a man dressed in all black—pants, sweater and ski mask—darted toward them, knocking her from the boys' hold. She fell backward onto a winter-brown grassy patch in front of a novelty store.

"What the..." Davey watched the guy race away before turning back. "You okay?"

"I think so." A shudder shook her body. Had the hit man found her?

"Here, let me help you." Davey reached out a hand and assisted her to her feet. He leaned close and picked a piece of grass from the sleeve of her sweater.

Kimberly brushed loose dirt off her slacks. She'd swear the man had called her *Satan's whore* as he ran by. A hired hit man wouldn't run off without finishing the job. And she doubted one would call her names.

It wasn't as if they filed a sail plan with the harbormaster in New Jersey anyone could follow. Only Sarah knew she crewed on *Sea Panther*. She'd remain safe as long as they kept sailing south. She had to believe that.

"You sure you're okay?" Timothy's face flushed and his gaze darted to where the man ran. With fingers curled into tight fists, he seemed torn between wanting to chase after the guy and wanting to stay and be her protector.

"Yeah. I'm good." She glanced in the direction the man ran. He had vanished into the dark night. "What do you think the guy was doing?"

"More than likely planned to rob one of the stores." Timothy took a firm hold of her arm. "Let's get back to the boat."

"Shouldn't we call the police?" she asked.

"The captain wouldn't want us to get involved." Timothy pulled her forward.

Davey grasped her other arm, and they made a beeline for *Sea Panther*.

No point in arguing. She wanted to get to the safety of the yacht as fast as possible and try to make sense out of what had just happened.

Satan's whore? Why had the guy called her Satan's whore?

* * *

After a night and day revisiting the episode in Chesapeake City, Kimberly doubted a connection to the rumored hit man, or to the break-in at the B&B. The incident had been nothing more than a case of mistaken identity. She'd been in the wrong place at the wrong time.

Redirecting thoughts to the present, she braced her feet on the deck while Colin steered *Sea Panther* toward a berth at the city dock in Annapolis. The chill wind blew loose hair from her face, and the first stars of the evening twinkled overhead, yet the captain hadn't made an appearance. He kept strange hours for a sailor.

There wasn't time to ponder his peculiarities though. She needed to concentrate on the task at hand. She eyed the entrance pilings with apprehension. When the yacht pulled clear, she relaxed and released the breath she'd held.

As much as she tried, it was impossible to stop thinking about the captain. Recalling his hot gaze when he barged into her cabin the other night made her ache with need.

"Hey! Pay attention." John jumped over the side onto the floating dock.

Kimberly wrinkled her nose and held the line ready to throw. When *Sea Panther* swung into position, she hurled the end of the rope. John snatched it out of the air and tied it to the nearest cleat.

After the crew secured the rest of the lines, he jumped onboard and gave her hair a playful tug. "Can't be gathering wool when we're docking."

"Sorry. I'll pay better attention next time."

"It's okay. The bay's calm tonight, but you'll need all your concentration on the task when the water is rough." He smiled and left her to her own thoughts.

Kimberly slid onto a bench in the cockpit and scanned the dockside restaurants and stores, their facades lit by a golden glow cast from old-fashioned streetlamps. The captain had meetings scheduled with a boat designer about a refit for *Sea Panther*. The plan was to stay in Annapolis for two nights. Not only would the crew have a chance to recharge the yacht's batteries from shore power, she'd have the opportunity to go ashore and purchase a few personal items.

As she rose to go below for her purse, a large raven landed on the boom.

"Shoo. Go away." She swatted at the bird. The nasty thing flew into her face, squawking and clawing. "Ouch! Get out of here." Kimberly used hands and arms for protection, but the damn bird scratched her right hand with sharp talons.

The captain appeared in a blur and reached for the mass of ruffled feathers. He handled the bird gently, removing it from Kimberly and setting it back on the boom.

"Sorry. I dinnae ken what has come over her. She is seldom aggressive without warrant."

"She?" Kimberly warily eyed the large black bird, which stared back with pure malice.

With an apologetic smile, the captain waved toward the raven. "This is Marion. She is my...my pet."

"Your pet attacked me." Kimberly cradled the wounded hand. Marion seemed a strange name for a wild bird. An even stranger pet for a yacht captain.

"She has drawn blood." He grabbed Kimberly's fingers, raised the hand to his mouth and ran a velvet tongue across the tiny lacerations.

Wow. Every molecule in her body clenched at the electric charge that raced up her arm and slammed into her chest.

A piercing squawk came from the bird. The captain staggered back a step. His eyes dilated. He must have felt the charge too. The raven leapt from the boom onto his shoulder, but kept its piercing stare on Kimberly.

"I apologize." Bowing his head briefly, the captain released her hand. "That was inappropriate." He whirled on a heel and disappeared through the companionway along with the bird.

"What the hell?" Kimberly stared after him.

CHAPTER FIVE

Robert sagged against the passageway bulkhead and attempted to focus his thoughts. The metallic tang on his tongue shocked him to the core. The tiny sip made his head spin with an erotic rush and his groin throb with aching need.

Desperate to hide his urgency, he straightened and limped to the privacy of his cabin. Marion leapt to her perch when he stumbled onto the bunk. Never before had he experienced such a potent reaction to the taste of blood. The rush coursing through his veins awakened the panther, and the vampire slithered from the dark recesses on the offensive.

Damn the raven. She frantically fussed, jumping and flapping pitch-black wings.

Robert's pulse quickened and his lungs burned. Each breath became a struggle. Chaos reigned within his body. Unable to prevent the onslaught of agony, he curled into a fetal position to ride out the torturous storm.

A ragged growl of pain escaped his lips when the big cat won the skirmish for supremacy. Pressure pounded at Robert's temples as tendons and muscles and bones constricted to reshape and accommodate the form of the panther. His garments shredded and fell from his body. Fur scored his flesh.

The big cat leapt from the bed to the floor, landing on all four paws. He stretched a sleek, muscled frame and released a wide yawn. His predatory gaze scanned the cabin until it landed on Marion.

She released a drawn-out croak.

"Relax. You can control the panther," Marion murmured the words in Robert's mind.

Robert concentrated and fought to seize dominance over the beast. The panther weakened. With a violent shudder, the cat collapsed, awkwardly attempted to rise, only to drop again into a quivering heap of fur.

Bones popped. Muscles stretched. Blood raged.

Wracked with god-awful pain, Robert lost touch with the mortal world as his body transformed back into the form of a man. His vampire-self took advantage. His sight sharpened and his fangs lengthened. He lunged for Marion.

She fled the perch, feathers flying. "Robert, force your control."

The familiar voice pulled him from the depths of madness to master the monster. Robert dropped onto the bunk and gasped for air. Damn! Colin had better bring the blood so desperately needed to keep the beasts at bay.

* * *

"What happened?"

Kimberly started at the sound of Colin's voice coming from behind her. She twirled around to face him. "A raven landed on the boat and attacked me. The nasty bird scratched my hand with its claws before the captain pulled it off."

She glanced at the hand. The marks were gone. Recalling the velvety touch of the captain's tongue, heat burned the back of her neck, yet a chill raced up her spine.

"I didn't know the captain had a pet raven."

Colin's features were inscrutable. His gaze briefly lit on the hand she cradled. "You must have frightened her. She'll get used to your presence in time."

"But will I become accustomed to her?" Kimberly flashed a half smile, making light of the incident.

Colin didn't smile. He glanced aft. "The lads are going ashore to a restaurant. They want you to join them. I have the night watch."

"I can't believe they want me to tag along again. Don't they want to pick up girls?"

"Doubt your presence will stop them."

"Come on, Kimberly, we're going for Tex Mex," Davey called from the dock.

She couldn't resist. She loved spicy food. "Give me a minute. I'll grab my purse."

As she stepped toward the companionway, Colin blocked her path. "I'll speak to Robert about Marion."

"Please don't. It was nothing."

"Are you sure? Her claws can leave vicious wounds."

Kimberly glanced at her hand hardly believing the marks had disappeared. "I'm fine."

"Then enjoy dinner."

She ducked below and grabbed her purse. On the way through the salon, an animalistic growl stopped her. The same disturbing yowl as from the dream. The noise came from the fore cabin. The captain's cabin. She stepped in that direction.

"Lads are waiting for you." Colin stood behind her. He must have followed her below.

Kimberly faced him. "Yes, I should be going." She couldn't help glancing again toward the passageway that led to the captain's cabin. *What made that sound?*

"Lass?" Although Colin's tone made the word sound like a question, he wanted to get her moving.

With a shake of the head, she shouldered the purse and headed for the companionway. "Have a good night," she called to Colin before climbing the stairs.

The boys met her on the dock. Together they walked the short distance to the restaurant. Near the naval academy, young sailors filled the bar. The hostess pointed Davey to the stairs, and Kimberly followed him up the steps to another bar area with tables. The boys ordered locally brewed beers. She ordered an Armadillo Margarita. Just the drink to have with hot spicy food, the lime flavor and kick of top-shelf tequila hit her taste buds with an *ahhhhh.*

She'd worry about the dent to the budget another time when not on edge.

After finishing most of the cocktail, a mellow sensation dulled her anxieties. Now would be a good time to ask the boys about the growling sounds, but even under the influence of alcohol, she couldn't get up the nerve. They'd think her crazy.

"Hey, Tim, isn't that Willy?" Davey glared out the window.

"Where?"

"I see who you mean." John pointed in the direction Davey stared. "Over there, standing with the group of guys outside the video arcade."

Timothy stood to get a better look.

"Never mind, he's gone," Davey said.

"Who's Willy?" she asked, vaguely interested.

"The guy you replaced." John scowled before forking up his enchilada and shoving it into his mouth.

She glanced at the young men on the sidewalk across the street. Dark hoodies over black concert tees and baggy pants hanging off their asses. For the most part—normal twenty-somethings.

"A real ass-hole." Timothy gulped a slug of beer.

"Really? What makes you say that?"

"Believe me. You don't want to run into him."

"Why?"

"You just don't. That's all." His expression turned sour. The conversation dropped, like a dud firecracker.

After dinner, the boys headed farther into town to hit the bars. Not inclined to join them in the carousing, Kimberly strolled the main drag where stores were open late for holiday shopping.

Glitzy seasonal decorations sparkled everywhere. The sight of animated Santa's elves plying their trade on high tech electronic toys behind the plate-glass storefront of a hardware shop made her chuckle.

Kimberly suppressed the urge to enter a brightly lit jewelry store. She couldn't afford to feed her fetish. But on approaching one of the trendy boutiques, the wintry window display drew her in. It was love-at-first-sight with the wool merchandise. While admiring a red cashmere sweater dress, her cell phone rang. Darn. She'd lost track of time.

Sarah's number lit the screen. Her sister's phone batteries must be good for a change.

"Hey," she whispered into the phone not wanting to disturb the other shoppers.

"Are you okay? I went to pick up your car. One of my guy friends went with me. Thank God. 'Cause someone broke into the car. And the cops—"

"Slow down. What happened?" Kimberly's pulse raced.

"I'm trying to tell you. Someone shot out the light on the lamppost over your car at the marina and smashed the passenger side window."

"You're kidding. Right?"

"I wouldn't kid about a thing like this."

Shit. Shit. Shit. Why would someone break into her car? She'd only left clothes in it.

"Kim? What where they looking for?"

"No idea. Tell me the whole story."

"The police searched the car. Lifted some prints. They're checking to see if any match the ones found in your room at the B&B. I told them about the hit man. They questioned Mr. Romano. Of course, he denies involvement."

"Oh, Sarah, you didn't. He'll never forgive me."

"What does it matter? He's not your client anymore."

Kimberly looked heavenward. Her sister didn't get it. Sarah didn't understand the importance of maintaining professional contacts.

"What else did the cops say?"

"They'll let me know if they learn anything from the prints."

"Was my car damaged?" The darn thing would probably cost a fortune to fix.

"Only the window and I had it repaired. And hey, all my friends think I look really cool driving around in a shiny black Beemer."

"Be careful. That car is the only valuable possession I have left."

"Yeah, it's a good thing you paid it off before Jerky

Jason came into your life."

"I don't want to go there," Kimberly murmured, tired of Sarah's constant reminders of how rotten her ex had been.

"Gotta hang up. Boss is calling for me. Be careful. Love you."

"Love you too." Kimberly pressed the End button and returned the cell phone to her purse. She glanced through the large plate-glass window into the street at the holiday shoppers strolling by. Unease tightened the muscles across her chest.

Just how much danger was she in? Was someone trying to scare her or was someone out to hurt her?

Needing a distraction from the mounting fear, she wandered to the next clothing rack and fingered the soft weave of a mohair cape. The tactile sensation soothed. Suddenly the hairs on her arms rose. Someone stood behind her. Heart pounding too fast, she spun to meet the captain's intense gaze.

"Ach, lass, I didn't mean to startle you." He stepped closer.

Kimberly released the breath she held and willed her pulse to slow to a normal pace. "It's okay. I'm not usually the nervous type. You must have caught me during a rare moment." She didn't want him to think she jumped every time a man came near.

The captain fondled the forest green cape she'd been admiring, and a delicious chill shivered along her spine. For a man with large hands, he had a gentle touch. What would those long fingers feel like caressing her skin? The thought of him massaging her breasts the way he did the wool caused a shot of lust to rush through her system.

Chills and fever. What a potent mix.

"This garment would look beautiful on you," he said.

"Thank you." She lowered her head to hide a flushed face. "I'm afraid I can't afford it."

"Will you tell me why a woman with a quick mind like yours is out of work and homeless?"

His question was blunt and to the point—a splash of cold water to raging hormones. How she'd landed in the current situation was the last thing she wanted to explain.

She raised a wary gaze to meet his. "Captain MacLachlan, I—"

"Never mind." He waved an arm as if to erase his words. "I did not mean to put such deep sadness into your eyes."

"Excuse me. We're closing," one of the shop's employees interrupted. Her gaze lingered on Robert as if to say, *you're welcome to stay*.

"We are leaving," he said to the woman then smiled at Kimberly. "Come. Walk with me."

She followed him out onto the sidewalk. Cars slowly drove by on the one-way street. If a hit man was after her, in truth, he could be anywhere. She tamped down on her nerves, feeling foolish, refusing to believe someone wanted to harm her. It didn't make sense. Her ex-clients were respectable businessmen. The burglaries had to be a bizarre coincidence. After all, she'd left the car in a nearly deserted marina. No wonder someone broke into it.

"I'm on my way to a jazz club. Care to join me?"

The invitation surprised Kimberly and she nodded. The captain probably felt bad about the bird incident earlier. He should, and she could certainly use a treat.

Still unnerved by Sarah's call, Kimberly flicked a glance over a shoulder and scanned the street behind them. No one seemed to be paying attention to them.

"Is something wrong?" The captain slowed the pace.

"No. Everything is fine."

"Are you sure?"

"Absolutely." She pasted on a smile.

"Glad to hear it."

They made their way along the street, past storefronts, and into a residential area of well-kept colonial homes. She relaxed. They spoke about trivial things. The weather, the next port of call, but neither mentioned the captain's pet raven, which was fine with her.

The warmth radiating from the captain made her fully aware of his overwhelming male magnetism. The pleasurable memory of the satiny glide of his tongue on her skin left her achy with need and fueled a growing desire to experience the sensual sensation again. She'd better be careful tonight. She felt vulnerable.

Kimberly frowned at the smooth skin of her hand. How had she healed so fast?

"Here we are." The captain's deep voice scattered her thoughts.

Several couples hung about smoking in front of a large colonial mansion turned club. The sweet sound of a jazz piano filled the air. The captain led her through the crowd loitering outside the door and into the foyer where he waved to the maître d'.

"Do you own this place too?" Kimberly asked as he assisted with her coat and handed it to the coat check.

"In a way. *Panther Enterprises* holds the mortgages on several bars and restaurants along the Atlantic seaboard. I try to visit them when we cruise near."

"Interesting."

"Hardly. Come." He grasped an elbow and guided her to the lounge entrance where the seductive voice of a jazz singer beckoned them to venture into the sultry atmosphere of the club.

Chrome decorated the elegantly appointed round room. She followed the captain through the crush. Black lacquered tables and red leather padded chairs encircled a small stage in the center of the floor. A handsome tuxedo-garbed Aryan man played a grand piano. In contrast, a tall, raven-haired woman dressed in a black cashmere v-neck sweater, tight black leather pants, and black spike-heeled boots sat atop the piano and weaved a sensuous web with the words from a Lena Horne song.

Kimberly joined the captain at a table near the front of the stage. Within seconds, a waiter brought an ice bucket with a bottle of champagne and two flutes. Robert poured, and they clinked glasses.

The song ended.

Leaning on elbows, the singer lounged provocatively on her belly, draped across the piano, while the piano player made love to her with his music and gaze.

The sensual scene made Kimberly perspire. There were only couples in the room; some openly fondled each other. Her discomfort increased as a woman licked her date's neck while stroking a hand over the bulge at the front of his pants. Heat raced along Kimberly's skin to the roots of her hair. What kind of place was this?

She nervously peered at the captain. He stared at the couple on stage. The piano player stood, bowed, pulled the singer into his arms, and dipped her backward over an arm. He gave her a lengthy, passionate kiss and nuzzled her neck.

Kimberly shifted uncomfortably in her chair.

A low growl came from the captain. He stood, knocking over a chair in his rush, and strode to the couple. When they broke apart, he grabbed the woman and shook her. The woman's high-pitched laugh grated on Kimberly's nerves. The captain wore a mask of anger.

Kimberly's chest tightened. She inhaled several deep breaths, trying to get her swirling emotions under control, to rid herself of the knot in her belly. What did it matter that the captain had a girlfriend? Or that he was mightily pissed at the woman.

* * *

Robert wanted to strangle his sister. She acted like a bitch in heat. He shook her, wanting to force some sense into her. "Raven, what were you thinking. Such a public display. You were about to allow Wolfgang to bite you in public. Have you lost all your sense?"

"You are the one making a scene." She struggled to pull free from his grasp.

He held tight to an arm and dragged her along a dark corridor, and into one of the private rooms. Once they were out of sight of prying eyes, he flung her onto the plush velvet sofa and took several deep breaths in an attempt to master his anger.

Her laugh enraged him more. How dare she take her improper behavior so lightly? The humans must never know her as a vampire shifter.

"Your conduct is appalling. And dangerous."

"'Tis you, brother, who puts us at risk, pursuing a cure for something incurable."

Robert ground his teeth.

"Why do you not embrace the power you've been

given?" Raven's gaze turned speculative.

"This is not about me."

"Are you sure?"

"Aye. 'Tis about you. You should not flaunt yourself on stage—" Robert's spine stiffened, his keen senses alert to the fact they were no longer alone. He spun around into a crouch, prepared to ward off an attack.

None came. Wolfgang leaned against the doorframe, a smirk curling his lips. "I would have cloaked us before we had sex."

"'Tis not the sex that worries me and well you ken it." Robert stood and glared at the man.

"Shall I go and take care of the human you left in the bar?" Wolfgang's lecherous grin stoked a primitive need within Robert to strike out at the threat to his mate. He swallowed hard and suppressed the urge to kill the bastard.

"I warn you, Wolf, stay away from her."

"You have not marked her." Wolfgang closed the door and glided into the room.

Robert stepped forward. He clenched tight fists. His blood roared. He wanted to fight.

The other male vampire laughed. "If I desired the drab *fräulein*, I would take her." He glanced at Raven. "I prefer my blood spiced with hot pepper."

"You will leave Kimberly alone."

"Not until you accept the gifts given you, will you be able to control your powers. Without doubt, until then, I will stomp you in battle."

Robert took another step toward Wolfgang.

"Puh...lease. Will the two of you stop the vamp posturing?"

Wolfgang plopped onto the sofa next to Raven. She slid onto his lap and suggestively stroked his chest.

"Fine. If the two of you plan to draw blood, do it behind this closed door where no mortal eyes will spy on you." Robert opened the door to leave, but turned back. "Raven, be aboard *Sea Panther* before dawn the day after tomorrow. The crew has orders to leave at 0800, with, or without you."

An open smile crossed crimson painted lips, exposing fully extended fangs. "Join us," she said before embracing Wolfgang and clamping her mouth on his neck. He reciprocated by piercing her pale skin with sharp fangs.

The desire to join in their erotic feeding overwhelmed Robert. With great effort, he forced himself to back away from the couple, refusing to participate in a perverted *ménage à trois* with his twin sister.

Sickened by the cravings of his vampire-self, he punched the doorframe. Fragments of splintered wood flew in every direction. A large piece stuck in his hand. He yanked out the rough sliver and morosely watched the wound heal.

Leaving his sister and her lover to their depravity, he went in search of the manager. Someone discreet would need to fix the door.

When he finally felt more in control and returned to the table in the lounge, his newest crewmember was gone.

* * *

Kimberly wandered through the empty streets of Annapolis. When she left the jazz club, she believed she knew the way to the yacht. Unfortunately, she'd made several wrong turns and now had no clue where she'd ended up.

Jazz club? The lounge would be better described as a sex club. The captain was a jerk for taking her. Especially since his girlfriend sang there. With each purposeful stride, Kimberly made an effort to release her irritation. It wasn't working. Her hands were actually curled into fists.

The captain had been rude to leave her alone at the table in the lounge while he went in the back with his girlfriend to...

Kimberly didn't want to guess what went on in the back rooms of the club. She quickened her pace as she entered a darkened street lined with warehouses and boat works. With the cloudy sky, not even the moon shed light on the street. She was almost clear of the worst of it when she sensed someone followed her.

Heart thumping a frantic beat, she burst into a run.

Before she got far, the pursuer grabbed her from behind and shoved her face into a brick wall. Pain shot through an arm as the attacker wrenched it up behind her back and trapped her with their body. A masculine body, heavy with arousal, the hard erection touched way to close to the crack of her behind.

"Satan's whore," the guy swore near her ear.

Kimberly kicked back at his legs.

He forced her into the bricks with all his weight, scraping her cheek on the rough surface.

"Why do you call me that?" she managed to ask between gasps for air.

"You're the Panther's whore, and he's the son of the devil."

"I'm not," she choked out.

"What?"

She stomped hard on the bridge of his foot. The guy groaned and lightened the pressure of his hold on her, but didn't let go.

"I'm not the Panther's whore," she screamed. Kimberly struggled, trying to wiggle her arms free so she could nail him in a soft spot.

The attacker tightened the grip, digging thumbs into her arms. "The Panther only takes woman aboard for perverted sex." The guy leaned in tight and rubbed his erection up and down. "You'll give me what you give him."

Kimberly felt the rapid pounding of his heart at her back. The sour stink of sweat surrounded her. But she refused to be overwhelmed by fear. "Not whore," she wheezed. "Hired crewmember."

He spun her around. Shoved her back against the wall. He was young and attractive with blond hair and blue eyes, and not what she expected. He seemed normal.

"Please, let me go. I swear I'm merely part of the crew." She fought harder to break free.

An animalistic growl thundered from the other end of the street.

"Shit! I'll be back for you. The life of one slut to avenge another." The guy let go and ran.

Her legs wobbled and she slid to the ground. Unshed

tears flowed unchecked over her cheeks. Through the moist blur, the hulking form of the captain approached, face contorted with rage.

CHAPTER SIX

Crimson streaks flared at the edges of Robert's vision. He forced the incensed beasts back into the murky recesses and shot into a sprint. His chest expanded with the super-pumped adrenaline surging through his veins. Kimberly had better not be hurt or all the vile creatures in hell would feel his wrath.

She huddled on the ground, eyes stained with tears and a cheek raw and already bruising. He reached out to touch her. When she laced her fingers through his, Robert's heart kicked hard against his ribs. He pulled her up and crushed her against his chest.

He stared in the direction the man ran. Dammit to hell, he wanted to chase after the attacker and kill the bastard for what he'd done. Kimberly's terror burned in Robert's nostrils. He couldn't leave her.

"What happened?" Fear for her made the words come out a gravelly demand.

Her trembling increased. Damn. He wasn't good at providing comfort. He removed his leather jacket and draped it around her shoulders then wrapped his arms around her and held tight. She fit perfectly pressed against him, as if he'd been born for the sole purpose of protecting her.

At a loss as to how to calm her, he rubbed her back and

made, what he hoped were, soothing sounds. "There, there," he murmured. "Everything will be all right. I am here. I have you now."

It took forever, but the trembling subsided. She pulled away and glared at him. "This was all your fault."

"What?"

"You heard me. Your. Fault. First of all, you took me to a club where everyone is doing— Never mind that. You took me to a club where your girlfriend sings. Then you leave me at the table, alone, while you go in the back to do...whatever with your lover."

"You thought Raven was my girlfriend?" He stared at her in disbelief.

"Well...yeah."

"She is my twin sister."

"You have sex with your twin sister?" Kimberly huffed.

If he weren't annoyed, he'd think the appalled expression on her face charming. "Hell, no. I took her to the back to give her a lecture." He ran a hand over his face, searching for patience. "I heard from an acquaintance she was hanging at the club, getting into mischief. I was trying to stop her from finding more trouble."

"Oh."

The O-shape of Kimberly's lips distracted Robert. Desire flashed red-hot. He mentally shook himself. Remembered she'd just been attacked. He needed to be gentle. "Tell me what happened."

"I got lost. Some guy followed me and shoved me against the wall. He called me Satan's whore, just like the last time. He said—"

"What?" Robert shouted not allowing her to finish. "You were attacked another time?"

"Not exactly. In Chesapeake City, when I was walking back to the yacht with Timothy and Davey, we startled a guy hidden in an alley. I think it was the same guy. He ran past us and shoved me to the ground. He called me Satan's whore then too."

"Neither Timothy nor Davey mentioned this."

Kimberly shrugged.

He would give the lads a stern talking to upon their

return to *Sea Panther*. Relieved to have Kimberly safe within reach, he took a deep breath and flexed stiff shoulders. His neck cracked, releasing some of the tension. "You have a nasty enemy," he said.

"No. You do."

"Me?"

"Yeah. At first, I thought he was the hit man rumored to have been hired by one of my ex-clients. But he called me the Panther's whore and *you* the son of the devil. He said you only bring women onboard *Sea Panther* for perverted sex."

"Really? Perverted sex? That is insane."

"I'm not making this up. He said he'd be back. Said he'd take the life of one slut to avenge another."

"What the hell does that mean?"

"Haven't a clue. Do you?"

"Nae." Robert scanned the street. "Come. Let us return to the yacht before we run into more difficulties. And what is this about a hit man?" He stopped walking and twisted to stare at her. "You neglected to mention that wee detail in your job interview."

* * *

Oops. Kimberly hadn't meant to let that tidbit of information slip. She swallowed and met the captain's gaze straight on. "On the merits of a financial tip I received from a trusted friend, I invested my money and the money of a couple of clients in an off-shore deal. The investment failed and we lost everything. After my firm fired me, I heard a rumor one of my clients put out a hit contract on me. But I can't believe he'd do such a thing. He's a really nice man."

"Was the loss great?"

"Yeah." Kimberly closed her eyes, swamped by the embarrassment of her stupidity.

The captain's fingers grazed her scraped cheek, leaving a trail of tingling sensation. "No man is *really nice* after he loses a substantial sum of money. His ego will compel him to lash out at the one who caused the loss."

"Is that what you would do?" Kimberly placed a palm where Robert had stroked, marveling at the tingling effect of his touch.

"Not if it were you, sweetling." He leaned forward.

Her pulse quickened. He placed a hand behind her head, slowly pulled her forward, and kissed her. A brief touch of satiny lips. Enough to cause a craving for more to burn within her breast.

She shouldn't allow him to kiss her. Shouldn't lean on him, but she was vulnerable. He felt so good. Kimberly wrapped her arms around his neck and kissed him back with all the pent-up passion within her demanding release.

His sharp intake of breath indicated his surprise. She took advantage, slipping her tongue into his mouth. He tasted great. A combination of champagne and berries.

He got with the program and angled his head, allowing deeper penetration.

She wanted to climb his body. Ride him.

He pulled away, leaving her breathless. A low growl escaped his throat, startling her. "What's wrong?"

"That will not happen again." He grasped her hand. "Come. I need to return to *Sea Panther* and figure out what to do about you."

* * *

Rays of golden sunlight shimmered through the porthole and Kimberly stretched lazily. Although Robert's kiss the previous night started out tentative, she'd responded with unrestrained passion. Who would have thought she'd had it in her? Certainly not her ex-fiancé.

Holding Robert in her arms had made her feel complete, as if he filled a void deep inside her of which she'd been unaware. She'd felt empty when he pulled away. She wanted to hold onto the good part, but the delicious memory of their intimate embrace faded quickly when she glanced at the clock and noted it was past noon.

Her alarm hadn't gone off. Someone should have wakened her. *Shit.* Had she blown it? Had Robert decided to fire her?

She pushed away the bed sheet, swung her legs over the side of the bunk, and chewed on her bottom lip. Would she be left to fend for herself in Annapolis? This late in the season, it would be difficult finding a crew position on another boat headed south. There wasn't enough money to get back to New Jersey. Besides, she wouldn't be safe there.

She couldn't go north.

Was it safe here? Would it be safer farther south? She'd be safe with Robert. And she didn't want to leave him. Not before exploring the new sensations he provoked.

Oh, God, what did he have planned? Could he be convinced to let her stay?

She threw on a pair of jeans and a t-shirt and raced into the galley. No one loitered there. There wasn't even a lingering aroma of bacon remaining from breakfast. No one lounged in the salon either. She climbed the companionway stairs and found Timothy sitting in the sun-warmed cockpit, reading. "Hey, where is everyone?"

He glanced up from a *Popular Mechanics* magazine. "Running errands."

"I overslept. Why didn't anyone wake me?" Kimberly swept un-brushed hair out of her face and attempted a smile.

"The captain gave orders not to disturb you. I think he turned off your alarm clock too."

"Why?" Her tense, bare toes gripped the deck.

"Maybe because you were attacked last night."

She touched the bruised cheek. "Oh. You heard about that."

"Yeah." Timothy made one of those annoying faces men give woman who they think are acting dumb. The knot in her stomach tightened.

"Does the captain plan to fire me?"

"Nah. He gave strict orders not to let you go ashore alone from now on. One of us is always to be with you."

Robert's concern thrilled her, but then...

"That's not fair. What right does he have to limit my activities?" For some foolish reason the domineering attitude pissed her off.

"Chill out. Two seconds ago, you were worried about being fired. Geez. The captain isn't restricting your behavior. All he said was one of us has to accompany you when you're away from *Sea Panther*. He's your employer, and while you crew his yacht, he's responsible for you."

Employee. After all, that was all she was to him. "I don't want to be babysat."

Her belligerent attitude was wrong, but she couldn't help it. Her emotions were on a roller coaster ride.

Timothy put an arm to his forehead and leaned back in mock horror. "What? Don't you like hanging with the twins and me?"

Kimberly released a heavy sigh. Now she'd need to stroke Tim's hurt pride. "It's not that. I like you guys. It's just...I don't need to be escorted everywhere I go." She reconsidered when she thought of the attack the previous night. "Well, maybe after dark." She would concede to that security measure.

"The captain said whenever you leave the boat. Don't even think of going ashore without one of us to carry your gear."

"Okay." She restrained the smirk pulling at her lips. "If you'll be my pack mules, I'll take one of you along. As a matter of fact, I need to go to a laundromat."

"Ouch." Timothy rolled his eyes. "That hurts."

Kimberly laughed. "Could go by myself."

"Nah. I'll go with you as soon as one of the others gets their ass back here."

The twins showed up a half hour later, and Timothy escorted Kimberly into town. They returned to the yacht after doing the laundry well after dark. Davey stood night watch. The rest of the crew had gone ashore. Timothy helped carry the bags of clean clothes below and then went back to the cockpit to hang with his buddy.

She sorted the laundry and placed each crewmember's on their bunk. Except for Robert's, his cabin being off-limits to crew. Why? She had to wonder. Curiosity always got the best of her. She carried his laundry to the door of his cabin and tapped lightly, though Davey had said the captain had gone ashore with Colin and John.

Of course, no one answered.

She tested the knob. Robert hadn't locked the door. *Should she?* She scraped her teeth back and forth across her lower lip. *Sure, why not?* In how much more trouble could she get? Besides, she wasn't planning to disturb anything, simply place the clean clothes on his bunk.

Maybe seeing his things would provide insight into the man. Kimberly opened the cabin door and peered in. The lavish cabin caught her by surprise, and she gawked. Dark green velvet covered the bunk. She shifted Robert's laundry to one arm and entered. Her fingers itched to touch the plush pillows made from luxuriant fabrics sitting atop the bed. While indulging in the tactile sensation, an indentation marring the fine wood bulkhead grabbed her attention. It appeared as if someone had thrown a punch. Robert likely slammed a fist into the wall.

She shuddered at the thought of such aggression directed at her. But to date, he'd only been gentle—even last night while angry after the attack, he treated her tenderly. Tenderly and passionately. Savoring the memory of their intense kiss, she brushed the fingers of her free hand across her lips. Why had he suddenly ended the kiss? He seemed to enjoy it.

Guess he wanted to avoid the employer-employee thing. She probably should too. An affair could get complicated in the tight quarters of a sailing yacht. Made good sense to keep a distance, but she couldn't convince herself not to pursue Robert.

Kimberly continued to check out his private space, feeling a bit like a voyeur. Two crossed cutlasses hung above the dent. On the wall over the leather settee hung a Scottish claymore. The two-handed sword looked like one she'd seen in a Celtic shop in Anderson Creek, North Carolina during the Grandfather Mountain Highland Games and Gathering of the Scottish Clans. How odd that Robert would display antique weapons on a modern yacht. The salt air couldn't be good for the aged metal.

Still clutching the laundry, she swung around. In a corner of the room, a large piece of dark exotic wood scarred with claw marks hung on ropes from the ceiling. Fortunately, there was no sign of Marion. Robert must have taken the nasty bird with him.

"What are you doing in my cabin?"

Kimberly dropped the clothes in a heap on the floor.

She twisted to face his stern countenance. "Sorry." She bent and picked up the messy pile of clean laundry, placing it on the bed.

"Did Colin not tell you this cabin is off-limits to crew?"

"He did." She quickly folded a shirt.

"And still, you chose to enter my private chamber?"

She ventured a peek at Robert. A red flush of color crept up his neck above the vee of the black tee stretched tight across his broad chest. Did he realize how much the size of him intimidated her in the tight constraints of the cabin?

Kimberly repressed the urge to dart past him and out of the cabin. It wouldn't do any good; there was no place to run. "I didn't want to leave your clothes in the salon." She gave him one of her famous speed smiles and shrugged, continuing to fold the clothes. "Door was unlocked."

"My mistake." His voice purred.

Kimberly placed the last refolded shirt on the bed and attempted to scoot past him. Before she could, he closed the door and blocked the way. His eyes flared.

"Let me show you what happens when someone chooses to disobey the captain's orders." He pulled her into his arms and captured her lips with a blundering mouth. The assault set her heart pounding at an alarming rate. Excitement and need shot through her veins along with the blood. She tasted his ferocity and returned it in kind.

They meshed, becoming one.

Fireworks exploded in her head.

When he pulled away, his breath came hard, as did hers, and his erection pushed against the buttons of his black jeans. "Leave my cabin and don't enter again without invitation. Do you understand?"

She raised her gaze from his groin to his eyes. Their unusual cinnamon color had brightened, appearing almost red. Weird. She shook her head, but his eyes were definitely red. "Your eyes—"

"Leave. Now."

She held fingers to her tingling lips and nodded understanding, but didn't move, mesmerized by the unusual light in his eyes.

He turned away and leaned forward with hands pressed on top of the desk. His knuckles whitened and his body heaved. Taut muscles rippled with each heavy breath.

"Go!"

Kimberly choked back a sob, rushed into the passageway, and ran to the refuge of her cabin. She'd made everything worse. How would she ever be able to face him again?

* * *

Robert stayed put, leaning against the desk, catching his breath, until Kimberly's footfalls faded. Releasing her from his embrace was one of the hardest actions he'd ever taken. The devil knew she could set fire to his loins with a mere glance.

When she'd given him that quick smile, he'd slipped into lust overload.

He ran his tongue over the elongated fangs and suppressed his vampire-self. Kimberly was the most damnable woman. She'd certainly turned things around on him. Her kiss demanded more than his had. What was he to do now?

He fell back onto the bunk and stared at the ceiling. He couldn't keep his hands off the spirited lass. When she was near, he lost what little self-control remained to him. Hiring her had been a monstrous error in judgment.

The panther yanked against its restraint, wanting desperately to mate. Having recently fed on nourishing blood, Robert forced the animal deep into the dark recesses within him.

How had he allowed himself to get into such a quagmire?

Inviting her to the club the other night had been a foolish mistake. Although he'd known Raven and Wolfgang would be trouble, he'd forgotten what a stranger would think of the reprobates that frequent the club. She must have been shocked.

Why else would she have run?

She used the excuse that she thought Raven was his lover. Why would Kimberly care? Did she have special feelings for him?

A knot twisted in his gut when he thought of the man who'd had her pressed against the wall of the warehouse. Robert refused to contemplate what might have happened if he hadn't arrived when he had. Nor did he want to think about what he'd do to the man when he found the bastard.

The man would prefer to be dead. Robert choked back a growl. From now on, he would maintain a friendly distance. It was the least he could do. They couldn't become lovers. She deserved much better than he could give her.

He could only bring heartbreak.

She'd seen the change in his eyes. He'd need to be more careful in her presence. Never be alone with her. The vampire shifted within the murky shadows in rebellion. Dread gripped Robert's heart. The monster had set his sights on Kimberly.

CHAPTER SEVEN

The sun peeked over the horizon as *Sea Panther* set sail. She made the way south, heading out of the Chesapeake. Kimberly worked alongside the boys and Colin to keep the sleek yacht sailing smoothly on course. Neither Robert nor his sister made an appearance on deck until after dusk.

Robert ignored Kimberly.

His sister... Well. She glared. Expected to be waited on. In general behaved unpleasant.

The rest of the crew was great to work with and Kimberly was beginning to consider them friends. A comfortable routine developed over the next couple of days. In the mornings, Colin gave the order to set sail. Kimberly shared duties with the boys, while Robert and his sister holed up in their respective cabins until sunset.

Sea Panther anchored offshore in the evenings. Colin ferried Robert and his sister ashore while Kimberly enjoyed dinner onboard with the boys. They took turns keeping watch, and whoever didn't cook cleaned up. After dinner, they played cards or read humorous stories aloud.

On Christmas Eve, they sailed into a public marina in North Carolina. As Kimberly finished securing the bowline to the floating dock, her cell phone rang. She waited for a thumb-up from Colin before answering. "Hello."

"I've been trying to reach you for days," Sarah complained.

"Merry Christmas to you too."

"Merry Christmas. But that's not why I called. Where are you?"

"Sorry. Cell service has been unreliable lately. We just sailed into New Bern. Why didn't you text me or leave a message?"

"I have news. Wanted to tell you myself. I'm afraid you'll be upset."

"Okay..." Kimberly inhaled a deep breath. "Spit it out."

"The fingerprints from your car match prints taken at the B&B. They belong to a known hit man named Dino Rizzetti. He's believed to be armed and dangerous.

"Shit!" Kimberly's heartbeat kicked into overdrive.

"Yeah. That's for sure. The cops also said he has no connection to Mr. Romano."

"I knew Sal wasn't involved. Did the police arrest this Dino character?"

"No. They haven't been able to locate him. They want to put you into protective custody."

"Why?" A lump formed in Kimberly's throat.

"I'm not sure. They want to know where you are so they can pick you up."

"No way." *No way in hell.*

"But you have a hit man after you." Sarah didn't need to remind her. Kimberly's stomach performed major somersaults without added stimuli.

John waved from deck. He was stocky and muscular. So was his twin. Timothy was wiry but strong. Colin claimed to have once been a Golden Glove boxer. Robert oozed power.

She didn't need cops. She sailed with five bodyguards. "I'll be fine. Love you." Kimberly ended the call and turned off the cell phone before second thoughts kicked in. Her sister would be angry, but Kimberly would make it up to her when this mess was over.

She climbed on deck and forced a smile for her crewmates.

"We have to decide who has watch." John handed over

four straws, one being shorter than the other three. "Hold these, and we'll each choose one."

"What about me? You guys always take watch."

John gave her one of those you're-being-stupid looks. "We can't leave you alone."

Of course not. Kimberly sighed and held out a hand. One by one, the boys drew a length.

"Damn." Timothy held up the short piece.

Davey slipped an arm through Kimberly's.

"Looks like you have the watch tonight, Timmy boy, while John and I have the pleasure of this pretty gal's company."

"No worries." John slapped Tim on the back. "We'll bring you something back from the pub."

"Thanks. Make sure it's something that's bad for me. The greasier, the better."

Kimberly grimaced.

"Sure," Davey said. "Cheeseburger and spicy fries?"

"How about rum cake?" Kimberly offered. "After all, tonight is Christmas Eve."

"Yummy." Timothy grinned, but then his expression sobered. "Be careful. The captain said to keep a close watch. He doesn't want strangers too close to Kimberly."

"How will I dance if no one is allowed near me?"

"You'll dance with us," the twins said in unison.

"Lead on, boys." She chuckled, pretending to be full of holiday spirit.

Kimberly followed them across the worn grayed planks of the dock to shore. Arms linked, they strolled along a charming street lined with houses draped in flickering holiday lights. When they reached the Main street pub, John muscled their way through the crowd. Luck was with them. They grabbed a semicircular booth as a family vacated it.

Kimberly slid across the turquoise vinyl to the far side and faced the bar. Davey and John took up residence to her left. From there they had a view of the front door across the half-high panel at her back, leaving the bench to the right vacant. While they chatted, the twins monitored the entrance and anyone who ventured too close. She chewed on the corner of her bottom lip. They were obviously going to hound her all night. Just as well, Sarah's news was disturbing.

A hit man could be anywhere. Here? Kimberly nervously scanned the crowd.

* * *

Robert paced the dock alongside *Sea Panther* and glared into the starlit night. The animal lingered at the edges of his consciousness, waiting for a moment of weakness. Marion circled above the yacht before landing on Robert's outstretched arm and releasing a lengthy croak.

When she whispered a warning in his mind, he tensed. "Keep a sharp eye out tonight, Tim."

"Something wrong?" The lad lazily dangled his long legs over the edge of the deck from where he sat.

"Perhaps." Robert glanced into the nearby woods and scratched the back of his neck. "Have a bad feeling."

Marion leapt from his shoulder, flew over Timothy, and down through the companionway. A few minutes later, Colin and Raven emerged from the yacht.

"Shall we go?" A wicked grin crossed Raven's crimson-painted lips.

Great. Robert cracked his neck. Whatever went down, his evil twin planned to enjoy. He grasped her elbow, and Colin fell in behind. "Timothy, stay alert."

"Aye, aye, Captain," the lad jovially called after them as they headed to shore."

"Something wrong?" Colin asked.

"Marion saw a dark figure with binoculars scoping the yacht from the trees near that outcrop of rocks." Robert pointed to their right. "When she circled, the watcher slipped deeper into the trees."

"What do you need of me?"

"Make the pickup and return to *Sea Panther*."

Colin inclined his head and strode off.

Robert frowned at his sister. The memory of how he'd found her remained a raw wound. After a hundred years of living the curse, he'd thought all of his family, including

Marion, had died after living out their natural lives. Then to find her at Waterloo in the midst of all the young soldiers' dead bodies with blood dripping from bared fangs had forced him to his knees. The rage still rode him.

She shifted into a raven and flew away from him that night. This evening, she would do his bidding, though he regretted using her. "Feed. Enough to sustain us both."

"'Twill be a pleasure." Raven entered the woods with a swish of hips.

Robert reached within for the transformation. Fangs burst forth, lengthened, and the vampire emerged. He would protect what belonged to him.

His yacht. His crew. His mate.

* * *

Willy moved away from the marina with as much speed as he could manage. He'd heard rumors the Panther owned a pet raven, and the darn bird had seen him. The evil creature possessed the same alarming stare as the captain.

Damn, he hadn't meant to show himself so soon. Willy reached into the fanny pack and rummaged for the tools. Holy water and a silver dagger given to him by a member of the slayer society he joined after learning of his sister's fate.

He'd avenge the slut.

His feet slammed against dead leaves as he weaved in and out of trees and dodged low-hanging branches. He needed to get away. As far away as possible. He ran for what seemed like forever—until his chest burned.

The forest thickened. Deciding he'd gone far enough, he stopped and bent over. Hands on thighs, he panted and gasped for oxygen. When he could breathe again, he looked up.

What the fuck? A sinfully sexy, raven-haired woman stood in front of him. The sexy-hot expression in her eyes made blood race to his cock.

"Like what you see?" She stepped closer.

"Yeah. We can have some fun." He licked suddenly dry lips in anticipation of riding the bitch and moved into her personal space. A long red fingernail dragged across his chest. Unexpected pain stunned him. His t-shirt shredded and blood oozed from a stinging cut. Excitement escalated. Didn't matter if she liked it rough. So did he.

She slowly wet crimson lips with the tip of her tongue. His was hangin'. Damn, if she wasn't a bitch in heat. She gave him a major hard-on. So sexed up, he was gonna explode.

She grabbed his crotch and squeezed. Oh, yeah!

He jerked his gaze upward. The woman's eyes changed color. Turned a frightening blood red. What? Too late, Willy spotted the fangs.

Vampire!

He tried to pull away, but couldn't budge. She licked her lips again and leaned in close. Willy struggled, but couldn't move leaden limbs. Those sharp pointed teeth hovered closer. Closer to the vein throbbing in his neck. Closer still.

Panic seized him. He had no control over his body.

She'd paralyzed him. He could feel sensation, but couldn't physically move. Acid choked his throat, and Willy learned the taste of fear.

Then...ecstasy.

* * *

His vampire-self scented fresh blood. Robert fought to maintain control over the fiend's actions as he cautiously approached his sister and her prey. Daintily licking the edge of her mouth, Raven tossed the human away. She grinned at Robert and her pupils returned to normal.

He hated himself for what he'd take from her—blood.

The monster must feed. The vampire rose to the surface and hissed at Raven.

"Easy, big boy." She laughed and held out an arm. "Take what you need."

He latched onto her wrist, sank sharp fangs into tender flesh, greedy for the nourishment she provided. His hunger proved voracious. The rich nectar on his tongue provided strength and renewed the vampiric connection between brother and sister.

She allowed him his fill. When finished, he grazed his tongue across the marks and closed the wound. Satiated, the vampire receded to a shadow in the background of Robert's mind. "Thank you."

He was truly grateful, but uncomfortable with the blood-taking just the same.

His sister smiled, reminiscent of the lass of their youth. Only for a moment, then the *Kick Ass Girl* returned. She used a metal tipped, booted foot to roll the intruder over.

"Willy?" Shock gut-punched Robert. He could hardly believe the lad he'd been kind to in the past stalked his yacht. The growl emerging from deep in his chest resonated betrayal.

Had the lad stalked Kimberly too? Probably.

"You ken him?" Raven asked.

"Aye, he crewed for me up north. I dropped him off in Cape May for a family emergency. That is when I took Kimberly on as crew."

"Foolish mistake."

Robert ignored Raven's rebuke and ripped the fanny pack from Willy's waist. He snarled at the contents. Tossing the vial of holy water to the ground, he examined the razor sharp silver dagger tilting it first in one direction then the other.

"Nasty little boy. Next time you will not enjoy my kiss." Raven kicked the lad hard with the metal tip of her pointed boot.

Willy moaned, but barely moved.

"What shall we do with him?" Raven reached down and stroked the lad's crotch. Terror-filled wide eyes looked back at her. "Shall I suck him dry and hang the corpse from a tree?"

Robert nudged her away from the lad and knelt over Willy. "Why are you here?"

The lad trembled as some of the paralyzing effects of Raven's scratch wore off. Struggling to speak, his mouth opened slightly, but no words came out.

Robert ground his teeth, waited. The tranquilizing effect would take time to neutralize.

"Y-yo-you kil-led my sis-sis-sister," Willy managed to burble after several minutes, a stream of saliva running along his chin.

"Pathetic." Raven shook her head and curled her lip.

"Go enjoy Christmas Eve, darling." Robert wanted to be alone with the young man to learn exactly of what the devil the lad was babbling about.

Raven's eyes flared red. "You sure you don't want me to take care of him?"

Willy pissed his pants.

"Leave him to me. I don't want you further involved."

"Fine." She tossed her long black hair over a shoulder and strutted off.

Torn between the need to punish the lad and the need to find Kimberly and ensure her safety, he glanced at the position of the moon. There wasn't enough time for both.

"Listen to me carefully, Willy. I have nae idea what you think I might have done. But I can assure you, I have not killed anyone." *At least not for the last one hundred years.* Robert leaned back on his haunches. "Most of the effects of our little encounter will wear off by sunrise. Would be in your best interest to forget about being here. About meeting us."

"Wha-at do y-yo-you mean m-mo-most?"

"Ach, now lad. You see, there is a small lingering effect of Raven's sweet kiss. She can track you. And through her, I can too. We will always be able to locate you. Talk to you."

Fear registered in the lad's eyes. Good.

"For now, lie here and rest. Come morning. Run along home." Robert stood. "I warn you, Willy, stay away from *Sea Panther* and her crew, or I will find you, and you will not enjoy the consequences."

Robert secured the silver dagger in its leather sheath and shoved it into the waist of his jeans at the small of his back. He strode in the direction of town determined to find Kimberly and ensure her safety.

With the lad incapacitated, the night should be quiet.

The confiscated blade and its significance would need to be dealt with soon.

* * *

Colin placed the perishable package under an arm and

hurried along the dock toward *Sea Panther*. Timothy leaned against the mast, under the glare of overhead lighting, gaze directed at two uniformed men approaching the yacht. When the lad noticed Colin, he acknowledged him with a slight motion of the head.

Good lad. Colin quickened his pace.

"Captain? Permission to come aboard?" the stockier of the sheriff's deputies asked, breath condensing as he spoke.

"Sorry, sir, the captain's ashore. Can I help you with something? I'm one of the crew." Timothy jumped from the deck onto the dock in front of the two men.

"Maybe. We're looking for Miss Kimberly Scot," the second, younger, deputy said.

"She's not here," Timothy said.

Colin approached the men from behind, and they spun around, hands on their holstered guns.

"Who are you?" the first deputy asked.

"Colin MacEwen, *Sea Panther's* first mate." Colin held his palms open to show he carried no weapon, while clutching the brown-paper wrapped package to his side with an elbow. "If you'll give me a moment to refrigerate this parcel, I'll try to help you."

"Give it to the kid to take care of."

Colin made eye contact with Timothy and handed over the blood. The lad inclined his head and went below, leaving Colin to deal with the men. "Will you explain your purpose, gentlemen?"

The younger deputy took out a pad and pencil. "We're to pick up a Miss Kimberly Scot. We understand she is a crewmember on this boat."

"She is, but she's not here now." Colin hoped Timothy understood what to do. "Has she done something wrong?"

"That's none of your concern. Do you know where we can find her?"

"Somewhere in town, celebrating Christmas Eve, I imagine."

The deputy's exchanged an annoyed glance and hurried to the patrol car parked at the end of the dock.

"Timothy?" Colin leaned into the companionway.

"Dialing." The lad held a cell phone.

* * *

Boisterous voices rose in joyous celebration around Kimberly. She pretended to have fun and smiled at John who raised a mug to clink with hers. In the bar area of the pub, a country fiddler played Christmas tunes, and the patrons sang the verses. Locals mingled with *yachtys*.

To say her mind was on overload would be a gross understatement, but the knowledge a hit man pursued you was more than anyone should have to deal with on Christmas Eve. She played with a cocktail napkin while Davey and John sang the chorus of *St. Stephen's Day Murders* along with the rowdy crowd.

The more she thought about Sarah's phone call, the more she realized the evidence didn't add up. A professional wouldn't leave fingerprints. A hit man would kill her, and that would be the end of it. Something else was going on, and she needed to figure out what.

The fiddler took a break. *Silent Night* played on the sound system. Voices lowered to a hum. Kimberly massaged the stiff muscles at the back of her neck. The effort to figure out what nefarious plot entrapped her brought on a migraine. Perhaps she should concentrate on something else for a while. The boys were in celebratory moods. Maybe they would shed light on the mystery shrouding *Sea Panther*.

"Why is the captain never around during the day?" she blurted out.

"Never around during the day?" Davey squeaked.

"You sound like a parrot," Kimberly said. "I've only ever seen him in the evening. Isn't that odd?"

"I've not noticed. Have you, John?" Davey hedged.

"No, I haven't," John said.

They were stonewalling, but she wasn't letting it go. Robert's behavior was peculiar. "I'm certain I've never seen Robert in the daylight."

The twins relaxed and gave each other one of those smug guy looks Kimberly hated.

"Robert?" John smirked. "Since when do you call the

captain *Robert?*"

Kimberly shook her head to brush off the question. "Sometimes, he seems warm and accessible, and other times ice cold. Closed off to others."

Davey's eyes widened, and he cleared his throat. Not once. Twice.

"What?" she asked.

"May I join you?" Robert said and slid into the booth next to her, not waiting for an invite.

Oh, God. Heat climbed from her toes to the top of her head.

She sneaked a peek to the right. Robert wore a wide grin that smoothed the scar on his cheek. Her pulse jumped. He looked lethal even when smiling. Far more handsome than any man had a right to look. She sipped from her mug to hide her embarrassment.

The fiddler strolled back on stage and played a merry tune. Couples got up to dance.

"Lads, go find partners. I'll keep Kimberly safe." He didn't have to offer twice. The twins disappeared into the thickening crowd.

Kimberly took another sip of her drink, wishing she had the ability to wiggle her nose and bewitch herself somewhere else. The fire burning deep within Robert's cinnamon eyes stopped her mid-thought, stopped her from glancing away, stopped her from wanting to slip away.

She desired him more than she dared. Their gazes held, and the barroom faded away. Sexually charged seconds ticked by with a slow sizzle.

CHAPTER EIGHT

A drunk banged into the table and broke the steamy spell holding Kimberly and Robert enthralled. She choked on a flat laugh. He cleared his throat.

The awkward moment thickened the air. Made it hard to breathe.

Kimberly twitched her nose. Now would be a good time to find a hidey-hole to crawl into. Perspiration glazed the skin between her breasts. God, her face must be the color of a ripe strawberry.

"I overheard you," Robert said.

"Did you?" *Just great.*

"Aye." His gaze dropped to the tabletop. He picked up a drink stirrer and fiddled with it.

Mesmerized, she watched large fingers nimbly tie the thin strip of plastic into a bowline knot. The naughty image of him using the same knot to tie a silk scarf around her wrists flashed in her mind. *Where had that idea come from?*

"What the rest of the crew has been trying hard not to tell you is I have a rare blood disease." Her wayward thought splintered at the unemotional statement of fact.

She gazed into his eyes, searching for something empathetic to say.

"I have to take it easy until my doctors can find a donor

with the right DNA makeup to help me. That is why I sleep a lot."

"I'm sorry." *Oh, that sounded lame.* Worse yet, she'd been thinking about sex. Kinky sex. My God, what had come over her lately? She'd never thought of having that kind of sex with Jason. Heat rose from toes to face. Thank God Robert couldn't read minds. She reached for her mug, but it was empty.

"Dance with me?" He grasped her hand.

She nodded, and followed him onto the dance floor. "When they find a donor, will they be able to make you well?"

His eyes clouded. "I hope so."

So did she.

He tucked her close, held her tight, smooth cheek against the rasp of whiskers, as they swayed with the other couples to the sweet melody of an Irish love song. She embraced hard muscle as she wrapped her arms around him.

How could a virile man like Robert be critically ill?

When the song ended, she pulled away, feeling awkward. He seemed uncomfortable too. They returned to the booth at the same time as the twins.

The moment Robert sat, his cell phone buzzed. He grabbed it from his belt. "Aye." A dark expression hardened his features. "Do what you can. Tell Colin to be ready to motor out and set sail as soon as we arrive."

Alarm pinched. Something bad must have happened.

He returned the phone to his belt and pulled her to her feet.

"What's up?" Davey asked.

"We have trouble." Robert pushed Kimberly through the crowd toward the back door. Davey and John followed. Once they were out in the night air, Robert answered Davey's question, "It appears Miss Scot is wanted by the sheriff's department."

Kimberly wanted to explain, but he cut her off.

"Colin is stalling the deputies, which will buy us some time but not much. You two..." He directed an intense stare at the twins. "Go to the boat and make ready to cast off on

Colin's order. I will borrow a launch, and we will rendezvous offshore."

John and Davey disappeared into the shadows.

"Come." Robert tugged on her arm.

They ran down the back alley away from the Christmas gaiety. By the time they reached the outskirts of town, Kimberly panted for breath. She still hadn't figured out how to explain the situation. "Captain, I—"

"Just answer one question. Did you break the law?"

"No." She shook her head with force. "Definitely not."

"Then you can explain later. Now, we need to hurry." He led her behind a waterfront hotel. They jogged across the manicured lawn to a private dock with a Zodiac tied to it. Luck was with them. Keys dangled from the ignition.

The inflatable boat raced out into the dark night. When the town with its twinkling lights looked like a miniature holiday village, Robert idled the engine, and they drifted.

"I'm sorry. I've done nothing wrong." Kimberly found it hard to believe the mess that had caught up with her.

"I didn't think you did."

"Robert, please let me explain." She needed him to understand she hadn't lied. She'd just neglected to tell all the details of her troubles. If she had, he never would have hired her.

He raised a brow. She flushed. It was the first time she'd used his first name to his face.

"Did you ken they would come for you?"

"Not really. My sister called earlier and told me the police investigating the break-ins want to put me under protective custody while they search for the hit man. I never imagined they'd send the local law enforcement after me here."

"I thought the hit man was a rumor. And by the way, break-ins were never mentioned. You better tell me the whole tale from beginning to end."

When Kimberly finished the story, she shook uncontrollably, not from cold, but from the realization of what she faced.

"You can count on me to protect you." Robert took both of her chilled hands into his warm grasp and squeezed.

"But I can only help if you are completely honest with me. If you continue to confide in me."

"I will from now on. I promise."

"Good. I vow to keep you safe." He gave her hands another squeeze before he released her and peered starboard. "Ah. Here comes our ride."

Searchlights from *Sea Panther's* deck scanned the water around them. Robert whistled, and the bright beam landed on the inflatable, blinding Kimberly for a moment.

He engaged the engine. The small boat motored alongside the now-idling yacht. After securing lines, they climbed aboard to the worried gazes of the crew.

"The deputies are searching for Kimberly in town," Colin said. "It won't be long before they learn we've gone."

Robert rubbed the back of his neck. "And now we are harboring a runaway and are accessories in facilitating her escape."

Kimberly stiffened. She hadn't considered she placed Robert and her crewmates into legal jeopardy. "I—"

He silenced her with a stern look. "Give me a moment to get some cash from my cabin then we will send the Zodiac back and be on our way."

Robert reappeared on deck a few minutes later and handed Davey an envelope along with the keys to the inflatable. "Return the Zodiac to the hotel and pay them for the use. Meet us in Charleston at the boatyard."

"Will do, Captain."

"And Davey." Robert patted his shoulder. "Do try to stay out of sight of those two deputies."

"You bet." Davey curled his lips into a cocky grin.

He jumped into the Zodiac, tossed lines, took off. Kimberly chewed on her lower lip as the small boat disappeared into the dark. She hoped he didn't land in trouble on her account.

* * *

A few hours later, Robert leaned over his desk along with Colin and glared at what might be a mage weapon. "What do you think?"

Colin ran his fingers over the gleaming silver surface of

the dagger.

"'Tis ancient. But that you already knew." He angled the blade back and forth in the lamplight. "Superb craftsmanship."

"I ken that too. What of its origin?"

"You'd know better than I."

"Arrrrgh." Robert slumped onto the settee. "Call Jagger. Have him find a thirty-two foot sailboat and rendezvous with us at Winyah Bay near Cat Island at high tide. He will ken the spot."

"What are you planning to do with Kimberly?"

"She will sail into Charleston with me in the smaller boat. After I have concluded my business with the builder, you and the lads can deliver *Sea Panther* to the boatyard. The authorities will expect her to be with you. By the time they realize the switch, Kimberly and I will be sailing for Florida and my compound. Hopefully, Jagger can pull in some favors and keep the law off our tail."

"'Tis dangerous."

"Not very. You ken the way around the shoals."

"You know that's not what I mean." Colin pursed his lips.

Robert ignored the disapproving look. "Give the lads shore leave with pay. You can rent a car and meet us at the compound."

"As long as I've known you, you've only fed from women who've thrown themselves at you. Like that vampire groupie in New Jersey with the purple hair. I believed Kimberly to be safe when I recommended hiring her. Now, I have doubts. I've seen the way you look at her, Robert. What are your intentions toward the lass?"

Robert bit down on rising anger. "I have vowed to protect her."

"I don't like it." Colin shook his head. "How will you hide your true self from her?"

"She sees my true self every eve'n. 'Tis the beasts of which she is unaware. I will keep them in check." Robert massaged the back of his neck. He didn't need Colin's censure at this moment.

"How will you feed?"

"Kimberly believes I have a rare blood disease. She won't question the bags of blood in the fridge."

"You can't go out in full sun. Do you expect her to sail the whole way to Florida alone while you hide in your cabin?"

"Nae. We will sail during the night and find a gunk-hole to hide in at sunrise. 'Twill be safer that way. She will understand we need to sleep during the daylight hours to avoid the authorities and the hit man who stalks her."

"She's a sweet lass in a ton of trouble. She doesn't deserve more."

Colin's chastisement cut deep. Robert had promised to protect Kimberly. That wasn't a vow lightly taken.

"She is a noble woman. I will protect her by any means required."

Even if that meant taking her blood? Robert shifted uneasily. He quieted his conscience, allowing the vampire to emerge and hiss at Colin.

His friend stood firm. "Be careful with her. She could too easily be hurt."

Colin was right, but that didn't change anything. "I will see nae harm comes to the lass."

"Your arrogance is showing."

Robert growled. Colin stared him down.

"Give me the damn blood."

Refraining from further speech, Colin handed Robert the crystal goblet. He accepted the glass of blood from his keeper and slowly sipped. The vital fluid didn't compare to the tiny taste of Kimberly's blood he sampled.

The vampire seized upon the memory. Robert could feed from her once more without initiating a transformation. The ability to track her movements and perceive her thoughts would assist him in keeping her safe. One more taste wouldn't cause her additional harm. He drank deep from the goblet, wishing it were her blood.

His conscience reared its unwanted opinion. Who was he trying to fool? He desired her with every fiber of his despicable being.

As a woman? As prey? As a mate?

A soft yowl escaped his lips, the panther uneasy. The

vampire slithered through the shadows, determined to have Kimberly. Robert forced the evil from his mind. What mattered most was keeping Kimberly safe.

* * *

Another Christmas day. Another overly bright diner with gaudy holiday decorations. Another job to do. Dino chuckled and lowered the visor of the baseball cap to shade his eyes. One could never be too careful when you were a hired gun, though he doubted the young deputy sitting at the next booth flirting with the waitress would recognize him from old mug shots. He'd undergone plastic surgery from his face to the tips of his fingers, changed the color of his eyes, and dyed his hair since his last incarceration.

He'd even changed profession—drug dealer to assassin.

Assuming the identity of a dead hit man was one of his most brilliant plans yet. And the fool that hired him was none the wiser. Dino couldn't wait to get the hundred grand for the kill. He took a sip of coffee and leaned back to better hear the conversation.

The girl giggled. "Maybe you could make it up to me tonight?"

"I'd love to, sweetheart, but I was up all night searching for a person of interest."

"But it's Christmas," she whined. "You promised."

"I know, honey. I'll make it up to you. I swear."

"Why can't you come tonight?"

"Would if I could."

"What's stopping you?"

"The woman we're searching for is part of the crew on that yacht, *Sea Panther*," the deputy said, changing gears.

"The fancy boat berthed over at the marina?" The girl's voice rose with excitement at the hint of gossip.

Go figure.

"Not any more. The yacht disappeared in the middle of the night around the same time *Hotel Jackson's* inflatable went missing. According to the hotel manager the Zodiac reappeared this morning with an envelope containing three hundred dollars cash."

"What's that to do with us spending Christmas night

together?"

"One of the guys from *Sea Panther* was seen leaving the dock after the Zodiac showed up. My partner is trying to get a handle on where the kid went. Then we're going after him."

"Don't count on me being available when you get back." The waitress stalked past Dino in a snit.

He threw a few dollar bills on the table for the coffee. It was doubtful the woman he hunted remained with *Sea Panther*. He'd done his homework. The yacht's billionaire captain had a reputation for being shrewd. Dino would find the kid from *Sea Panther's* crew before the sheriff's deputies. He planned to take him to his employer. The kid would talk if he wanted to live.

* * *

Sea Panther moored in a calm inlet on the Intracoastal Waterway. Kimberly snuggled within the folds of the new green mohair cape, allowing the unseasonably warm night soothe her. She'd slept in after their hurried escape and found the surprise gift late in the afternoon when she woke. No one would admit to being her secret Santa.

Only Robert could have left the large box wrapped in white paper with a large green velvet bow. Sarah would advise not to accept such a present, warning there might be strings attached. Kimberly didn't care if there were. She intended to keep Robert's thoughtful gift.

She leaned against the mast and inhaled deeply. Fresh air with a briny tang prompted pleasant memories of better times. She hummed as the evening sounds of the nearby salt marsh played a symphony.

Robert's grim expression when he appeared on deck brought reality crashing down.

In the time it had taken to reach the rendezvous spot, she'd tried to come to terms with her situation. The need to escape had ruined the entire crew's Christmas. She couldn't allow them to also risk legal retribution for helping her. She told Robert she didn't want him or the others to get further involved.

He wouldn't listen to reason. He insisted on doing

whatever was required to protect her and the crew. That was more than likely why he sent his sister on ahead to Florida. To Kimberly's relief, Raven had taken Robert's nasty black bird with her.

A mast light headed toward them along the channel. As it moved closer, Kimberly could make out the sleek lines of a smaller sailboat. She watched from the shadow of *Sea Panther's* boom as the boys secured the boat portside.

Dressed in wrinkled white linen—more appropriate for the sultry Caribbean—the man who jumped aboard after they'd finished rafting the two boats together was attractive in a rough sort of way. His messy, sandy-colored hair fell into sparkling golden eyes contained within a tanned, weathered face. Shorter and stockier than Robert, he had a powerful build, nonetheless. Intimidating, actually.

Bright white teeth snapped into a wide grin as he greeted Robert. That smile alone probably made most women fall at his feet. But he was in no way as handsome as Robert.

"Kimberly," Robert called. "Come. Meet my good friend Jagger. He's lending us his personal sailboat *Night Thrill*."

"That's kind of you," she said, joining them.

Jagger took her cold hand into his much warmer one. "So you're the woman everyone is after."

She shut her eyes unable to look at his teasing face. An awkward moment passed before he released her hand. "Well, I am glad to meet you." He eased away.

"And I, you." Although there was something about him that made her apprehensive.

A sharp pain at her temple surprised her and she reached up to massage the spot. With all that had happened, there was no wonder a stress headache kicked in.

Robert made an annoyed sound deep in his throat, startling her. He locked stares with his friend. The man shrugged. Robert draped an arm around her shoulder. "Ignore him, he's teasing."

The pain in her head subsided as if it had never been there. She smiled at him, comforted by his warmth.

Although she shouldn't read too much into Robert's actions, he seemed possessive all of a sudden.

They followed the others through the companionway and into the salon where refreshments waited.

"Please excuse us. I need a private word with Jagger," Robert said, and the two men turned toward the passageway to his cabin.

"If it's about me, I wish to join you." Kimberly didn't want Robert making decisions about the situation without her.

"Not now. Later," he promised.

"Typical. Men always think they know best." Kimberly flopped onto the settee.

The four men seated beside her, stuffing their faces with appetizers, cracked up laughing. Kimberly ignored them and stared at the passageway where Robert and Jagger disappeared out of sight. If only she could be a fly on the wall and hear what they discussed.

* * *

As Robert closed the cabin door, Jagger chuckled. "She will be a handful."

"Whisky?" Robert offered.

"Are you still trying to act as if you are fully human?" Jagger grinned and shook his head. "I gave up the effort to conform over two hundred years ago."

Robert snorted and poured three fingers. Although his friend would never admit it, Jagger hated their existence as much as he did.

"The doctors make progress." He drank the golden liquid in one gulp, enjoying the fire that raced down his throat. He'd be sick later, but it would be worth it to have enjoyed the human pleasure. "I believe they will find a cure soon. 'Tis why I am heading to the compound for more tests."

Jagger slapped his back. "I wish you luck."

Robert sobered. "You should not have probed her mind."

"You have not marked her."

Jagger's statement needled him. Wolfgang had said the

same. Maybe he wasn't doing Kimberly a favor by leaving her alone. Any vampire who crossed her path would smell Robert's presence yet know she remained unclaimed. Many vampires would relish taking her away from him. Not making love to her might be more dangerous than loving her and leaving his mark.

The thought of taking her blood while thrusting deep within her made him throb with need. But, he didn't want to cause her harm. "I will not defile another innocent."

"Yet you want her. And she is ripe for the taking."

"Aye. The desire to mark her and feed from her burns in my gut." Robert rubbed a hand over his face.

"You will be alone with her in tight quarters for some time after leaving Charleston. How will you curb your appetites?"

"Celibacy. Clinical blood bags."

Jagger grimaced. "Stale blood? Better you than me."

"'Tis palatable."

"Hardly." Jagger's eyes took on a knowing gleam. "You are in love with her."

Robert tensed. Was he? No. It was just he'd made a promise, which he intended to keep. He would ensure her safety.

"She is in danger from a hit man and a lunatic who thinks I killed his sister. And she is running from the authorities' good intentions. I have vowed to protect her."

"Then you will appreciate my news. I managed to get law enforcement to back off since she is the victim. All you have left to deal with is the hit man and the lunatic. Any idea why the nut case thinks you killed his sister?"

"Not a clue. His name is Willy Smit. He crewed for me up north before he got called home for a family emergency."

"Shit!" Jagger's cold stare bore into Robert. "You know the situation I helped you with in New Jersey?"

"Aye."

"The lady's surname was Smit."

The sensation of being gut-punched forced Robert back a step. Jagger referred to the vampire groupie with the purple tinted hair. Could she be related to Willy?

"Please. Tell me she did not die."

"She was very ill after—"

"Jagger!" Robert roared.

"She did not die, but she was quite ill and is still at the safe house recovering. Her family is unaware of her whereabouts. Maybe he is her brother."

"If so, I have been careless. They both know what I am."

Robert told his friend everything that happened the night he spent with the girl. Her seduction of him. The violent sex. The blood. All of it. Then he showed him the silver mage dagger Willy had carried.

"Damn. This is serious." Jagger pushed the blade away with a handkerchief as if merely touching it offended him. "Do you know what this is?"

"I fear I might. I hoped you would tell me my concerns are unwarranted."

"I wish I could, but I can't. The society must not have perished as we thought. If Willy is one of them, there will be an army hounding you from now on."

"Then you better stay away from me, before the society realizes what you are."

"You have saved me more often than I can count. I will watch your back, as you have mine. I will not abandon you because some misguided slayers are after you."

"You have been a true friend." Robert embraced Jagger. "Will you keep the dagger for me? I dinnae want it near Kimberly." He slid the ancient weapon of annihilation into its sheath.

Jagger's lips twisted into a distasteful frown. Robert thought he might refuse, but Jagger picked up the leather-encased dagger and stowed it in the satchel he carried.

"Drop me in Charleston. I will see what I can learn while you keep your lady safe."

Slayers? Satan damn them all. Robert never should have allowed Willy to go free.

* * *

Willy balanced on leaden legs. Yellow light from the late afternoon sun streamed through grimy windows along the upper section of one wall. He hated coming to the clinic.

Slayer's leader ordered he undergo a series of treatments in an effort to counteract the effects of the vampire bite. The society's doctor believed the drug cocktail would free him of the voices talking inside his head and stop the vampires from tracking him. The antidote hadn't worked yet.

"You know, it didn't hurt when she bit me. It was like the best sex I've ever had."

Cramps gripped his stomach, and he clutched his belly with a trembling hand. He clambered onto the cold metal gurney at the center of the antiseptic treatment room in the infirmary at the society's east coast headquarters and allowed the orderly to strap him in place.

"They keep talking to me, day and night. Can't sleep. They're driving me crazy."

The muddy brown, judgmental eyes of the Hungarian physician glared down at him. Why couldn't a nurse administer the serum? A dark haired woman with green eyes? The thought of the raven-haired vampire's emerald gaze turning fiery red, the bite, and the ecstasy that followed caused Willy's blood to race to his cock. He strained against the bonds.

He wanted the female vampire. He needed to escape. He thrashed wildly. The orderly used the bulk of his weight to hold Willy in place while the first needle pierced flesh. He slowly calmed as the drug relaxed him and eased the crazies.

When he went limp, the doctor jabbed the second needle into his arm and attached the intravenous bag. With the slow drip, it felt as if flames raced over his skin. He shuddered, loathing the thought of what would come next.

His skin burned as if fire ants marched across his flesh. He screamed. The terrifying sound reverberated off the chamber walls. The sensation of spiders crawling through his veins had him fighting the restraints.

The voices didn't go away. They laughed at him.

Hours later, he woke in a small bedroom, body soaked with sweat and throat raw from incessant screaming. Unbearable pain wracked his abdomen. He stumbled to the toilet before the vomiting began.

When the first round of spasms subsided, he leaned his forehead against the cool china bowl. MacLachlan and his whores must die.

CHAPTER NINE

Robert found it difficult to step away from the sensuous sight Kimberly presented while sleeping peacefully in the sailboat's v-berth. A band tightened around his heart. He laid the single red rose on the pillow next to her head with hope that when she woke, the token of affection would bring a smile to her delicious lips.

He remembered too well the taste and feel of that seductive mouth.

After allowing a finger the pleasure of brushing across a single brown curl, he yanked away an unsteady hand. She stretched and moaned in her sleep, exposing to his hungry gaze the tips of dark nipples through the sheer cotton fabric of a peach tank top.

The almost-constant pressure in his groin increased. Throbbed. His mouth watered and his fangs lengthened. To taste her blood again would be pure ecstasy.

He took two steps back, away from temptation, controlling the unwholesome urges. For three nights, he'd kept the monsters within him under tight restraint. His vampire-self relentlessly fought for control. Demanded he feed upon Kimberly. The panther, however, remained in the shadows of his mind, stalking, always watching.

Why did the animal not demand his mate?

Unease tightened Robert's stomach. He was well aware

Kimberly matched his soul. If only he still had a soul. Fate dealt them a terrible blow. For soul mates to be born in different centuries was one thing. To be immortal and meet the one woman meant to be yours, and not to be able to claim her, was more punishment than any man should have to endure.

He ground his teeth. The longer they waited to sail to Florida the more dangerous things between them would become. He ought to have Colin take her south.

Robert ignored the reproach from his conscience. He refused to give up what little time remained to be alone with her. Even if he couldn't seduce her, couldn't free the sexuality he sensed deep within her, he needed to keep her with him.

With a last glance at Kimberly, he whirled on a heel and climbed the companionway stairs to the deck. The full moon greeted him, and the monsters shifted. Robert inhaled a deep cleansing breath, forced them into the background, and stepped onto the floating dock.

He was eager to conclude the business in Charleston. The negotiations with the builder had taken more time than planned. *Sea Panther* and its crew still idled farther north along the coast. That was, with the exception of Davey. The lad hadn't surfaced, which gave Robert cause for worry.

Jagger worried too. He'd gone in search of the young man.

Robert left the transient dock and walked along the darkened streets. He prayed that if Kimberly woke while he was gone, she'd remember the order to stay below and out of sight. He didn't want her to risk being seen or recognized.

Before Jagger managed to call off the law, someone at the police department in New Jersey leaked her story to the press. Her picture, along with the suspected hit man's mug shot, was broadcasted over the national news networks.

Robert watched the story unfold on the small television in his cabin while Kimberly slept. He hadn't mentioned the broadcasts, not wanting to upset her further. The television stations showed interviews with ex-clients, one of which Robert knew well. Salvatore Romano. Robert planned to give the man a call after completing his business with the boat builder. Sal would speak frankly on the matter.

Others spoke well of Kimberly. They couldn't believe she'd done anything wrong. The interview with the ex-fiancé wasn't as cordial. The weasel accused her of investing in illegal overseas financial funds and of other unlawful practices.

She was no longer merely a victim of a crime but the subject of a criminal investigation.

Robert unclenched his fists. He didn't care much for the look of the man or for his unverified accusations. A smile tugged at his lips as he walked along the dock. Jason Reedman didn't know it yet, but he'd marked himself for retribution.

* * *

As Willy crept through the dark night, he repeatedly glanced over a shoulder to see if anyone followed. The secluded warehouse district near the Charleston docks gave him the creeps. He didn't want to be there, but the Slayer leader ordered him to come. One didn't disobey that psychopath.

Willy stopped in front of an armored steel door. The rusted light fixture overhead looked as if it hadn't worked in years. The surveillance camera, however, was new. Though he couldn't imagine it would pick anything up in the darkness. When he rang the bell, a lamp he hadn't seen blinded him with bright light.

He waited. No one answered. He would leave, but he didn't want to explain to the slayers why he hadn't met with anyone.

After an eternity, an aged security guard opened the door. "Whatcha want, boy?"

Willy leaned back. The man's breath reeked of cheap booze. "I was told to come here and meet with a gentleman."

The half-drunk guard eyed him suspiciously. "Know the man's name?"

"Nope."

The guard slammed the door shut. Willy pounded on it until his knuckles bled. Finally, the old drunk opened the door and glared at him.

"Come on, man. Let me in, they told me to come here," Willy said.

"Who?"

"Slayer."

The old man's rummy eyes widened. "Why didn't you say so to begin with?"

"You didn't ask."

"Don't be sassin' me, boy."

Willy forced himself to appear contrite. "Sorry. They didn't tell me what to say."

"You're the one they called about?"

"Guess so."

"Well, then. Follow me." A toothless grin crossed the guard's lips. "The boss didn't like them calling. Didn't like them knowing about him."

"I have no idea what you're talking about."

"For the best. The boss doesn't like people knowing his business."

Willy followed the guard into a poorly lit corridor. The smell of greasy chicken wings from a paper carton on the steel desk made him feel queasy and reminded him he couldn't eat. Favorite foods no longer tasted good. He cleared a tight throat and followed the man through a maze of passageways until they stopped in front of a metal door with a small tinted window reinforced with embedded chicken wire.

The old man opened the door. "Wait in there."

Willy walked into the room. He wasn't surprised when the door closed behind him, and the distinct sound of a lock falling into place grated his nerves.

He examined the glass in the door. It was one-way. Someone could observe him from outside, but he couldn't see out. What had he gotten into this time?

The windowless room was empty except for one marred metal chair. Willy sat and waited. Over an hour passed. He scratched a raw patch of skin on his arm. His health had declined since the vampire bitch bit him.

A rat scurried across the dirty floor. Willy moved uneasily on the cold seat. More time passed. He counted the dingy cream tiles on the ceiling for the fifth time.

Tortured masculine screams sounded from somewhere within the rickety old building. His stomach lurched. He swallowed hard and hoped he'd avoid a similar fate.

What was this place? Why had Slayer sent him here?

He must have dozed at some point because he woke to the sound of the creaking door. An upscale dressed man with gel-styled brown hair walked in. The security guard hurried in behind him with another chair. The man sat and stared at Willy through ice-cold silver eyes, an unreadable expression on his tanned face.

The inside of Willy's mouth felt as if an army had tramped through it. His body ached all over. He rubbed a hand over his jaw. Sandpaper. "How long have I been here?"

"A few hours. I would've met with you sooner, but I needed to oversee another interrogation...I should say interview." The man smiled with perfect white teeth and stretched long legs out in front of him, crossing silk covered ankles and tasseled loafers below the perfect razor edge crease of tan gabardine slacks. "I understand you once crewed on the yacht, *Sea Panther*."

"Yeah. What of it?" *What the freak is this meeting about?* What did fancy pants have to do with *Sea Panther* and Slayer. There must be more going on than Willy was aware of.

"How would you like to take a trip for me?"

"What's in it for me?"

"Money." The man glanced at a manicured hand before pinning Willy with an intense gaze. "I'll make it worth your while. If the contract I have for tonight fails, I need someone on the ground in Florida."

* * *

Around midnight, Robert examined diagrams and drawings, pleased with the most recent rendition of the proposed changes to *Sea Panther*.

"Well? What do you think?" Tom Sloan asked with a self-assured smile.

Robert studied Tom and considered the easy stance of the much sought after boat builder. Though much shorter, the dark-haired man had no qualms about maintaining eye contact. Robert had been impressed on their first meeting three years ago. Still was.

The builder neither questioned the need for the late meeting, nor complained about working into the night. He'd profit from the willing accommodation.

"These plans will work, though I would prefer a higher ampere generator with a backup."

Tom jotted a note on a yellow legal pad with a stubby orange pencil bearing his company logo. "Anything else?"

"Nae, I think we are good. Can you estimate when she will be ready to sail again?"

"Have to get back to you with a projected date, but I would expect the refit to take about six months."

Robert frowned and rubbed his chin. When he'd planned the refit, he hadn't thought beyond spending a month or two at the compound in Florida. He should have realized upgrades to *Sea Panther* would take longer.

After the blood tests were completed, he wanted to sail to Jamaica. He hadn't returned to the island since his turning. Recently someone or something had begun calling him there, a desperate whisper in his mind.

He'd ask Jagger to allow him to keep *Night Thrill* a while longer. His friend had mostly become a landlubber and wouldn't need the sailboat.

Robert filed a copy of the plans into his leather briefcase. "I will be out of reach for a number of days. Contact my office in Florida with the estimates."

"Will do."

As he grasped Tom's hand, Jagger rushed into the conference room, a dark storm raging within the depths of his golden eyes. Fear kicked Robert in the gut. "What's happened? Is Kimberly—"

Jagger held up a hand. Taking the hint, Tom stepped toward the doorway. "If you'll excuse me, I'll let you discuss your business in private."

After he left the room and closed the door discreetly behind him, Robert barely contained himself. "Well?"

"I found Davey in an alley by the docks," Jagger said. "Badly beaten. I took him to the hospital. He'll be fine, but my hunch is the hit man knows where to look for Kimberly."

* * *

Filtered light from a lamppost on dock streamed in through *Night Thrill*'s open companionway. The sight of the single red rose on the pillow beside Kimberly made her pulse quicken. *Robert.* If she didn't guard against it, she'd find herself in love with the sweet man. She brought the bloom to her nose and savored its soft scent. Who was she fooling?

He already held her heart.

She climbed out of the awkward shaped v-berth and dressed. It felt strange to sleep during the day and stay awake all night. The first day on the smaller sailboat, she tossed and turned on her bunk unable to fall asleep. The second morning, she agreed to take the melatonin Robert offered.

Once before, when she complained about jet lag, an associate at the financial firm where she worked at the time suggested the dietary supplement supposed to help regulate sleep and wake cycles. The little pill seemed to work. She slept through the day and was disappointed to have missed seeing Robert before he left for the meeting with the boat builder.

Robert had no problem sleeping while the sun was high. Of course, the aft cabin where he slept had a door, whereas the v-berth opened to the salon, to the bright daylight streaming through the Plexiglas.

Kimberly hummed as she brushed her hair. A twinge of guilt spoiled her good mood when she noticed the cell phone sitting in the top of a tote bag. Sarah more than likely seethed with anger. She would have worried at first, but her fear for Kimberly would ultimately morph into pure fury.

There was nothing to do about her sister's angst.

Kimberly didn't dare contact her. She couldn't risk putting Sarah in harm's way.

Kimberly plopped onto the settee and thumbed through a fashion magazine Robert had brought for her. After a while, the stuffy cabin made her feel like a prisoner trapped within the small confines of the sailboat. She needed fresh air.

Snatching the cape Robert gave her for Christmas on the way out, she stepped through the companionway and into the cockpit. Brisk reviving air filled her lungs. She glanced heavenward and searched for constellations in the star-filled sky. Finding Orion, the great hunter, made her smile.

A tinge of sorrow pinched near her heart. She'd often stargazed with her father when they'd sailed together.

"Ouch." A large insect whirred past her ear after biting her. She swiped at the bite and found blood on her fingers.

"Duck," a man shouted. It took Kimberly a few seconds to realize Jagger ran along the dock toward her. "Get down!"

She crouched in the cockpit and peeked over the edge. What was going on? In a blur of incredible speed, Jagger raced toward her, zigging and zagging with agility.

A man on the adjacent dock screamed.

Kimberly jerked her gaze in that direction. A large, tawny-colored cougar with canines bared leapt at a man holding a rifle. Reminiscent of her nightmares, she screamed. The man with the gun, along with the big cat, tumbled into the bay. A huge splash followed their fall.

She moved forward toward the bow of *Night Thrill*, but Jagger grabbed an arm, stopping her mid-step. "Let me go. Someone needs to help that man."

Feet pounded on the dock as people ran to see what happened. She fought against Jagger's hold. His free arm snaked around her waist, drawing her against a hard chest in an unbreakable grip. "Calm down and I will release you."

She elbowed him hard before weakening.

He swung her into the cockpit and set her on her feet, but didn't let go. "Get below before you are recognized."

He pushed her toward the companionway stairs. Anger hummed between them. In the salon, she moved away, scanning the room for a weapon.

His eyes narrowed. "Do not even think it."

"What?" She swallowed uneasily.

"I am not going to hurt you, little fool. On the contrary, I am here to protect you."

"What's going on?" Kimberly noticed her hand trembled as she rubbed her sore elbow.

Jagger reached out. She flinched, but before she could pull away, he brushed cold fingers across her ear. The hand he removed was stained with blood.

Her blood? She sank onto the settee and touched her ear. It was sticky.

Holy shit! She was really bleeding.

Her peripheral vision fuzzed. A deep breath kept her from fainting. She refused to allow panic to grab hold. "What happened out there?"

Jagger opened drawers and cabinets, slamming them shut, one by one, until he found the first aid kit. When he turned, the expression in his eyes softened. "Will you allow me to tend the wound?"

She chewed her lip and nodded consent, wondering what the hell bit her.

Crouching in front of her, he set the first aid kit on the settee and reached up.

The growl from the companionway stopped him mid-motion.

CHAPTER TEN

"I will see to Kimberly," Robert gritted through a clenched jaw.

Still feral from the change, he gripped the teak lip of the companionway overhead with both hands, making his knuckles turn white. The panther wanted to go for the jugular. Sink sharp canines into Jagger and rip the artery from his throat. Tear the hands his enemy dared to touch Kimberly with from his body. Rib the man to shreds.

Robert's chest heaved from the internal battle. He could almost taste his friend's blood on his tongue. With effort, he forced the wild beast down and stepped into the salon.

He scanned the tableau before him with irritation. Jagger sat back on his haunches, arms loose at his sides, a curl to his lips as if this disaster were humorous. Some friend. Robert wanted to smash a fist into the grinning face. He shook off the angry thought.

Kimberly lay against the cushions, body stiff, and gaze trained on him. Light from a lamppost on dock shined through the hatch above her head, emphasizing her worried expression.

The sight and smell of her blood made his heart pound erratically. The vampire pressed for release. Robert swallowed hard and pushed back against the monsters competing for control. He refused to allow them to make the situation worse.

Jagger moved away from Kimberly and leaned nonchalantly with one hip against the galley counter. Robert gave the man credit for being smart enough to get out of the way. He refocused on Kimberly, the only person on the sailboat of importance.

"What happened out there?" Her gaze shifted to Jagger then back to him.

Her strained frown emphasized her pale face. He feared she might go into shock. Grabbing a wool blanket from a cabinet behind the settee, he wrapped it around her, careful to avoid the blood clotting at the edge of her ear. He moved away quickly, so not to lose the battle with the panther and the vampire.

"The hit man found you." He rubbed his forehead to ease the emerging headache and frowned. "Dammit to hell, Kimberly, I thought I told you to stay below, out of sight."

"I was shot?" Her voice wobbled. She raised a hand to the injured ear. When she pulled it back, she stared at the blood on her fingers.

"Aye." Robert wanted to offer comfort, but couldn't trust himself. "I have ordered Colin to bring *Sea Panther* into port. He can dress your wound when she arrives. I dinnae think we can chance you going to the hospital."

"No need." Kimberly jumped up, dropped the blanket, and grabbed the first aid kit. She brushed passed him and stomped to the head. With a bang, the door closed.

Robert gritted his teeth. The lingering smell of blood overwhelmed his senses, made his stomach clench. At least the overall scent had changed. Good. He'd rather sense anger than fear. He retreated to the cockpit where the salty air tainted Kimberly's essence. There would be hell to pay if the monsters became provoked. Jagger followed.

"Damn you," Robert said. "Don't ever touch her again."

"The wound needed tending and I didn't know how long you would be. I never guessed she could tend to it herself. She's a strong one. You should be proud of her."

Robert sighed and the bluster left him. Disgust tightened his throat. "I let the man get away."

"Obviously," Jagger drawled.

"Too many people. It was bad enough I lost control to the panther and bystanders saw me. I could not let the story get out that a big cat killed a man on the Charleston docks, could I?"

"You are too close to the situation. Maybe you should let someone else take her to Florida."

"Like you, for instance?" Robert spat the question, possessive fury nearly strangling him.

"Maybe." Jagger tilted his head to the side and arched a brow.

Robert bared his fangs.

"An innocent suggestion." His friend raised his hands, palms forward.

Robert closed his eyes and swallowed. He clenched his fists, took several deep breaths, focused, forced his will and controlled the rising aggression.

The volatile air between them calmed. He raised his eyelids and took a step back. "I dinnae understand what has come over me of late."

"I do. If I were you, I would—" Jagger snapped his mouth shut.

Kimberly stepped through the companionway and joined them. "Okay, I made a mistake. I should have stayed below. I also understand I was shot." She tucked a lose curl behind the damaged ear, and her hand trembled. "What I don't understand is what a cougar was doing on the other dock. Who was the man it attacked?"

"Are you all right, sweetling?" Robert asked.

Kimberly's eyes widened at the endearment. Her gaze shifted from his face to Jagger's amused expression, to the floor. "The bullet barely nicked me. I don't know why you two made such a big deal over it. It hardly bled at all."

"Then you are sure you are well?" Robert scanned the length of her, searching for other injuries.

"Absolutely."

His black heart twisted. "I am glad."

"But you still haven't told me what a big cat was doing on the dock."

"I heard in town, a circus animal escaped." He kept his face blank as he told the lie.

"Oh my God. It attacked the hit man, didn't it? That was him with the rifle, wasn't it?"

"Lucky coincidence." Robert shrugged. "Too bad the man got away."

"And the animal?" Jagger asked, a slow smile curling his lips.

Robert shot him a scowl. "His keeper found him."

"What do I do now?" Kimberly placed a hand on his sleeve. "He'll try again, won't he?"

"Aye." He winced, wishing he could lie to her in this. Sugarcoating the truth wouldn't serve any good though. She needed to comprehend the danger.

He caught the gleam of moisture in her haunted brown eyes before she blinked and raised her chin. Jagger was right; she was a strong lass. She'd be fine. Robert wasn't sure he would be. Never before had he experienced such crippling fear.

"We sail for Florida." He brushed a strand of hair from her eyes, and allowed his fingers to linger against her smooth cheek. "Are you sure you are well?"

She nodded.

"Good. We need to leave before the authorities arrive, asking questions."

"I'm off. Call if you need me." Jagger jumped over the side onto the floating dock and strode away without waiting for a response.

"Thank you," Kimberly called after him.

He turned and waved then continued on his way, disappearing into the dockside hustle-bustle. Sirens blared in the distance. Time to leave. Robert reached over the side and cast off a line. He would keep Kimberly close until they reached the compound. But then what?

The question darted around in his mind, driving him mad.

* * *

Sleep filled days merged into pleasurable nights. Kimberly nearly forgot her predicament. Who would have thought Robert would turn out to be a fascinating conversationalist?

Stars glittered in the midnight blue sky. She held the wheel of *Night Thrill* and marveled over what she'd learned of Robert. He could speak on almost any subject. Business, economics, politics, music, art, though history seemed to be his passion.

"What would you like to discuss tonight?" she asked.

"Tell me about Fast Jimmy."

She inwardly groaned. Until now, they hadn't discussed anything personal, other than her current ordeal. She hated talking about her father. But since it was Robert's turn to choose the topic, she'd have to oblige.

"My father was born in Scotland, near Kilmarnock in Ayrshire. His family moved to Toronto when he was four. A couple of years later, they moved to Cranford, New Jersey."

"A good Scottish lad, was he?" Robert winked.

"I guess."

"How did he start racing?"

"He became good friends with the son of the reverend from the Episcopal church his family attended. Mr. Murray had a summer ministry on Long Island near Huntington Harbor. Since my father's mother worked, he spent the summer season with the Murrays and learned to sail on the Sound. I guess one thing led to another."

She fell silent for a moment and watched the sea. "Your turn," she said, turning back to Robert, wanting to change the subject. "Tell me about you and your sister and your family in Scotland."

A dark expression crossed his features then cleared. "Another time, perhaps. I will take the helm and you can go below and rest."

"I'll relinquish the wheel, but I'm not tired. I'd like to stay on deck."

"You are a vexing lass."

Kimberly suppressed a smile. "Tell me about your life. Please."

He didn't say anything, just gripped the wheel. She thought he wouldn't indulge her.

After five minutes of staring out to sea, he cleared his throat. "Raven and I were born in a castle on a sea loch on the western coast of Scotland to loving parents who died too early. Our much older brother and his first wife raised us. I grew into a man and became a successful merchant and secured the small fortune Raven spends on her adventures."

Merchant? Sometimes his word choices seemed archaic.

"There must be more to your story."

"Nae."

"What was it like to live in a castle?"

"Cold." His shoulders shook in a mock shiver.

Kimberly inhaled a deep breath of salty air and let it out sharply. She hated when he gave one-word answers. "Tell me more."

"Some other time." Robert chuckled.

To her surprise, he reached across the cockpit and grasped her hand. A companionable silence fell between them. Time passed...comfortably. They watched the sea swell and ebb until he finally broke the silence and released her hand.

"Tell me about your mother?"

Kimberly sighed. "Not much to say. She's remarried and belongs to a cult in New Mexico."

"You must miss her."

"No. She abandoned Sarah and me when my father died. Left us to fend for ourselves." Kimberly glanced away before Robert saw the pain and anger she still felt over her mother's desertion.

"I am sorry."

"Don't be. We were better off without her." She hesitated then continued. "That's why I worked so hard over the years. Why I took the stupid tip from Jason and used it to invest both my money and that of my clients in the off-shore deal he recommended."

Robert frowned and shook his head.

"On some level, I knew...I knew it was a mistake." She shrugged. "I was greedy."

"Dinnae be so hard on yourself."

She dropped her gaze, and he lifted her chin with the tip of a finger.

"You did what you thought was needed to survive and take care of your sister. Feel good about the successes. Think about all you have achieved rather than obsess over one mistake. You are a survivor. We will work this out together."

"Thanks. I appreciate the help."

They both fell quiet. The silence wasn't awkward—a nice surprise. Some of the weight had lifted off her shoulders.

"Tell me about your sister," Robert said after some time passed.

Guilt brought with it a flash of heat to her chest. Kimberly wrapped her arms around herself. She hadn't spoken to her sister in days. "Sarah is a loving, free spirit who's always there when I need her. She's probably frantic with worry."

"Do you want me to have Jagger contact her?"

"No. She'll be safer not knowing where I am. Don't you think?"

"Aye. There is truth in that."

Kimberly still couldn't believe what Robert divulged about the newscasts. He'd kept the information secret for a couple of days, but finally spilled the truth about the allegations against her so she'd understand the trouble pursuing her.

Jason was a full-fledged liar. If only she'd known sooner. Accusing her of illegal investment activities had been the last thing she expected from her ex-fiancé. He was such a rotten jerk.

She'd been a fool for believing in him. She'd have to stop running soon and go back to face the charges. Figure out a way to clear her name or never work again. Gullibility and stupidity were her only crimes.

Kimberly shivered. If convicted, she'd more than likely be sent to prison as an example, especially with the economy the way it had been over the last couple of years. She couldn't allow that to happen. No laws had been broken. As soon as she felt safe, she'd go back and tell her side of the ghastly affair.

The sky lightened on the horizon, and Kimberly took the wheel from Robert. While he went forward to drop the canvas, she started the *iron genny*. The engine hummed to life. After the mainsail rested neatly in the *lazy jacks*, he returned aft and eased around the large wheel to stand behind her.

The tips of his fingers brushed over her shoulders and slowly slid down her arms. Delicious chills tickled the skin beneath his touch, making her want to purr like a pampered feline. Hands over hers, he leaned in tight. The pressure from his erection caused her sex to clench. The evidence of her heightened desire dampened her panties, and she melted into him. "Robert, I…"

"Shhh, sweetling. Savor the moment. 'Tis all I can give you."

Life was unfair. He was trying to protect her. His illness stood between them. An unbearable sadness engulfed Kimberly. Robert hugged her as if he understood. They stayed like that, she steering, and he holding her tight until they reached the inlet.

He whispered directions while she navigated the sailboat into the sleepy cove. Early morning mist drifted above the water and wrapped around the two sailboats already secured there. Robert released her, and while the engine idled, he dropped anchor. Without a word, he went below.

Kimberly shut off the motor. She wanted to call him back. He would shut himself in his cabin and not come out until dusk. Tears burned her eyes. Their situation was hopeless.

CHAPTER ELEVEN

Night Thrill lolled at anchor. Robert leaned back against the cabin door with fisted hands. He sensed Kimberly's frustration as if it were his own. Even without the transfer of blood, a feeding would provide, he was more attuned to her than any woman he'd met in his nearly three hundred years of immortality.

Could such profound awareness have come from the one wee taste when he licked the scratch on her hand? If so, what would he experience if he were to drink his fill?

Fangs punched through his gums. Frustration wrapped around him and squeezed.

The tight confines of the cabin gave little room to maneuver. Not wanting to do something foolish, he locked the door. He clutched the bag of blood and removed the brown paper wrapping. His fangs penetrated the thick plastic, and he drank deeply from the unsatisfying contents. Nutrients coursed through his veins giving much-needed strength.

The vampire surged for control, wanting to break free before Robert stopped his heart and descended into the mindless deathlike sleep of his kind. Hunger satisfied, Robert easily confined the monster to the evil black place within him.

He slid a hand over the hidden latch on the bunk. To the

casual observer the bed looked like any other bunk in any other sailboat. On *Night Thrill*, as on *Sea Panther*, the bunk contained a secret compartment.

After releasing the catch, Robert lifted the hinged lid, stepped in, and lay down amongst the thin layer of nourishing soil Jagger had kindly provided with the boat. Most vampires preferred to sleep within the earth. Robert found the rhythm of the sea more to his liking. He closed the cover, taking solace from the absolute dark.

He needed to shut down his system and welcome the sleep of the undead.

The panther stirred, wanting to protect his mate. Robert willed the beast back into the shadows. The animal knew the truth. Robert couldn't embrace the regenerative slumber of vampires. If he did, who would protect Kimberly?

* * *

Kimberly stared through a window at the red fireball rising over the horizon. How did the old saying go? *Pink at night, pirates make delight. Red in the morning, sailors take warning.*

A bone deep chill shivered through her and she pulled on the cape Robert gifted her.

During the next two hours, both of the other sailboats motored out of the secluded cove. Kimberly paced the confines of the salon, knowing she wouldn't be able to sleep without help. In frustration, she swallowed one of the pills Robert supplied and climbed onto the bunk.

When sleep finally came, it was fitful.

She ran as fast as possible. Her muscles burned from exertion. She weaved through the trees, searching for a way to escape. The pounding sound of the man's footfalls spurred her onward. A steep cliff appeared. She paused and with hands on knees struggled for breath.

After glancing in both directions, she darted left. Too close to the edge, she skidded to a stop. Chest tight, she peered into the deep ravine. Fear spiked. She turned and raced along the edge of the cliff. Loose rocks tumbled down the slope.

Please, God, don't let me tumble over the side.

Twigs snapped behind her. The stranger must be gaining ground.

She glanced over a shoulder. Shit! The man was right behind her. Kimberly took a deep breath, sprinted full out, and jumped over a fallen tree.

Her foot caught on a branch. She fell hard. Pain seared an ankle, but she managed to push up onto sore knees. The stranger's body shuddered, contorted, stretched. Oh, dear God, what horror is this? The man jerked and transformed into a cougar.

Holy shit. She froze. The big cat bared its canines and leapt for her throat.

Kimberly woke with a racing pulse. Perspiration soaked her brow. Light streamed through the windows in the salon. She sat up and listened. Quiet. Robert's door remained closed. She hadn't wakened him. Her heartbeat slowed enough to settle the frantic thumping against her ribs. She settled back into the pillows. Exhaustion pulled her into oblivion.

Later, she woke again, feeling a subtle change in the motion of their floating home. The normal calm lapping of waves against the hull had turned into a persistent rocking. She quickly threw on a pair of jeans and a lavender t-shirt and scooted out of the cramped v-berth.

The door to Robert's cabin was latched open. He wasn't there.

After stepping into slip-on sneakers, she climbed the companionway stairs and found him scanning the entrance to their private paradise with binoculars. Ominous storm clouds covered the sun and a brisk wind blew from the south. White capped waves rolled across the surface of the water. Checking her watch, she was surprised at how early it was in the afternoon. Three o'clock, much earlier than they'd recently made a habit of rising. With the heavy gloom, the time seemed much later.

"Get below," Robert hollered. "We're about to have unwanted guests."

A brightly lit coastguard inflatable raced into the cove. Shit. Kimberly didn't wait to be told a second time. She scrambled below stairs and hid in the cabin.

* * *

Robert didn't need to check to see if Kimberly obeyed. He smelled her fear over the briny scent on the wind. He lowered the binoculars and made ready to greet their guests.

The coastguard Zodiac pulled portside. "Ahoy, *Night Thrill*."

"Ahoy," Robert yelled in return. "Problem?"

"Nasty storm headed this way. We're advising all boaters to take refuge in protective moorings. You should be safe here, but might want to put out a second anchor."

"Thanks for the forewarning."

"No problem." The guardsmen waved, and the inflatable sped away.

When the Zodiac cleared the inlet entrance, Kimberly returned to the cockpit. "Thank God, they're gone."

"Aye, I was in nae mood to try to outrun the US Coast Guard with a single-engine sailboat."

"Do you think they'll be back?"

"They will be too busy with the storm."

Kimberly raked her teeth along her lower lip. "Will we be okay?"

Robert ignored the blood rush to his groin and placed a palm against her cheek. "Aye, lass. Safe and snug within *Night Thrill*. Let us batten down the hatches. Shall we?"

She agreed and went to work. As a team, they prepared for the oncoming storm. Kimberly impressed him. She remained calm and focused while performing her duties. Bloody hell...if things were different, he'd be contemplating making her his wife. The mother of his children. His *lifemate*.

He swore under his breath.

"What?" She stopped to stare at him. "Did I do something wrong?"

"Nae. You are capable. I was frustrated with myself, is all. Here..." He reached for the other end of the rope she used to secure the extra water jugs. "Let me help tie that off, and then we will take ourselves below."

* * *

Wind howled, thunder rumbled, lightning streaked the sky. Rain pelted the deck. Yet Kimberly felt safe and secure holed up with Robert inside *Night Thrill.*

He discarded an eight-of-clubs. "Your turn."

She placed her cards facedown on the large coffee table. "Sorry. Not much into the game."

"Nae worries." He gathered the cards, shuffled them, and put them into the pack. "Is there something else you would rather do?"

There was, but she couldn't tell him what.

As if a mind reader, he motioned for her to sit beside him. She eased down onto the cushion, and he placed an arm around her shoulders. They snuggled together, silent, listening to the storm rage outside their little haven. When his fingers brushed across the bottom of a breast, her nipples hardened.

A hungry fire burned in his cinnamon eyes. Butterflies slam-danced inside her belly, and she self-consciously bit her bottom lip.

Robert made a strangled sound moments before his mouth ravished hers. She leaned into him. Every shift of pressure, every sensation, tore at her heart. Made her pulse race. She wanted to climb his body. Make love.

He scattered kisses over her face. Her neck. Her hair. A warm breath teased sensitive skin. He murmured against an ear, describing suggestive sensual positions they might try. She shivered in delight.

Erotic images played in Kimberly's mind as teasing hands roamed her body. Fingers plucked pearled nipples, drew her taut. He played her like a fine musical instrument.

First, the shirt landed on the floor. Then the bra.

Cool air prickled her skin.

He gave an encouraging smile. Two could play at this game. His shirt had to go. She reached for the bottom of the polo. His lips pursed and eyebrows arched as if he wasn't sure she could finish what she started.

Oh yeah, she could. Kimberly tugged the black cotton

up and over his head. Golden light from the lamp spilled across ripped muscle covered by beautiful bronze skin. She brushed fingers over the dusting of fine hair on his hard chest. Swept her touch over the washboard abs.

His body quivered. Was he as aroused as she?

Leaning over her, he pressed her body into the settee cushion as if in answer. He claimed her mouth again. This time, wet and deep, his tongue fervently stroked hers. Their intoxicating kiss lasted for what seemed like an eternity, and then to her disappointment, he left her lips barren.

Before she had the chance to complain, he drew a nipple into a hot mouth, surrounded the puckered aureole with satiny lips, and sucked. He laved the sensitized nub with his tongue. Grazed teeth across the heated flesh and nipped.

Gentle at first. Then rough.

She panted with each fierce sensation that spiraled through her system and clutched at her sex. Her heart pounded a tattoo. Not until the rough fabric of his jeans brushed against her thigh did she fully realize he'd removed her pants and panties while she'd been lost in a haze of pure pleasure.

She wanted him naked too. She reached for the buttons of his jeans.

He grasped her hands and held them still.

"Are you sure, lass? There will be nae turning back." His rough voice confirmed his desire.

"I'm sure." Kimberly wanted him more than she'd ever wanted any other man.

He didn't wait for assistance. He jumped from the settee and tore the pants from his body. Commando. She sat up and looked her fill. Tight abs, to golden vee of hair, to…

Oh. My. God. What a body.

Kimberly couldn't help but let a nervous giggle slip.

An assured smile curled his lips, and he sat beside her. Placing a palm at the back of her neck, he drew her forward for another wondrous kiss, the exquisite sensation sizzling all the way to her toes.

He pulled away, and she opened her eyes. He held a

black silk scarf. A trace of alarm tickled her nerves. She'd once imagined him binding her with a scarf using a bowline knot. How had he known?

"You can trust me. I will never hurt you."

Kimberly believed him. "Robert, I want to be with you, but we need...protection."

Understanding flashed in his eyes. "There is nae need lass. I'm sterile thanks to my affliction."

"I'm sorry." She touched his hand lightly. "It's not that. It's..."

"What?"

"Protection against STDs."

"Ahhh. I'm sure I'm safe, but Jagger must have some condoms around here. Give me a moment." A few minutes later Robert returned with a box. "Do you think this will be enough?"

She held her mouth tight, trying not to laugh.

He held up the scarf and raised an eyebrow. She nodded consent, feeling naughty.

Robert drew the silk across her chest. With the sensuous feel of the sleek fabric skimming her sensitized skin, excitement escalating, she gave him a game smile.

Robert wrapped the scarf around Kimberly's wrists and bound them together.

Hard and heavy, he fought for control. He had never wanted another woman with so much intensity. With such great need. Kimberly was open to him. The utter honesty with which she reacted to his touch left him humbled.

The vampire attempted to force his influence, to steal the pleasure for his own. Robert fiercely fought the monster back into the inky shadows, refusing to allow the beast to sully the purity of his desire for Kimberly.

He picked her up and sat her on the table. His hands shook from the effort to remain gentle as he laid her back against the wood and slowly raised her arms over her head. Maintaining eye contact, he secured the ends of the scarf to the handhold at the edge of the table.

His black heart ached as he admired the woman laid out before him. The way she moistened her lips sent pulsating blood rushing to his cock. Robert licked his lips. He could still taste her sweet kiss.

She lay across the teak like an offering to the gods. Only she was there for him. He could read the longing glistening in her eyes. His erection throbbed. A groan burned in his throat. He held it there, not wanting to frighten Kimberly with his animalistic need.

He skimmed fingertips along the insides of her thighs, enjoying the feel of silky smooth skin. She shivered. When he spread her legs wider and teased sensitive flesh, she squirmed with unabashed need. Her eyes grew darker and more lustful. Soft sounds escaped her precious lips.

Satan knew how much Robert wanted to possess her. He fumbled with the condom and snugged it over his erection. With a squeeze to his cock, sensation shot to his toes. He rose above Kimberly and entered her with a quick deep thrust. Wet and slick, she took him into her body easily.

On a slow draw, he pulled almost all the way out then thrust again. And again.

She met him stroke for stroke. Firm muscles gripped the length of him. Milked him. The sound of rolling thunder reverberated in his ears. Blind desire raced through his system and the thrusts grew frantic. Kimberly kept pace. The rhythm matched the rage of the storm as slick bodies met and withdrew.

He released her from her bonds. Pressure built. The tempest intensified. A dizzying sensation overcame Robert, and the lustful vampire reached for control.

Robert's musky scent tickled Kimberly's senses. His mouth was all over her, gentle and rough, kissing and trailing love bites over hypersensitive skin. She arched her back to give better access to her breasts. He laved first one nipple, swirling his tongue, creating a tight bud, then the other, using lips and teeth to best advantage to drive her to the edge of anticipation.

She barely had time to register the delicious sensation in one spot when she'd feel lips and tongue and teeth tease another needy place.

With each draw of his mouth, he thrust deeper, propelling her higher.

If the pleasure wasn't so mind blowing, she might be embarrassed by the mewing sounds escaping her lips. She didn't even care that tomorrow she'd be bruised with love bites covering her chest and throat. She'd known making love with Robert would be special. Though it was much more—a runaway roller coaster of erotic pleasure.

Robert nuzzled a particularly sensitive spot at her throat. He sucked hard, and she felt his teeth graze her skin. A sharp stab of pleasure-pain took her by surprise, and she bucked against him. Good-lord, she was going to explode.

The initial pulse of Robert's orgasm slammed into her, and her body shattered into a zillion pieces. Her soul soared through a star filled universe to a place of absolute bliss.

The vampire greedily drew Kimberly's essence to him. Her body convulsed. The violence of their orgasms rocked Robert, the man, to the core. Ambrosia pleasured his taste buds. Feminine blood rushed through greedy veins, sending him higher, over a dark precipice to another place, a world of light.

When he came back to reality, he felt weak. Kimberly slept peacefully within his embrace. He swished his tongue over the bite marks on her neck, using the healing properties in his saliva to repair the torn flesh. He slid from her warmth and tossed the condom to the side. Not that they needed the damn thing. Sterile vampires can't spread human diseases.

Wrapping them both in an afghan, Robert sat on the settee and held her in his arms, devastated. The vampire and the panther receded to the shadows; both well-pleased Robert had finally claimed and marked Kimberly. He supposed it had been inevitable since their first meeting on the street in Cape May. She, destined to be his mate. He, to ruin her life.

A hard truth for a once honorable man to swallow.

He brushed her hair with a gentle kiss. The scent of

green apples would always remind him of Kimberly, long after she left him. He couldn't bear the thought of living without her. Of never experiencing that moment of light again.

If he could keep her, how would he explain the monsters lurking within him? How could he explain the evil he had forced on her?

The lass would be fine. He had to believe that. One feeding did not a vampire shifter make. Though, what would she think of him when she recalled the feel of fangs piercing her skin? Her life essence rushing away? What would she think when she realized what he was and what the vampire within him had done to her?

Robert held her and waited for the fury of the storm to pass. The fury in his black heart would never leave him.

The sailboat gently swayed at anchor. He waited for the recriminations to begin. He waited for the disgust and hatred to mar her precious features. He waited to lose his love.

CHAPTER TWELVE

R obert embraced Kimberly and willed her to forgive
him. If only he had such power.

She opened sultry eyes. "Hello, sexy. You made my toes
curl."

The satisfied expression glowing on her face left him
breathless. Relief washed over him. She was unaware of
the unconscionable act he'd committed against her. He
hugged her, unable to let go, though guilt tainted the
pleasure.

Robert smiled, not wanting her to sense his regret. "Ah,
my love, you are a marvel."

She pinned him with a melted chocolate gaze. "What
made you change your mind?"

"About what?"

"Making love."

How to answer? "I couldn't resist you."

Kimberly blushed. When he released her, she leaned
back against the settee cushions. "What shall we do next?"

She comically wiggled her eyebrows like Groucho Marx,
making him laugh. She was such a miracle. And he—a
devil.

He swung his feet onto the floor. "A shower for me."

Too bad *Night Thrill* had a tiny head. Otherwise, he'd
invite her to join him and they could pretend they were

making love under a waterfall. He had better forget that pleasurable thought though. He couldn't risk another round of lovemaking until he had better control over the vampire. He would not take her blood again.

"Do you want to go first?" he asked.

She dragged the afghan over herself. "Go ahead. I plan to lie here for a while and bask in the afterglow."

Robert stood, took a couple of steps and his vision blurred. His world spun. *Bloody hell*. He attempted another step, staggered, and almost fell. He leaned against the galley counter, gasping for breath.

"What's wrong?" Kimberly tossed the blanket aside and jumped to his aid.

"I dinnae ken."

"Here, let me help you." She reached for an arm. "You're as white as the sails."

He held her off, stepped away, stumbled and almost fell again. He grabbed for the counter, a handhold, and knocked over a wineglass. The flute shattered. A shard pierced a finger, and blood oozed from a stinging cut. He gaped at the blood in disbelief as it continued to flow and drip onto the floor unchecked.

What was happening to him? The bleeding should have stopped immediately.

Kimberly grabbed the injured finger, placed it into her mouth, and swirled her tongue around the cut. The sensation jarred him. He yanked his finger from her mouth. The bleeding stopped.

"See, all better," she said.

Robert stared at his hand in horror. What had she done? He took a troubled breath. Thank God, there hadn't been enough blood to do her any real harm. He had to believe that. He forced himself to breathe evenly.

Kimberly's worried gaze locked on him. "Maybe you should lie down for a while. You look a bit green around the gills."

"Aye." He took a step and staggered again.

She placed his arm around her shoulder, supported some of his weight, and helped him to the cabin, where he collapsed onto the bunk.

"Do you think you're going to be all right?"

He nodded. The simple movement made him nauseous. He motioned to the door with his eyes, begging her to leave him to the weakness.

Kimberly's gaze followed his. "Um. Yeah." She moved to the doorway. "Call me if you need anything." She stood in the portal, a furrow in her brow, staring at him.

"I will be fine. Just need to rest." He managed to get the words out through chattering teeth.

"Sure." She stayed for a minute longer, worrying her bottom lip, looking skeptical. Then she left the cabin, and the door closed softly.

Robert didn't have the strength to get off the bed, never mind try to lift the lid and crawl into the soil that would help heal whatever damn affliction had overcome him.

A bloody disaster. How was he to protect Kimberly?

* * *

Two hours passed. Robert's condition deteriorated. Kimberly sat on the edge of the bunk and placed a cool, damp cloth on his fevered brow.

He opened his glazed eyes and clutched at the fabric of her blouse. "Promise me something?"

"Of course, anything."

"Dinnae radio anyone or phone anyone on your cell. The authorities might intercept the call."

"But you're ill. Let me call Jagger or Colin or your sister."

"Nae. There is too great a risk."

Kimberly chewed on the corner of her lip. She didn't want to agree.

"Promise me..." His grip on her tightened. "You will not make any calls."

"All right." She reluctantly gave in.

Eyes closed, he eased against the pillows. Kimberly watched him until his breathing evened, and he slept.

As she straightened the area around the bunk, she noticed an old wooden steamer trunk bolted to the wall. The lock hung open. She thought to put his discarded clothing in the chest, but when she opened the lid, she found the trunk already full. A large tartan lay on top. Curiosity took hold. She couldn't stop from rummaging through the contents. Beneath the wool plaid were the swords from Robert's cabin on *Sea Panther* and a set of antique pistols. Beneath those, men's period clothing.

What the hell? She was no expert, but could hazard a guess the garments were from the early eighteenth century. Delving deeper into the chest, she spotted a ratty black cloth.

Kimberly sucked in a breath at the sight of the grinning skull peering back from the lower left side of the fabric. A Highland claymore was drawn, complete with down-sloping quillons, blade pointed upward to the left from the bottom right, as if it were about to be brought down upon the skull.

She hastened a glance at Robert. He slept soundly.

Returning attention to the contents of the chest, a bit of red fabric caught her eye. She pulled out what looked to be a solid red banner of sorts along with what she presumed might be a well-worn British flag. That, too, had to be very old.

How odd. Why would Robert have all this stuff? Well, he did have a fondness for history. Maybe he belonged to an historical reenactment group and this gear made up his costume and props.

She carefully replaced the items as they'd been, folded Robert's clothing, and laid the bundle on top of the chest then left the small cabin.

Kimberly sat on the settee and shuffled the deck of cards. What had she heard at the *Rusty Scupper* that day that now seemed like an eternity ago? One of the salty old bar rats had accused Robert of being a pirate. Of course, that was absurd in this day and age. There must be a good reason why he had all that old stuff.

There had been problems over the last couple of years with modern-day pirates off the coast of Somalia. No way could Robert have anything to do with them. How ridiculous for anyone to think him a pirate.

Kimberly played an umpteenth game of Solitaire when Robert cried out.

She found him thrashing about on the bunk. His forehead burned hot with fever. In his delirium, his garbled words were difficult to understand and definitely not English. She detected a few French words spattered among another foreign language, the sound guttural. Gaelic?

She tried to calm him, but he lashed out, striking her in the chin with a flailing arm.

"Ouch." She moved her jaw from side to side. "Shit, that hurt."

His eyes flew open. Wild-eyed, he tried to rise from the bunk. Lacking the strength, he fell back to sprawl across the mattress.

"Man the sails. Laroux rides the waves," he bellowed in English. "Hoist the Jolly Roger."

Kimberly froze. Jolly Roger? What on earth?

"The red flag flies. The bastard will grant nae quarter." His eyes closed and his head tossed from side to side. "Have to outrun them or fight to the death."

Robert mumbled something else unintelligible before quieting. Then he released a loud snore as if the incident never happened.

Kimberly inhaled a deep breath, allowing her heart to slow to a normal rate. With the episode past, Robert slept peacefully. She laid a moist cloth on his brow and glanced at the trunk. Pirates? Was it possible? Could the rumors somehow be true?

Insane idea.

No. More than likely, he relived a part once played as an historical reenacter. Nightmares brought on by fever. Nothing more.

After two more days of dealing with Robert's delirium, Kimberly was ready to break the promise and call for help. She couldn't wait much longer. Too dangerous. She didn't know what effect the high temperature had on his blood disease or whether he had missed taking medicine. The thought he could die was more than she could endure. As with her father, Robert's death would be her fault.

Kimberly sat on the edge of the bunk for the longest time staring at him and contemplating the choices. Use the boat's radio to call the coastguard or use her cell phone to call 911. She had no way to get in contact with Robert's friends. He'd never provided their numbers. And his cell was password protected. She shook her head. *Night Thrill* had been at anchor in this cove for several days. Why hadn't one of his friends tried to contact them? Weren't they worried? Didn't they wonder where they were?

The sailboat was moored close enough to shore to get four bars on the cell. She'd call 911. Deciding to wait no longer, she gripped the phone, ready to dial.

Robert's weakened hand tugged on her arm. "Nae." His voice was hoarse from lack of use, and he made a chuffing sound deep in his throat. "You promised."

"Please, Robert. You're very ill. I need to call for help."

"Nae. Feel better. You must only call the authorities if *you* are in danger." He made an effort to sit, and she plumped the pillows behind his back. "Bring me a bag of blood from the refrigerator."

When she returned with the plastic container, he took it and slumped against the pillows. Smudges darkened the skin under his eyes. The rest of his face appeared sallow.

"I need more sleep." He grasped her wrist. "Promise me. You will not call anyone while I rest."

She chewed on her lip, unsure, not wanting to agree.

"Promise me." His eyes held a fierce command.

"All right. Damn you." She tugged her arm free and placed the wrist on his forehead. His temperature had gone down slightly. "How do I give you the blood?"

"I will take care of it. Just leave me for a while."

"Are you sure? You're still terribly weak."

"I will manage. Please, Kimberly, allow me some privacy to care for my personal needs."

Heat rushed to her cheeks. "Of course, how crass of me."

She turned away, but before leaving, she glanced back and frowned. His eyes remained glassy.

Robert ripped open the thick plastic bag with sharp fangs and greedily gulped the contents. Rich nutrients coursed through his system, repairing capillaries and collapsed veins. Tight fists uncurled. Circulating blood caused the fingers to tingle as sensation returned to his limbs. He inhaled several deep breaths and willed strength into his debilitated body. He tried to move his legs, but mobility came slower than he would have liked. Finally, after several attempts, he managed to slide off the bed, shuffle the few feet to the closed door, and twist the lock.

Robert gripped the handrail and leaned his forehead against the wood until the shakes subsided. Then he lunged back toward the bed. He used the wall for support while he gasped for breath. When the weakness passed, he opened the top of the bunk to reveal his sanctuary. He climbed in, lay within the fertile soil, and pulled some of the dark earth over his chest. With a pained thought, the lid shut.

Darkness engulfed him. The feel of rich dirt against flesh should have been comforting. Instead, frustration gnawed at his insides. The fact Kimberly cared for him, rather than him keeping her safe, irked Robert and made him want to climb out of his skin.

The healing properties of the earth would help cure him, but days of deep slumber would be required before he regained full power. During that time of helplessness, he'd have to trust Kimberly to honor her promise and pray she remained safe.

* * *

Kimberly sat with Robert in the cockpit of *Night Thrill*. Stars glittered in the midnight sky. They had been through a rough few days, but he seemed fully recovered from whatever bug had made him sick. Now they sailed out to sea to make up for lost time.

He skimmed his knuckles along her bruised jaw. "I am sorry."

"You didn't hit me on purpose."

"Nae, but I hate to see the damage I caused."

"It's merely a bruise. It doesn't hurt."

He stroked her hair. "You did not have much of a New Year celebration, did you?"

"I'll celebrate after I've gone back to New Jersey and

cleared my name."

"You do realize it will be a while before you can do that."

"Unfortunately, yes." She sighed heavily.

Robert gave a self-deprecating smile. "Was it that bad taking care of me?"

"I didn't mean... It's just..."

"Hush. I ken this is not easy for you."

"I'll survive." She would. Her problems seemed minor compared to the illness he faced. He could have fallen and died. The mere thought gave her a nauseous-queasy feeling in the pit of her stomach.

Robert stood and pulled her to her feet. "Why dinnae you lie down, take a nap, and allow me to watch over you? I will keep us on a steady course."

Her muscles ached from exertion, but she didn't want him to know what a hefty toll the past few days had cost. If she didn't get some rest, she'd probably collapse, and he'd know. She could hardly hold her eyes open.

"Okay. Wake me if you need me."

"I will."

A few hours later, Kimberly attained a semiconscious state. Something was wrong. An urgent need to wake tried to get through, but her mind had become encumbered beneath layers of sticky cobwebs. She mentally tore at the silky threads. Little by little, the haze cleared, and she sat up and glanced around.

"Kimberly, I need you now," blared from the intercom speaker.

The urgency in Robert's tone sent adrenaline humming through her system. She bolted out of bed and flew up the companionway steps.

Robert stood at the wheel covered from head to toe in rain gear. "Heavy weather coming. Don your foul weather gear."

She headed below and pulled on a thick fleece, heavy red storm pants and jacket, and ugly, white, foul weather boots. Shortly after returning to deck, the wind kicked up. At fifteen knots, Kimberly reefed the main sail. At twenty, she rolled up the genoa a tad and put a second reef in the main. The sea rolled with six-foot swells. When the wind reached a speed of twenty-five knots, she completely furled the genoa and *Night Thrill* sailed on the reefed main alone.

The massive squall hit like a tempest and slammed into them with vengeance. Horizontal rain bit into bare flesh. *Night Thrill* bobbed through white-capped waves like a child riding an unruly rocking horse. Robert manhandled the wheel.

"Drop the sail," he hollered over the din of the storm.

She tried, but the damn sail snagged on the rigging, and wouldn't release. A large wave crashed over the deck, drenching her from her hair to the tips of the rubber boots, making matters worse.

"Take the helm," Robert ordered. "I will go aloft, clear the rigging and free the canvas."

She shook her head. "Too dangerous in this wind."

"Nae choice."

Her muscles cramped from chilling fear. Kimberly held her breath while Robert used a climbing harness and the halyard to pull himself up the mast. He freed the sail, but as he lowered to deck, a line snapped and tangled around one leg.

"Shit!" He can't get free. Terror gripped her like a vise.

Robert yelled something, but the words were lost in the chaos of the wind. Kimberly locked the wheel. She'd have to go up after him. Her stomach roiled. What if she got part way up and froze? She'd never been able to handle heights. *Oh, God, help me. How can I do this?*

"You will." Raven's voice coaxed from within Kimberly's mind.

Kimberly twisted around, half-expecting to see Robert's sister standing next to her. She fought off the panic threatening to overwhelm her. With closed eyes, she inhaled a deep breath, and visualized what needed to be done. She heard Raven's encouraging words. Her father's voice joined in. Vivid images flashed in her mind. They talked her through each step required.

Reassuring warmth wrapped around her. The blood in her veins surged with energy. She released the fear.

Kimberly flipped her eyes open. She didn't question the strangeness of the experience. With disciplined efficiency, she placed the tools needed, including a sharp knife, into a small sack, and slung it across her chest. She pulled on gloves, secured the safety harness, and grabbed hold of a secured line. Then she climbed. Using hands and feet, she shimmied up the rope. Never once did she look down.

"Foolhardy wench." Robert cursed as she cut the tangled rope from his leg, freeing him.

It was dicey getting down with the wind tearing at the lines. After they both made it safely to deck, Robert pulled her into his arms, nearly forcing the breath from her lungs, and hugged her roughly. When they split apart, she trembled from the after effects of a powerful adrenaline rush.

"Your father would be proud of you."

"Thank you." Rain poured over her face. Years of guilt washed away with the stream of cold water. She smiled at Robert. But they weren't out of the storm yet.

Even with the biting wind and chill rain, Kimberly's smile brightened Robert's life like his youthful memory of Scottish sunshine shimmering on Loch Fyne. He didn't want to think of what would have happened if she had fallen and he couldn't get free to help her. Where was his vampire strength when it was needed? The experts in his employ had better find answers.

And soon.

With bare poles, the sails in the lazy jacks, he started the engine. His pride in Kimberly made him grin. Thankfully, it wasn't long before the storm's rage slackened.

The yacht continued to travel though rolling white-capped waves, and the sky remained dark, but the worst of the storm had passed. Robert held the wheel while Kimberly went below to change out of the foul weather gear. Then she took the helm while he removed his wet clothing.

When he returned to deck, he commandeered the wheel. Kimberly plopped onto a cockpit bench with a tired groan, though her cheeks were flushed with healthy color. He couldn't budge his gaze away. Pride filled his heart. She was his heroic savior.

Suddenly, a strange heat warmed his skin.

Night Thrill sailed into sunlight. Panic seized Robert and he let go of the wheel. It spun, jerking Kimberly from her perch on the edge of the cockpit bench. He reflexively covered his face with arms and hands, expecting the flesh to burst into flames.

Instead, he experienced the biggest shock of his immortal life. His skin didn't burn and disintegrate into dust. His eyes didn't tear. He tolerated the sun's rays without discomfort.

He stared at the fireball on the horizon, crimson merged with amber, brighter than he remembered. What had altered him so? Vampire shifters weren't supposed to get sick, and they certainly weren't able to withstand direct sunlight except in animal form.

Robert reached for the beasts. Both the vampire and the panther had receded deep into the depths of his subconscious. Why? He grabbed the wheel, bringing the sailboat under control.

Kimberly scrambled to right herself. "What's wrong?"

"Naught. I lost my grip for a moment."

She scrunched her forehead and looked at him oddly. Then she crossed arms over her breasts, drawing his gaze to her clingy floral print blouse. For the first time since his turning, he appreciated the profusion of colors. Bold reds. Bright yellows. Cooling shades of green and blue.

Glimmering light played with golden highlights accenting rich brown hair. Kimberly was a feast for his eyes. Her skin glowed. Her rose-colored lips—

"Now that the sun is shining shouldn't we find a gunkhole and get out of sight?"

The stunned revelations interrupted, he mentally shook himself. "Aye, I ken a place not far from here."

They raised the main sail, and Robert steered for a small cove he knew from previous trips south. Kimberly remained quiet, giving him ample time to reflect. His thoughts whirled around the questions, avoiding the most likely answer. Finally, he had to face the facts. The only possible conclusion to make—the key had something to do with Kimberly's blood.

Whether for good or ill, something in her blood altered the very core of his being. It was now more imperative than ever he reach the compound quickly and confer with the experts in his employ.

First, he would have one more evening alone with Kimberly.

CHAPTER THIRTEEN

Kimberly stepped through the companionway and her heart twisted. Robert had created a comfy haven in the cockpit. He'd removed the teak table from between the two benches and replaced it with cushions on the floor. Over those was placed a colorful cotton quilt.

He sat bare-assed on top, wearing nothing more than a predatory expression, like a cat about to pounce on a songbird. A thrill ran through her. Was she the prey?

Kimberly smiled on the inside—a secret smile—and held his hungry stare, letting the afghan she wore like a toga fall. Hot chills trailed his gaze as it slid over her bare skin. The deliberate visual appraisal teased a nervous giggle from her lips.

The desire reflected in his eyes made her feel sexy and maybe even a little bit beautiful. She dropped to her knees in front of him, surprised not to be the least bit awkward.

He placed his hands on her upper arms. "You are lovely."

Heat singed her cheeks, and she couldn't hold his stare. Maybe she was self-conscious after all. "Thank you," she murmured.

He grasped her chin, tilted it upward, and forced her to look him in the eye. "I mean it, Kimberly. You steal my verra breath."

Then he dipped his head and brushed her lips with his. He kissed her mouth with aching tenderness. Desire pooled in her belly. When his tongue slipped between her lips, she opened for him, inviting him to taste her passion. And she, his.

The raw yearning wrapped within Kimberly's response to the kiss tore at Robert's black heart. He twisted their bodies, her at his side where he could hold her while catching his breath.

"We have all night, sweetling. Let us take it slow." He drew the afghan over them. "Let us enjoy the starlit night."

Let us be as one.

Her heart raced as did his. He heard the blood rushing through her veins. Heard the pounding at her temples. Smelled honeyed desire. His fangs lengthened, and he struggled with the vampire for dominance.

He would not take her blood again.

Overpowered, the vampire receded, and Robert's fangs retracted. He relaxed and held Kimberly tight against his side.

"I love you, Robert."

His heart leapt along with hope. Was it possible? "You must mean someone else," he teased, unable to believe.

She rose onto an elbow and studied him. Honesty glowed in her chocolate eyes. "Nope. I'm definitely in love with you."

She leaned in and pressed sweet lips to his. He greedily accepted the offering and wrapped his arms around her. Reveled in the demanding kiss. Possessive need flowed through his veins.

Mine.

She belonged to him.

Robert ended the kiss, wanting to look upon his lover. A soft smile played on her lips. He swept a fingertip along the contour of a smooth cheek, admiring her beauty, which glowed from within. She was much more than he deserved. He inhaled a deep breath and took the leap.

"You are my mate. I love you," he said. "Always and..."

"Oh, Robert." Her smile widened and her eyes glowed

through a sheen of joyous tears.

His chest pinched and he pulled her close. "Forever," he whispered into her hair. He held tight, wanting to absorb her very essence. Introduce her light to the darkness lurking within him. He was damned. He shouldn't taint her purity. He needed to find a way to reverse the curse before she learned he was a monster.

Robert shook off the black thoughts and inhaled her sweet scent. The smell of green apples from the shampoo and body wash she used teased his nostrils. He nuzzled her neck, and Kimberly sighed. Until he found a cure, he'd take what solace he could from within her embrace.

A comfortable silence stretched. After a wee bit, she skimmed a fingernail along the length of the scar on his face. "How did you get this?"

He shivered and brushed the hand from his cheek. Grabbing the fingers, he held them over his heart. "'Tis naught."

How could he explain that he received the sword wound from a French corsair in 1715 on that dreadful night of his turning?

"Does it hurt?" She attempted to tug her hand free of his grasp.

He distracted her by laying siege to her mouth. They rolled across the quilt, their passion rising with each greedy touch of their lips.

Kimberly sucked Robert's lower lip into her mouth and took a playful nibble. He growled and rolled on top of her. He kissed her face. Her eyelids. Her temples. He made her wild for more. She panted, trying to catch her breath.

Robert loved her. She wanted to shout her joy to the world.

He didn't give her a chance. His tongue swept the outer edge of an ear, and she moaned. Her sex clenched, a primitive ache at the core of her femininity. Taut with need, she arched her back, lifting up off the cushions. He pushed her back with his hard body before slipping down her length and kissing her belly. The arousing kick to her system had her doing a shimmy.

Robert rose over her and knelt, straddling her hips. He lowered his head. His satiny lips found a sensitive nipple, and her breath caught. The pull of his mouth drove her crazy. She squeezed the firm muscles of his ass and held on, for fear if she didn't, she'd spiral out of control.

He skimmed hands over the curves of her body, setting fire to her skin with his touch. One hand roamed between her thighs and found the throbbing center of her need. When he slipped a couple of fingers within, she melted.

Kimberly dropped her arms and pushed against the cushions with her palms. She rolled her hips, pressing her pelvis against his hand, hoping to encourage him to give more.

Robert teased her sweet spot with torturous skill, pushing her closer and closer to the edge. She panted, clutching at the quilt beneath her, desperate for release.

He continued to toy with her until everything within clenched. She exploded, coming in glorious waves of ecstasy.

When she managed to catch her breath, she opened her eyes and took in his hooded expression.

Robert felt moisture seep from within the folds of Kimberly's pulsating sex.

Blood rushed to the head of his cock.

A blush spread across the length of her body as he yanked her forward on the quilt and lifted her legs up and over his shoulders. He would give her pleasure while teaching her to be less shy. His satisfaction would be all the greater for the effort.

He leaned in and swirled his tongue along the edge of her bellybutton. Licked the tender knot of raised flesh. Soft purring sounds spiked his desire, and he rubbed his erection against her softness.

"Please," she begged.

With the head of his condom-covered cock teasingly poised to enter her inviting folds, he lingered, increasing the anticipation to a screaming need. He tightened his jaw against the pressure demanding release. He held back until he could no longer bear the pleasure-pain and then thrust.

Kimberly's muscles gripped his hungry shaft in an erotic embrace and pulled him deep within her welcoming heat. Through the haze of pleasure, his heightened vampire senses detected the sound of a twig snapping on shore. He froze. Lifting his head, he quickly scanned the shoreline for a threat.

A ray of light from a searchlight spanned the port side of *Night Thrill*. Who dared interrupt them? He didn't like the answer. Adrenaline kicked in. Heart racing in alarm, he went on full alert.

Kimberly undulated beneath him.

He withdrew in a swift pull and lowered her legs, dropping to the floor at the same time.

"What's—"

He gently placed a hand over her mouth. "Quiet," he whispered near her ear. "We have trouble. Stay perfectly still until I return."

She nodded. He dragged the afghan over her, covering her completely. Cloaking their presence would do no good. The intruder already knew they were in the sailboat. His best tactic would be to take out whoever stalked them.

Falling into a crouch, Robert slipped past the wheel, and then scrambled up and over the transom, landing softly onto the diving platform on all fours. He slid into the water and swam beneath the surface, beaching south of where he detected the source of light. He threw off the condom and called the panther to the fore to claim his body. Robert shuddered as he allowed the transformation to take place. Bone and sinew contorted to accommodate the big cat's form. Fur covered his skin.

Well hidden within the tall grasses, the panther skulked through the marsh. He moved silently, rolling one cushioned paw at a time, over the muddy ground until he stopped behind the interloper.

He hunkered down to focus on the scent of his prey. Twisting ears forward, he detected the sound of the human's heavy breathing. He rose and advanced slowly. Froze. Crept forward a little more then sank into a predatory crouch. With the target eight feet away, the panther sprang, lunging for the man's jugular.

The man tossed him off, crawled a foot away, reached into a satchel. He rolled to the side, pointed the gun and fired. Missed. The panther growled, twisted his body, grasped the man's leg with his mouth and bit down hard. The man screamed, but managed to fire another shot. The blast echoed, then silence.

* * *

Kimberly remained motionless for the count of twenty. Her pulse raced at a frightening rate, but she refused to lie there naked and helpless. She groped around for a weapon. Finding nothing nearby, she concentrated on what she knew to be in the cockpit. The bag that hung near the companionway contained the crank handle for winding the winch.

She crawled closer and reached into the sack for the piece of metal.

A shot rang out. A man's scream rent the night.

Her breath left her lungs in a gasp. She clutched the cold steel to her bare chest and prayed Robert hadn't been shot. After wrapping the afghan around her nude body, she crept to the edge of the cockpit and peeked over the side. She caught a glimpse of two shadowed forms rolling together on the beach, everything else blurred into deep shades of gray.

A huge cloud swept over the moon, casting the land into complete darkness. An eternity passed. She tightened the grip on the crank handle and prepared to defend herself.

The lapping of water on the hull broke the silence, and she tensed. A loud splash off the starboard side sent a shot of adrenaline through her system. She raised her arm, ready to lash out with the makeshift weapon.

The moon suddenly escaped the clouds and brightened the sky.

"Kimberly, it is me." Robert hauled himself from the water and climbed onto the diving platform.

Relief overwhelmed her senses. She dropped the handle and rushed to him. "Are you okay?"

Water dripped from his glorious nude body. "The hit man found us," he said, his breathing labored. "The bastard got away, but I managed to injure him."

Her throat tightened and she couldn't speak.

Robert accepted the offered beach towel, but refused to make eye contact. He wore a hard expression. Jaw tight. "Go below and get dressed."

* * *

Less than an hour later, Kimberly stepped onto a run-down dock near St. Mary's, Georgia. Confused thoughts whirled in her mind. She gripped the tote bag tighter. Driving to the compound instead of sailing was a new development. Irritation tightened her muscles, and she stretched her back and neck to ease the kinks. Robert hadn't lied to her exactly. He'd just neglected to mention that Colin waited at a nearby motel, ready to drive them the remainder of the way south to Robert's compound in Florida.

Had they not been attacked, when would he have divulged the changed plans? She took a deep breath and loosened clenched fingers. Had Robert really declared his love for her?

She should be ecstatic. Instead, the contents of her stomach were performing gymnastics. Kimberly swallowed hard and tried to calm down. After several more deep breaths, she sighed.

Early morning light shimmered on the surface of the water. She inhaled the calming fragrance of the sea and turned away to the car parked next to the dock. Her reflection stared back from the darkened window of the black sedan. She glanced into the side view mirror and moistened swollen lips. Whisker burns reddened her cheeks. She attempted to detangle the snarled curls surrounding her face with her fingers, but there was nothing to do for it. She looked like a woman who'd just had *to-live-for* sex.

Only, damn it to hell, they hadn't completed the act.

Robert opened the car door, and she slid across the supple leather back seat. A few minutes later, he joined her, and they were off. They drove for hours in silence.

She stared at the scenery rushing by so she wouldn't

have to think. They passed mobile home parks and large shopping centers with massive parking lots. Housing and professional complexes, where every stucco building had an orange tile roof. Strip malls were too numerous to count. South of Orlando, the car zipped past newly built suburban retirement communities, their many-colored aluminum roofs glinted in the harsh semi-tropical sun.

Kimberly peeked at Robert from under her lashes. A shadow of whiskers covered his firm jaw, making him look all the more desirable. It was hard to stay mad when the subject of your snit sat next to you and was damn sexy.

So damn gorgeous, her sweet tooth hurt.

While they drove, her temper cooled. After all, Robert was only trying to be protective.

As if recognizing the change in her mood, he grasped her hand, and they laced their fingers. She'd sensed the sadness that overcame him after they left *Night Thrill*. She understood. Their adventure had ended. The hit man found her and probably would again.

Robert assured her protection. But how could he? She'd never before known this kind of all-consuming fear. To make matters worse, she worried about their new relationship. They'd declared their love to each other. Sure. But what effect would that have on their future? At his compound, there would be many other people. Would he treat her the same way in front of them as when they'd been alone these past few days?

Kimberly chewed on her lower lip—a bad habit she wished she could break.

She glanced at Robert. The now familiar pinch in her chest made her inhale deeply. Could their budding love withstand the uncertainty of her situation?

"You are thinking again?" He released her hand and dropped a palm to her knee.

She tried to ignore the fiery sensation his touch produced. "I have a tendency to think."

"Are you afraid the hit man will find you in Florida?"

"Partly." She couldn't tell him she feared for their future together. "Mostly, I worry about how I'll clear my name."

"Nae worries." He gave her knee a gentle squeeze. "I

have influential friends. I will obtain a good lawyer for you."

"I can't afford—"

"I thought we were beyond that. I will pay for your defense."

"But—"

"Nae argument." He leaned forward to speak to Colin.

The loss of his touch stripped Kimberly of all warmth, and she shivered. She couldn't accept the offer. She didn't want to take his money. Although, if she didn't, she wouldn't stand a chance of getting the charges dropped.

Robert settled back against the black leather and crossed his arms.

"I'll accept your help and any money you spend as a loan," she said. "I expect to pay you back after I've returned to New Jersey, gotten the charges dropped, and found a new position."

"There is no need for you to return north. You will be safer at my compound with me. Besides, the lawyers will need time to hire an investigator to collect information. Time to plan a defense."

Kimberly sighed. She must make him understand how important this was to her. "Robert, you have to understand, I've lost everything that defines who I am. If I don't go back and clear my name, I don't exist."

He grasped both her hands. "The hit man is still lurking out there. I will not lose you." He lowered his head and gave her a blistering kiss that burned her beguiled soul.

She poured more passion into the kiss. Robert took the cue, slanted his lips, penetrated deep. She moaned into his mouth. When he pulled away, he left her breathless. She allowed a soft laugh to escape and self-consciously glanced forward at the rearview mirror. Colin's eyes stared straight ahead at the road.

She couldn't believe she was making out in the backseat of a car like a sex-crazed teenager. With Colin as a witness, no less. Her cheeks burned.

Robert put on his sunglasses, wrapped an arm around her, and dozed. Kimberly envied his ability to fall asleep. She stared out the side window at the blistering sun.

Farther south, they passed citrus groves that gave way to cattle ranches. She smiled at two sandhill cranes strutting their stuff in a roadside ditch. After passing Lake Okeechobee, she caught the reflection of Colin's hazel eyes in the rearview mirror.

"It won't be long now," he said.

She nodded, and his gaze returned to the road.

After passing fields where the pungent odor from burning cane leaves permeated the car, Colin turned into a gravel road sided by cypress. The tree's knobby knees poked out of stagnant water. In another mile, the car passed a clearing with a rusted old mobile home. Indoor furniture decorated the deck. In the front yard, a brand new airboat sat on a pristine aluminum trailer. And atop the largest tires she'd ever seen on a vehicle, sat an older model jeep.

Robert stirred beside her. Noticing the direction of her gaze, he chuckled. "That is what the locals call a swamp buggy."

"What's it used for?"

"For driving into the swamp," he said as if she should have known.

"Why would anyone want to do that?"

He gave her one of those you've-got-to-be-kidding looks. "Because 'tis a beautiful place with many wonders to find."

The terrain they drove through was swampy. All she could imagine finding in the twisted snarl of vegetation was alligators and snakes and big bugs. Not a pleasant thought.

They drove several miles farther before Colin turned the car onto a new cement drive at odds with the native wilderness. After a quarter of a mile, they cleared the trees. The driveway circled in front of a large Spanish-styled mansion. In the distance, an amber glow surrounded the setting sun on the horizon.

"Home," Robert said, tone heavy with sarcasm.

Inside the front door, they entered an impressive foyer. Kimberly's heels clicked across Italian painted ceramic tile. She scanned the oversized room. Shades of autumn prevailed. Her gaze touched on the massive chandelier, before landing on Raven who waited at the bottom step of a grand circular staircase to greet her brother.

Unease crawled up Kimberly's spine. She still couldn't believe she imagined hearing Raven's voice while climbing the mast after Robert. In her fear, she'd also conjured her father's voice. *Ridiculous.*

Raven's curious gaze shifted from Robert to Kimberly and then back to her brother with intensity. "I sense a lot has changed since last I saw you."

He placed an arm around Kimberly's shoulders. "It has."

"Shall I show her to the master suite then?" Raven's eyes didn't express the sincerity of her smile. Her pleasant voice sounded fake too.

Robert's hold tightened. "I will see Kimberly to the guest suite next to mine."

"Then, I will leave you to it. I am off to Miami for a meal." She sashayed by, brushed a long crimson-painted nail across her brother's cheek in passing, and disappeared out the front door.

Kimberly released her breath in relief. There was something almost frightening about Raven. "Isn't Miami too far to go for dinner?"

Robert chuckled. "Not for Raven."

"Good eve'n to you both. I'm off to check in with the lads." Colin said, reminding her of his presence. "I want to make sure Davey is comfortable."

"Good night." Kimberly smiled at the burly man, wondering what he thought of her having *a thing* with Robert.

Colin placed a hand on Robert's free arm. "Call if you need me."

"Thank you," Robert said. "Enjoy your e'ven. Tell the lads I will speak with them on the morrow."

Inclining his head, Colin left.

"Hungry?" Robert asked.

"Famished."

"I will ask the chef to send something up after I show you to your rooms. One of the lads will bring our bags." He slid his arm along her spine, placing his hand at the small of her back.

As always, his touch thrilled her.

"Shall we?" He guided her up the stairs.

Disappointment assaulted Kimberly when Robert left her alone in the luxurious suite with nothing more than a kiss. Admittedly, it was a toe-curling kiss. She wanted more.

She'd assumed he'd stay the night and they'd make love on a real bed. She glanced out the French door of the balcony at the jungle of tropical foliage surrounding the grounds. Robert strode across the clipped lawn into the tangle of growth and disappeared.

CHAPTER FOURTEEN

Relief pooled in Robert's belly as he slipped away from the compound. No explanation required. No guilt. He jogged along the trails for over a mile, reveling in the solitude of the night.

Hoohoo-hoo-hoo, hoohoo-hoo-hoo-aw. A barred owl called. Night insects hummed. Robert seized the freedom to release the bonds on the panther.

He discarded his garments and fell to hands and knees. Bone and sinew stretched and reshaped to allow for the big cat. Coarse fur covered a lithe body. He yawned, raised haunches from the ground and pushed forward with forepaws. Needle-sharp, curved claws burst from their protective covering then retracted.

He sniffed the air. The fragrance of honeysuckle tickled his nostrils. He silently padded forward on big cushioned toes. The trail crossed a prairie. He sprinted along the worn path, racing away from himself and the strictures of civilization before slowing to a lope.

Near the edge of a slash pine forest, he stopped, attention fixated. He raised his head slightly, the tips of his ears prickled. An armadillo snuffled through rotting leaves for grubs. The panther proceeded into the tangle of palmetto. He sought larger prey.

Robert shifted the big cat's head from side to side,

surprised at the newfound ability to maintain his own thoughts while within the panther's form. He inhaled deeply, sampling the breeze with a feline nose. He entered the swamp by way of a game trail. Deeper in the quagmire, the scent of a rival male drifted to him on a puff of sultry air. His nostrils flared, and he snarled.

Farther along the trail, he found a scrape left on the path by the interloper. The mound of soil, leaves, and pine needles reeked of the other cat's urine. Yowling, Robert's panther-self scraped with hind legs, creating another pile with more leaves and dirt, and then to it added his own urine.

He sniffed the mound before moving on. He made steady progress through the swamp. Where he left the wet terrain, the trail meandered through wiregrass beneath slash pines. He hunted while traveling. Finally, he caught the scent of a deer.

Staying downwind, he stalked the prey, moving slowly without sound. At the right moment, he sprang. Teeth penetrated flesh, snapped bone. The small deer lay dead at his paws. He dragged the carcass several yards along a game trail and into the protective covering of a small thicket.

The feast began with relish. He gorged on flesh and blood. As the hunger waned, he slowed and nibbled on small pieces of raw meat. When full, he napped.

Several hours later, Robert emerged from the fog of slumber. The panther's facial muscles jerked, whiskers twitched, he opened his eyes a slit. He stretched his jaw with a wide yawn. Using a forepaw, he reached behind an ear to scratch away a biting tick. He licked at his fur, removing remains from the consumed meal.

The stale taste of blood had grown old during the cruise south. Satisfying his appetite in the form of the cat was a messy business, but preferable to the dishonor of feeding as a vampire.

Hunger fully sated, body well rested, the panther craved his mate.

Since he'd fed, Kimberly would be safer. Robert's vampire-self would be less tempted by her blood. He returned to the manse by a quicker route, constantly on alert for the interloper male panther.

He splashed into the deep end of the pool and swam to the shallow side, allowing the clean water to cleanse his fur of what remained of the meal. He padded up the steps onto the cement and shook off clinging water.

After entering through a private doorway, Robert pawed across the tile floor and skulked up the stairs. Silence met him in the hallway. Reaching her suite, he stood on hind legs and pulled down on the door latch handle with his forepaws. The fastener released. Silently, he dropped to all fours and used his muzzle to push open the door.

Kimberly slept fitfully.

He padded across the deep pile carpet and hunkered down at the side of the bed, watching, watching her breasts rise and fall with each breath. The panther curled his upper lip in a snarl at the thought of another male cat stalking his territory so close to his mate. He wanted to leap upon the bed and prove dominance.

Fear shot through Robert's mind. He couldn't allow the animal to take Kimberly in panther form, although the image in his mind had blood rushing to his cock. If the beast had her, she'd never recover from the shock. There was a good chance she might be physically hurt.

From within the beast, Robert did his best to maintain control, trying to keep the big cat from jumping onto the bed. The panther fought him and raised a large paw onto the edge of the mattress, ready to overpower Kimberly and take her as his own.

Robert forced his heavy-handed will, insisting the cat recede. He suffered grueling discomfort. Bones snapped and stretched. He emerged as a man. Ashamed of his naked state, and of what he imagined doing to the woman before him, he turned away slowly and padded from the room.

* * *

Perspiration coated Kimberly's skin when she woke in the morning. A mockingbird's stolen song sounded outside the window. She sat and ran a shaky hand through tangled hair. Sun streamed in through the screens of the open French doors. Even in the warm daylight, the nightmare seemed too real, too frightening.

The dream remained the same. A stranger chased her to the edge of a cliff before turning into a big tawny cat that attacked.

Inhaling a couple of deep breaths, she pushed away her unease. A shower and then breakfast would be just the thing to set her straight. Even though Robert had deserted her last night, she had no desire to remain hidden within these rooms. The mansion was huge, but surely, she could find the kitchen.

An hour later, she strolled down the stairs and into the foyer with a bounce in her step. She planned to enjoy the day.

From the back of the house came the rambunctious sounds of John, Davey, and Timothy. Glad to hear their voices, she headed in the direction of the laughter and found the boys in a casual dining room with floor to ceiling windows looking out on a tropical garden.

"Yo, ho. Look who's here." John jumped up and pulled out a chair, winking at her before sitting back down.

She suppressed a grin and sat across from Davey. She tried not to stare at the fading bruises covering his face and arms or at the cast.

"I'm doing much better," he said.

Heat flashed her chest. "I'm sorry you were hurt because of me."

He sported a crooked smile. "Wasn't your fault."

"Of course not," Robert said as he entered the room. He sat in the chair next to Kimberly and pressed a thigh against hers. Heat radiated through his slacks, heating the skin exposed below the hem of her shorts. Her breasts tingled and her sex clenched.

Damn the man.

All three boys quickly finished breakfast and made a beeline for the door. As they disappeared a handsome sandy-haired young male server dressed in black slacks entered the dining room. Kimberly made an effort not to stare at the taut muscles and thick arms covered by a charcoal gray polo. He served her a cup of coffee and placed a plate of bacon and eggs and grits in front of her. Then he inclined his head and left.

There had been a time when all the pumped-up testosterone from Robert's staff would have made her uneasy. Now, she felt protected.

She glanced at Robert. It was hard to remain aggravated with the man when he smiled as if she meant everything to him. He would keep her safe.

"Aren't you eating?" she asked.

"Nae. I have been awake for hours. I have already broken my fast."

Kimberly barely managed to keep a straight face. Sometimes Robert said the oddest things. "Then you're feeling well?"

"Aye," he answered. "When you have eaten your meal, we will take a tour of the research facility."

"Super," she said between delicious bites. "I'm really curious."

Robert grinned. "You? Curious? Never would have thought it."

Kimberly ignored the sarcasm and continued eating. After finishing the bacon and eggs, she pushed the plate away. She didn't care much for grits. "Ready when you are."

"Great, let us be on our way." Robert stood and pulled out her chair.

They departed the house by way of a plant-filled sunroom. With clasped hands, they strolled along a walkway weaving through the tranquil garden. Koi jumped in a small pond. The orange-red blooms of trumpet vine dangled overhead. The cement walk gave way to woodchips as they left the tended garden and entered a woodland. The scent of pine resin tickled her nose, and she stifled a sneeze. After a short stroll, they came to a large square building that matched the Spanish style of the mansion. A covered veranda wrapped around the three sides visible from their approach.

Robert dropped her hand and reached for the door handle. "This building contains offices, labs, and containment cells for sick animals. Two fifteen-acre enclosures are located elsewhere on the property for our resident panthers."

"I didn't realize you kept panthers here all the time."

"We have a couple of males that have become too comfortable with humans to be released back into the wild. We hope to mate them with cats from Texas."

"That's cool."

Robert smiled. "I think so."

He opened the door. A blast of frigid air struck Kimberly, forming goose bumps on her bare arms as she stepped into the air-conditioned building from the muggy outdoors.

"Are you cold? Maybe you should go back to the house for a sweater."

"I'll be fine once I get use to the temperature change." She gave him a smile and shivered.

"You're sure?" He looked doubtful.

"Sure."

"If you say so."

She nodded and followed Robert along a corridor of closed doors until he stopped in front of a plate glass window. Inside, a young woman fed a small cat with black spots from a baby bottle. Two other young cats sat in an animal carrier on a stainless steel lab table.

"I was told these kittens were rescued from the side of the road after a car killed their mother on a highway south of here," Robert said with a frown.

The kittens were beyond cute. It was hard to believe they would grow into full-sized panthers. Her nightmare from the evening before replayed in her mind, and she shivered again.

"You are cold."

"I'm fine."

He stared at her for a moment then turned. "Come on."

She followed him along the hall, past window after window where men and women, dressed in white lab coats, worked with test tubes and microscopes.

"All of this in an attempt to save an endangered species?" Kimberly asked when they stopped in front of a closed door. "You must be proud."

"Aye." Robert's cinnamon eyes glistened. "We have field biologists, veterinarians, geneticists, along with other specialists working on a solution."

"What about *your* blood disease?"

His hand froze on the doorknob. She took a step back when his hard stare locked on her, his emotions masked. "Doctors and scientists are working on a cure as we speak," he said softly.

"Sorry." Kimberly hadn't meant to remind him of his helpless situation.

He looked away and opened the door. "There is someone I want you to meet."

She followed him into a well-appointed office suite. Several nerdy types stood around a whiteboard, while others sat at a small round conference table. Absorbed by what they were doing, they didn't notice Robert and Kimberly standing inside the doorway.

Robert stepped farther into the room. "Doctor?"

Heads snapped up. Jaws dropped. Faces paled as if they looked at an apparition.

"Robert? This is a surprise." A very composed, platinum blond bombshell, dressed in a short black skirt, red silk blouse, and opened lab coat, rose from one of the chairs and walked toward them.

"Dr. Knight, I would introduce you to Kimberly Scot, one of my crewmembers."

Crewmember? Is that all she was to him? Kimberly tilted her head to look at Robert. His features were impassive. She returned her gaze to the other woman.

The doctor shook Kimberly's hand without making eye contact. The woman's green peepers had locked onto Robert and hadn't strayed.

"It's good to see you," she said rather breathlessly. "I didn't expect you...this early in the day."

"I will explain later," Robert said.

"What kind of doctor are you?" Kimberly blurted. She was probably rude to inquire, but the green-eyed monster had stung.

Someone coughed. Everyone in the office stared at

Robert.

He cleared his throat. "Is there nae work to do?"

All the geeks scattered, and one by one left the office.

"I'm an ethnologist." Dr. Knight's heavily tinted, red lips curved into a caricature of a smile.

"Patrice is sort of a psychoanalyst who interprets dreams," Robert interjected.

"Really? I've been having strange recurring nightmares myself. Maybe you could tell me what they mean?" Kimberly challenged.

"I'll certainly try. Tell us about them."

Idiot! Kimberly wanted to kick herself. What had she been thinking to travel down this path? "I didn't mean—"

"If you'd rather Robert not listen..."

"Are you keeping secrets from me, Kimberly?" he teased.

"No, of course not. I don't care if you hear."

"Wonderful." Dr. Knight waved toward the brown velour sofa in the sitting area of the office. "Please, take a seat on the couch and tell us about your dreams."

Kimberly chewed on the inside of her lip. Why had she impulsively asked the doctor to analyze the dream? Robert would think her crazy when he heard the details.

"I don't want to keep you from more important matters."

"You aren't. I'm very interested in...dreams." Dr. Knight gave Robert a penetrating look.

Since Kimberly couldn't think of an out, she sat. Pleasure sizzled when he joined her on the sofa and reached for her hand. Maybe he wasn't trying to hide their relationship.

The doctor leaned a tight ass against the front of her desk and waited.

Robert smiled encouragingly.

"I've always had a fear of heights," she said. "Even as a child."

"Many people do." Dr. Knight slid onto the edge of the desk and crossed one leg over a knee, giving Robert an eyeful of perfectly sculpted legs. "Please, proceed."

Kimberly bet the doctor exposed her assets on purpose.

Thankfully, Robert seemed unaffected. "I am verra proud of Kimberly," he said. "She overcame a long-held fear to climb the mast and rescued me when I got caught in the rigging during a violent storm."

"Indeed. How heroic." The doctor gazed at her with more interest than earlier. "The dream?"

"My nightmare always starts the same way." Kimberly nervously rubbed a hand over the fabric of her khaki twill shorts. "A strange man chases me through the woods. The dream seems to last forever. I run until I'm nearly exhausted and a steep ravine looms before me. In an attempt to escape, I dash along the edge, terrified I'll slip and fall."

As she spoke, the doctor snatched a notebook and pen from the side of the desk. Kimberly sneaked a peek at Robert. He gently squeezed her hand.

"Continue," Dr. Knight said when finished jotting in the book.

"Well. This is where it gets weird. The man morphs into a cougar and leaps toward me with bared teeth." Kimberly shrugged. "That's when I wake up."

She felt Robert tense.

Dr. Knight's eyes widened. She stared at Kimberly for a moment and then wrote furiously in the notebook. "Tell me, Miss Scot. Has the cougar always been a part of your nightmare?"

"No...I only recently started dreaming about the big cat."

"Do you remember when? Had anything significant happened in your life?"

Kimberly thought back. "It occurred the first night I slept aboard *Sea Panther*."

Robert stared at her, his expression unreadable.

"I'll have to give your dream careful consideration before I interpret its significance." Dr. Knight broke the awkward silence. She stood and placed the notebook back on the desk.

Robert dropped Kimberly's hand and rose. "There are a few things I need to discuss with Dr. Knight. Do you think you can find your way back to the main house?"

"I think so." She jumped to her feet.

The doctor stepped closer to Robert. "I won't keep him long."

The catty smile said otherwise. A cold chill crept up Kimberly's spine. Had Dr. Knight been Robert's lover?

* * *

Embarrassment and anger and jealousy battled for dominance in Kimberly's psyche. She shouldn't have allowed the doctor to get under her skin. She acted like a scared rabbit running along the wooded path from the research facility to the house. Slowing her pace to a brisk walk, she tried to breathe evenly.

In the garden behind the mansion, Davey sat on a bench in the shade of an old oak swathed in Spanish moss. Guilt warred with other swirling emotions. "How are you feeling?" she asked as she joined him.

"Much better. I'm getting lots of attention from the ladies." He shifted the plaster-covered arm and smiled. Blue eyes sparkled mischievously.

"I'm sorry you got involved in my mess."

With the unencumbered hand, he good naturedly poked her shoulder. "No need to apologize. I would do it again given the opportunity."

Kimberly swallowed her angst and allowed her gaze to drift to a bed of tangerine-colored New Guinea impatiens backed by the interwoven fan-shaped fronds of palmettos. An unusual brown and yellow swallowtail butterfly fluttered its wings, dancing on the warm breeze.

How had she made such loyal friends in such a short time? Kimberly's eyes misted and she blinked several times to clear her vision before addressing Davey. "Have you ever been here before?"

"Many times," he said. "We stopped visiting once Dr. Knight arrived. Not sure why."

Several scenarios ran through Kimberly's mind. None she cared to ponder. "What do you know of what goes on here?"

"Panther research," he answered too quickly.

"That's not all though, is it?"

Davey glanced around and seemed to carefully consider an answer. He leaned close. "You know the captain has a rare blood disease. Right?"

CHAPTER FIFTEEN

Robert sprawled on the comfortable sofa in Dr. Knight's office, his at-ease posture in sharp contrast to the chaotic emotions churning within him. Kimberly dreamt of a cougar attack. How could that be?

More likely, a Florida panther attack.

Did she subconsciously fear him? Was the animal within him more of a danger to Kimberly than he originally thought? Or had she inherited *the gift?* Psychic ability ran rampant in the women of his family. Even some of the men.

He scanned the panther's mind for animosity directed toward Kimberly. Found none. Only a desperate yearning to mate. The animal's frustration was understandable. Robert had been hard ever since they'd met.

"Robert?"

He started at the sharp voice, inhaled sharply, and shifted attention to the doctor. He hoped Patrice didn't mistake the bulge in his pants as interest in her.

As she often did, she sat across from him on top of the desk, legs crossed, emphasizing the sexy length of her limbs. The pose didn't excite him, though she intended it to. Why did she bother? He'd told her shortly after hiring her there would be no relationship between them.

"I'm surprised you hired a woman to crew on your

yacht." Patrice's eyes narrowed.

"She needed a job." He refused to take the doctor's bait. Though, in time, he'd have to come clean with everything that happened between him and Kimberly.

But not yet.

When he'd told Patrice about his recent illness and ability to go out in the sun, she wanted details. He'd explained he didn't have them. He didn't plan to reveal anything else about the changes within him until Dr. Lang, the staff hematologist, finished the analysis on his blood.

"Interesting dream, don't you think?" Patrice asked.

"Aye. 'Tis the first I heard the telling of the tale."

"Why did you lie to her and say I'm a dream analyst?"

"She doesn't know what I am. How would I explain an ethnologist specializing in Caribbean Voodoo employed by a Florida panther research foundation?" He shifted position on the sofa, disturbed by the conversation. "She believes I have a rare blood disease. Under such circumstances, I might very well work with a psychologist."

"I'm curious." Patrice studied him. "Why did you bring her here? You've never allowed anyone at the facility that didn't have personal knowledge of your affliction. Yet you've brought her and the young men from your crew to the compound. Why?"

"They are not your concern."

She tensed for a moment then her features smoothed into a calm mask.

He'd almost gotten past her guard. Interesting. But he needed to steer the discussion away from Kimberly. "Have you uncovered anything new from your research?"

"As I've told you before, I believe you were bitten by a vampire. I know we've gone over this several times, but let's try again. What do you remember of the events that occurred right before your turning?"

"I certainly dinnae recall being bitten. At least not by a man." Robert chuckled, pretending to make light of his situation.

"I'm serious. I've found no record of anyone ever being turned by anything other than the bite of another vampire."

Robert stiffened. He needed to find a cure. A way to be normal. He found it hard to believe another vampire bit him and he didn't remember. If that were the case, what chance did he have of finding a cure?

He held a hint of hope in his black heart he could become mortal again and spend the rest of his life with Kimberly. He wanted to grow old with her and die a happy man at a respectable age. "Are you telling me Zola's curse had nothing to do with turning me into a vampire?"

"No. But I don't think the curse directly caused the transformation."

"What are you implying?"

"I have a theory," Patrice declared.

"Well?" Robert stared directly at her, anticipation making him edgy. "What is it?"

She returned the intense look with her usual unruffled gaze. "I don't want to get your hopes up. I need to do more research before I can be sure. Tell me, again, everything you remember from the night you were converted."

Robert rubbed a hand over his forehead. He didn't want to relive that night of unbearable misery yet again.

"I know remembering is difficult. But I'm hoping we might find something we've overlooked before. Learn of some previously thought unimportant detail that will pull my research together and give us the answer we need." She leaned forward and the neckline of her blouse bulged to reveal an ample view of her breasts. Rose-colored nipples peeked through sheer nude-colored lace. "As you know, the magic of Voodoo has a strong basis in the African belief system. For every good, there is an opposing evil."

"Aye?" Robert jerked his gaze away from the enhanced breasts, unimpressed by the blatant display of her wares. "Similar to the Oriental concept of yin and yang?"

"Yes. So no matter how powerful the Voodoo sorcerer's curse, we can find a medicine man whose power is as strong or stronger and can reverse the spell. All we need learn is what curse Zola used."

Robert sighed heavily. "I know you are trying to help, Patrice. However, I dread revisiting that time."

"I could hire someone to hypnotize you. They could

plant a suggestion to forget what you've told us upon awakening."

Robert sat up straight. "I dinnae want anyone else brought on. 'Tis too dangerous. There are already too many people aware of my condition."

"Yet you brought your crew here."

"I have my reasons." He glared. How dare she question his actions? Little did she realize the lads knew exactly what he was. Hiring Willy had been a mistake. Aye. But the other lads were loyal without question.

Patrice held his stare for a long moment. A battle waged within her mind, reflected in her eyes. She wanted to snap at him. Put him in what she believed his place. Either fear or something altogether different stopped her.

"All right, lay down." She pressed the on-button on the tape recorder and picked up a notepad and pen. "Relax."

Robert closed his eyes, allowing his thoughts to jerk to that dreadful night.

"There was not a spot on my body not battered or bruised. Laroux's men had beaten me beyond endurance. I spent four days without food or water in the bowels of the Frenchman's pirate ship. I was verra weak. Why they dragged me through the swamp was beyond my understanding. Pain wracked my body."

"Excellent. The swamp is a good place to start."

He opened his eyes. *Excellent, my arse.*

Patrice jotted something in the notebook then glanced up to encourage him to continue.

"Somewhere along the way I lost consciousness."

"What happened when you came to?"

"I woke, free of the gag and bindings. I knelt on the dirt, held by two of Laroux's men. They left me, and I struggled to stand. Laroux said something about settling our disagreement with a sword duel. I managed to catch the saber he tossed to me. As I said, I was weak. I didn't stand a chance. He played with me, flaying skin with each slash of his sword. Each cut burned with an unholy fire."

"Tell us more about that." Dr. Kurt Nolen, his internist, had entered the office while Robert revealed the torment of the past.

"Like fire ants marched in the cuts." He inclined his head to the gangly man who plopped into a nearby chair.

"Poison. They'd probably coated the sword with a toxic solution," Kurt said.

"Yes," Patrice agreed. "Continue. Tell us what happened next."

Robert adjusted his weight on the sofa to get more comfortable for the rest of the tale. "Things are fuzzy. I must have passed out. I awakened later to the sound of drums, spread eagle, lashed upright to crossed logs."

Kurt cringed. "A vulnerable position for a man."

Patrice squirmed on her perch. "For a woman too."

"'Tis when I saw Zola, Laroux's lover, the Voodoo priestess with her pet panther."

"Okay. What happens next is important. Try to tell us as much detail as you can remember," Patrice instructed.

"Everything is real hazy. I had lost a lot of blood. And if Kurt is right, I had poison in my system."

"Tell us what you can," Patrice said.

"I heard chanting. People moved in and out of my sight like zombies. Zola held a snake in the air and said something about opening a door. I remember the words bloodlust and true love. I truly dinnae remember anything else said."

"Okay. Tell us what happened after that."

"A wind gust howled through the clearing. Everything went crazy. 'Twas like a crimson storm. Blood everywhere." Robert shuddered with the memory.

"Relax. Take deep breaths."

He took Patrice's advice, and the doctors gave him a couple of minutes to calm down.

"I know this is painful, but what else did you see?" Patrice pressed.

"I am sorry, I dinnae remember anything else."

"The memory must be so horrific you've blocked it from your conscious mind," Kurt said.

"What about your nightmares?" Patrice asked.

"Images. Darkness. A face with fangs. The panther lunging for my throat."

"A face with fangs? Robert, you've never mentioned that

before." Patrice sounded excited.

He grimaced. "It just occurred to me."

She glanced at her notes. Her brow wrinkled. "I think the Voodoo priestess intended to bring about your death and spread the word you'd been turned into a zombie. It makes sense. Zola wouldn't want your crew to come after her with revenge on their minds. If they believed you had become a zombie, your superstitious crew wouldn't search for you and they'd be more likely to vote in a new captain and set sail right away."

"Sounds plausible," Robert said hesitantly, though he had doubts, but he'd follow the theory through.

"However, I think something went wrong. The curse she used drifted to an ancient power and summoned a vampire," Patrice said.

Disappointment tasted bitter to Robert. "What are you saying? There is no hope to find a cure?"

"No, I'm not saying that." She paged through the notes. "Ah, here it is. I believe the one thing that can save you is true love."

True love. Robert doubted that had anything to do with his troubles.

"Don't look so skeptical. I believe blood from your one true love will break the spell."

He laughed. He'd never been in love until he met Kimberly. To what exactly did Patrice infer? A cure couldn't have anything to do with Kimberly. Could it? An uneasy sensation knotted his gut.

"Sorry. You wanted a cure."

"Aye. A serum or something."

"We'll continue to try to find a blood-related antidote," Kurt said.

"I'll bet Miss Scot's dreams have a connection." Patrice tapped the pen against her cheek and stared at Robert. "Maybe we should test your friend, Kimberly."

CHAPTER SIXTEEN

Willy cupped a hand over his eyes to block the glare from the late afternoon sun. Perspiration dripped along the side of his face and down the back of his neck. It might be late January, but it was hot as hell in this godforsaken swamp. He smacked at a mosquito that landed on his arm. Damn. Missed. With folded arms, he leaned against the rented jeep and waited for the other man to limp over.

Dino Rizzetti, the hit man from New York, was after the Panther and his whore too. The man's rifle sure looked efficient. Willy patted the satchel he carried. His weapons were more potent. It would take a special silver stake through the heart to kill Captain MacLachlan.

"You the kid JR sent?" Rizzetti asked.

"Yeah." Willy popped a clove of raw garlic into his mouth. The pungent flavor had become tolerable.

Rizzetti shook his head as if Willy were crazy. Maybe it was true. Willy frowned.

"You know anything about hunting? I'm out to kill a panther." Rizzetti smiled cruelly.

"I'm after the woman."

"Looking for a piece, are you?"

"JR wants me to take care of her." Thinking about what he planned gave Willy a major hard-on.

"Can't understand why JR sent you. He hired me to kill her. I can take out the woman and bag myself a big cat." The hit man caressed the rifle as a horny man might stroke a willing woman.

Willy certainly wasn't foolish enough to taunt a hired killer with the fact he already missed twice. The man thought the big cat a mere pet. The idiot didn't understand what he was up against. And Willy didn't intend to explain the truth of the situation to him either.

"JR thinks she has incriminating evidence that could land him in jail. He doesn't want her dead until I get the information."

"That sucks. I'm tired of this job. I want it over." Rizzetti spit on the ground near Willy's booted foot. "I searched her room and car in New Jersey. She doesn't have the fucking papers."

"Might be electronic."

The hit man scowled and raised the gun toward Willy.

"Watch where you're pointing that damn thing."

Rizzetti stared at him hard then lowered the business end of the gun.

"The panther do that to you?" Willy motioned toward the man's bum leg.

Hatred burned in Rizzetti's eyes. He rubbed his thigh. "Yeah. The big cat's good as dead."

Willy no longer cared what kind of death befell the Panther—man or beast—as long as Willy controlled the woman.

* * *

Kimberly walked through the garden to the house. She hadn't learned much from Davey beyond what she already knew. Maybe he wasn't telling her everything. Although she supposed it was unfair to suspect him. She had no reason to doubt him.

So what did she know? Robert had an obscure blood disease he might not survive. She swallowed hard. Kimberly didn't want to consider he might die. She jammed her hands into the pockets of her shorts. Okay. What else? In addition to the veterinarians who cared for the panthers, the research facility employed doctors who attended to Robert's health and scientists who attempted to discover a cure or at least a drug to extend his life.

That meant he at least had a fighting chance.

Dr. Knight was one of the specialists hired to make Robert's painful life tolerable. A good thing. Right? Then why did Kimberly feel jealous of the bitchy blonde? Other than the woman's obvious desire for Robert, the fact she was built like a pin-up model from the forties didn't help. Next to the voluptuous Patrice...

Kimberly cringed. Well shit, she was physically inferior. She was too thin and had tiny breasts. Not much to attract a virile man like Robert.

Yet he seemed more than satisfied with her body on the cruise south. Had he merely been temporarily sating lust? No. He claimed to love her. If she loved him, she needed to trust in his love.

* * *

Robert set Tom Sloan's letter aside and studied the blueprints. The refits for *Sea Panther* would take nine months. Too long for the planned trip to Jamaica.

He hadn't returned to the island in over two hundred years. Not since he gave up pirating. He'd never wanted to go back before. Too much pain. Too much hate. Too much regret. After the session with Patrice today, he was determined to return and try to jar his memory.

Jagger would certainly lend him *Night Thrill*. That would work out well. He could take Kimberly along. Keep her safe while enjoying time alone with her without censure. Robert smiled, looking forward to the trip for a change.

A knuckle knock pounded on the door. He raised his gaze expectantly. "Enter."

The door swung open and Colin approached the desk.

"Have a seat, my friend." Robert handed over the blueprints. "What do you think?"

Colin perused the plans, taking his time. Robert leaned back in the chair and waited, knowing his first mate would approve. Colin handed the prints back. "Sweet."

Robert shook his head. "You have spent too much time with the lads."

"What?" Colin grinned and raised his arms.

Robert rolled his eyes. Bloody hell, maybe he'd been spending too much time around them too. He set the papers aside along with the letter from Tom. "It will be months before she's ready to sail. Ask Jagger if *Night Thrill* is available for me to sail to the Caribbean."

Colin's jaw tightened. "What do you have planned?"

"A trip to Jamaica."

"Do you intend to take Kimberly with you?"

"I do."

"I don't think it's wise—"

Robert raised a hand to stop the lecture. "I promise to be careful with her." Colin sighed and nodded. Too easy, Robert thought. He was bound to get a good dose of Colin's mind before they set sail. "I need you to look into something for me."

"Of course."

"While out prowling last night, I came across a male panther's scrape on a game trail in Raccoon Swamp. Can you find out if any of the state collared cats are in my territory?"

"Sure. I'll make a few calls," Colin said. "Anything else?"

"Aye, but I dinnae ken what to do about it. My powers are diminished. Those remaining to me are oddly different. I can now maintain my own thoughts when within the panther's body, but have minimal control over the beast's actions. 'Tis why I prowled the swamp last night instead of staying with Kimberly."

The few moments he spent near her had almost proved disastrous. Could he trust himself as they sailed to Jamaica? Robert hardened his resolve. He would dominate the beasts, dammit. He had to make it work. He wanted Kimberly with him.

"And the vampire?" Colin asked, cutting through his thoughts.

"He has receded into a shadowy place." Robert exhaled sharply. "I can nae longer track Willy. The bond is broken."

"Shit!" Colin spat a few more, choice swear words.

"Where's Raven?"

"She has not returned to the mansion since we arrived and I can nae longer merge with her mind."

"Robert, the situation is becoming critical. Consider leaving Kimberly here. We'll see to her safety."

"I can't. I need her with me."

* * *

Patrice gathered the notes and files and shoved them into her briefcase. It was after five. Her sex throbbed and her breasts were aching to be touched. She wanted to scream. Have a hissy fit. She was so hot and so wet for Robert, and he...he barely noticed her. She'd practically offered herself to him on the desk and he hadn't responded. Damn the man.

Who was this bitch Kimberly? The slut obviously meant more to Robert than merely one of the crew would. She slept at the mansion, dammit. That gave her better access to Robert. That wouldn't do. Patrice stamped a foot. She was tired of playing nice while trying to gain his adoration. The gloves were coming off.

She stepped into the corridor and nearly collided with Raven.

"Don't fuck with my brother. You won't enjoy the byplay."

"What?" Patrice took a step back, spine tingling with alarm. "I don't know what you mean."

Robert's sister moved closer. Patrice winced. She hated Raven, but knew enough to fear the vampire bitch. Scanning the corridor, she sought an escape. There would be no running. Patrice stiffened her spine. As long as she worked for Robert, she was safe. Since she intended to become his wife once she found a way to cure him, there was no need to worry about Raven for much longer.

When Patrice thought of Robert shackled to her bed and all his delicious money in her control, fear morphed into an aphrodisiac. She got even hornier. Her sex oozed, and in a panic, she squeezed her thighs together, hoping to hide the scent of arousal from Raven.

It didn't work. The female vampire's nostrils flared.

"You know exactly what I mean." She pressed forward, hissing, revealing fully extended fangs. "Keep your tacky fingers off my brother."

Noise from a nearby conference room flooded the hall as several doctors exited and walked into the passageway. Patrice took advantage of the diversion to brush past Raven. "Dr. Lang, may I speak to you about doing blood tests on Robert's crewmember, Kimberly Scot?"

"Sure." The older man stopped as the others filed past, they shifted position until the hematologist had his back to Raven, partially shielding Patrice from the vampire's view. "I've been meaning to call you, Dr. Knight. We need to discuss..."

The boring doctor rambled on in a monotone, but she didn't bother to listen. She glanced over his shoulder. Raven watched them. Patrice tossed her hair and slowly smiled. She would figure out a way to remove the competition and have Robert.

Raven's red eyes narrowed before she strode off.

* * *

Kimberly relaxed in a comfortable chair in Robert's cozy sitting room. She raised her gaze from the fading page of a Scottish historical time-travel romance novel to the view of the tropical garden through the floor-to-ceiling windows. Elegant white flowers dominated over other receding colors. While she'd been engrossed in the story, afternoon turned into evening. No wonder her eyes burned.

She twisted the switch on the table lamp and froze.

Robert's sister leaned against the doorframe, watching her. The tall woman's eyes flashed red and her skin held a ghostly pallor.

Wait a minute. Her eyes were usually green. Kimberly mentally shrugged. Raven must wear tinted contacts to appear more Goth. In her tight black leather outfit, and with crimson painted lips and nails, Raven exuded pure sex. Kimberly glanced down at her own sage tank top, khaki shorts, and boat shoes. Her sporty appearance was less jarring against the casual mission-styled furnishings.

Raven's eyes flared as if she knew Kimberly's thoughts.

"I owe you an apology."

"I can't imagine why." When the woman glided into the room, Kimberly shifted on the plump cushion suddenly uncomfortable.

Raven slid into a chair. When she glanced at Kimberly, her eyes were green. Weird. Very weird. The fine hair on the back of Kimberly's neck tingled, and she wrapped her arms over her chest to shake off the chill. Her tired eyes must be playing tricks.

"I have treated you badly since we met," Raven said. "Given that my brother believes he is in love with you, and I care for him deeply, I would like to rectify the situation."

"There's no need." Kimberly inwardly smiled. Had Robert told Raven of his feelings?

"I believe there is." Raven ran one long enameled nail over the golden oak armrest of the chair. Her stare penetrated. "I would give you a bit of advice."

Kimberly placed the book on the side table and braced herself.

"Be wary of Dr. Patrice Knight. She has been dying..." Raven grinned wickedly and with an arched brow glanced up at the ceiling. "Not a bad idea."

"What?" Kimberly asked in confusion.

"Pardon me." Raven laughed. "The pleasant thought of Patrice dying in agonizing pain distracted me." Raven's gaze settled on Kimberly.

She shivered. The woman was frightening to the extreme.

"What I mean to say in the way of warning is Patrice has wanted to sink her claws into my brother ever since he hired her. She will stop at nothing to own him and his money."

"I don't know what to say."

"Watch your back and trust in my brother," Raven whispered.

"Ladies?"

Kimberly startled. Robert stood in the doorway. Dressed in black slacks and a white open throated dress shirt, he looked too handsome to be real. She felt a pinch near her heart when their gazes met. As he walked into the room, Raven leapt from her chair.

"Remember what I said, Kimberly." She sauntered past her brother and left.

Robert's gaze followed her and his brow furrowed. "If you dinnae mind my asking, what were the two of you discussing?" He shifted attention to Kimberly.

"Your sister felt she owed me an apology for her previous poor treatment of me."

Robert's eyebrows shot up. Kimberly chuckled. "Can you believe it?"

"Hardly." He reached for her hand and pulled her from the chair. "I have missed you."

A now-familiar electric current flashed through Kimberly. "It's only been a few hours."

Tucking her close to his body, Robert lowered his head and stole her breath with his sinfully scrumptious mouth. When they stopped kissing her legs wobbled.

"I have a favor to ask of you," he said.

"What is it?"

"The doctors wish to test your blood to see if you are a match for me." He held himself stiffly, as if she'd refuse.

Foolish man. "Of course, whatever I can do to help."

His arms were around her again. He kissed her...sweetly, lovingly. They slid to the floor. Buttons popped. Seams ripped. Clothing flew across the room. She lost herself to the magic spelled by his lips.

A breeze danced across her bare legs and she popped her eyes wide. "Robert, the door's open!"

The heavy oak panel slammed shut as if he commanded it. Her gaze flew to his. He smiled then distracted her with another titillating kiss.

Robert stroked satiny skin, touching every graceful curve. Her moans came louder with each caress of his fingers as he slid them in and out of her slick velvet softness. His erection grew iron hard. With his free hand, he fumbled with the stupid condom they didn't need. No matter. He would use it to relieve her worries.

He relentlessly teased Kimberly's most sensitive knot. When she spasmed and released a soft scream, he entered her with a powerful thrust.

The vampire wanted blood, but Robert controlled the monster.

He kept the pace slow, each motion calculated to ensure the rawest tantalizing sensation. Kimberly panted as she met each thrust, driving him harder. Deeper. Muscles strained. He held back, agonized to give more pleasure. With each stroke, he lost more of himself to the wonderful woman who'd stolen his heart.

They orgasmed in unison, driving Robert over a precipice never before taken. A tear leaked from an eye as Kimberly went limp in his arms. Joy filled his withered black heart. He'd experienced a wee bit of heaven.

The panther lurked within the shadows of his consciousness, the instinctual need to dominate his mate temporarily sated. Robert tightened the mental tether on the animal, praying it would hold him at bay, and picked Kimberly up into his arms. Her melted chocolate eyes gazed at him with more tenderness than he deserved. He was a louse for having messed with her life.

He refused to give her up.

"What are you doing?" she asked.

"Taking you to bed."

She struggled in his arms. "You can't carry me through the house like this. We don't have any clothes on."

"I promise no one will see us." He used his remaining vampire power to cloak their presence from the household.

She settled in his arms. "You can't promise that. You have a house full of guests."

He ignored her and carried her up the stairs, easing his hold as if he might drop her, and then tossing her upward, catching her before he took the next step. She giggled and cried out when he tossed her again. "Are you not afraid someone will hear you and come running to see what is happening?"

"No. You promised no one will see us and I trust you."

She awed him with her faith. A sharp pain stabbed Robert's heart. He didn't deserve her belief in him. When they reached her room, she unlatched the bolt with the brass door handle, and he kicked the panel open. He tossed her onto the bed and joined her, but he'd lost the playful mood. Self-loathing burned in his chest.

They briefly kissed before she fell asleep cuddled to his side. He remained there for several hours unable to sleep. Finally, he rose and slipped away. As he padded to his suite, the panther sought control. He wanted to feed.

Needing space too, Robert allowed the animal its freedom.

* * *

Kimberly woke and reached for Robert. He'd gone. Not for long though, the sheets still held the warmth of his body. She did her best to swallow the disappointment. He probably wanted to keep the gossip at a minimum. It was sweet of him to try to protect her from the censure of the others.

Moonlight spilled into the room through the French doors. She stretched. Her body tingled from their fierce lovemaking. She buried her nose in the pillow indented from Robert's head and inhaled his spicy scent. They obviously were sexually compatible. When she thought of the blaze of fire glowing in his cinnamon eyes as he suckled at her breast, she knew he was more than pleased with her assets.

It had been foolish to worry about Robert and Dr. Knight.

Before meeting her ex-fiancé, Kimberly had been comfortable with her body. When they first came together as a couple, he'd led her to believe the sex was great. After a while, he started complaining about her boy-like figure, demanding she get a breast enlargement. It was hard not to become self-conscious. Then when she refused, he ran off with his *stacked* administrative assistant. Kimberly had taken on the blame, hating herself for her lack of endowment.

She'd been foolish. Everyone knew Jason left because of the failed financial deal. And now the rat bastard had accused her of illegal dealings. How had she not known a creep lurked beneath his sophisticated facade?

Robert would never be unfaithful. He'd never abuse her

trust. She had faith in him.

Kimberly reached for the ivory silk robe draped across the bedside chair. As she donned the cover-up, the whisper-thin fabric teased sensitized skin, reminding her of all the places Robert had lovingly kissed.

The sweet scent of honeysuckle wafted through the open screen. She padded across the thick peach carpet to the balcony doors and leaned against the frame, gazing into the moonlit garden. From the corner of an eye, she caught movement, a rustle of foliage. Her breath caught in her lungs. The hindquarter of a big tawny cat with a long sweep of tail disappeared through the bushes. Her pulse raced. Could it be an elusive Florida panther?

CHAPTER SEVENTEEN

After several days of reviewing corporate contracts, Robert rubbed tired eyes and traversed the trail through the pine trees on his way to the research facility for an afternoon session with Patrice. Shadows were lengthening. He was late. Soon it would be sundown.

When he finished with the good doctor, he planned to search out Kimberly. He missed her. After all these years of living in the dark, being awake during the day kept him on edge. He needed her soothing touch.

He arrived at Patrice's office to find the curtains closed and the lights dimmed. He warily entered. She strutted from behind her desk to greet him. His hackles rose.

"Do you have the results of Kimberly's blood tests?" he asked without preamble.

Patrice's welcoming smile curved down into a frown, and she crossed her arms over her chest and leaned against the edge of the desk. "The lab believes she is the perfect match."

"What exactly does that mean?" Annoyed by her body language, he couldn't keep the bite from his voice.

The doctor's eyes narrowed. "Her blood has the right DNA makeup."

"A transfusion of Kimberly's blood will cure me?" *Could it be so easy?*

"Dr. Lang told me what happened on *Night Thrill*. I'm surprised you didn't see fit to inform me of such extraordinary occurrences." Patrice's lips wrinkled into an irritated pucker.

Robert tensed. He wouldn't justify his actions.

"No, in answer to your question," she continued. "A transfusion won't make a difference. However, on the basis of the blood match and my research, I do believe I know how to reverse the effects of the curse." She grabbed a notebook from the desk and flipped it open.

The now constant knot in Robert's stomach tightened. "How?"

"You need to take Kimberly's blood three times. The last feeding must take place at the exact spot where the curse occurred and within the quarter hour. You must force her to feed from you after you take her blood the last time. I believe that's when you will be free of the curse." Patrice glanced at the notes. "Let's see. You sampled her blood on the yacht when Marion...Raven attacked her. That would be number one. So you—"

"What?" Robert cut off the doctor's words. Panic seized his belly. He felt like he'd been gut-punched by a world heavy weight.

Patrice leveled her gaze on him unaware of the horror he experienced. "Your first taste of her blood initiated your possession. When you feed from her the second time, you will begin the transformation. Then when you arrive in the Caribbean..."

Dr. Knight continued to speak matter-of-factly, but Robert didn't hear the words. If the tiny taste he sampled started the process, Kimberly's transformation had already begun the moment he fed from her that first time they made love on *Night Thrill*. He prayed it wasn't true. If it was, he should have sensed a change in her. Wouldn't he have? No, he'd been blind with lust, cursed fool that he was. Now, what could he do?

"Robert, you're not listening to me. This is important. You must follow the steps precisely." Patrice's words sliced though his self-incrimination.

"What will happen to Kimberly?"

Patrice flung the notebook onto the desk and nailed him with a green-eyed stare. "I'm afraid you'll have to choose between her and living forever a shape shifting vampire. Because as much as you try to deny your existence, Robert, that is indeed what you are."

"Is it not possible a simple transfusion would reverse the effects of the curse?"

"No. You must go back in time to face your demons. You must take Kimberly's blood the second time as you return through the time portal."

"Time portal? Devil's blood, what the hell are you talking about?"

"The Bermuda Triangle."

Robert's heart stuttered, skipped a beat, and then raced. She couldn't be serious. "You are making a jest. Aye?"

"I find little humor in your situation."

What could Patrice possibly know of the complexity that was the Bermuda Triangle? He'd sailed through those cursed waters many times during his immortal life. He encountered all kinds of unexplained phenomenon. Yet not once had he been sucked through the infamous vortex into the past.

"Are you telling me, you believe in a time gate?"

"Yes."

"What makes you so sure? And if there is a gate, what makes you think I will find the precise spot and travel to the exact time and place of my turning?"

"I've researched the Triangle for years. I have the coordinates and you have the need."

"Ach, well, let us say Kimberly and I can travel through time and I follow your instructions and take her blood as we travel through the portal and then again at the site of the curse. What makes you certain I'll be cured?"

"A colleague sent me an ancient manuscript referencing the Séaghdha prophecy.

"What does Séaghdha have to do with me? He is naught but a legend."

"I'm positive Zola's botched curse opened a door to another dimension and the ancient Celtic vampire entered our world. In the ensuing chaos, he drank your blood and enthralled Zola's pet panther to do the same thus turning you into a vampire shifter like him."

Robert scraped a hand over his buzz cut and shook his head.

"The text states Séaghdha could shift into a hawk and used different animals in conversions to create fledgling vampire shifters. When Zola's pet Florida panther lunged into the fray, you took on his essence."

"This is not what I expected to hear from you, Patrice."

"I'm sure it's not, but you must face facts. I'm truly sorry to be the bearer of such uncomfortable news."

Robert hung his head and curled into himself. How would he make this right? "I wish you had a better theory."

"I've matched the prophecy information with research I've done on Voodoo curses, time travel, and the Bermuda Triangle. I'm positive Kimberly's blood and returning to the time and place of the curse is your answer." Hands on hips, she continued, "Robert, I've worked hard to solve your problem. I practically had to sell my soul to get that dusty old manuscript."

"I'm sure you've put in many hours and have been diligent. But if I believe you...if I go along with this crazy theory of yours and do as you say, will Kimberly become a vampire? A vampire shifter? Will she die?"

"What does it matter? You'll be cured."

The doctor's smug look provoked Robert's dark side. He curled the hands at his sides into fists, wanting to inflict pain. He swallowed hard and with effort kept the monsters from striking out at the doctor. He inhaled a calming breath. "It matters verra much to me."

"You have to face your reality. You'll have to choose between the woman you *think* you love and remaining a vampire shifter."

"Did I hear you right?" He massaged the growing knot at the base of his skull. "You want me to destroy Kimberly so I can live without her. What point is there in that?"

"You hired me to find a way to reverse the curse." Patrice moistened her painted lips and smiled. "I'm telling you the only way to succeed is to sacrifice Kimberly."

"Then I will remain a vampire shifter." Frustration

gnawed at his churning gut. To learn of a cure only to find the solution too deplorable to contemplate was more than he could bear.

Dawning lit Patrice's eyes." You've already started the transformation. Haven't you?"

"How do I reverse it?"

"Might be too late."

"Nae." Robert refused to believe he already condemned the love of his life.

"If you're not willing to try..."

"I will *not* risk Kimberly."

Patrice shrugged. "Then we'll have to find another way."

"Do you have an alternative?" A flicker of hope surfaced as he took a step closer to her.

"I need more information...perhaps..." Patrice's voice trailed off. "If only you'd let us hypnotize you."

"Fine, do it."

Patrice waved to the sofa then perched on the desk and reached behind her. When she turned to face him, she held a metronome. "Since you don't want me to bring in a professional, I thought you might allow me to put you into a hypnotic state."

Robert sat on the sofa, limbs numb. He didn't like the idea of going under hypnosis, but if they could find another way to reverse the curse, it would be worth it. If there was a way Kimberly could be protected, this wasn't the time to construct obstacles.

"Do what you must."

"Good," Patrice smiled cheerfully. "Now lie back and relax."

Robert reclined. He tried to force the tension from his stiff body. The metronome sounded a clock, clock, clock, at even intervals from the table beside him.

"Be calm. Concentrate on the sound of my voice," Patrice said. "Empty your mind of worry. Think only tranquil thoughts. Permit your body to relax."

She spoke in a monotone, voice soft. Robert allowed himself to let go.

"Send soothing messages to your muscles. Relax your toes, the soles of your feet, your heels. Loosen the muscles in your ankles, your calves, your knees." Patrice's voice soothed. "Allow your thighs to relax."

"Take a deep breath. Inhale through your nose. Fill your lungs with air. Hold it...now release your breath through your mouth. Push all the breath from your lungs." Patrice paused for a moment. "Again. Breathe deeply."

Robert inhaled, filling his breathing cavity with oxygen. Then he drove the air from his lungs.

"Again," Patrice coaxed.

He repeated the process.

"Loosen your fingers, your hands, your wrists. Relax your forearms, your elbows, your upper arms. Allow your shoulders to sag."

Robert concentrated on relaxing each part of his body upon Patrice's suggestion.

"Slacken your stomach muscles, your chest, and your neck. Soften your mouth. Allow your face to relax. Your scalp."

A weightless, floating sensation infused Robert's body.

"You're going down...down...down. There is nothing to fear. You will always be in control. If you wish to wake at anytime, count from one to three. On three, you will awake, feeling refreshed with a sense of wellbeing."

"Go down...down...down. Deeper. Deeper. Deeper."

He drifted in a haze of comfort. His mind roamed free within a place with no pain. A bright light hovered before him in the distance. Drawn to the brilliance, he floated toward the source of the glow.

Then something interfered with his comfort. His body came alive. Hot. Hard. Pulsating. He wanted something just out of reach.

"Tell me how you feel." The doctor's husky voice intruded from a distance.

"I am as randy as..." His calm shattered, replaced by flaming tension that drew his balls tight. It felt wrong. *One. Two. Three.* He jerked open his eyes.

"Bloody hell!" Patrice had undone the buttons on his jeans and straddled his thighs. Inside the silk boxers, fingers manipulated his sac, pumped a traitorous erection.

He grabbed her wrists and tugged the hands free. "How

dare you."

Her skirt bunched around her waist and the bitch wasn't wearing panties. The dark V of naturally colored brown hair pointed to her sex. She laughed, throwing bleached hair back from her face. Her blouse hung open, the front clasp of the red bra undone, her breasts spilled free, inviting attention.

"You've been enjoying my tender loving care." She tried to yank the hands from his grip. "I want to ride you to paradise."

He refused to release the hold on her, fearing she'd return to milking him. "Dr. Knight, this is highly unprofessional."

"Consider it research." She shimmied a bare bottom forward. His painfully stiff cock jerked, reaching for her moist opening.

"Nae. How the hell is taking advantage of me a way to find a cure?" He pushed her off and scrambled from the sofa. "We need to rethink our arrangement." Hands shaking with anger, he tried to fasten the bottom button of the fly over his engorged cock. A strangled feminine cry caused him to turn toward the door. A pallid Kimberly ran from the office.

"Satan's balls." He bolted after her while continuing to secure his jeans.

* * *

Kimberly ran blindly through the corridors of the research facility. She blinked away tears, refusing to shed them. The tread of Robert's feet echoed from behind. Darting around a corner, she found a closed door. She twisted the handle and slipped inside. Closing the door, she leaned her forehead against the cool metal. Thankfully, the sound of Robert's footfalls faded into silence.

Y...oo...www...llll.

Holy shit! Kimberly spun around, her heart pounding her ribs. The greenish-amber eyes of a large tawny cat stared at her from within an almost room-sized cage mere feet away.

Her shocked scream caught in a tight throat, and she

raised a shaky hand to her mouth. This must be the panther containment area. The panther staring at her looked so much like the big cat from the nightmares she could almost imagine it was the same beast.

Calm down, Kimberly. Breathe.

It couldn't be the same big cat. She'd never seen a Florida panther before visiting the compound. It's nothing more than a coincidence.

The cat released another ear-splitting caterwaul.

Kimberly reached behind her for the door handle. Facing Robert would be better than remaining here with her worst nightmare. She stepped into the corridor and came face to face with Dr. Knight.

"What are you doing here? This area is off-limits to everyone accept facility personnel."

Kimberly grasped hold of her courage. She refused to allow Robert's lover to intimidate her. "I took a wrong turn and ended up here by mistake."

The doctor's lips contorted into a mocking smile. "Really?"

She reached around Kimberly and opened the door, crowding, pushing her back into the room with the panther. Kimberly exhaled a ragged breath. "Who the hell do you think you are?"

Patrice continued to intrude on her space. "Did you ever imagine what you thought a cougar in your nightmare might actually be a Florida panther? From interbreeding, mature Puma *concolor coryi's* have distinguishing flaws. As you can see on our friend here, they have a crooked bend near the tip of the tale." She walked to the cage and pointed. "And if you look carefully you will notice a whorl of fur that grows along the center of their backs."

"Thanks for the zoology lesson, doctor, but I'm out of here." Kimberly cast her gaze over the animal one more time. The big cat in her dreams did have the described imperfections. Her curiosity spiked. "I've never seen a Florida panther until today."

She stepped closer to the beast.

"Of course not, Miss Scot. But isn't it worth considering? The same panther as in your dreams—here?"

The doctor's gaze moved past her shoulder. She stuck out an oversized chest, stood a little straighter, and plastered on a plastic smile.

Just great. Kimberly slowly turned around. As she'd suspected, Robert filled the doorway, arms folded across a broad chest, a deep frown cut into his hardened face. Anger radiated from him like heat from a furnace. She didn't know to whom he directed the hostility. Her or the doctor?

Kimberly wanted to get the hell out of there, but she pushed the idea into the corner of her mind and faced off with the two-timing SOB.

"Robert," Patrice's voice purred.

His clenched jaw twitched. He glanced from Kimberly, to the doctor, back to Kimberly. His gaze scorched her. "Kim—"

"Robert, I must have a private word with you," Patrice interjected before turning to Kimberly. "Would you be a sweet girl and run to my office." She combed fingers through her mussed bottle-blond hair. "I left an important file on my desk. If you would get the folder for me, I'd appreciate it. The file is important to Robert's case. I want to review the report tonight at home so we can start therapy tomorrow."

"Dr. Knight, 'tis nae longer your place to give orders." Robert glared at the woman.

Tension lay heavy between them. Kimberly shifted her gaze from Robert to Patrice, feeling confused, wanting any excuse not to deal with him or the betrayed emotions the sight of him sparked.

"Sure, what the hell, I'll run to your office and meet you in the parking lot with the file."

As she scooted past Robert, he reached for her. "Lass, I can explain."

She easily avoided his grasp, and quickly made an escape. Dr. Knight was good, Kimberly thought as she walked back to the scene of the lovers' tryst. A true manipulator. She gave the doctor points for that.

Several minutes later, she stared at the large envelope lying in the center of Dr. Knight's desk with Robert's name neatly printed on the front in boxed lettering. She shouldn't look, but...

Biting down hard on her lip, she dropped into the swivel chair and slid out the manila folder contained within the envelope. The red stamp mark CONFIDENTIAL glared at her. She couldn't remember a time when she'd felt more betrayed. It had hurt when Jason deserted her, but Robert's indiscretion cut deeper. She should have known he would leave her like every other man in her life. Her father. Jason. And now, Robert dropping her for Patrice.

A fancy designer desk clock ticked off the seconds. Kimberly could feel her heart pounding in her ears to the same beat. Reflux burned her throat. She needed to calm down.

Her father's death wasn't her fault. Jason's infidelity had nothing to do with her. And Robert had made no promises other than protection.

She ran a palm over the smooth surface of the file folder. Curiosity had gotten her in trouble before. Often when she was a child. And since...

On that night on *Sea Panther*, when Robert had punished her with a toe curling kiss. Damn the man. How dare he be with Patrice?

Kimberly glared at the folder. The bold red ink glared back. Grasping the corner of the cover between a thumb and forefinger, she hesitated. She had no right to read his personal health records. Such things were private matters between doctors and patients. Though a lot more went on between Robert and Patrice besides a mere professional relationship, and Kimberly had been privy to the disgusting details.

Nausea gurgled in her stomach. Dammit, she loved the man. Even if she was angry with him, she still needed to learn how serious his illness was. She'd worried so many times he might be near death. The need to know just how sick he was drove her crazy.

A dull ache throbbed near her heart. She took a deep breath. Calm down. Think clearly. Her hand trembled as she opened to the first page. No matter what had taken place between Robert and Patrice, Kimberly wanted to know just how sick he was.

The first couple of pages showed the comparative results of blood tests. She skimmed through that. Then she turned to Patrice's summary notes and started to read.

At nearly three hundred years of age, Robert MacLachlan's uncontrollable transformation to and from a Florida panther seems to be the direct result of a Voodoo curse.

A sharp pain pierced Kimberly's heart. *What the fuck?* Robert? A panther? Ridiculous. Patrice must be insane. Did she think Kimberly stupid enough to fall for her ploy? The file must be a fake. The manipulative bitch was messing with her again.

Could be true? It would explain the big cat on the dock in Annapolis. And the Florida panther Kimberly thought she saw last night outside her room. She focused on the page and read the next sentence.

However, his blood lusting seems to imply a bite from a vampire.

Holy shit. A vampire? A shape shifter? Kimberly looked desperately around the room, gaze landing on the surveillance camera. Why did a panther research facility need almost as much security as a military installation?

She thought about the strange hours Robert kept. His dated speech patterns. Their strange sleeping arrangements. Kimberly trembled, unable to get her reflexes under control. She couldn't read any more.

Vampire? Panther? Bizarre enough to be real. She had to leave.

Her legs did the Elvis shake, almost giving out on her as she stood. The report dropped to the floor in her haste to escape. She ran from the office, darting through the halls to the building's entrance, and out onto the veranda.

Robert and Colin stood a few feet away, conversing. Kimberly scanned the area for a way past them. If she could make it to the trail that led into the swamp, she could get away. Run away. Far away. As she was about to make a dash for it, Robert glanced up, and her stomach lurched. He appeared relieved to see her. Her heart twisted, causing her to clutch her chest.

"Lass, I need to talk with you." He stepped forward. "Why are you shaking so? I can explain everything."

Kimberly didn't believe he could. She took a couple of steps back.

"Where are you off to in such a rush?"

She attempted to pull herself together. "I need some time. I thought I'd go for a jog."

"Please, let me explain about Patrice." Robert's eyes pleaded. "It is not what you think."

If she didn't get away from him, she'd melt into a puddle of jellied nerves.

Panther? Vampire?

Kimberly swallowed. "I need to calm down before I can talk to you."

"It is getting dark."

"I won't be gone long." *And shit, if you are a vampire, the night is yours.*

"Please, trust in me." He leaned in, lowered his head, and gently brushed her lips with his sensuous mouth. "Come back to me, my love," he whispered.

Her heart burst into a thousand shattered pieces like a broken mirror. She ran to the start of the swamp trail and twisted around for one last look. Dr. Knight stepped through the entrance onto the veranda, and Robert strode toward her. He seemed to grow in stature. Fear sparked in the doctor's eyes. Kimberly took an awkward step backward and a dead twig snapped under her foot.

Robert spun toward the sound. His eyes blazed blood red. Sharp fangs marred the beauty of his mouth. *Vampire. Shit!* She darted through the foliage into the swamp.

CHAPTER EIGHTEEN

A bright moon spilled a ghostly glow over the swamp trail. Night insects screamed at Kimberly as she darted through jungle-like vegetation. A pain burned her side. She stopped to get bearings unsure how far she'd run. In places, the thick canopy cast a heavy shadow and the trail became nearly impossible to see.

Fear prompted her onward. She reached deep within for strength and sprinted through the marshy tangle of trees. He'd follow. He wouldn't let her leave.

She ran blindly. Clawing fingers from the underbrush tore at her clothes. Scratched exposed skin. Breathing came hard. Her pulse raced.

Oh, my God. Robert had fangs. He was a monster with blood-red eyes.

She had to get away, far away. At a clearing, she slowed. Changed directions. Sped up. A twig snapped behind her. Spurred her forward. Fangs and blood flooded her mind. She must escape.

Before her loomed a large pond bordered by deep mires forming dangerous traps. An alligator slid off a log into the water. Kimberly swerved. Raced along the edge. Slipped on the wet clay, caught herself, and kept running.

Her flight reminded her too much of the nightmares.

Hands grabbed her. She screamed. A man wrestled her

to the muddy ground. Pinned her arms. Not Robert, a stranger. The stalker had found her again. She fought with all her might, kicking, scratching, biting.

"Satan's whore." He spat as he spoke, the reek of garlic heavy on his breath.

With an adrenaline-induced burst of strength, Kimberly pushed him off and started to rise. A hard slap stunned her. He pushed her back. Forced her to the ground.

It was definitely the stalker, though he looked different. Ugly. His face was swollen, pocked, blotchy. His hands roved over her body, gripping at her clothes, bruising skin, touching intimate places through the cloth.

"Get off me!" she wheezed.

The buttons on her blouse popped. No way. This was *not* going to happen. She kicked up and caught him in the balls with a knee.

"Bitch," he hissed. He fell to the side, clutching himself.

Kimberly scooted away. As she got to her knees, a threatening growl rumbled. Her attacker turned toward the sound and paled. Panic filled insane eyes. She followed his stare. Robert crouched. His body shuddered, his clothes shredded, and he morphed into a big tawny cat. He lunged for the attacker, canines bared.

The man screamed. Cloth tore. Somehow, he managed to crawl a few feet away from the snarling cat.

Kimberly drew in great gasps of air and picked up a heavy limb from the ground. She had to help the man. She couldn't allow the panther to rip the guy to shreds. Before she swung, a warm breeze blew across her cheek, the touch of feathers, and then Raven appeared from behind. Robert's sister grabbed the end of the makeshift weapon and stopped Kimberly's momentum.

The big cat circled the quivering man, hissed, and then loped toward the trees. The panther stopped, slowly twisted his head toward Kimberly, and burned her with a greenish-amber stare. He yowled mournfully before disappearing into the cypress trees, leaving an impressive paw print in the wet marl.

Raven released her hold on the limb and moved to stand over the young man.

"Why did you stop me?" Kimberly asked. "Robert has turned into some kind of monster. He might have killed the guy."

"Florida panthers must be protected," Raven said. "Besides, this punk intended to rape you and who kens what else." She picked the guy up by the front of the shirt and held him against a tree with unnatural strength. Then she snapped her gaze to Kimberly. "Leave us."

Kimberly took a shaky step back. "But...what about Robert?" She pulled the sides of her blouse together to cover her breasts and tied a knot at the center with the loose ends. "And you? You appeared out of...nowhere."

"Go. Now!" Raven hissed. Her cinnamon eyes glowed red like Robert's had earlier.

"Don't leave me here with her. She's a monster too," the guy shrieked.

Shit! Another vampire? "Are you..."

Raven smiled pleasantly. "I only plan to have a wee talk with the misguided youth."

Kimberly glanced from Raven to the stalker, frozen in indecision. Whatever trouble Raven gave him, he deserved. Kimberly had problems of her own. She couldn't go back to the compound. What she learned there was near impossible to believe. The nature of things was not as she'd been taught. Frightening dark secrets...

She inhaled a calming breath. Monsters existed. Vampires and shape shifters existed. And she didn't want to imagine what else existed.

"Go," Raven said. "Go now."

Kimberly bolted, leaving the guy to his fate. She had to get as far away as possible, as quickly as possible. Taking a bend in the path, she stumbled on a loose stone. A snake slithered out of the tall grass near her foot. Kimberly curbed the desire to scream and jumped away from the reptile. The slithering creature was the least of her worries. She jogged along the trail toward the sound of a car engine. Headlights flashed in the distance. Maybe at the highway she could hitch a ride. She flicked a clump of mud from her sleeve. A passing driver might take pity.

A large owl flew through the trees, its wings whirring as

it passed. Then the wooded area became eerily quiet. Kimberly stopped and stared back at the path. Was she wrong to leave the young man with Raven?

She had to. She had no other choice. There was too much danger to go back for him. Besides, he wanted to hurt her. Kimberly ran toward the headlights.

A gunshot sounded in the silence. She frantically spun around, searching the shadows within the tangle of plants surrounding her. Then she darted around a large tree and ran into a rock hard chest.

* * *

Dino Rizzetti held an armful of squirming woman. Before she could detangle from his hold, he braced one arm behind her back and pressed her securely against his chest. He felt the rapid-fire of the bitch's heartbeat through his shirt. The pressure from hard nipples jazzed him to a sharp edge. His balls tightened.

He grabbed a fistful of hair and jerked her head back. Frightened brown eyes stared at him. His quarry looked like a doe caught in headlights. She opened her mouth, inhaling air deep into her lungs, making ready to scream.

"Don't." He yanked hard on the hair he held.

Tears filled her eyes. She didn't shed a drop though. A strong one. Impressive.

He twisted her around, forced an arm up into an awkward position then pushed her toward the rental car. Lady luck had kissed him. The kid JR sent hadn't shown up.

The woman whimpered at the sight of the dead panther lying in the beam from the headlights. A victory thrill ran through Dino. He'd bagged himself a big cat and caught the woman. He would find out what she had on JR then kill her. It would be entertaining to coerce the information from her before her life ended with a bullet between the eyes. The hit payoff would be enough to retire on.

He repositioned her to the side while opening the trunk. She struggled, and he almost lost hold, but he wouldn't let the bitch get away. Not from him.

"Get in," he ordered.

"No." She wriggled and fought like a wild cat about to be dropped into a barrel of water.

He pulled his handgun from its holster and slammed the grip against the side of her head. She slid to the ground, out cold. Dammit. His bum leg hurt like hell and now he'd have to lift dead weight to get her into the trunk. He struggled, breathing hard, but managed to lift the body. He dropped it into the car, and reached for the hood.

Y-oo-www-llll.

Alarm raced up his spine. A second yowling spooked the hell out of him and he hit his head on the trunk hood. He glanced at the dead cat. It hadn't moved.

He turned around warily, hand trembling on the grip of the gun. Another panther lunged for him, its sharp teeth bared. Dino fired a shot into the beast. The big cat grabbed hold of an arm, sinking canines into flesh, but suddenly weakened and let go. The sound of many approaching ATV's forced Dino to hobble into the cover of the swamp. He clenched his teeth against pain. His leg and arm hurt like blazing hell as he worked his way deeper into the bush. He refused to allow the compound's security detail to catch him.

Fuck the money. This job wasn't worth what JR was paying.

* * *

Bright lights hurt her eyes and Kimberly shut them tight. Her head thumped like the drumbeats performed by her favorite Scottish tribal band.

"Kimberly, wake up, lass." Colin's voice coaxed as if from a distance.

Someone gently slapped her cheeks. Muscular arms slid under her. She fought the assault.

"Stop!" Colin shouted next to her ear.

She jerked her lids open. "What the hell?"

A blurry Colin obscured her vision, and the pounding in her skull increased in magnitude to an intolerable agony. She closed her eyes again, allowing him to lift her into strong arms while she concentrated on dulling the pain in her head.

"I'm taking you to the compound where a doctor can check you for injuries."

She managed to utter the word, "no," but not with much force.

A soft chuckle cut through the misery. "You might have a concussion."

How had everything gone so wrong? Despair overwhelmed her.

"Robert's dead," she said before blessed blackness engulfed her.

* * *

Willy stiffened within the female vampire's grasp. Urine ran down a leg and soaked the crotch of his pants. He would die, or worse, be turned into a monster.

She held him firmly against the rough bark of the tree with one hand pressed to his chest. His feet hung loose, a foot off the ground. He squirmed, trying to get away. The effort was futile. With a swish of a red fingernailed hand, his worn shirt tattered into strips and slid from his body.

The bitch scratched his chest, a single sharp nail cut deep. He thought he remembered what to expect. But this time, the intense burn lasted longer, nearly causing him to pass out. His heart slowed then raced, pumping toxin through his system. He felt the poison flow through his veins, slowing body functions. The sound of a sporadic heartbeat terrified the shit out of him.

His limbs froze in paralysis. The only things he could move were his eyes and mouth. That meant he could only see what was directly in front of him, and gasp in fear.

The woman's teeth grazed his neck. Several times. His skin ultra-sensitive, every nerve ending zinged at her touch. She played with him. Teased.

Blood rushed to his cock. *Damn the bitch to hell.*

Although he couldn't move, he felt every touch with heightened senses. She rubbed against him, making him hot, needy. She leaned in, flicked a pink tongue along the seam of his closed lips. He opened wide, craving more. She refused him.

His erection throbbed to the point of pain. "Please," he

begged. "Bite me."

She threw her head back and laughed. Then she sank sharp fangs deep into his throat. Fireworks exploded in his mind as an intense orgasm rolled down the length of his cock.

Then she dropped him like a piece of unwanted garbage before disappearing into the swamp. He slid the length of the tree to the ground and wept. When no more tears remained, he tried to move. Unlike the previous time, he could. He laughed hysterically. She hadn't turned him into a vampire.

The Slayer doctor had the wrong information. The Hungarian told Willy the second bite would convert him into a vampire. But nothing had changed. He felt fine. Better than fine.

His senses seemed sharper. Swamp sounds played music for his ears. He tromped through the woods on a silent step. The moon slid behind the clouds, yet he could clearly see the armadillo foraging through the decaying vegetation. His stare locked on the animal. Willy's stomach clenched from hunger. He rubbed his tongue over his teeth.

What-the-fuck? Fangs emerged from his gums.

Willy woke in a cold sweat. The nightmares were worsening. He'd soiled another pair of boxers. The sheets. The mattress too. He sat on the edge of the bed, limbs gripped by lethargy. He forced himself up, staggered to the bathroom, and looked in the mirror. Bloodshot eyes stared back. Opening his mouth, he ran his tongue over the upper gum. No fangs. He released the held breath. When he returned his gaze to the mirror, his heart kicked into overdrive.

Behind him stood the raven-haired vampire.

* * *

"Kimberly, lass, wake up."
"Let her sleep."
"But she's been sleeping for two days."
"I gave her a sedative. She needs rest in order to heal."
Voices in the shadows. Kimberly didn't understand

what they were talking about, although she knew they referred to her. She attempted to shake the fuzz from her brain. Why couldn't she remember anything? She glanced around, but could only make out dark shapes, everything covered in a flowing gray fog. Where was she? Tendrils of pungent smelling vapor surrounded her, wrapped around her, skimmed across her skin.

The air thickened, making it difficult to breathe. She reached up and tore at elusive fingers encircling her throat. Strands of gossamer fiber seemed to cloud her thoughts. She clawed at layers of sticky mental cobwebs, fighting to be free from the imprisoning gloom. Finally, the haze cleared, and she stood in a familiar corridor. Why couldn't she concentrate? The lights dimmed. With a strong shake of the head, she tried to un-jumble her thoughts.

Oh, yeah. Colin. She was supposed to deliver a message from Colin.

She stepped forward. The corridor stretched out in front of her, elongated into an endless tunnel. The ghostly white walls pulsed as if breathing. Kimberly's heartbeat stuttered in her ears. Dread became a heavy weight pressing against throbbing temples.

Kimberly moved as if in slow motion, each step more difficult. She tried to focus. Her fingers curled into fists. She needed to deliver the message to Robert.

After what seemed like an eternity, she could see the end of the passageway. A sickly yellow glow illuminated the hall outside the open doorway of Dr. Knight's office. Kimberly's throat constricted and she gasped for breath. Intuitively she wanted to flee. Only sheer determination kept her moving forward. One-step at a time. Robert was there. She needed to give him the message.

The last leaded step brought her to the threshold. She peered in, eager to see Robert.

No. The word screamed in her mind. She gripped the doorframe as denial burned her chest. Robert reclined on the sofa, body stretched taut, eyes closed, lips parted in masculine rapture. Patrice straddled his thighs, her hands caressing the erection inside the boxers exposed by the unbuttoned pants. The doctor spied Kimberly and whispered something to Robert. His eyes popped open, and he reached for Patrice. Her breasts spilled over the top edge of lacey bra cups and she leaned into him.

Kimberly strangled on an involuntary gasp. Robert's gaze flipped to her, guilt evident on his flushed face. She whirled around and ran blindly through the corridor. She raced around a corner, stopping in front of a steel door to catch her breath. The long stride of heavy footsteps pounded toward her.

She opened the door and backed inside the dark room. As quietly as she could manage, she shut the panel then leaned her head against the cold metal. She couldn't face Robert. Her heart ached at his betrayal.

A light flicked on behind her.

Kimberly spun around, and gaped at the man standing a few feet away.

"You didn't believe he loved you, did you?" Jason's white teeth flashed—a perfect contrast to his well-kept, tanned appearance—and his lips slowly stretched into a mocking grin. "Did you expect him to be faithful to a plain Jane like you?"

"What are you doing here?" Kimberly couldn't believe the audacity of her ex-fiancé to show up, here, now, after she'd been gut-punched by the sight of Robert with Patrice.

"Don't you want me to take you back? You begged me to stay with you before I left for the Caymans." He stepped forward. "You always begged."

Y...o...w...l.

Kimberly took a step backward at hearing the frightening sound and bumped into the closed door. She bit her lip and slid her gaze over Jason, to the nearly room-sized cage behind him. Her heart kicked in her chest.

Jason dissolved, leaving her alone with her worst nightmare—a big tawny cat with greenish-amber eyes and a sardonic smile. The animal opened its mouth and yowled again, the sound grating along nerve endings like chalk on a blackboard.

She'd rather face Robert. She reached behind and grasped for the knob, opened the door, and spun into the hallway right into Patrice. Another mocking smile.

"Did you think he would want a sexless woman like you?"

Kimberly's fingers fluttered at the base of her throat with the horror of the woman's comment. Robert appeared behind Patrice, pulled her back into him and wrapped his arms around the doctor's waist.

"You didn't believe my lies, did you, Kimberly?" They both laughed.

Kimberly tumbled backward and kept falling as if she'd plunged into a bottomless pit. Her scream got lost in a chaotic cacophony of sound.

A nightmare. Must be a nightmare. Wake up. Please.

She hit the ground hard. Held still for a moment, breath knocked from her lungs. She needed to get a move on before *he* found her.

Kimberly got up and ran. Scratching fingers grabbed at her from the dark. The thud of pounding footfalls sounded from behind. He'd lied to her. He was a monster with blood red eyes and fangs.

This wasn't right. She must be having another terror dream. She tossed and turned, becoming tangled in damp sheets. She ripped at the cotton. Come on. Wake up!

When she opened her eyes, he stood in front of her. Robert morphed into a panther and lunged for her throat. She leapt out of his path and landed with a thud on...

On a thick carpet?

Her eyes felt dry, stuck shut. She forced them open and focused. She lay on the thick peach carpet in her suite at the compound. Her pulse slowed, and she took a deep breath.

Then adrenaline kicked into her blood stream as an uneasy sensation swamped her. She wasn't alone. She twisted her head and gasped at the sight of a pair of large brown man's loafers. She quickly raised her gaze to tan khakis, to a stripped polo shirt, to the man sitting in her bedside chair.

"Good, you're awake." He dragged fingers through disheveled graying hair as he looked down with empathetic hazel eyes at her position on the floor. "I was beginning to worry."

"Who...who are you?"

His lips curved into a grave smile. "Dr. Nolen, your doctor."

Kimberly swallowed to ease the tightness in her throat. "Are you here because Robert is dead?"

CHAPTER NINETEEN

A mourning dove cooed outside the open window, and Kimberly glanced through the screen. During the night, a cold snap blew across the states below the Mason-Dixon Line, its chill reaching deep into south Florida, making air conditioning unnecessary.

Such a shame. The less than hardy potted flowers on the veranda had succumbed to the lower temperatures. Kimberly wrapped the tartan shawl around her shoulders and gazed back at the patient.

Robert lay in panther form on a gurney next to her chair. Leather bindings strapped him to the stainless steel. For the past two weeks, the veterinarians had given him heavy doses of tranquilizers to keep him from biting at the stitches marring his massive chest.

She ran a palm over the coarse tawny fur of his thick neck. His chest rose and fell with each breath. The research facility's chief veterinarian assured that Robert wouldn't die. She prayed the doctor spoke the truth. Robert's condition had yet to improve. Even with a lower dosage of sedatives, he remained semiconscious.

A tear slipped and landed on the panther's face. His whiskers twitched. His lids cracked a slit and he yawned, extending a long pink tongue. His eyes opened wide.

Kimberly held still, swallowed, and tamped down hard

on her remaining fears. A sad greenish-amber gaze slid over her face. Her apprehension was pointless. He didn't struggle against the bindings. Instead, he closed his eyes as if reconciled to the current circumstance. Had he given up?

If only she could explain her feelings. Make him understand she accepted his unusual and somewhat frightening nature. She had to try. "I'm not sure if you can hear me." She stroked the panther's neck. "If you can, I'm not sure if you'll understand my words. But I need to tell you how sorry I am that I ran from you and caused you to be shot while trying to protect me. I'm no longer afraid of you." She sighed. "I accept what and who you are. I accept you as a man. I accept you as a panther. And I..."

She swallowed thickly. "I accept you as a vampire." Kimberly rested her head on the big cat's shoulder. "Love you," she murmured. She rubbed her nose into the stiff fur, inhaling the musky scent.

A soft purr vibrated along the panther's chest. Maybe she was getting through to him.

"Colin told me the truth about Dr. Knight. I know she tricked you while you were under hypnosis."

The purring stopped. Kimberly squeezed her eyes tight. She wouldn't cry. Dr. Knight had set the stage to push her away from Robert. The bitch almost succeeded. Kimberly had acted out the part scripted precisely as directed and made a mess of things. If only she hadn't run.

Her reaction made sense at the time. Who wouldn't have tried to get away from a predatory and bloodthirsty beast? Her sense of reality had been destroyed. She'd thought the chances against a hit man were better than those against a vampire shifter.

"Robert, I wish I hadn't run." She slid fingers through the fur with steady strokes, needing to assure him of her love.

The last two weeks had felt like an emotional roller coaster ride. After she recovered from the concussion and trauma of what happened in the swamp, confusion continued to jumble her thinking and nightmares. She'd been ready to escape the compound and all the crazy people who made up Robert's scary world.

That was before she met Dr. Kurt Nolen. He befriended her and explained everything.

She continued the even strokes over Robert's fur. The purring began again. Good. At least he still enjoyed her touch.

Kimberly had never given psychoanalysis much credence before, but although Kurt was an internist, he dabbled in psychotherapy, and was good. He'd forced her to face reality. He helped her work through the fears that revolved around Robert's less than normal state of being and the guilt over her father's death. Emotionally, she felt better than ever.

Although, she still resented the fact Robert wasn't the one to explain his peculiar malady. A thoughtful frown crossed her lips. Perhaps she should continue attending counseling sessions.

The purring quieted when she drew her hand away. She leaned back in the chair and rolled her head from side to side, hoping to ease a stiff neck from sitting for so long.

She owed thanks to Dr. Nolen. He had reminded her of the man Robert was. Of his innate goodness. Of the code of honor Robert embraced. Kurt explained about the monsters haunting Robert. How Robert did everything in his power to control the evil he believed lurked within him. And how all the scientists on the staff researched a cure to save Robert from giving in to the dark side because he was a man they respected.

She respected him too. When he got well—she had to believe he would—she'd make him suffer for not trusting her with his secret. Had he told her and made her understand, he would have saved them both a lot of anguish.

Colin entered the room to stand beside her. "How's the patient today?"

"He seems...resigned."

A furrow appeared in the big man's forehead. "That doesn't sound like Robert."

"He's not tugging against his bindings. That's a good thing, right?"

"Not necessarily. He should have regained his strength

by now. Without a will to fight he may not recover."

"Isn't there anything else to be done for him?" Kimberly chewed on the edge of her lower lip. She had to believe he'd get well.

"I'll talk to the vets. Maybe they should stop doping him completely." Colin motioned to the door. "Come away now, lass. You need to keep up your strength. It's the chef's day off and the lads have prepared lunch."

"I don't want to leave Robert alone." She brushed fingers over his fur once more."

"I'll send one of the veterinarian's assistants in to watch over him."

Kimberly rose and followed Colin to the door. She glanced over a shoulder. "I'll be back."

The panther's penetrating gaze bore into her.

* * *

Robert waited until Kimberly and Colin were gone. The panther's body convulsed several times before the man emerged from the beast. Using his restored vampire powers, he forced the drugs from his system through the pores and burst the restraints holding him. He gritted his teeth against searing pain as the wounds on his chest instantly healed, leaving nary a scar. His breath released as a relieved sigh.

He sat up, threw his legs over the side of the gurney, and scanned the sterile room. A bundle of clothes lay atop a metal cabinet. Good man. Colin had known he might shift at any time. Standing, Robert grabbed for the jeans. He had to get out of there. The offensive odor lingering from Kimberly's fear burned his nostrils.

She'd said she could accept him as he was, but she lied. To herself, and to him.

As he pulled the black denim over his hips to his waist, a female gasp sounded from behind. With fingers still fastening the top button of the jeans, he spun around expecting to see one of the veterinary assistants.

Kimberly's brown eyes were too large within a too pale face. She wore her hair longer now. The soft strands dusted her shoulders where her family colors draped a low cut floral blouse that exposed a glimpse of cleavage. His heart slammed against his ribs. The short black skirt dragged attention downward along a length of slim leg, to an ankle, to a turquoise flip-flop displaying toenails painted bright tangerine. He glanced away and swallowed to clear the tightness in his throat while he finished buttoning his fly.

When he looked again, Kimberly gave a tentative smile. White knuckles clutched the doorframe though. She feared him but didn't flee. She deserved credit for that at least.

An awkward silence hung thick between them. Her head lowered for a moment. When she raised it, tears glistened on the tips of thick lashes. "I'm sorry."

Damn, his chest pinched, he couldn't stand to see and hear her pain, knowing he was the reason for it. He should have never gotten involved with her. From the first, their bond had been a mistake. The loss would kill him, but he needed to end their relationship now, before he caused more hurt. He would send her away. Jagger could protect her better.

"None of what happened was your fault. I take full responsibility for all that has transpired." Robert snatched the shirt and shrugged it over his shoulders. He buttoned the front of the black linen and walked toward her and the door. "Now, if you will excuse me, I have phone calls to make."

"That's it? That's all you're going to say?"

"Aye. For now."

Kimberly grasped his arm. A jolt shot through his system as he tried to pass. *Damn her*. She let go, but didn't step out of his way. "We need to talk about everything that happened."

"Not now."

"Then when?"

He shoved his hands into the jean's pockets. "Dinnae push me, lass."

"Or else, what?" Kimberly's forced laugh cut deep. "You'll turn me into a vampire?"

Robert's hiss escaped from between clenched teeth. Kimberly took a step back. It wasn't smart to yank on a tiger's tail. Or in this case, a panther's tail.

For god's sake, a vampire stood before her. Was she certifiable? Yup, must be. She stood on the balls of her feet to seem taller and pulled on the open edges of his linen shirt. He allowed it. He even tipped his head forward and permitted her to kiss him.

Kimberly took encouragement from the acquiescence and leaned into his hard body. She slid her tongue along the seam of his lips. He stiffened but didn't stop her. She wrapped eager arms around his neck, took his bottom lip between her teeth, and nipped the flesh.

He exhaled sharply, the air rushed over her moist lips, making her shiver. His nostrils flared though he still held himself in check. In frustration, she pressed tighter against him and slipped her tongue between his lips and into his mouth. He responded by dueling with her.

She was delighted when he removed his hands from the jean's pockets and used them to cradle her ass. Okay, now they made progress. What did she need to do to push him a little farther, to get a stronger response from him? She grazed her tongue along the edge of his top teeth. A rumbling sound erupted from his chest, and she felt his fangs elongate.

Holy shit. She tensed, and he started to pull away.

"No." She kept her arms firm around his neck. If she loved him, she had to accept him as he was. "Bite me."

She leaned her head back and exposed her neck while still gazing into his eyes.

His eyes glowed crimson red. He had her up against the wall before another thought entered her mind. His hands expertly roamed her body, touching everywhere, thrumming her need. Moisture pooled at the juncture of her thighs and she rode his knee. He released a harsh growl and grazed sharp teeth along the base of her throat.

A prickle of fear made her tremble. She forced the unwanted emotion away and tilted her head to the side to give better access, curious to feel the prick of his fangs.

He bunched her skirt around her waist and pushed her panties aside. His fingers plucked, and teased sensitive flesh, bringing a quick and explosive orgasm.

By the time she caught her breath, he was gone. The door slammed with finality. Damn the man. She wasn't about to let him get away with walking out on her. She adjusted her clothing, smoothed her hair, and stalked into the passageway.

CHAPTER TWENTY

Robert stepped behind the desk and took a deep breath. The realization of what he'd almost done had instantaneously deflated his desire.

Damn. When Kimberly's scent altered from fear to arousal, he lost control. Once again, she'd turned the situation around on him. Her irrational plea had been nearly impossible to resist. What the bloody hell had she been thinking to invite a vampire to feed? He almost performed the unforgivable deed and taken her blood for the third time.

The consequences of such a foolish act would leave her life in ruin.

He couldn't live with being the cause of her pain. He needed to learn more about the damn curse and Dr. Knight's crazy theories for a cure. The report had to be there somewhere. Robert shuffled through the paperwork on Patrice's desk.

"How dare you walk out on me?"

He glanced up. Kimberly stood in the doorway, hands on hips. The peppery scent of anger mixed with feminine zest drifted into the office. Robert kept his lips closed tight to keep from uttering the curse burning in his throat.

She marched into the room, stopped in front of the desk, and leaned forward, pressing palms against the polished cherry. "Who the hell do you think you are?"

The wooden barrier between them prevented him from pulling her into his arms, which would be disastrous for them both. Robert dropped onto the chair and slid his lower body under the desk to hide his renewed interest.

Maybe Kimberly's position, standing above him, would keep fear from overpowering her nerve when he explained everything. He placed his hands in plain sight on the surface of the desk in another attempt to lessen the chances of frightening her. "Hear me out."

"All right. But it better be good."

Robert cleared his throat, stalling. He steepled his hands in front of him and looked into her furious eyes. Instead of keeping the advantage of height, she sat in one of the guest chairs across the desk from him.

"As you are aware, I am a reviled vampire."

"Hardly reviled." A smile pulled at her mouth. She fought it and gripped her upper lip with her teeth instead.

He glanced away to gather scattered wits. "I will leave the adjective in place for now," he said, returning attention to Kimberly. "You ken, 'twas my fault the insane young man stalked you."

"Colin told me you almost killed the guy's sister."

"Aye. I did."

"But you didn't. You made sure she received medical treatment and emotional counseling."

He flipped a hand through the thick air, dismissing the import of the comment. "Dinnae you understand what I am trying to tell you? I hunt to feed. I cannot always control the bloodlust."

"You've been drinking clinical bags of blood."

He couldn't help the grimace that twisted his lips. "'Tis not verra appetizing. But aye, I have other methods of feeding besides drinking blood from humans."

"There. You see? I have nothing to fear from you."

"I am a monster." He shouted the words.

Kimberly cocked her chin. "Not to me."

He shook his head. How could she be so foolish? "Have you forgotten that I am also a shape shifter?"

"Your panther form is magnificent." She scorched him

with a direct gaze. "But that doesn't give you the right to abuse me the way you did in the treatment room. Especially after I risked my heart admitting I still love you."

He held his breath. Could she mean those words? "There is nae future with me."

"Of course there is. You're immortal."

He shook his head.

"Robert, listen to me. I. Love. You."

"Dinnae you understand?" He dragged a hand over his face. "I have endangered you."

Kimberly pursed her lips.

"I am not a nice man. Bloody hell, I am not a man." He glanced at the ceiling. "Satan curse me, I am a beast, not a man." He banged a fist on the desk.

"But, Robert—"

"Dinnae you understand? Are you nae listening to me?" He hung his head, spent.

When he glanced up, Kimberly smiled.

"What?" He rubbed his chest, trying to ease the discomfort burning there.

"You've told me your opinion. Would you like to hear mine?"

He nodded. What else could he do, facing her sincerity?

"Here's what I know." She pegged him with a look that stole his breath. "You are a good man, a gentle man, a loving man. The beasts within you are like a disease. All we need do is find a way to heal you."

"You dinnae understand of what you speak."

"Oh, I do. I've had many long discussions with Dr. Nolen. He believes the solution to your problem is buried somewhere in Dr. Knight's research notes. It's a matter of finding the correct notations. He's in his office, reviewing the files right now."

"Where is Patrice?"

Kimberly's eyebrows rose in a feminine arch. "Patrice is it?"

"You told me you knew the truth."

"So you did hear and understand me."

"Aye. Where is Dr. Knight?"

Kimberly shrugged. "Disappeared." Her smile glowed, and although it shouldn't, the sight warmed the chill within the deep shadows. "Shall we go see Kurt?"

"Kurt is it?" A possessive blast shot through Robert's veins. The panther awakened, demanding to surface and enforce his ownership. Robert held the animal back, wanting to make his own demands.

"Dr. Nolen and I have become good friends."

Robert growled then stalked around the desk to tower over Kimberly. "You will become non-friends."

He pulled her up and into an embrace, renewing his claim. She wrapped warm arms around his neck, leaning into him, sweet lips pressed against his cheek. The panther quieted.

"I love you with all my heart." Robert kissed her once, fiercely, to remind her that he was the one she loved. Then he released her. "Shall we visit Dr. Nolen?"

Her thoroughly kissed, dazed expression made his black heart pound a joyous rhythm.

"Come." He grasped her hand.

She laced her fingers through his, sending a gentle thrill through him. When she touched him like that, he almost believed everything could be resolved between them. Robert tugged on their joined hands, and they left the office together.

Being a sunny February Sunday, minimal staff worked at the compound. Robert steered Kimberly through the quiet corridor toward Kurt's office. They walked side-by-side, hands clasped, a single unit.

He squeezed her fingers gently, unsure whether he meant the gesture to reassure her or himself. Though her acceptance gave him hope.

The door to Kurt's office hung ajar, and they entered without knocking. Kurt uncharacteristically slumped, bent over one of many file boxes cluttering the corner of the office. He spun around with a hand held to his chest when realizing they stood behind him. "Damn. You startled me."

"Sorry, old boy. Kimberly said you have Patrice's notes and you think a solution to my, er..." He glanced at Kimberly, and she smiled reassuringly. "...problem might be noted within." Robert shifted his gaze to the abundance of cardboard file boxes. "What is all this stuff?"

"Patrice's research." Kurt ran a hand through unkempt graying hair. "Books on vampires, shape shifters, the Celts, Voodoo, Hoodoo, cults, the Bermuda Triangle." He waved an arm over the cardboard boxes. "Journals and interview notes. And...well, a lot of reading material."

"Can we help?" Kimberly asked.

"Sure." Kurt straightened, relief vivid in his hazel eyes.

Robert grabbed one of the notebooks. "Tell us how you wish us to proceed."

"Just read. I think you'll recognize anything important."

Kurt dragged a box full of books across the floor to the sofa for Kimberly. Robert tossed the notebook back into the box, picked the thing up, and followed Kurt.

Kimberly sank onto the cushions and selected a thick book from Kurt's box. "Oh, yay, Dracula."

"I don't think we need to read the fictional novels." Kurt selected a nonfiction book and held it out. "Here, read this one on Voodoo."

"Cool." Kimberly's lips curled into one of those quick-then-it's-gone smiles. Then she discarded the Bram Stoker classic and accepted the other book from Kurt. "I always wanted to learn how to put a curse on someone."

Hours later, Robert rubbed tired eyes. The words on the page had blurred.

"What the hell?" Kurt raised his gaze from the journal he was reading. "Patrice wanted you to convert Kimberly into a vampire?"

Kimberly's gaze shot to Robert.

He returned the stare. "I told Patrice it was never going to happen."

"Why would she want you to convert me? Oh yes, I get it, she wanted you for herself."

"According to the notes in this journal." Kurt shook the offensive bound document. "She believed if Robert took your blood three times, the third time being at the exact location and time of the curse, you would become a vampire shifter and Robert would be cured."

"That's insane."

"Aye, 'tis." Robert grabbed her hand and cradled it to his chest.

"You'd also have to take his blood in between each of his feedings," Kurt added.

"Ick. I don't think I could ever do that." She wrinkled her nose then squeezed Robert's hand. "I'm teasing. I know you would never hurt me."

"That is not exactly true. I have already hurt you."

"No you haven't." She shook her head adamantly.

He twisted to face her fully. "Aye, I have. Do you remember the day my, er...pet raven scratched your finger?"

"Yeah."

"Ach, well. When I licked the wound, I ingested some of your blood."

"Does your saliva have special properties? Is that why the scratch healed so quickly?"

"Aye. But to get back to my taking your blood..." He glanced at Kurt and felt his face flush.

"Do you want me to leave?" Kurt asked.

"Nae. You already ken most of the sordid details."

"Sordid?" Kimberly tugged on her hand.

"I dinnae mean the lovemaking, sweetling. I am referring to the despicable things my vampire-self did to you when I lost control."

"Despicable things?" she asked, looking confused. "What did you do?"

He held her gaze. "When we made love the first time, I pierced your flesh to feed as we climaxed. That was the second time I ingested your blood."

"Oh." A scarlet blush colored her throat and cheeks.

"I fear if I lose control again. Feed from you again... Ach, well, I am not sure what will happen."

"Patrice believed three exchanges of blood would produce a vampire shifter," Kurt interjected.

"But how would that cure Robert?" Kimberly looked to the older man for answers.

"We believe your blood contains special properties. That your blood has altered his quintessential vampire traits. That's why, all of a sudden after he fed from you, he could tolerate the sun. Anyway, Patrice believed your blood would convert Robert back into a mortal man and you would become a vampire shifter to replace him."

Robert moved uncomfortably on the sofa. "Kimberly..."

"It's okay, Robert, I know you won't harm me. I wondered about your ability to withstand the sun." Kimberly took a deep breath. "After I licked his injured finger, Kurt, I didn't feel anything strange. I didn't feel different."

"We don't understand everything about what is happening with your blood or Robert's."

"Kimberly, I never meant for any of this to happen," Robert said, his regret nearly strangling him.

She squeezed his fingers hard before dropping his hand. "I know."

"Kurt, we haven't had a chance to talk since I was shot. Before I went under hypnosis, Patrice presented a theory about what would cure me."

"Well, what was it? That is, besides exchanging blood with Kimberly?"

"Patrice seemed to believe if we traveled back in time to the date of the actual curse and I took Kimberly's blood there and forced her to feed from me, I'd be cured."

"Wow!" Kimberly's eyes rounded.

"Aye. Wow is right. I told the woman to forget it. I will not endanger you." He flicked his gaze to Kurt. "But what if I could travel back in time? What if I could travel back in time and change the events leading up to the moment Zola performed the curse?"

A knock sounded at the door. After a brief moment, Colin stuck his head in. "Raven left a message on the answering machine."

"What is it?"

"She's off to Scotland."

"You're kidding me, right?" Great. He didn't have the luxury of time to deal with his evil twin.

"She also said she's taken care of two of your problems. The rest is up to you."

"I can only imagine what she means." He shook his head. Could his life get more complicated? "I appreciate you coming to bring the message."

"No problem. I thought you would want to know right away."

"Aye. Thank you."

Colin left and closed the door.

"What do you think the message means?" Kimberly asked.

Robert shrugged. He didn't want to guess. His sister was certainly up to no good. Scotland? He hoped she wasn't foolish enough to search out Séaghdha. According to Patrice's notes, he had a lair somewhere in the western islands.

He should go after his sister, but he and Kimberly's situation had to come first.

"There is something else you need to know." Robert placed an arm on the back of the sofa and leaned into Kimberly. "Raven and Marion are one in the same. Raven is my twin, but she is also my pet bird, Marion. Her real name is Marion MacLachlan. She followed me those hundreds of years ago when I left my home in Scotland to sail for Jamaica."

"How did she become a vampire?" Kimberly asked.

"Men kidnapped her, and because they thought her a lad, they pressed her into service on one of His Majesty's ships. She refused to tell me how she was turned. Just that she was bitten by a vampire. After reading Patrice's notes, I suspect it was Séaghdha, a verra ancient vampire of legend. He must have converted her into a vampire capable of shifting between the forms of a raven and a beautiful woman."

"I always thought her frightening."

"Okay, now Kimberly knows everything," Kurt said, eyes focused in that inquisitive mad-scientist way. "Let's get back to this time travel theory of yours. What made Patrice believe you could travel through time?"

"Before we get back to that, I better tell you that Patrice believes Séaghdha converted me."

"But how?" Kurt asked.

"She believed Zola's curse went awry and opened a door to another dimension or to the underworld. She believed

Séaghdha slipped through, used Zola's pet panther to create the monster I have become."

"Interesting."

"You think?" Robert couldn't hold back the sarcasm.

"Actually, the theory explains a lot. I often wondered how both you and your sister had become vampire shifters through different means. It never made sense to me. But after Séaghdha fed from you, he would have easily been able to track your twin. Your DNA makeup is similar."

Robert blew out a heavy puff of air. It was his fault his beautiful sister had been transformed into a deadly monster. Pain slammed into his chest, forcing a grunt from deep in his throat. He had blamed himself all along, but this revelation added weight.

"Are you all right? Kimberly reached for his arm.

"Aye." If piercing self-hatred was all right.

"Now, getting back to our earlier discussion, what made Patrice believe you could travel through time to the exact time of the curse?" Kurt asked, bringing Robert back to the topic at hand.

"She said she had the coordinates and I had the need."

* * *

Raven soared high over the immense gray ocean, enjoying the cool breeze ruffling her feathers. She targeted the single black dot below and descended. While making several circles over the Scottish freighter, her keen gaze scanned the decks. Her cargo remained secure. She croaked in exhilaration.

Gagged and bound, Patrice and Willy sat in awkward positions lashed to pipes on the upper deck. Poor humans. Or in Willy's case—poor sort-of-human.

Raven released an ear-piercing croak, an avian cackle. The bitch and the boy-toy must be uncomfortable. Damp and dirty.

Raven could hardly wait until the boat made port. Oh, she planned to enjoy Patrice's humiliation. When Raven finished punishing the Voodoo doctor for toying with Robert, Séaghdha would appreciate the broken woman as a gift.

Then he would owe Raven. Big time.

As for Willy, even now, in her bird form, she could almost taste his blood. *Orgasmic.*

She would complete the conversion and have him forever. Though she'd need to keep him well hidden from Wolfgang. The wolf must never learn about her new plaything.

Raven inhaled a deep breath of the briny sea air. Well pleased, she circled one more time, sent out a cry on the wind, and flew for the coast.

The ping of guilt tightening her chest caused her bird form to falter and drop a few feet. She refused to question her resolve. Raven pushed the good-girl thoughts into dark recesses in her mind and caught an upward thermal.

* * *

Kimberly dropped another book on the teetering pile in front of the sofa. They'd made a mess of Kurt's office. Papers, reports, dirty dishes lay scattered on most surfaces. She stretched in an attempt to ease the kinks in her neck and spine from sitting for too many hours.

She took a sip from the coffee cup and nearly spit it out. Cold. She placed the mug on the end table and glanced at Robert. Her heart fluttered and her sex clenched just from the sight of him. She bit her lip. She needed to concentrate on the problem at hand. "Have you ever sailed through the Bermuda Triangle?"

Robert raised his gaze from the notebook he examined. "I have."

"Well? Tell me about it."

His jaw tightened, and he placed the spiral bound book onto the other cluttered end table. "'Tis different than anywhere else on earth."

She hastened a glance at Kurt. He had his nose buried deep into one of Dr. Knight's journals and seemed to have forgotten she and Robert were in the office with him.

"How is it different, Robert? Are any of the rumors true?"

"Do you mean of a paranormal nature?" He raised an eyebrow.

She stifled a grin and nodded.

"Not sure." He hesitated and his brow wrinkled as if he recalled uncertain memories.

"You must have heard things over the years. Seen things?" she persisted.

He cleared his throat. "I have heard tales of wormholes and time portals, though I have never found any." He lifted his feet onto the glass-topped coffee table, and leaned back against the sofa's tan leather. "And I have experienced glitches with my gadgets and electronics while sailing through those cursed waters."

Kimberly reached for a book about the Bermuda Triangle filled with sticky notes, laid it on her lap, and opened to the first yellow tab.

"The Triangle is an unnerving place," Robert continued, arms crossed over his muscular chest.

"Unnerving? How?"

"'Tis hard to explain...unusual thick fogs, hazes, strange lights hovering where there should be nary a one. Sometimes a soul can hear voices whispering in the fog and hear whistling."

Kimberly tapped the opened page of the book. "More than one hundred forty planes have disappeared since 1964 and only God knows how many ships have been lost."

"Aye. Ghost ships have been found for centuries in the Triangle. Some dating back to the Phoenicians."

"Some of this reads crazy." Kimberly held up the book. "A clairvoyant and his followers believe Atlantis sank into the depths of the Bermuda Triangle when the civilization abused its resources. The theory states their advanced power sources may still be active in the area, causing modern equipment to malfunction. Other accounts point to alien intervention."

Robert chuckled. "Do you believe in aliens?"

"I don't know. Maybe. I never believed in vampires or shape shifters before and where did *that* get me? I think we need to keep an open mind."

"*Touché.*"

"I've got it," Kurt said.

"What?" Robert said in unison with Kimberly. He gave

her a wonderfully warm smile before shifting his gaze to the doctor.

"The coordinates for a time gate," Kurt said, his face animated with excitement. "A place where time warps and sends ships to other time periods."

"The past?" Robert asked.

"According to Patrice's notes."

"Ach, bloody hell. Then that is where I shall sail."

"I'm coming with you." Kimberly wasn't about to let him go without her.

"Nae. I go alone."

"I'm coming with you."

"I will not take your blood," he said, expression firm.

"I didn't think you would. But maybe my presence will be enough to alter the series of events leading up to that horrible witch cursing you."

"Nae."

"Please." She wasn't beyond begging. "Pretty please."

"Kurt, say something." Robert glared at the doctor.

He shrugged. "I think Kimberly should go with you."

CHAPTER TWENTY-ONE

The preparations didn't take long once they decided to set sail for the Caribbean, so on a glorious March morning, Kimberly stepped aboard *Night Thrill* and inhaled the taste of the pre-dawn sea air. Sultry temperatures had returned to south Florida and even at this early hour, perspiration pooled between her breasts.

Robert followed her onboard. They'd risen early and traveled to Miami to meet up with the sailboat. Jagger having sailed *Night Thrill* south from Georgia after Kimberly and Robert left the boat behind weeks ago to travel to the compound by car.

Shortly, she and Robert would sail southeast, into the Bermuda Triangle and, if Patrice's research findings were correct, through a wormhole into the past.

Her stomach tight, Kimberly let her gaze settle on Robert and linger. He'd dressed all in black like the pirate swashbucklers from the Errol Flynn era movies. The sight of him made her shiver with yearning.

A furrow crossed his brow and he frowned. "Are you having a change of heart, lass?"

Kimberly sensed his concern. He still didn't believe she wanted to travel to the past with him. There was no way she'd let him go alone.

She grasped both of his upper arms and swayed forward

onto the balls of her feet. Their gazes met and held. Heat flashed within his eyes. Kimberly took it as encouragement and leaned in and pressed her lips against his, loving him with a gentle caress. Fire sizzled at the intimate contact. The sensual burn seeped into her soul and claimed her. She gave Robert more, everything, all the emotion within her.

A panther's purr rumbled from his chest when she deepened the kiss. As she finally pulled away, he chuckled. "Guess that was my answer?"

"It was."

"Anytime you feel the need to answer me in such an exquisite manner, please, go with those feelings." A sexy smile slipped onto his face.

She punched his arm playfully. "You look handsome, but I doubt eighteenth century shipmasters dressed completely in black."

His grin widened. "How would you know?"

"I looked it up on the internet."

"Damn technology." His gaze appraised her. He swept a hand in a circle. "Spin around for me."

She twirled and waited for his reaction.

"Not bad. The lad's garments we pulled from Raven's chest of period clothing look great on you, revealing fine assets. And with your hair longer and pulled back in a queue, well..." He cupped a palm on a butt cheek and squeezed. "You steal my verra breath."

His touch started a chain reaction, and her sex clenched. She gasped, feeling a blush creep up her neck. Several moments passed before she could articulate the words, "Thank you."

He raised his eyebrows knowingly and removed the hand. "Ach, well." He cleared his throat. "Shall we run the pre-sail check?"

"Aye, aye, Captain." She saluted.

He looked away quickly then gave a swift sideways glance before making busy, checking the safety equipment. Kimberly watched him for a moment then smiled and went below to ensure their gear was properly stowed. She checked the seacocks on the toilets and sinks, making sure they were in a seagoing position. Then she returned to the deck to remove the canvas covers and prepare the sails. Robert started the engine. Kimberly released the lines, and they motored out of the marina.

"The weather forecast is ideal," he said when she joined him in the cockpit. We should have smooth sailing all the way to Bimini Island."

"Is that where we're headed?"

"Aye, lass, 'tis." His expression sobered. "We will reach the coordinates Patrice noted as we pass Andros Island on the approach to Bimini."

Her stomach did a little hip-hop, and Kimberly swallowed awkwardly. *Holy shit.* They were going to try to sail into the past.

After a thirty-hour sail—a pleasant passage—they neared their destination. The tropical azure sky displayed no more than a wisp of a cloud. Kimberly tilted the wide-brimmed hat to better shade her eyes, glad for the gauzy long-sleeve shirt covering her pale arms. Given the chance, the noon sun would burn exposed skin.

A mirror image of the sky overhead, the Bahamian waters glistened in the sunlight. She loved the changing palette of color from clear blue to transparent turquoise, allowing glimpses of the coral below. A gentle wind blew out of the northwest. Kimberly inhaled the pleasant scented sea air.

Night Thrill made steady progress, flying only the main sail. Robert handled the helm as they rounded Andros Island on a heading for Bimini. She reveled in the indulgence of watching him. Robert had discarded his shirt when the sun rose and the temperature soared. Her gaze slid over his torso. Sleek tanned skin, glossy from a sheen of perspiration, pulled taut over tight muscles that flexed with every move. Desire gathered low in her belly.

He looked over from the wheel and smiled. Her breath hitched and she felt love for him in every cell of her body. She wished they could sail like this always. To somewhere else though, not to their current destination.

Without warning, the breeze quit. Completely stilled. Kimberly jumped into action, tending the sail while Robert engaged the engine. He shot her a strange unnerving glance as he shrugged into a black linen shirt.

She swallowed apprehensively and moved to stand beside him. "What is it?"

"The compass is going haywire. Spinning wildly." His tone of voice revealed growing excitement.

Kimberly chewed on the edge of her lip, taut with anticipation. They'd been waiting for something to happen, though she hadn't really believed the stories. The contents of her stomach shimmied. Was she ready to confront the unknown?

A cool mist advanced, quickly developing into dense fog, which expanded into an enormous semicircle not five hundred yards off deck.

"The RPM's are dropping," Robert reported.

The boat slowed to a near idle. Kimberly's stomach lurched. She glanced at her watch. The second hand had stopped moving. She tapped on the crystal. Nothing.

She reached for Robert's hand. "It'll be okay," she said, lacking true confidence.

Robert squeezed her fingers. "That's my brave lass."

The eerie fog swirled, encircling the sailboat yet kept a distance of about three hundred yards. Kimberly glimpsed the clear sky in the center—bright blue with no clouds. It was as if they were caught in the eye of a mellow storm.

Without warning, a large mass burst through the edge of the milky fog to hover about thirty feet above the surface of the water off their port side, throwing a huge shadow. The air smelled different. Like after a thunderstorm.

"What the hell is that?" Kimberly whispered.

"I dinnae ken." Robert wrapped an arm around her shoulder, pulling her tight to his side.

The elliptical shaped *thing* began to vibrate. She held her breath. A soft whirring broke the unnatural quiet. Lights on the bottom of the object flashed, alternating between red, green, blue, and white.

Off the sailboat's bow, a hole opened in the fog, exposing a tunnel of sorts with swirling mist walls. Before Kimberly could blink, the floating object entered the opening and vanished. Just as quick, the tunnel entrance closed.

"Wow. Was that real?" Kimberly asked.

"I am not certain, but I read an eyewitness report within Patrice's notes describing a similar sighting."

"Do you think it was a UFO?"

"I hope not. If it was, then *this* isn't a time portal." Robert gave her arm a squeeze.

"It could still be. If the portal could take us back in time, why couldn't it also bring someone, or in this case, an object from the future to our time?"

Robert released her and rubbed the back of his neck. "This is all a wee unnerving, though, you make an excellent point. But then again, it could have been from another galaxy or a dimension of which we have nae knowledge."

Kimberly retrieved the cell phone from a hidden pocket in the boy's pants she wore. Robert's eyes narrowed. He probably thought she planned to call for help. Even if she wanted to, they weren't close enough to land.

"You shouldn't have that. If we make it to the past... Ach, well, I hate to think what would happen to you if someone found your cell phone."

"I didn't plan to take it with me. Just wanted to see if it still worked." She depressed the On button. Nothing. "It's dead." She tossed the useless phone into a small compartment under the wheel.

Time dragged. The fog slowly swirled closer. Kimberly kept checking her watch, but it wasn't working. She took it off. "I guess I shouldn't be wearing a watch either."

"Get rid of anything from the present time."

As she checked her pockets to ensure she hadn't accidentally picked up something that didn't belong in the past, the amount of blue sky overhead shrank to nothing more than a small circle over the cockpit. Then the milky haze overtook even that tiny bright spot.

A fine mist moistened her face, and she tasted salt on her lips. The fog rolled across the deck, thickening and becoming darker and heavier as strands of vapor swirled around equipment and through openings. Visibility declined to mere inches.

Kimberly felt as if chilly fingers reached for her from

within the ominous fog. She grabbed Robert's hand. "Please don't let go of me. I'm frightened."

"I will keep you safe." He wrapped muscular arms around her and pulled her back against his broad chest. "Remember to talk in the lad's voice you practiced and if we get separated, tell anyone who finds you that you are my nephew, Ian, my cabin lad."

"Okay."

Abruptly, she heard whispering within the fog.

"Ahoy there. Is anyone aboard?" The disembodied voice made her shiver.

Kimberly pressed tighter against Robert and the heat of his body. "Did you hear that?"

"Aye," he said, voice muffled against her damp hair.

Within the fog, someone whistled a jig-like tune. The haze dissipated slightly. Three men dressed in old-fashion aviator gear stood off the bow of the sailboat as if they walked on water. One saluted, and then they all vanished into the vaporous mist.

"Oh. My. God." Gooseflesh prickled the length of Kimberly's arms. She leaned into Robert's strength. "You did see that, didn't you? I read about flight crews being lost in the forties."

"I saw." He gave a gentle squeeze. "I am certain we will see more unusual sights before our adventure is complete. Are you still willing?"

Kimberly took a deep, settling breath. She wasn't letting him go alone. "Yeah."

"Good lass." He brought her down with him, and they settled on a cockpit bench.

The temperature dropped. Her blouse became soaked from the moist air and the cold seeped into her bones. Her teeth started to chatter.

"You're freezing." Robert opened the storage lazarette beside them, drew out an oiled canvas jacket, and helped her into the sleeves. When she was snug within the fabric, they resumed position with Robert hugging her from behind.

"Have I told you recently how much I respect you?" Love glowed in Robert's tone. "How brave I think you are?"

"Thanks for the reminder."

He kissed the top of her head, brushing lips across her hair. His arms wrapped her within comforting warmth. She sighed with contentment and burrowed closer.

Secure within Robert's arms, Kimberly dozed until he stiffened. She flipped her eyes open. Not five feet off the starboard side of *Night Thrill* floated an intricately carved, wooden sailing vessel. The entire ship lay swathed in long strands of clinging seaweed, even the three rows of unmanned oars.

"What is that?"

"A Corinthian trireme...I think." The boat rammed the side of *Night Thrill*, tossing them onto the deck. Robert clambered up only to lose balance as the two boats bumped again. He finally got his feet under him and stood. "Dinnae move."

"Don't leave me. I—"

The fog twirled, spinning fast, picking water up from the sea, tossing *Night Thrill* on its side. Long tendrils of kelp wrapped around Kimberly and tugged her away from Robert as seawater rushed across the deck. She reached for his hand, but their fingers slid apart as they both toppled overboard. A strong force dragged at her body, pulling her downward through a spiraling tunnel comprised of the oppressive haze.

She choked on the scream of terror caught in her throat as the world spun.

CHAPTER TWENTY-TWO

Port Royal Harbor, Jamaica, 1715

Robert landed hard, the wind knocked from his lungs. A haze engulfed him. Distorted voices teased his mind. *Kimberly.* Where was Kimberly?

He shook off the numb fog. Sensation returned slowly. With it, long forgotten memories. The touch of wet homespun against skin. The comforting strength of the oak deck beneath his arse. And pain. Skull splitting pain.

His head throbbed. His chest ached. His hands stung.

He inhaled, but found it difficult to breath. Rough hands grasped his shoulders and dragged him into a sitting position. Seawater splashed over his face, ran into his eyes. He choked and coughed and spit out foul swill.

With effort, he cracked crusty lids. His eyes burned, as did his palms. When his stinging vision cleared, he held up his hands to see why they hurt. He stared in surprise at the unexpected cuts and rope burns. Slashes across the palms oozed blood.

His blood? He reached deep within for the healing power of the vampire. Nothing. *Satan be damned.* He was no longer vampire. He searched his mind for the panther and found no beast within. The animal was gone. He'd really traveled to the past, to a time before the curse.

A coughing spasm wracked his lungs. Through tears, he glimpsed his grinning men. The quartermaster, Mr. Cox, held the wooden bucket from which they had doused him. Robert shook his wet hair like a shaggy dog, spraying those who didn't scramble away with enough speed.

His hair? What the devil? Wet strands stuck to his face. No longer clipped close to the scalp, his hair hung long, the way it had when he'd been a young man.

"What happened?" Robert demanded. A strangled chuckle escaped Cox. He reached out and Robert grabbed hold of the offered hand, allowing the man to pull him to his feet.

"Ye were fixin' the riggin' and fell."

"Where is Kimberly?"

The seamen glanced at each other uneasily.

"Kimberly?" Jamie Cox looked dubious.

"Aye. The woman with whom I traveled."

"Captain, ye must have done damage to that hard head of yers when ye fell if yer thinkin' there is a woman aboard this ship."

A tight band wrapped around Robert's heart and squeezed. Where in blazing hell was Kimberly?

"Kimberly!" The name tore from his throat and he shouted it into the wind.

Fear crawled around in his gut, stealing his breath. Panting, feeling frantic, Robert grabbed the nearest crewmember by the front of the shirt and lifted him above the deck until his feet dangled. "You have not seen my woman?"

The man's eyes bugged, and he shook his head.

Strong arms seized Robert from behind and dragged him back. Even though he no longer felt the panther within, a growl erupted from deep in his chest and he dropped the mate to fight off the one who held him in a powerful grip.

"What the hell has come over ye, Captain?" Cox spoke close to his ear. Like a switch snapping on, sanity returned.

"Release me," Robert said, the tone a quiet demand.

Cox's hold lessened. Robert shrugged off the man's grasp, inhaled a deep breath and looked at the wary men scrutinizing him as if he were crazy. He spun and pinned the quartermaster with a fierce stare. "Where is my cabin lad?"

The man shifted his feet, glanced at the gaping men, and murmured softly, "Ye dinnae have a cabin lad, Captain."

"Aye, I do." Robert swept a glare over the men watching him. "Dinnae you have work?"

The seamen scattered, mumbling under their breaths as they went back to their duties. Bloody Hell. He acted a fool in front of the crew. He had better come up with a plausible reason why he'd thought there were a woman and a cabin lad aboard.

"Mr. Cox, precede me to my cabin and I will explain about my missing stowaway."

* * *

A couple of days passed yet Robert didn't find Kimberly. Fear clawed at his insides. She had better be safe somewhere or he would kill anyone who dared harm her.

And if she didn't make it through the time warp? Well, he refused to even consider the consequences. His fingers curled into fists from angry frustration as he followed Mr. Page along the quiet corridor to the Governor's private office.

"Your cabin lad is lost, you say?"

"Aye. Have there been any reports of a lad, a stranger to these climes, wandering about?"

Mr. Page made a nasal sound, a snort of sorts. "Lads run away all the time and disappear. Many take up with pirates."

"My nephew did not run away."

"That as it may be, we have heard nary a tale." He stopped in front of a small door. "Here we are."

Robert rubbed the ache in his chest and clenched his jaw. No one he'd spoken to admitted knowing anything about a strange lad roaming the island. What had happened to Kimberly?

"Captain MacLachlan to meet with you, Your Excellency," said the somber little deputy secretary after he opened the door.

Robert ducked his head and entered sideways to fit through the narrow threshold to the office.

His Excellency, Lord Archibald Hamilton, Governor of Jamaica, stood and dipped into a quick bow. "Welcome."

Even though much shorter than Robert, and slighter of build, the man exuded his noble lineage by the arrogant way he held himself. His tightly curled brown wig hung loose to the shoulders of a faultlessly tailored long coat of the finest blue cloth. Dark judgmental eyes peered at Robert from above a sharp nose and full lips.

"Thank you, Your Excellency." Robert bent at the waist and held the bow for a moment longer than the governor had as a sign of respect.

"Archibald. Please. Use my given name, and I shall address you by yours. Nae need for formality between fellow Scots of a like mind. At least, not here in my office. What brings you to our island, Robert?"

Robert tilted his head, indicating the deputy secretary.

"There is no need for you to remain, Mr. Page. Go about your business." Archibald followed the man to the door.

"May we speak freely?" Robert asked once Mr. Page's footsteps faded.

Archibald closed the heavy wooden door. He motioned to a chair for Robert and sat behind the ornately carved desk. "Proceed."

Robert undid the lower buttons of both his long coat and waistcoat and, flipping the flaps out of the way, sat. *Damn bothersome garments.* He brushed a piece of lint from his breeches and looked into the expectant gaze of His Excellency.

"Campbell's men dogged my steps in Glasgow, making it impossible for me to further our cause," Robert said. "Arrest was eminent. My brother feared they'd make an example of me to discourage other would be rebels."

He inwardly cringed, never having liked to think of what he'd risked, running arms from France to Scotland. A gruesome punishment awaited a convicted rebel in the Britain of the early eighteenth century. Hung by the neck until you passed out. Revived. Forced to watch as they ripped out your entrails. Then to be sliced into pieces for public exhibition. Not a romantic fate.

Though one faced by many a Scottish hero.

"My brother thought you might find a use for my ship and my services."

"How is Lachlan?"

"Ach, well, he plans to lead the MacLachlan men when James lands in Britain."

"Splendid. What do you ken of my plan to finance a wee Scottish navy with His Majesty's funds?"

Robert made an effort to appear surprised. He'd sailed around the world, partaking of despicable activities after his turning, but actually knew a great deal about Lord Hamilton's Jacobite plotting, having had nearly three hundred years to research and analyze every historical detail of the failed rebellion. He wanted to tell his fellow compatriot that their efforts would only cause heartache. However, Patrice's notes provided a stern warning not to change history.

He must only alter events directly related to the Voodoo curse.

There had been a time, before he knew better, when he believed participating in the secret plot to overthrow King George I of Britain and replace him with James Stuart, the Old Chevalier, a noble duty. Now Robert's life was more complicated.

He would play his small role in history, find Kimberly, stop the Voodoo priestess from performing the curse, and return Kimberly to her own time. His gut tightened. He'd never explained his belief to her. But he felt certain, once the curse was reversed, he would live the rest of his days in the eighteenth century without the love of his life. Maybe he would even die for the Jacobite cause.

Because of the curse, Robert's name didn't appear anywhere within the written history of the time. He often wondered what role he was to have played had LaRoux and Zola not interfered.

"Would it meet with your approval to serve as a privateer in my fleet?" Archibald's question jolted him from the morbid thoughts. He sat up straight to listen.

"I see I've spurred your interest." The governor smiled broadly before continuing. "When the local merchants came to me, complaining of the seizing of Jamaican vessels by Spanish armed pirates and demanded of me armed protection," his dark blue eyes gleamed with excitement, "it occurred to me to replace the naval warships that have been called back to Britain with privateers."

The sound of footsteps from outside the closed door caused both men to stare at the heavy wood panel.

"Perhaps we should continue our discussion in my library at home this evening."

"Aye." Robert stood.

"Of course, you'll join us for dinner afterward. My lovely wife, Anne, has planned a soiree to introduce her new ward to our friends and associates. The gathering will provide the opportunity to meet both our supporters and our adversaries."

Robert swept into a low bow. "I look forward to the occasion."

* * *

While attending the governor that evening at his great house, fear festered within Robert's soul. What had happened to Kimberly?

A humid waft of air rustled the sheer curtains at the open window and twilight shadows played across the garden beyond. The alluring floral perfume, heavy in the air, twisted Robert's gut. He needed to find her. Protect her. Make things right for her.

He'd made a bad decision. He never should have allowed her to attempt passage to the past. She'd been a brave lass. He prayed to find Kimberly soon, unharmed, and send her back to the future where she belonged.

Though the separation would break his heart.

Carefully handling the glass in his hand to avoid spilling its contents, he turned from the tropical display of pristine white blooms and dense foliage. Away from thoughts of his love. He needed to concentrate in order to play his role tonight. Human wolves prowled the room.

Memories of his past—present—were faulty at best. The

only recourse for how to react to the emerging events was to rely on instinct. Earlier, before the others had arrived, he'd agreed to accept the commission offered by Lord Hamilton. Robert wasn't sure where such an act would lead.

He prayed he'd know when and where it was the right time and place to alter events that would keep Zola from performing the Voodoo curse. He must stop her from unleashing Séaghdha on the unsuspecting world to rampage and bring about destruction.

Robert eased his grip on the glass before he broke the damn thing. Ivory lace draped his wrists, spilling from the turned back cuffs—heavy with embroidery—of the knee-length green velvet long coat he wore. He'd forgotten how much he despised the formal garments of his past. Especially the silly stockings. He missed his black jeans, silk shirts, and sleek leather jacket. Robert tapped a foot. He'd much prefer to be wearing heavy modern boots rather than the ridiculous buckled shoes that pinched. He swallowed hard and kept the grimace from showing on his face.

He had to keep a clear mind. On the morrow, he would join the ranks of Captains Barnet, Jennings, and Fernando. Robert and his crew would harass the Spaniards and hunt pirates and, if luck was with him, secure a bounty to help finance Archibald's navy. However, for the moment, he would glean all he could from the proceedings.

Robert discreetly observed the political interplay from where he leaned against the library wall, mastering a pose of boredom, pretending a greater interest in the ruby liquid in the tumbler in his hand than in the dozen well-dressed men attending His Excellency. It was amazing how quickly the game of intrigue came back to him. He enjoyed another taste of wine, savoring its rich flavor, something he couldn't enjoy as a vampire shifter without the wall of his stomach shredding to pieces. He drank the last of it and deposited the empty glass on a passing server's tray.

Dressed in pristine livery, the ebony-skinned man didn't flex a facial muscle as he moved on.

Robert's gaze drifted to Mr. Heywood, a member of the

governing council, and Robert quickly decided the man wasn't to be trusted. He surveyed the others. Several of the men, merchants mostly, complained to the governor, demanding immediate action to protect the trade of the island from piratical design.

"The hostilities perpetrated by the Spanish backed pirates continue unhindered. The seas are now more perilous than during the war." The rotund Mr. Proctor's voice rose and his face mottled to a deep purple. "And that barbarous Frenchman, Jacque LaRoux, terrorizes the waters off our coast. Last month alone, I lost a large vessel richly laden with cargo to that cutthroat."

LaRoux. A tremor ran along Robert's spine and he gnashed his molars. His fateful run-in with the notorious red-haired Frenchman had set into action the events that changed Robert's life for eternity. Several years ago, prior to the time where he currently found himself, Robert had come upon the corsair while running goods—tobacco mostly—between Virginia and Glasgow.

The redheaded pirate had attacked Robert's ship, raising the skull and crossbones along with the red flag, declaring a battle to the death. Robert had turned tail and run, not wanting to endanger his men or the precious cargo. LaRoux stayed on him. The ensuing battle turned fierce, until a lucky cannon strike hit the powder reserves in the hull of LaRoux's ship and it exploded into toothpicks. They'd found no survivors. LaRoux escaped before the blast. The man held a grudge and a burning desire for vengeance.

The paneled doors swung open, ending Robert's reminiscing. The butler called the men to join the ladies for the evening meal, thus concluding the savage talk of depredations and plundering and robberies at the hands of pirates.

Robert entered the hall and suffered the sensation of being gut-punched.

The young man to his right snickered. "I see this is your first glimpse of our delicious new belle, Mistress—"

"My God!" Robert rushed forward, but stopped short. Her eyes went wide and her beloved features marred with confusion.

"Do you know me, sir?" The familiar voice trembled.

His Excellency laid a hand on Robert's arm. "Do you ken the lass, MacLachlan?"

The hopeful expression Kimberly wore cut Robert to the core. He didn't want to deny her, but needed to understand their situation better before revealing himself or exposing her.

"My apologies, Mistress. I thought you were someone else."

His chest tightened with the disappointment clouding her melted chocolate eyes. Eyes, he missed gazing into. Damn, their journey in time had gone afoul.

What had their time traveling set into motion? He hoped she wouldn't say or do anything foolish that would indict her as a witch.

"I'm afraid I've had an unfortunate accident, sir." A haunted gaze settled on His Excellency's wife, Lady Anne.

The petite woman put a protective arm around Kimberly's waist and smiled at Robert. "Mistress Kimberly was thrown into the sea and washed up on our beach where several of our workers found her. She cannot remember how she came to be here, or from where she came. Nor can she remember a family name. We hoped you might know her."

Robert inclined his head politely. "I am verra sorry, Mistress Kimberly. From a distance, you reminded me of someone I once kenned. On closer inspection, I see I was mistaken. You are far more beautiful." He reached for her gloved hand. "Now that we have met..." He kissed the air above the fingers. "I hope in the future you will consider me as your champion."

Kimberly blushed, lowering her head as she withdrew the hand. "Thank you, sir. You are too kind."

When she raised her gaze, Robert experienced that familiar ache in his heart. He had to make things right.

During dinner, it was impossible to keep his gaze from drifting to Kimberly. God had designed her body to wear the costume of the time and lure men to their untimely demise like mermaids in seagoing myths.

Her rose-colored gown was more than fetching. Not that he minded the pants or shorts or short skirts, or the colorful blouses she usually wore. But damn, the way the silk of the gown hugged her curves and plunged low at her breast with a crimped frill was sinfully decadent, yet she exuded a hint of innocence with her hair piled atop her head in glistening brown curls, pleasantly devoid of the smelly powder most women wore.

He shifted in his seat and clenched a fist under the table. If the cad to her right didn't remove his gaze from her bosom soon, there would be one more eunuch limping through its life.

"Captain MacLachlan, are you enjoying the swan?"

Robert inhaled a deep breath and forced a civil smile for the blond chit sitting beside him.

"Aye, that I am, lass." Though it was the beautiful swan across the table he enjoyed, not the meat on his plate.

His dinner partner chattered on disclosing inconsequential gossip about the planters and merchants who made Jamaica home. Bored beyond endurance, Robert returned his gaze to Kimberly, and she blushed. Thank the good Lord. She was still attracted to him.

How would he survive the rest of the damn meal? Watching her made his breeches tight. He shifted uncomfortably and forced a smile at something his dinner partner said. Finally, the men rose from the table to retire to the library to smoke and drink brandy. Robert lazily followed. When he passed Kimberly's chair he nonchalantly leaned in.

"Dance with me later," he whispered near her ear.

She gave a quick nod, and he watched a blush creep up her lovely neck.

Before Robert left the room, he noticed a speculative expression sweep across Lady Anne's gracious features. Did he have an ally?

* * *

Heat flashed across Kimberly's chest. Man, she wanted to grab him, curl up into his body and stay there. Like the others, Robert believed she had amnesia. If she weren't scared, she'd tease him for a while, letting him continue to believe she didn't remember him.

It wasn't the terrified-out-of-her-mind kind of scared. Kimberly knew she wasn't in danger of physical harm. Her fear was more of the holy-shit-what's-coming-at-me-next kind of scared. She desperately needed to feel Robert's arms around her. Have him assure her everything would be all right. When they danced later, she would tell him the truth.

Kimberly never had the chance to pretend she was a ship's cabin boy as they'd planned. She fabricated a believable story after she awoke naked in bed at the governor's home and learned Lady Anne had already discovered her gender. The lost memory story popped into her head when Anne explained how slaves found her unconscious on the beach, wrapped her in cloth and delivered her to an aide of the governor.

Not only did faking amnesia explain why she didn't know how she ended up in the ocean, but she could also blame it for a lack of knowledge of the cultural mores of the time.

Her skin prickled and she glanced up. Lady Anne stared at her, an assessing glimmer in intelligent gray eyes. Kimberly bit her lip. Maybe she wasn't a very good actress.

"Ladies, shall we retire to the ballroom and wait for the men to tire of discussing business and politics and join us?" Lady Anne gracefully rose while a servant held out her chair.

"If we wait until then, we will never see the men again," Lady Strafford quipped, flicking a fan open as she, too, displayed inbred poise while rising from her chair.

The younger women giggled behind the flash of their bejeweled fans.

Kimberly worried her bottom lip. She wasn't comfortable with the period gown or shoes or accessories. Though thankfully, when the servant slid her chair back, she managed to stand and follow the others from the dining room without falling on her ass and causing an embarrassing scene.

As a kid, she'd loved to play dress up. But trying to act

the part of a genteel early eighteenth century lady seemed far beyond her acting ability. These women made it an art.

She perched on the edge of an ornate sofa, hoping to be left alone. Unfortunately, the young woman with the tight powdered blond curls who'd been partnered with Robert during dinner joined her in a quiver of silk cloth.

"Mistress, Kimberly, I ken I am being forward, not waiting for an introduction, but I wanted to meet you after hearing about your situation. Must be harrowing, not kenning who you are. Oh, I should introduce myself. I am Jane, daughter of Lord Chalmers."

Kimberly swallowed. How had Lady Anne instructed her to address a Lord's daughter? Oh, what the hell. "A pleasure to meet you."

"Is it true? You dinnae ken where you came from or who your father is?"

"Not at the moment." The irony of the situation brought a half-smile to Kimberly's lips.

"Captain MacLachlan is taken with you," Jane said as she settled in. "He watched you all during dinner."

"I don't think—"

"You have only been here a couple of days and you have already captured the interest of the only eligible bachelor on the island worth pursuing." Plump lips produced the most precious pout. "My father will be annoyed with me. He wanted me to catch the captain's eye."

"Why?" The word flew out of Kimberly's mouth before she could stop it.

"For a match, silly. Father had hoped for a joining of our clans." Jane spread the skirt of her ice blue gown out to drape around her as if she were getting ready to have a picture taken. "Dinnae worry, I will not compete with you. The others will try to gain his attentions, but I promise I will remain your friend. Captain MacLachlan is too dark and dangerous for me. I want to marry a sweet man with a poetic heart."

"How lovely."

"Scandalous, actually."

Kimberly's expression must have given away her confusion because the twit felt the need to explain.

"Captain MacLachlan, I mean. He never wears a wig or powders his hair. Disgraceful. Oh, I am sorry, you dinnae powder yours either."

"I'm allergic. Makes me sneeze."

The young woman wrinkled her nose then leaned in close, blue eyes glistening.

"I should not tell you this." She glanced at the other ladies who were absorbed in coy conversations.

Kimberly smiled fully. Of course, the simpering fool would tell her what she didn't care to know. She pretended interest.

"I should not even know about the place, but there is an alcove in the garden behind the house designed for lovers," Jane whispered from behind the ivory and blue silk fan she expertly fluttered for effect. Then she proceeded to describe the garden and explain how to find the secluded niche.

God, these women flirted. With the way they acted, it didn't matter whether the men joined them. The women seemed more intent on impressing each other than attracting a man.

The doors opened and three men entered carrying musical instruments. After tuning the strings, they started to play. Shortly afterward, the male guests filed into the room. Kimberly searched for Robert, but he wasn't with them nor was the governor.

Couples danced in a country style. She remembered seeing similar dance steps when attending a dance demonstration at a Scottish festival at Old Westbury Gardens in Long Island while visiting friends of her father. She started tapping a high-heeled, slippered foot to the music and an awkward uneasiness settled in, making her feel a bit like a wallflower as she had in grammar school when no boys asked her to dance.

Then she caught the eye of the gentleman who'd sat next to her at dinner. Just great. The conceited jerk would probably ask her to dance. She glanced around nervously, planning to escape before he approached.

She rose to flee and almost ran smack into Robert's broad chest. She'd been so intent on watching the dancers and then her dinner partner's approach she hadn't seen Robert walk up from the side. Thankfully, he grasped an elbow, steadying her, keeping her from falling.

After releasing her, Robert bowed. "Will you honor me with this dance, Mistress Kimberly?"

She bobbed her head and allowed him to escort her to the floor, positive she was making a big mistake. How would she dance in the heavy long skirt? She could hardly walk without fear of tripping. However, after he bowed and she curtsied, she quickly picked up the steps as the movements resembled line dancing, and the skirts flowed with her as she swirled. They merged and stepped with the other dancers, separating and coming back together.

He looked marvelous in the period clothing. The high collar of the forest green velvet coat and the ivory cloth at his throat set off a dark tan, making him appear more handsome than ever. He smiled. Oh, my. He no longer had a scar across his cheek. The tawny long hair pulled back in a queue—that would make any modern woman envious— enhanced the now smooth skin of his face. Her stomach did a little hop.

Their fingers briefly touched. A thrill tingled along Kimberly's arm. Her breath caught as their gazes met. She couldn't hold the contact. The concern evident in Robert's eyes made her feel guilty for the charade, but she'd explain things as soon as they had a moment alone.

She noticed Lady Anne standing beyond the dancers, speaking with her husband. Kimberly swallowed awkwardly, hating she'd deceived the sweet woman.

Robert danced off as they changed partners again. Kimberly laughed, amazed she hadn't tripped over her skirts. The stress from days of worrying and fearing for Robert slipped away and she smiled at him when the steps brought the dancers in a circle to return to their original partners and the music ended. Without a word, he placed a hand on her lower back and whisked her away, through the open doors and onto the terrace.

CHAPTER TWENTY-THREE

Kimberly's warmth penetrated the flesh of Robert's palm as he escorted her to the far edge of the terrace. A shot of lust tightened already-taut muscles.

"I ken this is highly improper. I should not take you away from your chaperone." His voice too gravelly, he cleared a dry throat. "Ach, well, I hoped we could share a word in private."

"I know of a secluded spot in the garden where no one will overhear us." Kimberly's brown eyes held a curious gold glimmer. Mischief?

Was she flirting?

Robert flicked his gaze toward the candlelit room beyond the open doors. Yellow light fell onto the stone of the terrace near the doorway, fortunately he and Kimberly where well hidden from view within the shadows. No one seemed to have noticed their departure.

"Will you show me the way?" he asked, hesitant, the teasing gleam in her eyes making him uneasy. For God's sakes, she didn't know him. She shouldn't be looking at him that way.

Her tongue slipped out and moistened her lips, causing his insides to flame. His need to hold her close chased away all doubt.

"Please." He wasn't beyond begging her favor.

She took his hand, and he followed along after her like an obedient puppy following its beloved mistress. Robert kept a smile to himself, glad Kimberly didn't know how to behave properly. A well-bred lady of this time would never take a man, stranger or not, alone into a garden unless...

She planned to be ruined?

Hmmm. Was it possible Kimberly believed she was an eighteenth century lass and planned to trap a wealthy husband? Robert grinned. Now there was an idea.

Torches burned throughout the garden to light the way. They walked along a path laid with fragments of shells, through a courtyard with a fountain where carved stone mermaids swam, to a secluded garden alcove with a stone bench and tall shrubbery for walls. Kimberly yanked him within and before he took a breath, her lips pressed against his and stole the air from his lungs.

Blood rushed through his veins, heading south. Their tongues met, and all he knew was texture and sensation and the fire in his loins. He slipped arms around a slim waist, lowered his hands until he felt the luscious curve of her bottom through the layer of skirts, and drew her forward against a stiff arousal. Instead of pulling away and slapping him, as any young lass should, she melted into him.

His conscience flared. But if she didn't know who he was, she shouldn't be kissing him, dammit. Anger replaced the feelings of guilt, and he released her from the embrace, ending the kiss and stepping away.

"God, I missed you," she said breathlessly.

"What?" Sluggish to process the meaning of the words, he slowly un-flexed the fists he'd unconsciously formed.

"I was scared I'd never see you again." She grabbed the lapels of his long coat and kissed him again. Hard. A kiss that branded his soul.

When the kiss ended, he took a moment to compose himself before speaking. "I dinnae understand. I thought you did not recognize me. That you did not ken who I am or anything of yourself."

"I'll explain." She led him by the hand to the bench and sat. Then she patted the seat beside her. "Please, sit with me."

Confusion made Robert dizzy. Maybe he should act upon the suggestion and join her on the bench. He slapped back the flaps of his coats and sat. "Mistress, I—"

She placed a gloved finger to his lips for a brief moment. "I know who you are."

"You do?" His voice sounded strangely shrill.

"Of course, I'm only pretending to have amnesia or *brain fever* as they call it." Kimberly removed her gloves, placing them in her lap.

A rush of relief allowed him to breathe more easily. "What happened?" After she explained the circumstances of the rescue from the beach and the later meeting with Lady Anne, he understood the sense in the lie. "Good thinking."

"Thanks. Why do you imagine we became separated?"

"Could be my ship acted as an anchor for me and you did not have anything in this time to draw you, to ground you in this time."

"Glad that's over." Kimberly ran a hand over his smooth cheek. "Your scar is gone."

"Aye. The French pirate cut my face the night the curse transformed me." Robert chuckled. "I could have used my vampire powers to disguise the disfiguration, but instead I chose to leave the damaged flesh visible."

"Why?"

"Ach, well. The clumsy attempts of strangers not to stare reminded me of my blunder. 'Twas a warning never to underestimate an opponent."

"You were too hard on yourself."

Robert released a breath and shook his head. "Nae. LaRoux is dangerous and I was a fool."

"Have you heard any mention of him since you've returned?"

"Rumor has him stalking the coast."

She sighed, exhaling a heavy flow of air, and lowered her gaze.

Robert removed the hand from his cheek and brought the palm to his lips. Kimberly shivered in response. Then she tugged the ribbon from his hair. The strands fell around his shoulders in waves. She grasped a handful and playfully tugged. "I like it."

Did he actually suffer the heat of a blush burning his cheeks? She'd unman him if he let her.

"Robert, I can't bear waiting another moment. I need to feel you inside me."

"Here?" Of course, his throbbing erection proved he wanted her too. But not here. Not where someone could stumble upon them.

The hair ribbon dropped from her fingers. The green velvet fluttered to the ground to land beside the bench. Her rose-colored gloves followed.

He met her gaze. Golden flecks sparkled within the brown, hinting at the sexual hunger burning there. His chest tightened and he found it hard to breathe.

"Please." She slowly raised her skirt hem, inch by excruciating inch.

The mere sight of her ankle made his arousal hard as stone. The line of her calf—

"Bloody hell, Kimberly, I dinnae think we should." He dragged a hand through his hair.

"I don't see why not. It's dark, and I'm not wearing any panties under this gown. I need to feel you're real and not a figment of my imagination."

His cock spasmed, and he groaned. She was killing him with her logic. He rose from the seat, and she hiked up her skirt over her knees, showing more leg as she straddled the bench. When she started bunching the rose fabric at her waist, he looked away and released a strangled breath. He scanned the area surrounding the alcove.

"Not here." He took her hand and pulled her up from the bench. "Come." The word was a guttural command.

Kimberly stood, skirt dropping to hide her tantalizing flesh. He led her along another garden path and onto the manicured lawn.

* * *

Lady Anne stifled an unpleasant shudder when she glimpsed Lord Chalmers' young daughter approaching. The lass looked as if she were a pampered cat who'd swallowed her mistress's favorite canary and knew no punishment awaited. The girl dropped into a quick curtsy.

"Lady and Lord Hamilton, I would not normally tattle on an acquaintance, but I fear for the reputation of Mistress Kimberly." The veiled accusation rushed from pursed lips.

Anne gasped. How dare Jane start a scandal?

"What has happened?" Archibald asked. "Explain yourself, lass."

"I am sure 'tis naught to concern us, dear." Anne placed a soothing hand on her husband's arm, hoping to cool the heat of the girl's jealous words.

"Oh, but it is. I observed the infamous scoundrel, Captain MacLachlan, boldly escort Mistress Kimberly from the terrace into the shadows of the garden. Someone must protect her from the likes of him."

No one needed to protect Kimberly from Robert. More likely, he would shield her from others who would prey on a lost woman. He was known to be of unquestionable honor.

"Do you accuse Captain MacLachlan of indecent action against our ward?" Archibald demanded.

Jane Chalmers sniffled and raised a hand to her chest in a good imitation of feminine concern. "I am so verra afeared for Mistress Kimberly. She doesn't seem right in the head, if you ken my meaning. She might not understand the need to resist a wayward advance."

Archibald stiffened. His face flushed red. "The man dares to take advantage of my hospitality?"

"Let us not come to a hasty conclusion. Kimberly is probably only showing the good captain the gardens." Anne attempted to lighten the dramatics. She dropped the hand from Archibald's sleeve and glared at Jane.

"The brain fever has obviously impaired her good sense," Archibald said then turned to the Chalmers girl and patted her arm in a fatherly fashion. "Dinnae worry yourself, lass, I will personally handle the situation."

"Now, Archibald, I think you overreact." Anne loved her husband dearly, but once he got a bur in his breeches, he was impossible.

"You must come with me, my dear, in case a woman's touch is required. Heaven knows, I have been accused of being too gruff on occasion and your ward is of a sensitive nature." He gently grasped Anne's elbow. "We will find Mistress Kimberly and ensure her safety."

Archibald escorted Anne through the doors and onto the terrace. To her annoyance, Jane followed in their wake. Fortunately, none of the other guests noticed the commotion and joined in the search.

The crunch of shells beneath their feet grated on Anne's already annoyed sensibilities. She'd never cared much for the Chalmers lass and the girl had given Anne more reason to dislike her. They strode the garden paths in all directions and found no sign of the young couple.

Anne tugged on her husband's arm as they entered the mermaid alcove. "See, Archibald, false alarm, they are not in the garden."

Jane released a squeal of delight and bent to pick something up from the ground.

"Well, they *were* here." She held a green velvet ribbon, a color matching the long coat Captain MacLachlan wore, and a pair of rose-colored gloves as if she'd won a prize at a fair. Anne stifled a smile, recognizing the gloves as the ones she lent to Kimberly. Maybe she wouldn't need to push the couple together.

"Give me those," Archibald demanded. "Mistress Jane, return to the house."

The girl reluctantly relinquished her treasure to Archibald, and he slapped the gloves against a thigh. "My lady and I will ensure nae harm comes to our ward."

* * *

Kimberly's heels sank into the lawn. She kicked off a shoe and bent to remove the stocking, wobbled and slowly rolled the thick silk down her calf and off, dropping it on the ground. A strangled masculine gasp made her smile and she looked at Robert from beneath lowered lashes. His nostrils flared, and he groaned. Although he sounded like a wounded animal, laughter danced in his eyes.

"Come here. Let me lean on you." She flipped off the

second rose-colored silk slipper.

Kimberly held onto Robert's upper arm with one hand and slid the remaining stocking off with the other, tossing it onto the lawn to join the first. The cool grass tickled her toes, not the luxurious softness of Kentucky Blue, more the coarse feel of Bermuda grass, but pleasant all the same. They waltzed across the lawn, holding each other close, and Kimberly laughed aloud as Robert whirled her into the tropical forest. He chuckled, too, the husky sound pure pleasure to her ears.

She breathed in the unique scent of ocean and woods and gazed at the man she loved. "I was terrified when I thought I was lost in time, alone. Afraid I'd never see you again, Robert. Afraid I'd never return home. Afraid... Well, enough to say, I was frightened."

"I am sorry. I never should have allowed you to accompany me on this quest."

"I don't want an apology. You had no choice. I wasn't about to stay behind." She gave him one of her speed smiles. "Now that we've found each other everything will be okay."

"How can you say that? We have my worst night terror yet to face."

"Then we'll face the worst together." She grasped his upper arms and squeezed before releasing him. "No more talk about nightmares, at least for now. I want to make love. Please, Robert."

"I am yours to command." He waved an arm with a flourish and bent into a low bow.

She giggled, actually giggled. "You're playing the gallant to the max."

"Ach, well." He stalked toward her. A devilish twinkle glittered in his cinnamon eyes as he slowly backed her up until her rear rested against the rough bark of a large tree. He leaned in close. Heat radiated from his body as he pressed against her, surrounding her in loving warmth.

God was she glad she hadn't allowed Lady Anne to talk her into wearing one of those hoop petticoats—supposedly all the rage on the streets of London. The tight corset was bad enough.

Robert's mouth slanted over hers, and she forgot about women's undergarments. Their kiss—wet, potent, deep—made her bare toes curl into the dirt at the base of the tree. She could feel each quick breath he took as if it were her own. The rhythm of their hearts raced at the same breakneck speed.

He tasted delicious—the peachy fruit of the brandy he'd drank. He smelled good too.

She felt a moment of loss when he stopped kissing her. Then his tongue caressed an earlobe and she moaned from the exquisite sensation. Desire swept through her to pool low in her belly, and lower in her womb.

"Now." She wasn't beyond begging, and she tugged on his silky hair. "I can't wait any longer."

He chuckled and lifted her skirts. Then it was as if the world thudded to a stop, faded away. The satiny rasp of his hard length entering her nearly pushed her over the edge. Pure bliss. She fought the release though, wanting the sinfully sensual sensations to last forever.

The gentle glide transformed into a frantic race. Two hearts pounded a tattoo together. A growl erupted from deep within Robert's chest, the vibration making her shiver. It wasn't the yowling of the panther but a very human, very masculine declaration of ecstasy.

Kimberly lost all control and plunged over the precipice to experience a bursting exhilaration greater than she could have imagined. When she finally floated back to earth, Robert gently held her within his embrace.

"Wow," she said when able to breath and speak again. *The single word summed up the experience nicely.*

"Indeed." Robert's exhale whispered over her damp skin.

They held on to each other, even after their pulses slowed to a normal pace. Robert didn't seem to want to let the moment go any more than she did.

When he did pull away, a chill teased her moist thighs before she dropped her wrinkled skirts. With a couple of tugs, she adjusted the bodice of the gown back into place.

Robert fiddled with the silly looking breeches, and a new blast of lust shot through her system. He took a good look into her eyes and stepped back. She caught the smile he tried to hide.

"We had better return to the party. They will have missed us by now," he said, his husky tone echoing the desire bulging against the fabric at his groin. He pulled her tight against him and gave her a hard hug before releasing her.

Robert cleared his throat and clasped her hand. They walked across the lawn, swinging arms, to where Kimberly dropped the shoes.

"I must look a wreck," she said. Hair had fallen from its pins and she tucked a wisp behind an ear. "They'll all know what we've been doing, won't they?"

Robert dropped her hand and slid a heavily lidded gaze the length of her, sending a lick of desire coursing through her body yet again. Geez. No matter how sated she was, a mere look from him made her all hot and bothered. She fanned herself.

"You look exquisite in dishabille. But you are right, 'tis obvious what we were doing."

Robert leaned in and kissed her. A quick peck then he released her. "Do you think you can sneak to your room without anyone seeing you?"

She bit her lip. "A maid told me there is a back way."

"Good." Robert reached down and picked up the discarded shoes and stockings.

"What is the meaning of this?" His Excellency, Lord Hamilton, and Lady Anne stepped from the shadows. "Captain MacLachlan, I expected better from you. You dishonor your clan, your father's good name, your position. You take advantage of my hospitality."

"I intend to make amends."

"Then you will wed?"

"Aye. 'Twill be my honor to wed Mistress Kimberly." Robert raised his chin and stared into Lord Hamilton's hard eyes.

Kimberly had never meant... She glanced at Lady Anne, hoping she would intervene. The woman shook her head. Crap. She'd only wanted to be with Robert. Kimberly couldn't let him alter the fabric of time. Endanger their quest.

She pinched his arm. "No, Robert."

The look he gave her made her close her mouth and swallow hard. Hurt flickered in his eyes before all emotion disappeared. "Dinnae you wish to marry me?"

"Yes, of course, but I thought if we married, you know..." She pleaded with her eyes, hoping for understanding. "I always thought I would get married at home."

"'Twill be a long time before we can return to Scotland." Robert continued to play the role. "I believe Lord Hamilton suggests we marry now to save you from ruination. And I must concur with him on the matter."

"I demand it," Lord Hamilton blustered. "I might not ken who your father is, my dear, but I am sure, no matter his station, we would be in complete agreement on this matter."

"Oh." She attempted to wrap her mind around the situation. If they married here, in the past, their marriage wouldn't be real. Maybe it wouldn't affect the flow of time. They would only be play-acting. Robert would be free once they returned to the twenty-first century, if he wanted to be. "Well, then, Captain MacLachlan, I accept your proposal."

A secret smile played on Robert's lips. He was probably thinking of the wedding night. She bit her lip so she wouldn't grin.

"Good. Good. All settled," Lord Archibald said in a gruff tone then turned to his wife. "Can we make arrangements for tomorrow?"

"Yes, husband." She clapped her hands close to her chest. "I believe we can." A twinkle of laughter lit the woman's dove gray eyes.

Kimberly snatched her shoes from Robert, curtsied, and fled for her room, leaving Robert to deal with Lord and Lady Hamilton and *the arrangements*. She briskly strode across the lawn to the manor house and then slowed to walk along the length of the back wall. Where is it? She knew the door the maid mentioned had to be there somewhere. She ran a hand over smooth stone. Even though it was hard to see in the shadow from the building, her fingers felt the change in texture indicating the wood panel.

As she found the metal door handle, she detected movement at the edge of her peripheral vision. She twisted to look and glimpsed a man stepping from behind a large palm tree about a hundred yards away. She froze in place until the thought occurred to her that she was acting foolish. She sucked in a breath and moved closer to the house, hoping to hide in the gloom.

The large man paced a short distance toward the garden at a different place then from where she'd come from. When he stepped into the moonlight, she choked on an intake of breath.

Holy shit. Could he be Robert's pirate nemesis?

All she needed do was open the damn door to find safety within the manor house, curiosity had her staying put. She shrank against the wall when he turned. The man certainly looked like a swashbuckling pirate. Heavy muscle flexed beneath the tight fabric of light colored breeches as he walked. His booted stride ate the distance back to the palm, a long sword swinging at the hip. He twisted, shifting his weight, giving a better view. He wore an ivory shirt, open from waist to throat, beneath an elegant dark-colored coat with huge turned back cuffs. A large gold medallion hung from a chain around his neck. She shivered at the sight of the harsh features carved into his face. Power and danger.

Was it a play of the moonlight or did the man have red hair tied back with a ribbon? Robert had said LaRoux was known for the flaming color of his hair. Without thinking, Kimberly almost stepped from the shadows, but caught herself when a guest of the governor exited the garden and walked across the lawn to join the stranger.

The men spoke in loud whispers, the words unclear, though it was obvious by the emphatic gesturing the one from the party was angry. Then the governor's guest returned to the garden the way he'd come and disappeared from sight.

Kimberly stared for a moment at the one who remained,

but as the moon slid behind a cloud, the manor grounds went dark. When the light returned, the stranger was gone.

Her hand shook as she eased open the heavy wood door. Kimberly hesitated. Was that the swish of a silk skirt? She squinted into the gloom and shook her head. Must have been palm fronds rustling in a puff of air. Feeling exposed, she rushed inside and slammed the panel shut. No other female had been there; the breeze had caused the sound and it had been misinterpreted by her imagination.

She leaned back against the closed door and inhaled a deep breath, wishing there were a lock. Her pulse raced, as did her thoughts. What had she seen? Should she report the meeting to someone? Maybe something illicit was taking place.

Should she find Robert and tell him? Or should she go to her room and forget the whole affair? She hated indecision. Kimberly pushed away from the door and walked along the dimly lit passage toward her bedroom. The sense of urgency faded.

She didn't feel up to facing any of the guests' disapproving stares while she searched for Robert. She could tell him tomorrow. Besides they weren't supposed to alter history, only stop the curse. Surely, the conversation about whatever it was she'd seen could wait until morning. She didn't know for sure the man was a pirate.

When she reached the bedroom, she focused her thoughts on the mundane activity of undressing and preparing for bed with the help of a maid. The young woman gave Kimberly shrewd glances and complained at length about the crumpled and soiled condition of the borrowed gown.

Fearing her cheeks were scarlet, Kimberly slid between the bed sheets. The maid continued to grumble under her breath as she straightened the room. The glare the girl gave the stained gown before leaving had Kimberly biting her lip to keep from laughing.

Kimberly burrowed deeper into the soft mattress. It didn't take long for thoughts to return to what she'd seen in the moonlight. Had the purpose of the clandestine meeting between the two men been criminal? Had she seen a pirate? More specifically, LaRoux?

She punched the pillow to plump the down filling. She'd tell Robert first thing in the morning. With a twist, she rolled onto her belly and sought sleep, but she stayed awake for hours, tossing and turning, and worrying about tomorrow and the wedding.

CHAPTER TWENTY-FOUR

The bright tropical sun glared over the gathering from a clear cerulean sky and a constant ocean breeze rustled nearby palm fronds. Kimberly startled when someone coughed and she returned her attention to the clergyman.

"Captain Robert Iain MacLachlan of Strathlachlan, son of Archibald, fifteenth Chief of Clan MacLachlan, and brother to Lachlan MacLachlan, sixteenth Chief of Clan MacLachlan, wilt thou have this woman to be thy wedded wife to live..."

Lack of sleep made Kimberly's mind fuzzy. She clutched and released the peachy-pink fabric of the overskirt to her wedding gown. Words blurred in her mind and a tremor whisked down her spine.

Robert clasped her hand and gave the moist fingers a gentle squeeze. His touch soothed. She remembered to breathe and inhaled a deep breath. The sweet scent from the flowers woven through her hair tickled her nose and she sniffed back a sneeze.

The lanky clergyman's somber eyes peered from over the pages of the prayer book, and the man frowned, though he continued to speak the words without missing a syllable, "...as you both shall live."

"I will." Robert inclined his head.

Kimberly tilted her neck and stole a long look at him

from the side. God, he was magnificent. He wore a cottony ivory shirt under a great kilt of red and green plaid. Muscular calves wrapped in fawn leather below the hem, broad chest and wide shoulders above. The ornately handled knife in the sheath tucked into the thick belt was a bit ominous yet added to the masculine effect. No wonder, romance authors wrote about Highlanders.

What mattered most, though, was what shone on his handsome face—an open expression of love. Her heart did a joyous leap.

"Repeat this promise before the Almighty Father and these witnesses: I, Robert Iain MacLachlan, take thee Kimberly..." The man's monotone voice went silent and he looked at Robert in confusion.

Robert cupped a hand to his mouth and leaned forward to whisper.

The clergyman cleared his throat, making an abrupt sound. "Highly irregular," he glanced at Lord Hamilton—lord and lady stood as witnesses—his lordship nodded, "yet I will proceed."

Although the preacher continued, his shoulders sagged. "...to be my wedded wife, to have..." His voice droned on.

When he finished, Robert repeated the words, ending with, "I pledge thee my troth."

Kimberly swallowed compulsively. All of a sudden, the marriage felt way too real. It wasn't that she didn't want to marry Robert. She did. It was just...she'd hoped to marry him in her own time after she'd cleared her name.

The clergyman stared. She ventured a glance at Robert. His intense gaze was on her too. Self-consciously, she bit her lip. He smiled encouragingly.

"Kimberly." Again, the clergyman made an unpleasant noise in his throat, clearly displeased he didn't have a list of names for her. He continued anyway, "Wilt thou have this man..."

When he finished, she said the expected, "I will."

He spoke the words she was to repeat, and she began her vow.

Back in December, when at the B&B in Cape May, she never imagined she'd be standing on the steps of a small, whitewashed church in 1715, reciting wedding vows. Her voice hitched and tears threatened as she gazed into Robert's cinnamon eyes, full of longing.

"...and thereto I give thee my troth," she finished, meaning every word.

The clergyman laid aside the prayer book, picked up a silver tray containing two gold rings encircled with Celtic etchings, and held the plate out to Robert.

Robert picked up the smallest, stepped and turned to face Kimberly fully. "With this ring I thee wed, with my body I thee worship, with all my worldly goods I thee endow."

A thrill raced through her, and she picked up Robert's ring. When she placed the gold band on his finger, she said, "With this ring I thee wed, with my body I thee worship, with my heart I thee love."

The hairs on the back of her neck stood on end and she felt as if she'd received a blessing from *fate*. Robert was her destiny. Now, if only they could make things right here and return to the future.

The clergyman scowled. She ignored him and grinned at Robert. He bent his head and kissed her deep, curling her toes in the flimsy borrowed shoes she wore. She swayed, and he braced her with an arm to keep her from falling. They turned in unison to face the assembled and descended the steps.

A rag-tag group of seamen from Robert's ship and a couple of their host's acquaintances offered congratulations as they passed. Lady Anne squeezed Kimberly's hand when she reached the bottom step. "He will keep you safe."

Goosebumps pricked Kimberly's upper arms and she glanced at Robert who stood several feet away, speaking with Lord Hamilton. Then she smiled at Lady Anne, even though the woman's comment was unsettling.

"I'm sure he will," Kimberly murmured.

Over Lady Anne's shoulder, she noticed Jane Chalmers speaking with the man she'd seen in the garden the previous night with the...pirate. Shit. She'd forgotten to mention the meeting to Robert. Oh well, it would have to wait. There were too many people around now to broach the subject.

She accepted well wishes from one of the seamen and waited for Robert to finish his conversation. The morning ceremony might not have been the wedding of her dreams with Sarah as the maid of honor. Nevertheless, with Robert as the groom...well, the wedding ceremony was more special than any she imagined. And exceedingly better than the one planned with Jason.

Damn, she didn't want to think of that jerk, his betrayal, or the mess she needed to face in the twenty-first century. She wanted to concentrate on Robert and share her happiness. Tomorrow, she could worry about the future. About pirates, a Voodoo priestess, and an ancient vampire. About a lying ex-fiancé, trumped up charges, and proving her innocence.

Today, she would live for the day.

Robert joined her. She raised her chin and smiled at the man who held her heart. He lowered his head and branded her with another scorching kiss. "I have a special surprise for you."

CHAPTER TWENTY-FIVE

Where the hell is she?

Robert shifted the bulk of his weight from one leg to the other, yet again, and glanced at the mid-day sky. Bright sun. Blue sky. Weather would remain clear. He returned his stare to the outside of the ballroom's double doors as if force of will alone would make Kimberly appear.

He'd been waiting for her on the terrace of the governor's home for what seemed like an eternity. In reality, no more than a half-hour passed. After a quick post-ceremony toast to their nuptials, she'd gone to her room to change into a simpler gown.

Preferably, a garment easy to remove.

Soon she'd be all his. He chuckled. The governor had snickered like a fool and poked him in the ribs when he'd informed Robert of the romantic glen and waterfall in the hills above the great house. The secluded pools were ideal for swimming in the raw, or so Archibald said. *A perfect spot for a tryst.*

Robert wanted time alone with his new wife. He cracked a smile. *Wife*—he liked the sound of her new title.

After too many tedious minutes, Kimberly joined him. Her simple yellow frock with purple embroidered flowers made a striking contrast to her dark coloring, but he didn't plan for the dress to remain on long. He couldn't wait to have her naked in the spray of water cascading over rocky outcrops, and over her luscious curves. An image of rosy nipples hardening in the breeze teased his thoughts. He almost tasted her moist skin on his lips.

Her furrowed brow caused his sexual fantasies to shatter. The muscles across his chest tightened. "Where is your smile, lass? Are you already regretting wedding me?"

Mischief lit her eyes and her lips trembled before stretching into a grin. "I'm wondering why you're still wearing your plaide, but don't get me wrong, I love the way..." She raked the length of him with a hot gaze. Tingles followed in its wake. "Well, you are the epitome of every girl's Highland dream. Though, I'm surprised you're still dressed in your great kilt with that knife tucked in the belt."

He released the breath he held then accepted the large picnic hamper collected from the kitchen and hefted it onto a shoulder. "My costume is perfect for an alfresco lunch in the woods." At her expression of doubt, he added, "You will see."

She snorted. Ignoring the lack of respect, he preceded along the path through the tropical pleasure garden toward the forest.

"Where are we going?" she asked.

Robert couldn't wait to witness her reaction to the falls. He looked over a shoulder and quirked his lips. "'Tis a surprise."

She wrinkled her nose. "Are you referring to the same surprise you mentioned after the ceremony?"

He chuckled and turned all the way around. With his free hand, he grasped her fingers and tugged her through the trees to the trail that led into the hills.

"Slow down. These ridiculous silk slippers weren't made for hiking."

"Shall I carry you?" He lifted a brow in challenge.

The impulse to throw her over a shoulder and run the remaining distance to the waterfalls made him feel like a sex-crazed barbarian. His cock jerked beneath the fabric of the plaide, and he stifled a groan before it roared from his throat.

"Definitely not," she said. "You would drop me and ruin our lunch."

"Dinnae underestimate me." He stalked close.

"I never do." She rolled her eyes. "I can walk just fine if you'll slow the pace."

They climbed the winding trail rising through the rain forest without speaking. He shortened his steps when she struggled for breath.

"Aren't they beautiful?" she said after a deep inhale.

Jewel toned parrots screeched and flew from tree to tree ahead of their approach as if the birds directed the way. "Aye, lass. They are."

Robert set the hamper on a rock to help Kimberly climb through a particularly difficult section strewn with boulders. He returned for the basket, and they continued along the trail. Little sun penetrated the leafy canopy and the air cooled as they climbed becoming more comfortable. Still, the day was hot.

"Not much farther," he yelled over the roar from the hidden cascades.

"Waterfalls?" Kimberly's voice bubbled with excitement.

He raised a shoulder and bit back a grin.

Her pace quickened when they entered the clearing at the base of the lowest falls. She ran toward the edge of the small pool and bent to dip fingers into the crystal-clear water. As he drew close, spray moistened his skin and wet his hair.

Kimberly straightened and pleased him with a smile that brightened her face. "Beautiful." She reached up and pinched a blossom from an overhanging vine. "I don't know what kind of flowers these are, but I love the citrus fragrance."

He leaned forward to inhale the bloom, though her feminine scent was what drove him wild. The fabric of her gown became translucent from the mist. Pert nipples pressed against the sheer bodice and a shadowed V taunted from between her thighs. Bloody hell, she'd taken his suggestion and wore nothing beneath the frock. He forced air in and out of his lungs as blood rushed to his already hard erection.

She stuck the bold yellow flower behind an ear. "Such a lovely place for a picnic."

He tamped down on the sexual urges. "Not here. Come. 'Tis only a wee bit farther to the special place the governor told me about." His voice sounded like it had been scraped across jagged rocks, and he attempted to clear his throat.

With arms outstretched, Kimberly twirled in a circle. "This is the perfect spot."

"Archibald claims there is a better place."

"Okay, let's go. Lead on."

He rolled his eyes to make her laugh. When she did, the husky sound grabbed his balls and squeezed. He struggled to draw another breath.

"Thought we were going to another spot," Kimberly said, tilting her head. The damn sexy woman knew exactly the effect she had on him.

"We are," he croaked.

Bloody hell. Tides, currents, depths—he ran boring data from memorized nautical charts through his mind in an effort to reel in the lust.

She followed him up a steeper climb. Where the ground leveled off, he moved aside a huge fern frond and waved Kimberly through. Her pleased gasp warmed his chest near the heart.

* * *

The governor had been right. The forest room, decorated with abundant foliage and tropical flowers and cascading water, was perfect for an afternoon picnic. Kimberly kicked off slippers, hiked up her skirts, and waded into the tranquil pool at the base of the lowest falls.

She danced in the shallows, turned to kick water at Robert, but stopped at the sight of the sharp-looking knife he pulled from under his kilt. Another appeared. They'd probably been strapped to his thighs. He laid the two weapons beside the hamper and retrieved two more from his boots. Then he withdrew the leather sheath with the fancy handled knife from his belt and added it to the pile.

Her eyes nearly popped when she recognized the pistol he yanked from behind his back and added to the pile of weapons. The gun was one of the antiques she'd found along with the other pirate paraphernalia while searching the sea chest on *Night Thrill*. He'd have no need of any of it. They would stop Zola before the curse turned him into a vampire and a shifter.

"Planning for war?" Kimberly rubbed a palm over her belly, trying to make the queasy sensation go away.

"We are not in *our* time. The past is fraught with danger."

She understood, but pushed aside the unpleasant implications. The last thing she wanted to worry about was why he carried weapons or what they had yet to face together. "You do believe you belong in the future."

He hesitated, staring at her with one of those annoying unreadable expressions. "I belong with you."

In an attempt to make light, she tried to imitate his Scottish dialect. "Ach, you ken how to make a lass swoon."

They both laughed, but her smile faded when Robert dropped his belt and unpinned the brooch holding the plaid fabric at the shoulder. She let her gaze follow the fabric as the great kilt pooled at his feet, leaving only the long shirt remaining to cover his assets. The muscles in his thighs flexed when he knelt and spread the wool over the ground like a blanket.

Her insides clenched with desire. She couldn't hold back the groan that escaped. His lips quivered into a smile in response to the desperate sound. He plopped onto the ground covering, pulled off the primitive boots, and got comfy.

"I told you my costume would come in handy." He reached for the picnic hamper, opened the lid, and rummaged through the contents. A flask and two pewter mugs appeared, and he poured them each wine. "Join me."

He tilted his head toward the spot beside him. She stepped from the water and walked toward him. Their gazes met, a promise passed between them. She sat beside him within a circle of silk, arranging the fabric as best she could.

He handed her a cup and raised his own. "To my wife."

His toast made her warm and fuzzy. "To my husband."

The clink of cups could hardly be heard over the roar of the waterfall. When they finished the wine, he removed a small package from the basket. Paper ripped and a bar of soap fell from the wrapping.

"Lavender from France," he said. "I thought you might enjoy a shower."

"How?"

"I was told there is a hidden cavern behind the highest falls where the spray is quite refreshing."

"Where? Up there?" She pointed to the largest cascade about sixty-feet above them. The queasies came with a vengeance to swirl in the pit of her stomach. What was he thinking? He knew she hated heights.

"We will climb the falls together."

She swallowed hard. She could do this. After all, she'd proved she could control the fear of heights when she rescued Robert from the rigging on *Night Thrill*.

With a flick of a wrist, he sliced a chunk of soap off the bar with one of the knives. He stood and pulled the tunic over his head. "Undress."

She slid her gaze from his face, over the broad chest, and lingered on his erection. Pure lust hit her hard, pooling low and thick, replacing any remnant of fear. The urge to caress the silk encased steel had her raising an arm and reaching for him.

"Undress," he growled, gaze intent.

The husky demand made her pulse quicken. She stared, arm hanging in midair.

"Hurry, lass."

She rose, and Robert spun her around so her back was to him. "Let me perform this service for you, sweetling."

Deft fingers made short work of the row of tiny buttons holding her gown in place, several flying off to scatter across the forest floor. Her heart hitched as the dress slid to the ground and she stepped away from the silk. Robert draped it over a rock then smiled. She crossed both arms over her chest, feeling exposed and vulnerable in the warm sunlight, but wanting him with all her heart.

"Dinnae cover yourself. I love looking at you."

Heat burned her cheeks, but she dropped her arms. It

wasn't as if he hadn't seen her nude before. Why today felt different was beyond her. Duh. Marriage.

A devilish grin formed on his face, and she had the urge to pinch him. Before she could, he grasped her hand and dragged her toward the base of the falls, to the edge of the pool where water gently lapped the shore.

"You have to be kidding. I can't climb up there." He was nuts. No way would she make it to the upper falls unless he knew of a path along the side through the foliage that wasn't visible.

"Come." They plunged into the water up to their knees. Her skin prickled with goose bumps, the cooling effect much appreciated after the heat of the day though it didn't quell the warmth of desire. He splashed her and she splashed back. She laughed aloud. Hardly able to believe she frolicked out in the open with no clothes on.

They waded across to the base of the first little falls. Robert said something, but she couldn't hear over the roar of rushing water. She leaned closer. "What?"

"Step where I step. Archibald described a way through the rocks, and I think I have found it." He stepped up and over a moss covered rock.

She followed, and as they climbed, he guided her around slippery-looking rocks, mini cascades, and larger spills. The firm grip he kept on her hand was reassuring. Silt squished between toes. Bubbles shot up from beneath the surface to tickle her ankles, bringing a smile.

Wet skin glistened golden across Robert's back in the sunlight. Muscles flexed with each stride. The sight of his tight butt had her wetting dry lips. She swallowed and tore her gaze away to focus on the upper falls, their destination. A shiver of anticipation teased. Losing her balance, she slipped and swayed. Her breath caught. The fear of falling made her twist awkwardly and she flung her free arm forward.

Robert released his hold on her hand, whipped around and grabbed both of her shoulders. Their gazes locked. Affection shimmered in the depth of his eyes. She would always be safe with him. Need swelled. She wanted him to kiss her. She tilted her head, lifting her lips to him. The peck to her nose took her by surprise.

Robert leaned away and grasped her fingers. "Are you all right?"

"Yes. I love this place," she yelled over the rumble of the falls.

"I am glad." He flashed pearly white teeth free of fangs.

She nodded and they continued their climb. When they reached the uppermost falls, he disappeared through the silver wall of tumbling water. Unsure whether to follow, she waited until a hand appeared, and he pulled her through the spray to join him in an amazingly quiet space. Under the falls, sound muffled.

After a few moments, her eyes adjusted to the filtered light. Years of gushing water had carved a bench of sorts at the back of a small cavern. She threw an arm out—the spray danced over her skin like a cool shower. "Now what?"

"I wash my wife."

The expression in his hooded eyes made her edgy with desire. "Sounds...wonderful."

Robert lathered the soap and squatted. He lifted her left foot onto a knee, and she shifted her weight for better balance. When he finished washing the first foot, he paid special attention to the second, tickling her till she begged him to stop.

A giggle gurgled up her throat and she laughed with delight. He joined her with a rough chuckle of his own. He wrapped large hands around each of her calves and massaged the tired muscles. Her legs weakened when his touch slid higher, the friction sending electric tingles upward to coalesce at the core of her sex.

His soapy fingers teased sensitive flesh on the inside of her thighs. Her thoughts scattered. When she swayed, he grasped her hips and lifted, laying her on the edge of the bench. He wrapped an arm around her back, protecting her skin from the rough stone. With breathtaking tenderness, he toyed with the folds protecting her sex until she nearly went insane with need.

Magic fingers stroked, teased, persuaded.

Breath coming in sharp little pants, Kimberly arched

her back, silently begging for relief.

He splashed icy water over her thrumming sex, rinsing away the fragrant soap. Before she inhaled a shocked breath, warm lips replaced his fingers. When his tongue licked and delved and drew her taut, her moans grew louder than the muffled sound of the cascading falls. She frantically grasped for something just out of reach.

The contrasting sensations of cool mist and hot mouth were almost more than she could bear. An orgasm flared, creating sparklers shooting bright rainbow colors. Blues and purples and greens—so vibrant. Sensual reds. Bold yellows and hot orange lighting her up from within. Her scream of release echoed the intensity of the sizzling climax.

Robert wasn't finished with her though. He lathered his hands again and paid particular attention to her breasts. Her desire swelled, but she wanted to drive him wild. Before he argued against it, she slapped his hands away and stole the soap sliver. "My turn to push you over the edge."

* * *

Robert groaned when Kimberly swept the soap and teasing fingers over his rock hard erection. His breathing ragged, he tried to hang onto his control.

Damn, she was killing him.

He sought her gaze and held it as she rinsed him with a splash of cool water. The chill did nothing to ease the burning need. Instead, desire flamed.

While her lips surrounded his width and she sucked him deep, he gripped the edge of the stone bench beneath him. She stroked and licked, circling the head of his cock.

Kimberly's loving awed him. She was so much more than he deserved. He wanted to stay with her, have children with her, grow old with her. He wished he could find a way to follow her into the future after they settled things here.

When gentle fingers caressed his balls at the same time as a velvety tongue rasped the length of him, his heart slammed into his ribs, and he lost the ability to think.

Robert bucked, arching his back and thrusting with his hips.

Instead of taking him back into her mouth, she used her lips to tease him to the edge of endurance. Then she took him into her mouth, sucked him deep into her throat. He held tight. Stayed with her. He was close...so close. Each breath wheezed through gritted teeth. The sensation of moist satin gripping his flesh coaxed him toward the point of no return. The erotic pull drove him insane. He panted and strained.

She withdrew, returned, teased, pushed him to the edge. The orgasm that followed rocked him to the core as it rolled down his length. Colors flashed behind his eyelids. Every shade of love burst like fireworks across a July evening sky. He exploded into her mouth and she took all of him. Every drop. She released him for a moment to swallow then sucked his entire length back into her moist recesses and wrung him dry.

Every muscle limp, he basked in the afterglow.

A feminine laugh of satisfaction made him raise his head. He opened an eye to the sight of his grinning wife. Rather pleased with herself, she was.

He babbled, actually babbled, before speaking a coherent word. "I dinnae think I can move."

She grabbed a hand and yanked him to his feet. "I can't stay here any longer, my skin is pruning."

Returning to the sunny glen was fine with him. He'd never get enough sun now he was no longer a vampire shifter. What he wanted to do more than anything, though, was cuddle in the sunshine with his naked wife, enter her silken sheath, and make love until stars dotted the midnight sky.

* * *

The fabric of Robert's great kilt was soft against Kimberly's bare back. She inhaled his musky scent and sighed. His responding chuckle muffled against the skin of her throat where he nuzzled and nipped near her vein.

He raised his head. "Hungry?"

The softly spoken question nudged her from a haze of

bliss. "The food is long gone."

They'd enjoyed the picnic lunch after returning to the clearing. She stretched to ease the exquisite aches in her muscles from hours of mind-blowing sex. The insatiable man made love to her numerous times, in every imaginable position, plus some. She shivered as the sun faded behind the treetops and the clearing fell into shadow.

Rolling unto his back, Robert wrapped an arm around her, and pulled her tight against his side. His contented sigh warmed her as nothing else could.

Mine. A possessive swirl of pleasure tightened her spine. He belonged to her. She closed her eyes and allowed the knowledge to sink in.

"Are you happy, lass?"

"I am. I'm not sure why a ceremony should make a difference—especially one that isn't going to mean anything when we return to the future—but I believe we've bound our love together."

"The vows we made are forever. Your needs shall always come before my own."

She squeezed his hand. He said the sweetest things.

They lay quietly for a while. Kimberly listened to the rush of water and birds calling from the trees. She ran fingers through the fine hairs on Robert's chest, feeling lazy enough to doze. She spaced for a bit, letting her mind roam free. When she once again became aware of her surroundings, she noticed the quiet. The birds had stopped their chatting.

A calloused fingertip traced the curve of her lips. "You're frowning again. You think too much."

"I feel exposed. I've had an unnerving sensation ever since I landed on this island as if someone is watching me." She raised her torso and stared at the trees edging the clearing, scanning the shaded darkness beyond.

Robert sat beside her. "Are you sure 'tis not nerves from journeying through time?"

She searched the tree line again then shrugged. "I suppose."

He reached for the wicker hamper and withdrew a brown paper wrapped package tied with string and handed it to her. "Your wedding present."

Her eyes teared up. "I've nothing for you."

"Nae matter." He patted an arm. "Open the gift."

She pulled at the string, peeled the paper back, and fingered the exposed fabric. Soft. She unfurled the cloth and held up a whisper thin slip of fine lawn with ecru lace edging. "It's beautiful. Where did you get it?"

"My ship. Bruges before that." He ran a hand through his loose hair, tucking the long tawny strands behind an ear. "I purchased the chemise along with other garments to sell in Glasgow. Only I wasn't in the city long enough to conduct business before I was forced to leave rather than be arrested."

Nothing more needed to be said.

"Thank you." She wished she had something for him.

"Ach, well, put it on." While she slid the slip over her head, Robert grabbed his tunic and tugged it on.

"'Tis getting late. We should return to the great house." He reached for the matched pair of knives and strapped them to his thighs.

"Must we?" He nodded and Kimberly stood, grabbed the dress from where it draped a rock and slid the silk over her head. After the gown flowed over her shoulders, Robert made short work of the buttons. She spun, and he leaned in and planted his lips on her mouth.

Soft and sweet and oh so deep.

She was immersed in sensation until he ended the kiss and leaned back. "You ken, lass, we might have a bairn in about nine months."

Kimberley flipped her gaze to his. "Why do you say that?"

"As a vampire shifter I was sterile. As a man, well..." He hesitated. "If for some reason I couldn't return with you to the future, would a babe be a problem?"

Kimberly frowned. "What do you mean? You're returning with me."

"Aye, if I can. But we need to be realistic. We must be prepared—" He raised a hand, and although she wanted to interrupt, she held her tongue— "in case something goes afoul when the time for averting the curse arrives."

"I don't want—"

"Will a babe be a problem?"

The force of her exhale blew fallen strands of hair from her face. "As much as I'd love to have your baby, you don't need to worry. I have a contraceptive implant."

"You do?" The expression on Robert's face revealed disappointment.

"I'll show you." She raised the arm and bent it at the elbow, placing the palm on the back of her head. With the fingers from her other hand, she felt along the inner side of the upper arm. Her stomach dropped to her toes and her mouth fell open. "Shit. It's gone!"

Not that she'd mind having Robert's baby. A satisfied masculine smile crossed Robert's lips before he blanked his expression, so she kept her smile private.

"Why would you think you're not returning with me?" She pinned him with her best glare.

Robert shifted his weight uneasily. "We dinnae ken how this time travel folly will turn out, do we? Your birth control apparatus must have disappeared going through the time warp. Who kens how fate twisted from our actions?"

He couldn't tell her his fear that once they stopped the curse he would no longer recognize her. Nor would he be immortal. Nor live in her time. Robert planned to stop the Voodoo priestess from casting the black magic. He'd already instructed his quartermaster to kidnap Kimberly afterward and sail with her into the Bermuda Triangle.

He prayed once there, the time portal would suck her back to the future.

He would do his best to make it up to her during their short time together—before he faced Zola. He swallowed hard. Damn, it hurt to think about her returning to the future without him. He pulled her close and kissed her deep. When she opened her eyes they were unfocused, then they widened.

Adrenaline surged, his body primed for danger. Robert pivoted on a heel. In one fluid motion, he released the daggers from the sheaths strapped to his thighs, and positioned his bulk in front of Kimberly, ready to face the threat.

He didn't see any danger. "What the—"

"I thought I saw someone running through the trees."

"Are you sure?"

"Not really. I saw a flash of bright blue. A blur." She sounded embarrassed.

"Could it have been your mind playing tricks on you? A bird?"

"Maybe. I've been nervous ever since I saw that redheaded pirate near the garden."

"What?" Robert yelled.

"Oh, I forgot to tell you." Kimberly bit her lip.

"Maybe you should enlighten me." He uncurled the fist he hadn't realized he'd made.

With her gaze glued to his shoulder, she replayed what she'd seen the prior evening.

"The red-haired pirate must be LaRoux. The man you describe him meeting with might be Mr. Page, the governor's deputy secretary." Robert scrubbed his face with a hand. What a tangled mess. "Dammit, Kimberly. I can't believe you forgot to tell me you saw a pirate on the grounds of the governor's great house."

"I had other things on my mind. Like getting married. Remember?"

"Bloody. Brilliant."

"That's unfair." She bunched her hands on her hips and scowled.

"Did you forget what we came here for?" He couldn't believe she neglected to tell him something of such import.

"No." Kimberly stared at the ground and slid her toes through the blades of grass at her feet, refusing to look at him.

"I should have never let us become distracted from our goal. Our only goal." He grasped her chin and lifted it. "Look at me. We are here to stop Zola from performing the curse. For no other reason."

The stare she shot him sizzled. "You're right. But no worries, you won't need to divorce me when we get home because we're not legally married by twenty-first century standards."

"Dammit, Kimberly, I dinnae want a divorce." He released her chin, crossed arms over his chest, and held her glare.

She stepped back, putting space between them. He would have none of that. He reached for her—

Pain exploded at his temple, and he crumpled.

CHAPTER TWENTY-SIX

As Robert fell to the ground, breath shot from Kimberly's lungs. Pressure from the thick arm squeezing her chest sent panic screaming through her system. A sweaty, giant of a man jerked her from her feet and swung her to the side, trapping her in an unrelenting grip.

Kimberly couldn't inhale enough air to scream. Her vision blurred. When her eyes refocused, she was hanging stomach-down over a hard shoulder with her hands secured behind her back, tied with rope that chafed her wrists. Though it hurt like hell, she craned her neck. Robert lay with his face planted in dirt at the center of the once-peaceful clearing. A gash at the temple oozed blood. Worse, the barrel of a pistol pointed at his prone form.

"No!" she screamed.

The red-haired pirate from the night before snapped his head up at the raspy shriek. His eyes flared. Greed and hate and something she didn't want to define burned in the intense stare. She bit down on her back molars, refusing to succumb to fear.

She'd screwed up and both their lives were in danger.

"Damnation. Ye drivelin' codfish. Get the wench the hell out of here," the pirate bellowed.

The man who held her turned on a heel and strode into

the trees. She thrashed in his grasp to no effect. He carried her squirming weight as if no burden at all. After several long steps, she was tossed in the air and repositioned on his shoulder. A sharp jolt to her stomach on landing made her want to vomit.

The bile she swallowed churned in her gut along with fear and anger.

After several agonizing minutes, her captor threw her over the back of a horse and tied her in the most uncomfortable position—belly down. Blood rushed to her head. Muscles stretched and burned as the horse pawed the earth.

No point in screaming. They were too far from the great house for anyone to hear, nor reach them in time to help. Moments passed like eternity. Foul-smelling animal sweat and manure tainted each inhale. She tensed when the horse moved forward in a slow walk.

Tied to a lead horse, her horse followed along. Aching muscles made every minute stretch. When they finally cleared the forest, the animals broke into a trot. Agony tore through Kimberly's limbs and dangling neck with each jarring step the horse took. Head pounding, she threw up lunch.

Closing her eyes, she wracked her brain. How would she get them out of this mess?

Caught in cobwebs of time, panic escalated. Her pulse raced. Overwhelmed, her vision went from fuzzy gray to black. Dammit, not again.

She ran through the jungle. The stranger chased her into the dense foliage. She tripped on a loose root. When she fell, he morphed into a big cat and lunged.

Kimberly froze, breathing hard. A scream threatened to explode from her lips, but the cat dissolved in mid-leap.

Her mind whirled, trying to understand. Although the nightmare had returned, waking brought the dread of reality.

Kimberly stayed still, not wanting to alert anyone who might be watching that she was awake. Taking inventory, she ached from head to toe, but ropes no longer bound her wrists. She still wore the damp gown and her feet were unencumbered.

Where was she? She must have passed out. A gentle rolling motion along with the briny tang of the sea aggravated an already-sour stomach. Could she be on a ship?

She lifted crusted eyelids a mere crack. Light burned her retinas, forcing her to blink.

When her vision cleared, she opened her eyes. Rays of hazy sunlight penetrated grungy panes of glass. The size of the window confirmed in whose cabin she'd landed.

Other women in such a situation might think themselves fortunate to be ensconced in the captain's cabin. Kimberly might have agreed, if said cabin belonged to Robert. She didn't consider being held prisoner in LaRoux's cabin a good thing. Although, the alternative might get her tossed to his despicable men. She didn't have any misconceptions about possible fates.

Considering the sunlight, she must have been out cold the whole of the night. She was in a dire situation, but fear for Robert tore at her heart.

Her muscles cried when she rose to a sitting position on the bunk. The bed was rather opulent like what she imagined one would find in a fancy bordello of the period. An abundance of jewel toned silks and velvets—garnet, emerald, sapphire—draped the mattress along with luscious pillows. Gold cords with tassels pulled open gauzy fabric hung from hooks in the ceiling.

She touched her chafed wrists, raw from the rope bindings. Okay, she needed to get out of there. Now. Her legs wobbled when her feet hit the cold floor. She stood for a moment to regain balance. Drawing strength from deep within, she rushed to the heavy oak door and yanked. Locked from outside. *Double shit.*

The window.

She ran across the cabin, climbed up and kneeled on the cushioned window seat. She leaned against the glass and peered through. Wow, the cabin sat high in the ship. What remained in her stomach did a somersault and a wave of nausea forced her to sit back onto bent legs, clutching her belly. When the sick sensation passed, she clamped down on her fear of heights and looked out the window again.

The ship sailed a short distance from land. Unfortunately, the damn window had small panes. Even if she broke the glass she wouldn't be able to climb out. But if she managed to break the glass and bust the frame in-between the panes, she might be able to shimmy through, dive into the water, and swim for shore.

She twisted around and searched the cabin for something hard she could grip. On the desk sat a bronze-like object that looked just the thing. She raced to the desk and picked up the heavy piece of metal. Latin words were engraved into the flat, round end along with a sailing ship. Must be one of those seal thingies used with hot wax to secure documents.

Kimberly tested the weight. Perfect. She wrapped some cloth around the seal end to muffle sound and slammed it into the window. Glass shattered, a few pieces falling free. She paused. Had anyone heard the noise?

Laying the seal on the window seat, she crept to the door and listened. Quiet. She rushed back to the window, picked up the seal and lifted her arm to swing. Footsteps sounded in the corridor outside the door.

Shit! She slipped the matrix under a cushion and swung around to face the door.

The door slowly creaked open and a small face with wide brown eyes appeared from behind it. A runt of a boy slipped into the room. He never removed his gaze from her as he clumsily set a bowl, pitcher, and cloth on the desk. "The captain says ye stink."

No news there. She smelled worse than the locker room after a particularly vigorous exercise class at the health club she belonged to before the financial fall from grace. Kimberly eyed the boy then the open door and took a step in that direction.

"Hey. Nice to meet you," she said, trying to set him at ease while taking another step toward the door.

The boy's eyebrows rose into a crusty hairline. He shook his head. "The drivelin' codfish is a wait'n for ye ta run."

She almost laughed. Did everyone call the clod who'd captured her a drivelin' codfish?

"Miserable bastard likes ta hurt the skirts."

Kimberly swallowed hard. She needed to get out of there. And fast. Lifting the pitcher, she poured water into the bowl, wet the cloth with a shaky hand, and glared at the boy. "You don't plan to watch, do you?"

The young boy's cheeks blushed red. He darted through the door and slammed it shut.

Water from the cloth she held to her chest dripped between her breasts, wetting her gown, reminding her how difficult it would be to swim with all the fabric weighing her down. Impossible.

She yanked on the bodice, ripping free the few buttons remaining from when Robert undressed her by the waterfall. After quickly stripping to her new chemise, she lunged back to the window seat and grabbed the seal from its hiding place. Heart hammering, she took another shot at the window. More glass broke free, but hardly any damage to the wood frame. She hauled back and swung fast. The wood splintered, making a loud cracking sound.

A couple of more swings and maybe she'd be able to squeeze through. She leaned forward and looked at the turquoise water far below. Keep tight. You can do this.

She inhaled a deep breath and hit the sash hard. Holy crap. What remained of the window broke free and fell from the ship. As Kimberly stared at pieces of the frame floating in the water, an unsettling thought took hold. What if Robert were held prisoner somewhere in the ship? She shouldn't jump. She should try to find him.

Ka-bam. The heavy wood of the cabin door crashed against the wall behind her.

* * *

The sour taste Robert woke with from the foul smelling gag wasn't as disconcerting as the rancid water teeming with vermin chewing his skin. Gagged, and bound hand and foot, he was at a disadvantage.

A trace of yellow light entered from cracks between the boards overhead. Once his eyes adjusted to the dimness, he still couldn't make out much of the dank cell. The rolling motion and groan of timbers confirmed his guess though.

They held him prisoner in the hull of a ship. If everything had gone as before—Laroux's ship.

What happened to Kimberly?

Dammit. He'd made a mess of things. He couldn't dwell on his fear for her though or he'd go mad and be of no use to either of them. Stiff muscles and joints screamed each time he attempted to move. Festering sores burned his skin. How much time had passed? He couldn't guess.

Where were they taking him? He knew the answer to that question too well. He'd already lived this nightmare. They were taking him to the other side of the island where Zola would perform the curse.

He kicked bound legs in an attempt to dislodge the rodents. A particularly large rat with shiny pink eyes hovered close, waiting for the thrashing to stop. If only he were still a vampire, he could control the wee creature's mind. Force the rodent to chew through the ropes rather than ravish his wounds.

He shimmied to and fro, searching for something to use to break free. Time might be repeating itself, but he refused to allow the same outcome. He wouldn't become a member of the shifting undead. A minion of Séaghdha.

That monster couldn't be permitted to enter the earth's realm. God, when Robert thought of Raven, his once sweet twin, pressure weighed on his chest. He couldn't allow the guilt to immobilize him. He needed to escape, find Kimberly, and stop Zola.

Robert almost wished himself still cursed, able to call the panther to the fore. The transformation to the big cat would have shredded the rope securing him, freeing him of the bindings.

Footsteps from outside the cell made him stiffen. The door swung open and blinding light shot at him. He blinked several times to clear his vision.

The swabbie who entered jarred Robert's memory. Something struck him as different. An uneasy sensation swirled in his gut. The last time he went through this, he'd been left alone until they reached Zola's lair. This time he wore his plaide from the wedding, not the trews he'd worn when captured previously.

Traveling through the portal to the past *had* changed things—disturbed the flow of time. He couldn't expect everything to go as before.

The lad pulled a sword from its sheath and stuck the point under Robert's chin, drawing blood. "Make no move, *Captain.*"

What the hell? Robert flinched, but quickly masked his chaotic emotions. A second lad, big and burly, entered the cell and tossed a cloth bundle into the muck beside Robert before unsheathing his sword. Rats scattered then eased closer.

Teàrlach, one of his men, stumbled in, a sword at his back, eyes large with fear. Swollen purple bruises marred the poor lad's face. Obviously, an unwilling participant in whatever drama was to be performed.

Bloody hell. Robert surged against the ropes. Had the bastard pirates raided his ship? Or had they plucked the mate from a tavern? He cursed against the gag in his mouth

More importantly, where had they taken Kimberly?

"Captain, pardon the insolence." Teàrlach wearily eyed the others. "I am to dress ye fer yer trial."

CHAPTER TWENTY-SEVEN

Kimberly didn't spare a second to learn who entered the cabin. She leapt away from the ship in a dive that built in momentum, forcing her deep into the depths.

When the downward force lessened, she swam in an arc and glided upward. Her lungs would explode if she didn't reach the surface soon. She kicked with everything she had. Pressure built as she propelled through the water. With a final stroke, she burst free and gasped for breath.

A wave washed over her head, sucking her back under. Surfacing again, she blinked several times to clear blurry vision. Breathing hard, treading water, she cupped a hand over her eyes to deflect the afternoon glare and dared to take time to monitor the ship as it sailed past.

Something heavy hit the surf beside her. The splash hit her face and water shot up her nose, causing her to sputter and choke. Without waiting to find out what or who landed in the sea, she kicked hard and swam toward shore as if the devil himself gave chase.

A large hand wrapped around an ankle and dragged her back. Although she fought the hold, she ended up crushed against a hard male body. She felt every ridge, every muscle. Pale green eyes devoured her. She'd been caught by the *devil*.

She struggled like a mad woman, but having had little to

eat for strength against the brute force, she quickly weakened.

"Foolish wench. If you swim for shore the reef will cut you to shreds."

"How dare you?" Kimberly struggled more, yanked on his hair, but made minimal progress escaping the iron grip.

"Do not try my patience, mademoiselle."

"Let go of me, you...you, blackguard." She had a moment's urge to roll her eyes. Instead, she kicked at his shins.

Captain Laroux laughed despite the anger radiating from him. He sobered quickly though. "Do not force me to knock you out."

The whispered words close to her ear made Kimberly tense. She couldn't afford to be unconscious again. She'd never manage to escape.

With her body held tight to his side by one arm, the pirate kicked and used the other arm to cut through the water toward the longboat rowing for them from the ship.

When they reached the rescue boat—capture boat— rough hands pulled her over the gunwale and tossed her against one of the benches. She scrambled onto all fours, crawled toward the edge and gripped the gunwale. Hope of diving over the side ended when one of the crew manhandled her onto the floor and held her down with the weight of a sweaty body. The smell of onion breath curled her nose when the man flipped her over and got right in her face.

"Go ahead. Try again." Missing and heavily stained teeth made the man's leer worse.

Eyes full of lust, he stared at her breasts. Before she could cover the hard nipples showing through the sheer wet fabric of her chemise, he lowered his head and suckled a breast.

Kimberly screeched and beat curled fists against his back. The man squeezed the air from her lungs. She gasped, fighting to breathe. By the time her lungs filled with briny air, the man had been ripped away and swam alongside the boat.

The dripping wet Laroux glowered as if it were her fault

the mate attacked. He grabbed a piece of sailcloth from one of the men and shook it. "Cover yourself. I will not have you causing a brawl." He held the makeshift cover-up to her. "If any shall have you, 'twill be me."

Not if she had anything to say about it. Glare for glare, she prayed to find Robert soon.

* * *

Trial by battle. Not that Robert had broken any laws. LaRoux wanted to even the score, as he put it, for Robert blowing up his ship. The shock of seeing Kimberly in the damn pirates clutches was a damaging blow. Robert staggered.

His opponent's sword slashed, drawing more blood. Stinging fire raced from the wounds, blazing through Robert's system. With the agony, his system began to shut down. Releasing an anguished croak, he glanced at Kimberly and fell to his knees. Strength gone, unable to rise, he landed face-first in the dirt.

Kimberly screamed. The horrific sound sliced through his delirium. He raised his head and stared through blurry eyes, burning her image into memory. It was heartbreaking to think this would be the last time he ever gazed upon her precious features. They'd been prisoner in the same ship for days. Kept apart.

He had to fight to save her. He pushed at the ground with the heel of his palms, but couldn't raise his body more than an inch. Something was terribly wrong. This shouldn't be happening. His wounds weren't that serious. Dammit to hell.

Poison. As Kurt surmised, Laroux had coated his blade with a poisonous substance. Robert's cuts rendered him helpless. He'd never be able to save Kimberly.

His body trembled uncontrollably. Many hands grabbed at him. Four men raised him in the air. "No!"

As they carried him over their heads, their skeletal faces morphed, elongating into that of frightening creatures. Monsters. Zombies. Robert's heart stuttered, having difficulty pumping blood through veins. His mind fuzzed. Where was Kimberly? He needed to beg forgiveness.

Panic charged through him. *Please, God, let me save Kimberly.*

Darkness wrapped its comforting arms around his soul. When he came to, pain wracked his body. Every nerve. Every muscle. Every tendon burned. Drums pounded a primitive beat. Voices chanted in ancient tongues.

He used every ounce of energy remaining to open his eyes. Several minutes passed before his vision adjusted to the fire glow. The sight before him was out of a bad B-movie.

Torches burned, lighting a circular area. Black skinned men wearing short loincloths, feathered headpieces with horns, and bracelets and anklets made from seeds and bones, undulated provocatively as they danced around the outer edges of the circle. Their harsh voices joined by others hidden in the dark.

They had tied him spread-eagle to logs forming an X, his arms painfully stretched to the upper V, while his legs were secured outward at the bottom. The most vulnerable position a man could find himself in.

Dancing continued. More torches were lit. Then he saw Kimberly on the other side of the clearing, tied to a single stake with arms lashed above her head and toes dangling inches above the ground. She wore a short loincloth around the waist and only strands of beads draped from the neck covered her breasts.

He prayed for this insanity to be a nightmare. A bad dream that would soon end. He would wake and find himself on the bunk in his cabin on *Sea Panther* with Kimberly safe in his arms.

The rhythm of the beating drums quickened. The gyrations of the men became frenzied. Robert's pulse raced in tempo with the drums. He tugged at the ropes binding him, thrashing to get free.

At the sight of Zola, he stopped struggling. The Voodoo priestess entered the clearing. A serpent wrapped the length of an arm, circled her neck, its head draped over one shoulder. The pet Florida panther walked at her side. Behind her came LeRoux, wearing a smug expression. He strode to Kimberly, fondled a breast, and said something close to her ear.

Something Robert couldn't hear. He arched his back and renewed the struggle against the ropes, but there was no way he could break free. "Get the hell away from her!"

Kimberly swallowed the bile choking her, hating the touch of the leering pirate. Hating they forced Robert to watch the man grope her. LaRoux rubbed a nipple with a calloused thumb, causing the flesh to harden. Unwanted sensation clenched her sex, tightening all the muscles in her body. She hated the man. She hated herself.

"I will free you once MacLachlan is dead and make you my mistress." The pirate's breath teased the tiny hairs on the back of her neck, causing them to stand on end. "You will dress in beautiful gowns. Wear precious jewels. Except for when you adorn my bed. There, I will free your passion." He brushed several fingers along the side of her face in a promising caress.

She spit in his face. He threw back his head and roared with laughter, ignoring the spittle on his cheek.

"You will enjoy my plundering. And I will enjoy taming you." He forced a hand between her legs.

She cringed at the unwanted intimacy. Wanted to vomit. Didn't want Robert to witness her humiliation. He bellowed. The sound that of an enraged beast.

The maddening beat of the drums quieted. The chanting continued as the dancing men removed reeds from the center of the clearing exposing a large ditch. Zola unraveled the snake and held it in the air with both hands. The dancing men heaved the heavy logs to which Robert was tied onto their shoulders as if the wood was the weight of kindling. They carried him toward the pit.

"All powerful Da call upon your messenger Legba to open the portal to the gods. Receive our sacrifice. Flesh for flesh. Blood for blood. Reversed only by the blood of true love," the Voodoo woman screamed the words.

All hell tore loose.

The wind whipped crazily. Ominous fog swirled through the clearing, its chilled fingers brushing across Kimberly's exposed skin, the sensation—pure evil.

A caricature of a man dressed completely in black appeared in a vortex within the fog. Deeply carved sockets in a face void of eyes. Stained fangs hung from ripped flesh where a mouth should have been.

Kimberly recoiled from the surreal scene. My God. Séaghdha.

The men raised the wooden cross into the air near the edge of the pit. Robert's body strained. The veins in his neck expanded as he heaved against the ropes, fighting to get free.

Kimberly knew a fear like none imagined in her most insane nightmares. She stared at the grotesque figure of the vampire and all peripheral sight faded. She couldn't faint. Not when Robert needed her most. She fought to stay conscious. Concentrating on him, she prayed.

He renewed the effort to break free and strained against the binding ropes.

"All powerful *Da* call upon your messenger *Legba* to open the portal to the gods. Receive our sacrifice. Flesh for flesh. Blood for blood. Reversed only by the blood of true love," Zola repeated the curse.

Séaghdha's image sharpened. Flesh knit together. His substantial form loomed over those gathered. He raised his arms, and lightning cracked.

The panther yowled and leapt into the pit. The cross bearers dropped Robert and ran. Men darted in all directions screeching with fear. A wide-eyed Zola threw the snake into the hole and started to run from the clearing. Laroux fought with her, trying to drag her back. They fell into the pit.

Unearthly screams rent the night.

A large raven flew into the commotion. Glistening black feathers were yanked free and caught by the breeze as the vampire grabbed the bird in a clawed fist.

Kimberly struggled against her bounds with every ounce of strength she could call forth. With an all-encompassing effort, she thrust her body forward. The straps holding her prisoner snapped. She smacked the ground hard. Pain shot up her left leg. She lay there numb for a moment, a bone surely broken. Using her arms and one good leg, she dragged herself across the dirt. With sheer will driving her, she lunged for Robert. She fumbled, fingers stiff, laboring to untie the ropes holding him to the damn cross.

"Hurry."

"I'm working as fast as I can."

"Faster. We need to get out of here. I'm too weak to fight."

When both hands were free, Robert tried to help untie the ropes at his ankles, but he was so weak she had to free both legs. She attempted to help him stand, but when he leaned his weight on her, she went down. With an awkward twist of her body, Kimberly's head hit against a rock with a terrible thud.

Through blurred eyes, she witnessed Séaghdha's attack. Too weak, Robert succumbed to the vampire's bite.

Heartsick, Kimberly lost the battle to stay conscious.

CHAPTER TWENTY-EIGHT

Current Year
New Jersey

E arly on a cool, late April morning, Sarah woke with a racing heart. What the hell? Taking a deep breath, she flicked on the bedside lamp with a trembling hand. Nausea bubbled in her belly, a consequence of her so-called gift. She sat up, swung her legs over the side of the mattress and wrapped her arms around her chest in a reassuring hug.

As if on autopilot, she pulled on leggings and an oversized concert t-shirt—both black. Then she slipped her arms into the sleeves of a favorite hoodie. Dark purple, her favorite color. Well, except for black. She always wore black. Her signature non-color—black.

A quick visit to the bathroom to brush her teeth ended with a splash of cold water to her face. Sarah slid into a pair of purple Crocs by the bedroom door and was off.

Driven by an insistent compulsion, she grabbed the keys to Kimberly's Beemer from the counter and headed for the parking garage on the bottom floor. With a press of the key fob clicker the locks popped. She slipped into the black leather driver's seat and twisted the key in the ignition. The engine purred like a content kitty even after sitting idle in the chill of the night.

Sarah eased the car out of the exit without a backward glance. She drove for a distance before her muscles relaxed. The digital readout on the dash read 4:48. What the hell was she doing driving south on the New Jersey Parkway at five in the morning on a Saturday?

Of course, she knew the reason. A sense of urgency. A compulsion.

She glanced at the hand on the steering wheel. At the amethyst ring. Her birthstone. The gem was supposed to bring good luck. Unlikely when *the dreams* haunted her.

Vision dreams had disturbed her sleep for as long as she could remember. When she'd wake, an acute need to act always pushed her to do things she wouldn't normally do.

She swallowed compulsively and kept her gaze on the road, driving the same speed as the rest of the sparse traffic. Even at this hour of the morning, cars zipped along the parkway, hurrying to God only knew where.

At the exit for Route 34, she slowed for the tollbooth, took the ramp, and cruised onto the local highway. *Eleven miles* the sign at the side of the road stated. She'd be at her destination in less than twenty minutes depending on the damn traffic lights.

Great. Just great.

Only an occasional car drove by as she passed sleepy strip malls. Green lights most of the way, so an hour after leaving the apartment, Sarah navigated the cloverleaf and stopped at the orange cones blocking the entrance. The park was open from sunrise to sunset, but someone had already knocked over two of the cones. She maneuvered the vehicle around the one remaining and entered Sandy Hook National Seashore.

A fool's errand more than likely. What were the chances of actually finding Kimberly where the dream indicated?

Sarah passed the entrance booths, the small buildings still shrink-wrapped for protection against harsh winter storms. She drove the old road, past first one then two lonely beach pavilions. She passed the parking lot for the *Crow's Nest* bar where she and Kimberly used to party and pulled into the small lot for the Historical Society.

Nuts. Certifiably. She dropped her head on the steering wheel. She had to be nuts to have made this trip. What were the chances of finding her missing sister on a beach in New Jersey when Kimberly disappeared in the Bermuda Triangle a couple weeks ago?

Sarah got out of the car, the noise from the closing door overly loud. The only other sounds were the cackle of gulls and waves breaking on the beach. She kicked off her shoes and walked across the cold sand to the water's edge as the sun crested the horizon with white-yellow light. All around her was sand and water and beautiful sky. She glanced up and down the beach. Why had the compulsion brought her here?

She took a deep breath of salty ocean air and walked along the beach, the view of the New York skyline across the water becoming more evident with each step. She stopped and scanned the sand, the dunes, and continued her trek.

Movement further ahead on the beach attracted her attention.

Oh my God! She ran.

* * *

The white light drawing her nearer exploded into fragments of blue glitter then vanished. Gray mist encroached, swirling around Kimberly, whirling close, invading her mind. Her chest tightened as she plummeted, freefalling through a dark abyss.

Kimberly jolted eyes wide as she landed on all fours. Wet sand squished between fingers and toes. Lapping waves wrapped spume around her body. She wanted to roll into a ball and cry.

Robert was a vampire once again.

She wasn't sure how long she stayed huddled on the beach with tears flowing down her cheeks before she heard her name shouted from a distance. Shivering, she managed to stand on unsteady legs. The wet fabric of the torn gown clung to weak limbs. Bright light from the early morning sun reflected off the water, blinding her.

Torn gown? The last thing she was wearing—

Pain throbbed. She rubbed her temples. What was she trying to remember?

"Kimberly?" Someone called her name again, more earnest now. Closer. She shaded her eyes with a hand and searched the dunes then the beach.

Long silver-blond hair fluttering behind her, Sarah jogged across the sand toward her. Kimberly took a shaky step and fell into her sister's outstretched arms. Thank God. She'd returned to her own time.

But without Robert? It didn't matter if he was vampire. She wanted him.

She pulled away from her sister and frantically scanned the beach, the dunes, and the water's edge. Oh, shit! He hadn't made it back. They had failed to stop Séaghdha. Robert would be a vampire forever. A panther forever. And she would be alone, without the love of her life. Forever.

"Where have you been? I've been worried," Sarah said.

"Lost. In another world." Kimberly sobbed the words.

"I had a dream I'd find you here."

A tremor wracked Kimberly's body.

"You're freezing." Her sister removed the hoodie she wore and held it out.

Kimberly slipped it on, but the sweatshirt didn't provide much warmth. It would take a lot more to crack the ice that encased her heart.

"Let's get you home." Sarah tugged on her hand and led her across the sand toward the parking lot without asking more questions. Although, she must have a ton. Kimberly certainly did.

She glanced back to the beach. How would she live without Robert?

A large flock of laughing gulls scavenged along the shore. From within their number, a single black raven called to Kimberly with a drawn-out croak before flying out to sea.

* * *

White light flashed, leaving Robert blinded. Séaghdha threw him back against a tree. Pain exploded in his head. His body convulsed. The bite sent fire rushing through his veins. His vision spun. By the time the pain lessened, and his vision cleared, Kimberly had vanished.

Séaghdha flew off, Raven clutched within his grip.

The ache in his heart debilitated Robert more than any wound. He stared at his palms. Blood from Kimberly's head injury, mixed with his blood, covered the fingers. He touched the hands to his face. Bloody hell.

Tears combined with blood.

A healing blue glow wrapped around his body, radiating heat inward. He shuddered as the pain and grief eased. He inhaled several deep breaths and his heartbeat regulated to normal. Energy and strength pulsed through his veins.

Kimberly's blood healed him.

Robert surveyed the remains of Zola's botched spell. Little remained except a crater of scorched earth where the pit had been. Laroux and Zola and all their minions were gone. Hopefully, to hell.

Robert stood and stared into the crater. The scene that caused the devastation flashed through his mind. Raven? He hung his head. His dearest twin was doomed. His chest tightened with anger, but there was nothing he could do for her. She owned her fate.

Releasing a sad sigh, Robert strode through the trees to the beach and began the long trek to the harbor and his ship. As he walked, all he thought about was Kimberly.

Reversed only by the blood of true love.

Kimberly's blood had been the key all along. Combined with his blood and tears, her blood had healed him. Their bond of love was strong. He would find his way to her. Their love was their destiny.

CHAPTER TWENTY-NINE

Robert flipped the data stick he found in Kimberly's valise between two fingers and sat at the desk in his cabin on *Sea Panther*. Although he wanted to respect her privacy, he couldn't. He plugged the thumb drive into the laptop and opened the file manager program. The system listed several file folders. He scanned the list for any titles with the word *offshore* in the name.

"Ach, there it is." Maylock Global Offshore Transaction.

He clicked on the file folder. Sub-folders appeared.

Rubbing his jaw, he mulled over the hunch. The hairs on the back of his neck had stood on end whenever Kimberly spoke about her ex-fiancé Jason Reedman. Each time, Robert had all he could do to keep the panther down. The vampire had wanted to create a blood bath. At first, Robert thought he was stricken with male jealousy and the panther's need to stake its claim.

After a couple conversations since his return from the past with his good friend and Kimberly's ex-client, Sal Romano, Robert felt certain his screaming intuition was correct.

A list of documents populated the screen. He scanned the titles as he scrolled through the list. The answer was there somewhere. He'd bet his newfound freedom on it.

He clicked the find icon and typed the name Jason

Reedman. Robert would let the search program locate the files he believed to be there within the business buzz of contracts and correspondence.

Twenty-four hours later, he had the evidence needed. He clicked Print and the machine hummed. Fifty-eight pages would be enough to clear Kimberly's name and indict the bastard who'd hurt her.

She had possessed the incriminating information without realizing.

Robert slipped the mound of printed-paper into a brown clutch folder, flicked the attached elastic, and dropped the bundle into his briefcase.

"Dinghy is waiting." Colin stood in the doorway.

"How did you know I was ready?"

"Heard your war cry from up on deck." Colin grinned. "Figured you found what you needed to get our lass out of trouble."

"The bastard will pay." Robert raised his gaze to the claymore and the two antique cutlasses hanging on the bulkheads. Reedman should consider himself lucky they were unable to meet in the past.

"Robert?"

"Aye." He nodded at Colin. "Time to correct the wrong done to Kimberly."

Robert grabbed the briefcase and followed his first mate out of the cabin, through the salon, and ascended the companionway stairs. He rubbed his chest. Without Kimberly, *Sea Panther* seemed empty.

Topside, the lads jumped up from where they lounged on cockpit benches and slapped his palm with excited high fives. Timothy glanced at the briefcase. "Did you find enough evidence to put the SOB behind bars?"

Robert smiled. "Aye."

John grinned and slapped Timothy on the back. "Told you so."

A steady breeze blew salty air along the river, jingling rigging on *Sea Panther* and the other sailboats docked in the New Jersey marina. A short boat ride across the Hudson, a meeting with the DA, and Robert would see the charges against Kimberly dropped.

"You gonna bring her back?" Davey asked.

"Damn right."

* * *

"I don't want to pressure you into a decision. It's only been a short time since the charges against you were dropped." Kimberly held her breath and waited for Mr. Romano to finish speaking. "The job is yours if you want it."

She still marveled over the unexpected turn of events. A week ago, the prosecutor's office did a one-eighty and dismissed the charges against her stating new evidence had surfaced. The unexpected turn of events also baffled her lawyers.

"Kimberly, are you still there?"

"Your offer is very generous," she said, hedging. She bit her lower lip and switched the phone from one ear to the other. Was she ready to go back to work?

She needed money. She needed time.

"Take your time. Think about the opportunity. You can give me an answer next week."

"Thank you, Mr. Romano. I don't—"

"You used to call me Sal."

"Thank you, Sal."

"That's better. My wife and I are hosting a party on Saturday night for a friend who's been away for a while. I'd love for you to join us."

"I don't know if—"

"Sylvia would enjoy your company."

"All right, then. I'll come."

"Good. We'll see you at eight and please think about accepting my job offer."

"I will. Thank you."

Kimberly hung up the phone and stared out the window. Red-orange oriental poppies fronted an evergreen hedge in the garden. She'd been back for three months and all she could think about was Robert. She rubbed her extended belly. The precious life growing within her womb would always remind her of his love.

"Hey. Can I borrow your blue sweater?" Sarah asked as

she entered the living room of the apartment they now shared.

Kimberly twisted to face her sister.

Sarah rushed to her. "What's wrong? You look horribly pale."

"Mr. Romano offered me a job and invited me to a party."

"Super."

"I don't think I can—"

"Why not?"

"I don't know if I'm ready." She lowered her gaze to the oak floor.

"Oh, Kimberly, you have to start living your life again."

"I know."

"Go to the party. Take the rest as it comes."

* * *

The high-speed private elevator hummed as it ascended the forty-eight floors to Sal's penthouse apartment. It jolted to a stop, and Kimberly patted coiffed hair. Why had she agreed to come to the party?

She didn't want to be here. She wasn't ready to face people yet. Especially people who knew her before the scandal.

Her host met her at the door. "I'm glad you decided to join us."

She followed him through the foyer and into the large chrome and black leather decorated living room. Surprised to find the room empty, she scanned the modern art on the walls. Cubism—probably Picasso's—not to her liking.

Kimberly suppressed the urge to fidget. She hadn't expected to be the first to arrive.

"I asked you to come early so I could reintroduce you to a friend." Sal grasped an elbow and escorted her toward the windows.

Who? A man sat on one of the leather sofas with his back to them. The room wasn't completely empty after all. Hairs rose on her arms. She sensed something familiar about the man. An unexpected tingle of hope sped her heart rate. It couldn't be possible. Could it?

The man rose and slowly twisted around to face them. The breath shot from Kimberly's lungs with a powerful whoosh. Oh my God. The room swam, and she swayed.

"Are you all right?" Sal grabbed an arm to steady her.

She attempted to speak, but no words left her suddenly dry lips. She nodded.

"I'll leave you two alone then," he said though his voice sounded as if he spoke from a great distance.

The man who looked too much like Robert rounded the sofa to stand in front of her. It hurt to look at his cropped tawny hair, cinnamon eyes filled with something she couldn't fathom, and firm square jaw. The thin scar across his cheek. She turned away.

Kimberly chewed at the edge of her lower lip and gazed out the floor to ceiling windows. The Chrysler and Empire State buildings towered over the rest of the cityscape and she tried to use them as a ground. Damn, her eyes burned. She pinched them shut.

"Look at me, lass."

That voice—so familiar. She couldn't look at him or she'd collapse into unstoppable tears. He spun her around and held her by the upper arms.

"Are you happy I'm here or do you wish I never came into your life?"

"I never expected to see you again."

"Tell me you are glad to see me."

She tossed off his hold, and Robert dropped his arms. Kimberly placed a palm on her belly bump as if she could protect the life within from her tumultuous emotions. A roller coaster ride with peaks of joy and free falls into fear.

"Why won't you look at me?"

"I'm afraid you'll disappear." She kept her chin tucked. She couldn't look at him.

He gently raised her chin with a fingertip. "Please, Kimberly, let me see your eyes."

"How is it you are here? I saw Séaghdha—"

"I'm sorry you had to witness that." Robert gave a sad smile. "But your blood healed me. I am as mortal as you."

"Thank God." She hiccupped on a sob and tossed arms around his neck. "I was heartbroken when I got zapped back and you weren't with me."

"I knew I would find you again." His lips crushed hers in a toe-curling kiss. When the kiss ended, he clung to her. "You are my destiny and I yours."

They dropped onto the sofa and ignored the sounds of the other arriving guests.

Kimberly held his hand, unwilling to let go. "Somehow when I hit my head I was pulled into the time portal. I must of thought of Sarah and the beach where we used to hang out 'cause that's where I was dumped. How did you get back through the time warp?"

"We sailed my ship into the Triangle and lowered the longboat. I went adrift in it. After my men set a course for Jamaica, I rowed to what I believed were the coordinates of the portal. A storm blew in and tossed me about then I got sucked into the vortex. A cruising motor yacht found me in the water clinging to a piece of wood. I spent a month in a hospital before remembering who I was and what needed to be done.

"You were ill?"

"Aye. Out of my mind with fever." He raised their joined hands and kissed hers. "I called Sal. He helped me get home. I hired a firm to investigate your ex-fiancé and—"

"But why—"

He held up a hand. "I couldn't tell you I was back until I cleared your name. I didn't want to give you false hope if the hunch was wrong."

"You're the one who got the charges dropped?"

"Aye. They arrested Jason Reedman this morning. I found the evidence on a data stick in the valise you left at my house in Florida."

Kimberly felt a knife sharp pain in her chest. Jason's betrayal cut deep. But when she gazed into Robert's loving eyes, moisture spilled from hers. This man sitting beside her, loved her, would cross centuries to be with her.

"Robert, there is something I need to tell you."

"What, love?"

"We're going to be parents."

His eyes slipped to her belly. When he raised his gaze, a broad smile crossed his face and his eyes glowed.

"I couldn't be happier." His lips brushed hers in a gentle kiss.

"I love you," she said.

"And I will love you forever." Robert held her hand over his heart.

* * *

A half hour later, Robert sipped champagne wishing Kimberly would hurry. How long could one woman take to powder a nose?

"Whatcha doin here? This ain't no Halloween party. How'd you get past the guards downstairs?" one of Sal's boys shouted.

The muffled response got lost in the noise from the chatty crowd.

"Who the fuck do you think you are? You. Can't. Come. In. Here." Each syllable, spoken with a heavy Italian accent, escalated in anger.

Sounded like there would be a fight. Robert craned his neck to see what caused the disturbance near the entrance to the penthouse. A Hollywood actor regaling admirers with stories of a recent trip to Venice blocked Robert's line of vision.

Sal's bodyguards, always on alert, went into action. One whisked his wife away while the others muscled through the crowd toward the door.

More words fired off in the heavy accent. Robert searched the crowd for Kimberly. She exited the powder room where she'd gone to wash the tearstains from her face when the other guests began arriving in earnest. She lifted a hand in a finger wave.

"He's got a gun," a woman screamed.

Kimberly's head swung toward the commotion by the door. One of the bodyguards leapt from the crowd and tackled her. Their limbs tangled as they fell. Robert lunged forward.

The pop of a gunshot added to the noisy commotion. Panic twisting his gut, Robert kicked a table of hors d'oeuvres over in an effort to reach Kimberly. She waved him off.

Another of Sal's bodyguards exchanged punches with the gunman. When the bodyguard went down, Robert grabbed the hooded man, swung him around and punched him in the stomach. Guests cheered him on. Fists flew.

After several punches, Robert pulled the rubber Dracula mask off the man's head and exposed the battered visage of Dino Rizzetti, the hit man who had chased after Kimberly and shot Robert while in panther form.

"Who hired you?" Robert shook the bastard by the shoulders. The hit man spit blood and a tooth. Robert raised a bruised fist as if to hit the bastard again. "Tell me."

"No more." Rizzetti held up a hand. "It was JR. Jason Reedman."

Kimberly gasped. Robert flipped his gaze to her. Her hand covered her mouth and she stared back through wide eyes. Other than that, she looked healthy. Thank the good Lord the shot missed her.

Sal approached with a couple of policeman. The cops took Rizzetti away in handcuffs.

"Thank God that's over," Kimberly said.

"Aye. Now I can take my wife home."

"To *Sea Panther?*"

"Aye. Forever and always." He drew her into his arms and kissed her with all the love burning in his heart.

EPILOGUE

One year and six months later

With a silver tray laden with three champagne flutes in hand, Kimberly swept through the French doors onto the tile terrace. Robert and his sister stood near the bougainvillea-draped railing overlooking the tropical garden.

"Don't bite any of my guests tonight," Robert admonished Raven. "'Tis Madelina's first birthday and you wouldn't want her to be traumatized.

His sister smiled brightly, hand poised on Robert's sleeve. Fangs slipped over red-painted lips as she leaned into him. Alarm clenched Kimberly's heart. Raven had never shared the details of her imprisonment by Séaghdha. Did her inner goodness remain? Would she hurt Robert?

Raven laughed softly and kissed her brother's cheek then glanced at Kimberly. "I'll behave. I promise."

Kimberly released a silent sigh and handed them each a glass of champagne before placing the tray on a nearby table.

"A toast to the future." Robert held out his glass. In turn, she and Raven clinked his flute with theirs.

"I'll regret drinking this later, but it's delicious." Raven smiled. "When do you set sail again?"

Kimberly exchanged a conspiratorial glance with Robert.

"Not until after the *bairn* is born," he said.

Raven's eyes glistened. "Another baby?"

"Aye. A boy. Our heir."

"Heir? And what about our daughter?" Kimberly put hands on hips and glared at her husband. "She's our first born."

"Can't we have two heirs?"

"You really are an ancient." She rolled her eyes and stroked Robert's cheek.

The love shining in his gaze warmed her heart and even though they weren't alone, she stretched up on tippy toes and planted a hard kiss on his lips.

When she pulled away, his sultry expression promised pleasure for later.

"Shall we drink to the future generation?" Robert held up his flute. "May they be free—"

"To freedom." Raven raised her glass. "And to Séaghdha's demise.

Just Beyond the Garden Gate
Book One, Highland Gardens Series

by Dawn Marie Hamilton

Time Travel Fantasy Romance

Determined to regain her royal status, a banished faerie princess accepts a challenge from the High-Queen of the Fae to unite an unlikely couple while the clan brownie attempts to thwart her.

Passion ignites when a faerie-shove propels burned-out business consultant Laurie Bernard through the garden gate, back through time, and into the embrace of Patrick MacLachlan. The arrogant clan chief doesn't know what to make of the lass in his arms, especially when he recognizes the brooch she wears as the one his stepmother wore when she and his father disappeared.

With the fae interfering at every opportunity, the couple must learn to trust one another while they battle an enemy clan, expose a traitor within their midst and discover the true fate of the missing parents. Can they learn the most important truth—love transcends time?

Journey from the lush gardens of the Blue Ridge Mountains of North Carolina to the Scottish Highlands of 1509 with *Just Beyond the Garden Gate*.

Just Once in a Verra Blue Moon

Book Two, Highland Gardens Series

by Dawn Marie Hamilton

Time Travel Fantasy Romance

What happens when a twenty-first century business executive is expected to fulfill a prophecy given at the birth of a sixteenth-century seer? Of course, he must raise his sword in her defense.

Believing women only want him for his wealth, Finn MacIntyre doesn't trust any woman to love him. When, during Scottish Highland games, faerie magic sends him back in time to avenge the brutal abduction of his time-traveling cousin, he learns he's the subject of a fae prophecy.

Elspeth MacLachlan, the beloved clan seer, is betrothed to a man she dislikes and dreams of the man prophesized at her birth, only to find him in the most unexpected place— facedown in the mud.

With the help of fae allies, they must overcome the treachery set to destroy them to claim a love that transcends time.

Journey from the lush gardens of the Blue Ridge Mountains of North Carolina to the Scottish Highlands of 1511 with *Just Once in a Verra Blue Moon.*

Future Works:

Time Travel Fantasy Romance

Just Wait for Me
Book Three, Highland Gardens Series

Just in Time for a Highland Christmas
A Highland Gardens Novella

Paranormal Romance

Raven's Revenge
Book Two, Crimson Storm Series

Dawn Marie Hamilton dares you to dream. She is a 2013 RWA® Golden Heart® Finalist who pens Scottish-inspired fantasy and paranormal romance. Some of her tales are rife with mischief-making faeries, brownies, and other fae creatures. More tormented souls—shape shifters, vampires, and maybe a zombie or two—stalk across the pages of other stories. She is a member of The Golden Network, Fantasy, Futuristic & Paranormal, Celtic Hearts, and From the Heart chapters of RWA. When not writing, she's cooking, gardening, or paddling the local creeks of Southern Maryland with her husband.

Visit Dawn Marie on the web at DawnMarieHamilton.com.

www.ingramcontent.com/pod-product-compliance
Lightning Source LLC
Chambersburg PA
CBHW020237180626
46810CB00006B/2232